SWORD OF FIRE AND SEA

The Chaos Knight
BOOK ONE

ERIN HOFFMAN

an imprint of Prometheus Books
Amherst, NY

for Brenn and Kristin—
two very talented ladies who believed

Published 2011 by Pyr®, an imprint of Prometheus Books

Cover illustration © Dehong He.

Inquiries should be addressed to
Pyr
59 John Glenn Drive
Amherst, New York 14228–2119
VOICE: 716–691–0133
FAX: 716–691–0137
WWW.PYRSF.COM

15 14 13 12 11   5 4 3 2 1

Library of Congress Cataloging-in-Publication Data

Hoffman, Erin, 1981–
    Sword of fire and sea / by Erin Hoffman.
        p. cm. — (The Chaos Knight ; bk. 1)
    ISBN 978–1–61614–373–2 (pbk.)
    ISBN 978–1–61614–374–9 (e-book)
    I. Title.

PS3608.047768S96 2011
813'.6—dc22

                                                                2011006883

Printed in the United States of America

CONTENTS

// CONTENTS //

Part Three: Sapphires

PART ONE
EMERALDS

CHAPTER 1

A DEAL IN SIANE'S EYE

Though the coastal island of Siane's Eye was lush with whispering palms and tropical flowers too exotic for the names of men, the wind that swept ever outward from its alabaster monuments came chill as a lifetime of penance. It prickled Vidarian's skin, but he hardened himself to it; the Sisters would not see a Rulorat captain hiding his hands like a saltless boy.

He turned to salute the *Empress Quest*, waiting far below in the green harbor waters. A signal flag acknowledged his safe arrival, and that the crew would await his return.

One last bridge separated the small viewing ledge from the white temple of the goddess of the air, but now that his stomach expected its sway, it was harder to cross than the first. The only sea or land access to the Eye was via an arcing bridge of interlocking alabaster blocks. Whatever bound them was supple, free to the play of the cold wind, and though it bore carved handrails, the memory of its lurching—unfriendly foliage all that awaited after a plummet thrice the height of the *Quest*'s mainmast—would be with him some time.

Setting courage between his teeth, he boarded the second bridge, locking his eyes on the waiting temple, willing his legs to interpret the sway of the bridge as the rhythm of a deck. Familiar. Safe.

Then he was across, the yawning green that haunted his peripheral vision swallowed by secure earth and smooth cobblestones. A figure wrapped in gauzy robes perpetually at the play of the temple wind stood by to greet him.

Upon reaching the first white arch of the temple Vidarian covered his surprise at the aged face beneath the diaphanous hood by bowing smartly from the waist and removing his tricorne. He did not know what he found more peculiar: the lines etched like weathered sandstone against the woman's cheeks, or the strange striped lizard that coiled tightly about her left forearm. The little beast was pale green, skin like pebbled sand, and its many-striped eyes moved independent of one another.

"Welcome, Captain." The priestess's voice was like vellum crumpled and straightened many times, latticed and soft. Her eyes were the translucent grey of a winter sea. "Priestess Endera awaits you within. We of the Eye are pleased to bring water and fire together once more."

"I wondered at that. I should have thought the priestess would call me to Val Harlon," he ventured. The lizard's near eye tracked him.

"For undertakings of import, the air sisters have ever been the conduit for the volatile elements." She gestured to the alabaster. "We are the bridge."

"Truly extraordinary engineering," Vidarian said with genuine appreciation. "What substance is it that holds them together?"

She blinked; lambent, alien. "Why, air, of course."

And so they had swayed, the bonds of all the elements not as strong as they once were. His stomach gave a lurch as he involuntarily imagined those bonds failing at just the right moment. He thanked the air priestess and pushed his thoughts along; if she did know what Endera had planned for him, she would hardly give any sign. "Please lead the way," he said instead, and she smiled and turned on soundless feet toward the next temple arch.

Hanging from the ceilings, arches, and indeed every available surface of the white alabaster were feathery fronds of olive-green vegetation that dropped no roots, though they clung in places to the stone. They drank thirstily from the air, lifted by the breeze that came from the temple's core. Tiny golden blooms no larger than Vidarian's thumbnail peppered some of the plants, and from these danced slender black butterflies, their wings shimmering blue in the dim light. Here and there another of the strange striped lizards clung to a vine or alabaster column; wherever they passed, each tracked Vidarian with one weirdly telescoping eye.

The pressure of the moving air grew stronger as they passed further into the temple, born from the Windwell at its very center. His companion's light robes, made of wound scarves, now lifted steadily behind her like so many pennants from a festival barge. At the next hall, its vaulted ceiling easily three times the height of a tall man, she turned and led him down a quieter passageway out of the wind, and thence into a carpeted reception room lit by lanterns of blue oil, their crystal chimneys throwing shards of pale light in shifting starbursts against the white walls. The air priestess bowed, lifted a hand unburdened by reptile, and turned back down the hall.

At a delicate table of pale maple wood sat Endera, whom Vidarian had met only once before and that two decades ago. Her voluminous wine-red robes defied the gentle delicacy of the air temple, as did the rich gold of her skin and eyes. She motioned him to the seat opposite her, and poured him a cup of tea that, by the gold leafed embossing on its nearby shipping packet, would have kept the child of a merchant family in silk for a year. Vidarian sat.

"Well, priestess? Your little waifs were quite—insistent—that I meet you here, and I have the bruises to prove it."

White teeth flashed beneath the velvet hood. "*Well trained*, dear Captain, is the term I believe you're searching for."

"Of course." He picked up his tea. Inhaling deeply of its sweet, subtle fragrance, he took a gulp and tried not to think about the price of the hot liquid that slid down his throat. As it reached his stomach, a secondary flavor—just a touch of floral bitterness—bathed his tongue, but it brought with it a welcome awakening of the senses.

Siane's Eye was neutral territory. Though Vidarian would have liked to ignore the summons from Endera, certain obligations forced his hand, but his cordiality only went so far. He enjoyed the tea as much as one might, but waited without speaking long enough for his impropriety to become clear.

The fire priestess's carnelian circlet glowed suddenly as she leaned forward into the lamplight. Even in shadow her face was statuesque, suspended in the agelessness of long-held authority. "I have a task for you, Captain. Your ship and lineage make you uniquely suited to it, and I am willing to pay well." Vidarian was about to make a quick retort that he was not to be "tasked," but the air stopped in his chest as Endera began to move one arm across the table.

With casual grace, the priestess turned over her hand, emptying a black velvet pouch into the air. Vidarian's breath moved again, drawn swiftly inward, as a pair of slender cabochons each the size of his thumb clattered down onto the table.

The green stones glowed, and not from the blue light of the lanterns. Vidarian's hand moved toward them out of pure human reflex—but he withdrew just in time. Still, the heat that he knew they held seemed to burn on his fingertips. More wealth sat before him than any ten of his comrades had ever seen. "Sun emeralds," he said, breath ragged in his throat. "Dear priestess, who have you taken under your wing that could possibly be worth such a price?"

"She was under my wing already."

"You can't possibly mean—"

"I do." No hint of any emotion colored the priestess's face as she lifted her teacup to her lips and sipped, cradling the porcelain in long-fingered hands. This Vidarian saw peripherally, locked as he was on the stones lest they disappear, knowing envy greener than sun emeralds was alive in his eyes. "She requires escort to my sister in the Temple of Zal'nehara. Circumstances demand that this route move along the western coast." For only a moment Vidarian glanced sharply upward; to tour the western coast to get to the Temple of the Sea was to make a trip of perhaps twenty days take several months. But his attention was drawn magnetically back down to the emeralds, and Endera smiled, catlike. "Lovely, aren't they? And near priceless." Her voice was sweet music in his ears, a persuasive spell.

Abruptly Vidarian pushed back from the table, his spine sinking into the plush seat cushion. A faint sneer twisted his lips as he stared at the table, morbidly fascinated. "Not on your life, Priestess. Those gems are worth more than I am, more than the *Quest* and all her crew. That's dangerous."

Endera's hands froze around the cup and her tone dropped a few degrees. "Then name your price."

A thousand prizes leapt to mind, dizzying him. A ship to mate his *Empress*, swift as a gull and strong as a kraken—five ships, ten! He could be Admiral Vidarian Rulorat, and he knew that if he asked it of her, Endera would make it so. Those two emeralds alone would purchase enough wealth to keep him fat and rich for the rest of his days. But . . .

"There's no price could be worth such madness," he said, pushing himself to his feet. "I'm sorry, Priestess. My crew would have me tossed if I brought a fire priestess on board; you must know that. Much less for a tour through the Outwater, full of pirates and Nistra knows what else. Good day to you." He turned and strode for the exit, making a break as quickly as dignity would permit.

"Sit down, Captain."

He stopped in the threshold but did not turn, riding the swell of temper that threatened to break over his composure.

"I am a very busy woman, Vidarian. I had no intention of calling you to this meeting to waste your time and mine with fruitless negotiations." Endera slowly finished her cup of tea, but there was no warmth in her voice. "I had hoped this wouldn't be necessary. Seventy years ago your great-grandfather made a commitment to my predecessor on behalf of the Rulorat family. The Breakwater agreement. You know of it."

Vidarian sat down. The swell had died to a bubbling tide of dread.

"I am invoking that commitment, yet I wish our engagement to remain cordial. So let me try this again." She leaned forward. "Name your price, Captain."

His throat was dry, but the teacup was empty, and he did not move to refresh it. He permitted himself a brief clenching of both fists, then dove in, protocol be damned. "What makes you think, Priestess, that I should abide by an agreement dormant these last thirty years? It was not an agreement I made, nor my father."

He'd pitched his voice to rattle her, but she didn't even pause. "Our last renewal was indeed thirty years ago," her voice like tumbled glass, "two years before you were born, dear Vidarian." At her maternal, understanding smile he clenched his fists again below the table. "I certainly know this must be difficult for you, but think what your father would have done."

Of that there was no question. And yet . . . "He'd have known to cross the Outwater with a Sharlin priestess on board would be madness too, Priestess."

"A risk, most certainly. For which you are offered very generous compensation, Captain."

The compensation sat on the table between them, still glowing, and not with reflection. A wildness seized Vidarian. "Binding magic. Those emeralds, tied to my life—destroyed when I am."

Endera was silent for a long moment. After a small eternity she reached forward and placed her hand across the priceless stones. A smile turned her scarlet lips, dazzling and dangerous. "You are an intriguing man, Captain," she said, and there was laughter in her voice. "I agree to your bargain."

Then, without speaking, she focused intently on the jewels beneath her cupped hand. Bright golden sparks kindled in the depths of her eyes, and a glare like summer sunlight speared through her fingers from the emeralds, leaving dark spots spangled across Vidarian's vision. For one wrenching moment he felt as if the breath had been drawn out of his chest—then all was as it had been. The light was gone from beneath the priestess's hand, and from her eyes. She withdrew her hand.

"It is done."

This time Vidarian did not stop himself when he moved to take up one of the stones. Its immediate surface was cool to the touch, but the heat that burned within stirred his very soul.

An ocean of light swirled inside the polished stone. The sun emerald was green only around the outside, winking golden when turned in the lantern light. It was heavy—heavier than any other jewel he'd touched. Only reluctantly did he slide it into his left hand and pick up the next.

As soon as he touched it he knew something was wrong. This stone was not heavy, and the light that danced within it formed twisting flames. His eyes darted up to Endera. "What is this?"

"Such an observant lad," she smiled.

"What did you do?" he asked sharply, dropping both jewels back on the table without a care for their value.

"Be careful, Captain," the priestess warned, golden eyes suddenly sharp. "All things come with a price. This emerald is not bound to you. It is bound to the priestess you will escort, and both will remain in my possession until you return. You privateers call it—insurance." Endera reached again across the table and brushed a golden fingernail across the first of the emeralds. A cold shiver ran up Vidarian's spine. "All things with their antithesis," she murmured, regarding the stone with disturbing intensity. Her eyes were lazy, thick lashes low as she looked back up at him. "The cardinal rule of spirit magic, and indeed all magics, holy or not. In order to bind that stone to your life, I had to bind some of your life—just a little part—to the stone." Her smoldering gaze sharpened with her voice. "You will escort Priestess Windhammer, Captain, and you will see her safely to the Temple of Zal'nehara and the protection of my sister, where the sea will mask the fire within her." She picked up the first of the emeralds and tucked it into the black velvet pouch. When she held it out to him, he accepted it without thinking, numb. "Then you will return here, and I will give you not only the other emerald but also two sun rubies of equal size. You will be a rich man, and Priestess Windhammer will be safe."

Vidarian stood stiffly, dumbstruck. Before he could think, Endera spoke again in a clear dismissal: "She will meet you at Val Harlon's east pier tomorrow evening, number ten."

Still rebelling at how thoroughly he had been caught in the priestess's web, but unable to refuse with the offer of the stones now doubled, even if his life did *not* depend on it, Vidarian managed, "So be it, then." He did not offer his hand; the bargain, as she had put it, was already sealed entirely too tightly for his liking.

Endera smiled.

Giving a stiff bow, Vidarian turned to stalk away, but the priestess's voice caught him just as he lifted the velvet curtain.

"One more thing, Captain."

Vidarian froze.

"You will have no steel that bears a polish near this priestess. The Vkortha who seek her are telepaths, and can sense any such metal when it comes near the life flame of a fire priestess. It acts as their eyes."

"Priestess, you can't possibly be serious. Our anchors, the fittings for the ship—"

"Are all salt-encrusted and infused with the energy of the sea. These are no risk. Only any *polished* steel that your crew may bear will be. Steel, well cared-for, retains the memory of its origin; it recalls the flame that birthed it. Each fire priestess past the initiation rite carries within her a thread of the great Mother Flame, and it calls to all its brethren."

Unthinking, Vidarian reached for his sword, and Endera's eyes followed his hand. "This sword was my father's, and his father's before him. I'll not leave it in any port."

"Then keep it," she said, "but keep it covered at all times when you are in the presence of Priestess Windhammer. Any consequences that follow should you fail are yours to deal with—but if there's anything left of you when the Vkortha are through," she tapped her fingernails on the table, and for a moment they flared like tiny suns, "there won't be when I am."

Vidarian bowed again, tight-lipped, and strode through the arch before he could ensnare himself further. The priestess's soft voice came to him as he paused to return his hat to his head, as if it were his fate.

"Protect her well, Vidarian."

⌇⌇⌇

Vidarian left the Eye as though propelled by its unceasing wind. But as he passed through the final archway, the old air priestess lifted her narrow hand, and he stopped, just short of stumbling.

"I would never question a sworn Sister," she said without preamble, gently stroking the chameleon's back. "Yet I have known Endera for many years. Her movements are her own. And she did not come here under the command of Sher'azar." She drew a tiny crystal whistle from her wide belt. "Take this. If it hasn't yet faded, it summons a powerful wind, the Breath of Siane." As she smiled, her eyes vanished into the vast wrinkles above her cheeks. "You cannot imagine its value. Carry it wisely."

As she passed him the whistle its tightly coiled strand of braided linen came unwound, and Vidarian lifted his hat, partly in salute to the air priestess, partly to allow the whistle around his neck, where he tucked it behind his neckerchief. The thought of returning to his crew with this errand had thrown his thoughts into a gale, and he felt a rush of gratitude for the kindness from this priestess of that turbulent element.

"Go with the blessing of Siane, Captain, though your winds be fierce or fair." Her pale eyes were distant, but deep within them, as in the gullet of a hurricane, there was the glow of distant lightning. She smiled. "I suspect you'll need it."

CHAPTER TWO

THE CREW OF THE EMPRESS QUEST

Marielle, the *Quest*'s first mate, was waiting at the alabaster bridge.

Vidarian bit back a sigh as he saw her. In truth, the sight of her was steadying, but they'd agreed her responsibility was with the crew, not on the island. And from the set of her shoulders, at the moment she was not Marielle, First Mate, but Marielle I-Changed-Your-Swaddling-Clothes, Captain Sir. He averted his eyes from her aggressive grey stare out of reflex, only for an instant, which of course made things much worse.

"Dare I ask, Captain Sir, what you have gotten us into this time?"

Batten and caulk. And forge ahead.

"We've taken a commission with the Sharli Priesstesshood, an escort mission to bring one of their number to the Temple at Zal'nehara, where the Nistra followers there will take charge of her welfare." Marielle's eyes widened at about every fourth word.

"Direct through the bloody Outwater? I presume you told them how mad an idea that is?"

"She invoked the Breakwater, Marielle."

Marielle crooked three fingers in the sign of Nistra, warding. "A name your granddad had no business agreeing to! It's a bad affair, getting between goddesses, to say nothing of a call-the-waves-down-on-me bloody agreement name like that."

As with all true many-decade friends, Vidarian and Marielle had small, specific, manageable habits that drove each other insane. For Vidarian,

Marielle's was her unavoidable religious affectation. He battened down some more. "Please try to be reasonable, Marielle. Your superstitions—"

"Are nothing of the sort, they are concrete and provable and as old as the sea herself. The crew won't have it, sir, and I don't allow as I should either," Marielle bristled, gripping the ends of her waist sash in agitation. "'The Wake knows they've plenty of ships of their own, these priestesses. Why the *Quest?*"

"They do have their own ships. And you know my obligation to them."

"Your granddad building some ships really don't—"

"This truly isn't up for discussion, Marielle." He stared her down, and her mouth clicked shut, but sternly as ever. "I'm sorry. I don't like it any better than you do. But I can't take my family's name and ship without their obligations. You've sailed with enough Rulorats to know that."

Her angled eyebrows said she was almost convinced. "Will you at least consent to asking the sea witch for Nistra's forecast on this? I'll warrant you weren't foolish enough to take this on without advance payment."

Vidarian folded his arms, instinctively moving to brush the velvet pouch in his front pocket, surreptitiously. "I'll allow it if you insist. Though nothing changes, Marielle. The *Quest* is committed already."

"It'll be a forewarning, at least. Captain Sir."

∿∿∿

Marielle's cabin was as large as Vidarian's, being in previous generations allocated to his grandmother, when she and his grandfather had captained the ship together, all except in formality. Marielle had it so stuffed with gear and paraphernalia that it looked perhaps a third its true size.

In the back of the cabin, bolted to a table near the bed cabinet, was a large glass shelter that contained a currently purple-spotted green octopus and a large quantity of salt water. Marielle had acquired the sea witch, a peculiar southern sea creature quite famously expensive (and invaluable on ships of any merit), in a wager many decades ago.

Wordlessly, Marielle pulled her prayer book from a shelf beneath the table and opened it to the section on prophecy via sea witch. Nistra followers had discovered the sea witch's unique capabilities over a hundred years ago and instituted their use wherever possible. They needed a steady diet of small crustaceans, fresh and alive, which presented some problem to followers that lived too far inland, but Marielle kept a ready supply pulled up from the sea floor at all times. Now she pulled a leather pouch from a rack beside the bookshelf and dropped a handful of calcified sand into the water. The witch turned completely and unsettlingly transparent.

Still not speaking, she reached out a hand, palm up, toward Vidarian. He frowned just to register his disapproval and pulled the velvet pouch from his pocket, then slid the emerald from it and into her waiting fingers. Without looking at it, as if she instinctively knew its hypnotic properties, she dropped it into the tank.

From the initial flash of bubbles the emerald dropped straight down, sinking with barely a drift to right or left to rest, glowing, among the rocks at the base of the tank. The octopus writhed, reaching for the glass borders of its tiny domain like a man thrown overboard in a tempest. Then it turned the deep red of a flesh wound aged in the sun.

Marielle's face was impassive as she quickly turned the wax-slick pages in her prayer book. Carefully inked illuminations played out identical octopi in a spectrum of colors. When at last she came to the shade that closest matched the octopus's current color, with some flipping back and forth of pages to be sure, she froze and bent over the description. The prognosis was not good. Vidarian only caught the words ". . . except in great defiance to your safety of mind and body will . . ."

He prepared for the explosion as she gently, carefully closed the book. But her voice was unexpectedly low and soft.

"It ain't never come to good, your family and Sharli, Sir. Never."

As the sun bloodied the sky to the west of Val Harlon the next evening, the *Empress Quest* bobbed in green water at dock nine. A slender black knife of a rivership bearing the banner of Temple Kara'zul rested beside her, and as twilight settled in, a hooded figure descended from the ramp next to the dock ten marker.

Endera's charge wore a sweeping skirt of burgundy crushed velvet and a cloak of the same, seeming not to notice the cloying heat that kept all of the sailors and passersby displaying maximum skin, even in the wind-chased evening. A belt of carved onyx cinched her narrow waist, matched by a glittering pendant around her neck. Where Endera had been a polished, silvery flame with alabaster skin and golden hair and eyes, this Priestess Windhammer was a dusky ember, dark gold her complexion and raven black the long braid whose tail brushed past her hips.

"Ariadel Windhammer," she said, hesitating slightly upon reaching him. She extended her hand—a small, petite thing. Delicate though she might be, the priestess had a strong, firm grip. She was complete and total trouble.

Finally, he managed, "Vidarian Rulorat, captain of the *Empress Quest*."

Her smile was morning breaking over the eastern sea. "Rulorat, truly? I should have trusted Endera to find me a stalwart guardian. Your family is renowned on the seas."

Vidarian was about to answer when a soft, plaintive mew echoed up from one of the crates stacked beside the pier.

Ariadel blinked. "Do you hear that?"

"Just a dock cat."

"Nonsense. I doubt if its eyes are even open yet." Like a predator herself she crouched and listened intently, moving silently among the crates on the dock. The source of the mew made the mistake of scuttling from one crate to the next, and Ariadel pounced.

She pulled it from the crates as one might an unsuspected treasure. The molten light of the setting sun flashed in the kitten's green eyes, and then across Ariadel's dark ones.

Vidarian blinked, then squinted suspiciously at the kitten. It was more a ball of grey fur than a creature, though punctuated with pink ears and nose. Despite being fluffed into a rather rotund shape, bones showed through its skin where the patchy fur exposed it. Doubtful it would be much of any use at all as a mouser.

"I feel she must come with us," Ariadel said, curiously fixated on the creature's eyes.

He nodded, diplomat enough to hide his skepticism. One picked one's battles. "If it's your will, Priestess." Vidarian swept his arm in an invitation toward the gangplank ahead.

The *Empress Quest* was a sleek double-masted schooner of eighty-five feet in length, carved from red teak, light and strong. Shallow-bellied for a seagoing ship, she rode high in the water, with pennants snapping in the breeze. She was currently one of the larger ships in the harbor, built for the rugged coastline, barnacled where her waterline had once been higher from prolonged exposure to rough waters. There was nothing in the world lovelier than the sight of her bobbing at port, and so it was with some misgiving that Vidarian observed the priestess's reluctance to board.

Finally he held out his hand to her, and she stared at it for a moment before accepting his assistance. As she stepped onto the plank, she murmured, "Pardon my moment. I've never been on the high sea before," but it was with the curious calm one would observe a foreign delicacy at dinner. Still, her grip on the kitten gave her away—its eyes looked about to pop out in her firm grasp.

"Windhammer," he said, partly to distract her. "Strange name for a fire priestess. Have our families met before?" She did not look at him, but seemed bent on taking in every detail of her surroundings as they stepped onto the *Quest*'s fine deck.

"My father's name," she said distractedly. "The fire in my veins is from my mother. A remote cousin of Priestess Endera's. Oh!" She exclaimed in surprise as the grey kitten suddenly squirmed loose (likely in protest to her death-grip, though Vidarian certainly wouldn't say so) and landed on the deck with a thump. In a shot the kitten was off, streaking toward the galley as if it knew exactly where it was going.

Vidarian watched in chagrin. Then, raising a hand to his cheek, he called out, "All hands prepare for sail! Ms. Solandt, bring us out!" The sudden loudness of his voice startled the priestess slightly, but she recovered, watching the stream of men that poured out of the forecastle with slightly narrowed eyes.

"Oughtn't I meet the crew?"

He grinned. "After we're settled on route. My *Empress* grows impatient if docked too long. Shall we?" He raised a hand toward the main hold, and she followed his gesture, but somehow managed to make it look like it had been her idea all along. Trouble indeed.

∿∿∿

The forecastle's anteroom, by his grandmother's tradition, was as ornate as a wealthy landsman's stateroom, and used to honor individuals of the crew on special occasions. Heavy mahogany cabinets and a massive matching table, all intricately carved with water nymphs and merfolk, were bolted to the polished teak deck, their fixtures hidden by carved clawed feet. A pair of runners covered the deck to either side of the table, patterned in the voluminous chrysanthemum designs peculiar to the continent-island nation of Targuli. Each was of thin but surprisingly soft silk, woven at an astronomical thread count and also stapled discreetly to the boards. Vidarian shut the thick door behind them, cutting off the bustle of the crew's quarters.

Ariadel took it all in with cool aloofness, thick lashes masking her half-closed eyes. She, of course, was used to much greater splendor than this—but Vidarian guessed that the watery theme was not quite her cup of tea.

Speaking of which, he moved to a silver tea service that he'd asked Marks to lay out prior to their journey. Sitting in a polished rack fixed in the center of the lacquered table, the teapot was a tall silver affair rimmed with filigreed roses. Two matching cups sat on silver saucers nearby, and Vidarian deftly measured out portions of dark honey-colored tea for both of them. Ariadel accepted her cup gratefully, exclaiming over the detail and skill of the worked metal. "My mother's," Vidarian explained, not diffident, and Ariadel turned her attention to the tea.

However, as she took her first sip, she worked quite obviously to avoid spitting the liquid back out. "It's cold!"

Vidarian cleared his throat to hide the start of a laugh. "Your pardon, Priestess. The tea is from Insartia, and intended to be enjoyed chilled. It's been quite warm out." Taking up his own cup, he swallowed a mouthful of the tea, enjoying its herblike, minty overtones. "We'll be under way shortly, and I'm afraid I must leave you to attend the launch. So if you'll pardon my directness—" he looked over his cup for permission, and continued at her cautious nod, "you are not, of course, obligated to tell me, but why are they searching for you?"

Ariadel stared into her cup as if the answer would rise from its glassy surface. After a long moment she said, hollowly, "I know where they live."

Vidarian frowned. "You are only one person. Surely others know the location of their operation. They must have spies, staff, orderlies?"

The priestess shook her head, increasingly subdued. "Not that simple, I'm afraid. They migrate, but they have a single unmoving fortress on an island in the Farwestern Sea. I happened to stumble upon its location, and they read the signs of my presence." She took a quick draught of the tea. "It was not intended that they should be able to do so."

Cradling his cup between his hands, Vidarian traced the silver roses with his eyes for a moment. "I gather this is somehow Endera's mistake."

"She knew the risk." Ariadel abruptly set down her cup. "The knowledge was worth it. And she knew that her sister at Zal'nehara would protect me. The Daughters of the Sea have been searching for the Vkortha fortress unsuccessfully for years."

Knowing it would be futile to mask his ignorance, Vidarian simply asked: "The sea is their domain, and they could not find the island? And if you have told others, why are you alone hunted?"

"Their domain was their weakness. They are too familiar with the environs of water, and the Vkortha have many layers of telepathic camouflage on the island. It took fire to penetrate them, for they were woven in with the patterns of the ocean itself, with which the Zal'neharans were too familiar. And I have told no one else. Endera has a certain latitude from Kara'zul, but they would not have approved of any such official cooperation with Zal'nehara, and know nothing of my efforts or hers."

Vidarian shook his head, with a terse smile. "I won't pretend to understand temple politics." He would have said more, but three tones from a brass bell atop ship cut him short. Setting the cup aside, he offered his hand to Ariadel. "If you'll excuse me?"

Her touch was like fire—not surprising, perhaps, if one had time to think about it. Vidarian hadn't. And like fire, it didn't let go easily. "Captain, I have little doubt that Endera tricked you into this."

Vidarian laughed softly, dodging her earnestness by dint of a quick step backward and a respectful half-bow. "It was my own folly, Priestess, and I intend to make the most of it. The *Quest* and her crew have no equal on the sea, I promise you that."

CHAPTER THREE
A Bold Display

For the next two weeks Ariadel could rarely be seen abovedeck, plagued as she was with seasickness. Or it was certainly sickness, and certainly from the sea travel, but unlike any Vidarian had ever seen. She spent most of her time in meditation, and was friendly if demure at meals with the crew—she had even entirely won Marks, the cook, to her side by dint of her willingly shared Velinese cooking techniques.

No one on a Rulorat ship would be intimidated by ability, but Marks, an old stick of a ship's cook who had served under Vidarian's father, had a certain pronounced discomfort when it came to revealing admiration for the priestess's particular expertise. When pressed, he was a stoppered bottle uncorked—"And her knife skills, Captain—I know chaps'd pay good honest scratch at the academy to watch that woman shred ginger!"—but each admission came with guilt more worthy of an eastern cathedral. Because only Vidarian of all the crew knew that Marks had, in his youth, aspired to be a land chef in one of the imperial courts, he was the sole recipient of the cook's confessions, and so over the course of those first early weeks acquired, not quite willingly, a rather thorough education in the culinary comparison between the Velinese mainland and the sprawling southeastern empire.

When not administering jovial cooking lessons, and instead caught unsuspecting by a knock at her door, the priestess's eyes had a furtive look, pinched as if all the world were pressing down upon her. But by the third week she'd improved significantly, enough to explore the ship in earnest. While making the rounds one morning Vidarian noticed a suspicious amount of handiwork being done aft on the main deck: net weaving, sail patching, minor woodwork—someone had even hauled a barrel up from stowage for recaulking.

He found Ariadel at the eye of the storm, whispering to the lamps. The sight brought him up short, and he only realized he was staring when Calgrath, a spry and time-wrinkled topman who as far as Vidarian knew hadn't actually aged in a decade, addressed him in an awed mutter.

"Somethin' else, ain't it, Cap'n? She been at it all morning—already fixed the row lights along the port corridor." Vidarian almost quailed to hear the reverent note in Calgrath's voice; he'd seen the man stoically extract sea urchin spines from a cabin boy's foot, fight a pirate with only a flying jib to his back, and laugh through a storm that sent half a dozen salted sailors back to land permanently. In fifteen years only the moonlit glaciers of Val Morhan had awed him.

As the priestess whispered to each lamp, the cuffs of her velvet robe hiding her raised hands and obscuring her words, the flame within leapt up like a loyal puppy to a long-missed master. She left a trail of bright flames behind her, and yet with every invigorated flame the assembled crew collectively held its breath.

Vidarian cleared his throat sternly, and the spell was broken. Crewmen and -women jumped in startlement, then made a good show of shouting duties to one another as they returned to their assigned work. Vidarian did his part by glaring in dissatisfaction, but he couldn't help being relieved for all their sakes that it was him who caught them gawking and not Marielle. The first mate had been efficient and professional as always, but one swore the skyglass climbed whenever she and the priestess were within ten feet.

Having completed charming the lamps, the priestess was asking Revelle Amberwight, munitions lieutenant, about the location of the stored powder when Vidarian closed enough to make out her words. The officer colored, her high cheeks darkening, and made her apologies as Vidarian approached, claiming urgent duty on a staff inspection, or surely she would be glad to give the priestess a personal tour. It might even have been true. She saluted as she hurried past.

"Something I can help you with, Priestess?" Vidarian asked, to defuse the puzzlement on the priestess's delicate features.

"I'd thought to look over your powder," she said, courteous but not masking her eagerness. The curiosity of the priesthood was legendary; few he knew had much experience with the followers of Sharli, but by the priestess's demeanor he assumed they must be much like the Nistrans, endlessly fascinated with poking at their chosen element and documenting how it twitched. Merchant vessels rarely complained—their curiosity was a generous one, and filled many a captain's purse. "My temple has been studying the dwindling potency of firearms enhanced in the last decade. We believe we may have a remedy."

"I am not, as you might imagine, anxious to see my ship turned into a laboratory," he prevaricated, thinking of Marielle and swallowing his immediate hope and greed. It was true, what she said: the past two decades, not just one, had seen the accelerating decline of distance weapons. It meant closer battles, when they couldn't be avoided. Uglier ones.

"It could mean a great difference to your defenses," the priestess argued, echoing his thought. "I am, of course, eager to lend any assistance I may for your crew's welfare, and my own."

"You'll want a sea test," he allowed. "A hand cannon would be enough."

"It would suit perfectly," she smiled.

The scuttlebutt flew quickly, as it always did. By the time Vidarian had collected a hand cannon and gauge, a collection of observers had gathered at the windward bow. Marielle, by fortune or her own design, was relieving the quartermaster at the helm and thus out of sight.

Ellara Stillwether, munitions officer, accompanied Revelle and the priestess, observing the process carefully. She and her lieutenant took careful measurements, assisted by Lifan, their little windreader. The priestess had been shocked at first to discover a child on board; Vidarian, in turn, had been surprised that she was unfamiliar with the custom. Lifan was Ellara's cousin, and fiercely guarded; Ellara herself had served as windreader on the *Quest*, when she could—the ability faded with the onset of adolescence. Ariadel assured them that no such parallel existed for fire, which typically appeared *after* adolescence if at all. For Lifan's part, she was as brightly intelligent as her protector, and showed a steady knack for figures that made Vidarian sure she would one day follow in Ellara's footsteps, if the land didn't lure her away.

After a full battery of initial calculations was complete, Ellara meticulously loaded the hand cannon, tamped it, laid its neck across a mark on the bow, and fired. The shot echoed over the calm water, and when it finally arced down to splash into the blue, Revelle called out a time and trajectory estimate.

As they prepared for the second shot, Ellara solemnly passed the flask of powder to the priestess. What followed was significantly more satisfying to the attentive eyes of the crew than her earlier performance with the lamps. On the deck she spread a linen cloth, and upon this spread a measure of powder. With her hands just above it, but never touching, she began a rhythmic chant, twitching her fingers to its beat. Vidarian would admit to no one that his own heart lurched when the powder began to glow; the gasps of the crew were enough.

Gradually the glow faded, and the priestess tipped the powder back into its flask by rolling the linen into a funnel. She handed the flask back to Ellara, who accepted it with reverence barely masked by her outward veneer of skepticism, and wadded the linen away into a pocket, of which her robe seemed to contain many.

Without ceremony Ellara directed Revelle and Lifan to take their readings again, and they complied swiftly. Then Ellara loaded the cannon once more, her movements as measured and diligent as if she were at her officer's test again.

The crew erupted in a furor as the shot sailed out across the water, easily a third again the distance of the first. Some whooped with delight, others murmured appreciation or amazement—and above them all, Ellara voiced a strident cry that checked the others. "Captain! Our calculations!" Her dark eyes were flinty with concern, darting as they doubtless racked through the hundreds of adjustments that the priestess's powder implied for their defenses.

"Ms. Amberwight," Vidarian spoke without turning from the water. "My quarters. You'll find a red leather book on the third shelf. Fetch it, please." The priestess's head tilted in inquiry as the lieutenant saluted and hurried off. "My grandfather's log," he explained. "He had a fascination with munitions. The middle section is entirely devoted to trajectory calculation tables. Outdated, we thought, even in my father's time." He laughed.

In moments Revelle had returned with the requested volume. She offered it to Vidarian, but he gestured instead to Ellara, who looked about ready to pounce. Or explode. She was too professional—narrowly—to seize it from her lieutenant's unprepared hands, but neither did she waste time in finding the page Vidarian directed her to.

"The measurement is quite close," Ellara said, her eyes intense on the text when they weren't darting to her wax tablet for comparison. "We'll want to run more tests . . ."

"There should be enough of the new powder for several," Ariadel offered. She seemed slightly fatigued, but satisfied as a housecat, leaning against the bow.

The sun was beginning to drop over the water to the leeward side, and here the forecastle cast a long shadow that just reached them. Celer, one of the two cabin boys, had fetched a lamp and now bore it up near them, a fine excuse to get a close-up look at the powder that his height had not previously afforded. A glint from the priestess's hands caught Vidarian's eye; a pale blue residue clung to her palms. Vidarian wouldn't have noticed it if not for the flickering lamp, but as she lifted her hand, the residue glittered like powdered graphite. And yet she had not touched the powder.

"The tests, I'm afraid, should rightly wait for tomorrow, and daylight," Vidarian said, and though both Ellara and Revelle looked as though they'd like to object, they could hardly slow the sun, and quelled their objections. Ellara surely was mentally concocting some way to float lamps on the sea's surface so as to prolong the experiment, but she would have to settle for poring over the elder Rulorat's book into the deep hours of the night, as she doubtless would.

"Priestess, if I may?" Calgrath offered, and Vidarian turned to him in surprise. He gave a little bow, excusing himself, but continued, "Our medical kit? Surely—"

"It would take a trained specialist in the medical arts to adjust those. I dare not risk imbalancing them," Ariadel apologized, and added, "I'm sure your ship's mender has them in the best condition possible." This won a smile from the old seaman; the priestess could not know that the mender in question, currently on a watch shift if Vidarian recalled the day roster, was Calgrath's younger brother-in-law; but the keenness in the old man's eye when it came to medicine should have told her enough.

"Priestess, a word, at your convenience?" Vidarian ventured, and Calgrath bowed himself away.

"Of course, Captain."

Back in the wood-varnish embrace of the forecastle anteroom, Vidarian sat quietly, not speaking, while Marielle, off from her shift at the helm, delivered the familiar silver tea service from the galley, almost certainly prompted by Marks. The grey kitten, which had been confined to the forecastle after three times managing to raid the galley (and nearly losing its life to the cook on the third) slept soundly, curled on a brocaded chair.

"Will you be liking anything else?" Marielle asked coolly, once she'd settled the tray. She was a scant degree off, in the angle of her hips, from body-checking the priestess, as if to deny her presence.

"No, thank you, Ms. Solandt."

"Very good, sir," she nodded, and finally spared a glance for the priestess, out of protocol. "Nistra's peace." She bowed, and left, shutting the door behind her.

The priestess permitted herself a soft laugh once the door was safely closed.

"Something amuses you, Priestess?" Vidarian couldn't quite keep the frost out of his tone.

Her laughter stilled. "Just an odd expression, it strikes me," she said, and leaned forward, folding her hands self-consciously. "It seems I've done something to offend you, Captain."

"Only insofar as you've been playing tricks on my crew, Priestess," Vidarian said. "Neither they, nor I, deserve such."

The priestess's eyes widened; her etiquette training surely did not cover direct confrontation. Better, Vidarian thought, that she learn sea ways quickly—he reined in his anger to a cold implacability, but was startled, himself, to find that there was disappointment there as well.

When she didn't answer, Vidarian continued, "There was something on your hands. You added it to the powder."

She stiffened. "I said that we had a remedy, not that it was supernatural."

"But the chanting, the hand-waving, the glowing. The lamps. Trickery, yes?" As he spoke he heard his father's anger in his own voice, the rumble of distant thunder.

"They're not fairly 'tricks,'" the priestess insisted hotly. "They do work." Now her hands came together under the cuffs of the robe, vanishing.

"But it's nothing to do with elemental manipulation."

"It's nothing to do with my elemental ability," she corrected, but reluctantly, a deer brought to bay. "It *is* manipulation."

"Why?" he asked simply.

She surprised him by sliding to her feet, rising gracefully as a courtier. She inspected her upturned palms ruefully, then brushed them against the velvet robe. A pang of uneasy guilt shot through him at the distressed curve of her shoulders, the set of her jaw. He'd meant to chasten her, to demand forthrightness, but not to wound her. "I've never been skilled with the necessary deceptions," she sighed.

"Necessary?" His voice was sharp again, and he took a deep breath. "Why should deception be necessary?" he continued, willing his grandmother's civility, calling up arduous etiquette lessons from his childhood.

She turned, the robe swaying gracefully with her, but with more weight, his sharper eye concluded, than velvet should account for. "Your people have noticed the fading of your tools, you've said as much yourself—over decades." He nodded, but rather than pursuing her case, the priestess bafflingly turned away again, and then back to him. She searched for something in his eyes, boring into him until he could feel his cheeks heating. "What I'm about to say would have me confined to Sher'azar for a decade, if Endera or anyone else found out," she began, but now that she had committed this much did not hesitate. "The tools aren't simply fading. Our ability to manipulate the elements has also been dwindling—not merely for decades, but for the better part of a century."

A cold fist of dread clenched in his stomach. "The sea wars—"

"—were the beginning of the unrest," she agreed. "A great change is coming. We've seen this dwindling accelerate in the last decade, and now—"

"—the Vkortha," he finished for her, and again she nodded.

Silence stretched between them. The kitten, according to the enigmatic internal logic of cats, had slept through their heated discussion, but now awakened and stretched. The priestess picked it up, coaxing a rattling purr out of its thin chest with a few strokes of its back, and settled herself on the chair it had just been occupying.

"Strange doings," Vidarian said at last, folding his hands. "I can't begin to comprehend them. But I also have never seen willful deception come to a good end. I still do not now see why this cannot be explained to my crew."

"Do you tell your crew every smallest detail of your charting decisions, your courses, which contracts you accept and which you do not?" she asked, scratching the kitten behind its ears. It purred louder, then rolled under her hand, kicking upward with its feet and attacking her playfully. She wrestled back for a moment, then released it onto the carpet.

"Not every detail," he said, bound by his own honor to honesty, though unsure what he was admitting, exactly.

"Yet they follow you, because you are their captain," she said, looking up at him again. "If you were to democratically decide every detail, the ship would never move."

"I do not demand their deceived belief," he said. "That's something else entirely."

"But we do not truly deceive," she insisted, and the intent sincerity in her wide eyes was more disarming than he'd have liked to admit. "The benefits that I have provided to your ship are genuine." That he could not deny, and the fervor in her voice was not sternness but ardent conviction. "Captain, you must believe me, that what I have seen as a priestess of Sharli, again and again, is that the priestesshood is needed. The priestesshood alone retains the records of these fluctuations in elemental energy, and if we are to survive, we require the support of the common folk, which comes only when they believe that we are still capable of our foremothers' deeds."

"I will not argue against that cannon shot, and I am grateful," he said. "But can you really be so sure that the priestesshood knows best?"

She smiled, asking with her eyes if *he* was so sure about baiting her. He smiled back. "I'm never sure of anything," she said. "As the philosopher Veldaus said, 'the sure mind is the closed one, capable only of repetition.'"

"You certainly seemed sure of him," Vidarian said, nodding at the kitten, which was presently attacking a tasseled end of the table runner.

"Her," Ariadel corrected absently. "I apologize for unsettling you," she said, her head tilting in what Vidarian was sure was sincere puzzlement. "I don't know what came over me. It's against my training to hold with such impulsive superstition."

He laughed before he could stop himself. "A fire priestess? Trained against superstition?"

She colored slightly, but her smile was gentle; the sudden thought of Endera even attempting such an expression surprised Vidarian with its absurdity. This Ariadel was obviously unlike any fire priestess Vidarian had known. "You must have little experience with priestesses," she said, echoing his thought. "Although the common folk—"her eyes dropped to the tray Marielle had brought in, surely unconsciously"—permitted and, yes, even encouraged their superstitions, the priestesshood rigorously trains against such things."

"Yet I must bear them in my crew." He sighed, and at her worried glance, smiled again, wryly. "Fear not. I will not betray your secrets. But I will appreciate your honesty in private, at least."

"That I can promise you," she said, and he gave a little half-bow of thanks from his seat.

Beneath them, the ship was moving, turning on its course. Vidarian's stomach clenched again, for he knew their place on the chart. They angled southwest, the prevailing south wind dropping from belled sails; in such fashion did the *Empress Quest* enter the Outwater. And her lights blazed bright against the great dark sea of the night sky.

CHAPTER FOUR
A FIRE AT SEA

One week later Vidarian sat closeted in the aft cabin, door firmly shut and commanding officers instructed to ensure that the priestess stayed on the other side of the *Quest* for a brief duration. When he was satisfied that all was secure, he settled down on the bench bed and drew his sword.

Since Endera's description of steel's "remembrance" he couldn't quite look at his ancestral blade the same way. The longsword, light and strong with the slightest arcing curve to the blade, was as old as the *Empress Quest*—five generations past, and Vidarian was the sixth. If what Endera said was right, some fraction of his grandfathers' souls remained in the blade.

Sunlight filtered down through the blue and green stained glass set into the back portholes of the cabin, bathing him in gentle aquamarine light. It slid across glimmering steel like foam along a beach as he turned his arm, feeling the familiar weight of the three-quarter-tang blade and its mahogany-covered hilt. As always it felt like an extension of his hand, the weight of his family settling like a protecting mantle about his shoulders.

The square of flattened steel just above the sword's silver-plated cross-guard bore six names—and when Vidarian fathered a son, his name would be chiseled in below them at the boy's thirtieth birthday. Seven generations did not make for an ancient tradition, but theirs was sound, and its weight rested heavily in Vidarian's palm.

As was sometimes his habit, he sat contemplating the names for a time; having long since memorized every serif and curve, the letters were familiar, almost mesmerizing. He was still staring at them when the first shouts rang out abovedeck, pierced by the emergency cry of the boatswain's pipe—*ship sighted, ship closing.*

Vidarian sprang to his feet and only just remembered to sheathe the blade before thundering out the door of the cabin.

High afternoon sunlight lanced his eyes as he ran out onto the deck. Men were boiling up the ladders at either end of the ship, and Calgrath, perched in his customary position in the crow's nest, was bellowing down.

"Captain! Ship sighted off th' port bow! It's the *Starless*, sir, and she be closin' swift!"

Spitting a curse, Vidarian began roaring commands. Fast as the *Empress Quest* was, she was no match for the *Starless Night*, a pirate vessel known for breaking speed records as a matter of annual sport. And she'd been lurking, to appear so suddenly. Off to port was a collection of tiny islands wreathed by perilous shoals, all but invisible in the dark waters; it was madness verging on suicide to plant a ship there, but that was a fair description of Vanderken's strategy.

Marielle met him at the wheel. She was already shouting orders to the rest of the crew, but paused to exchange a few low voiced words with Vidarian. "Captain, these're not *Starless* waters. She hasn't been seen in these parts for over two years! Mighty odd if you ask me."

"Right now it's best not to ask, Ms. Solandt. Just get me every cannon aboard aimed at that loveless craft!" Taking a sighting from the compass at his right, Vidarian spun hard on the wheel, bringing the *Quest* about as hard as she would bear, swinging her slender bowsprit around to face the *Starless*. "Solandt!" he shouted, remembering something. Marielle answered with an "Aye?" from across the deck. "Get someone to the priestess—keep her below deck! Once she's secure, get back up here and unlock the fore starboard chest—I'll not have these men meet Vanderken with rusted weapons!"

"Aye, sir!"

The orders were rapidly carried out, and well for it, too, as the *Starless* was closing with disturbing swiftness. Within moments, it seemed, cannon-fire boomed on the distant waves, falling short of the *Quest*, but not nearly short enough.

The wind was against the opposing vessel but she plowed on unconcerned. The *Quest*'s arc shortly brought her around nearly ninety degrees to her own wake, presenting her gallant and cannon-studded port bow to the rapidly closing *Starless*. "All cannons fire when ready!" came the distant shout from Marielle, and Vidarian held the wheel firmly on course.

A resounding *BOOM!* shook the deck as the *Quest* opened fire, the priestess's augmented powder performing superbly; the crew roared to hear such play. The *Starless*, steady on her approach and moving too swiftly to accurately gauge position, could not avoid the shot in time, and took a hit to her highest mast. Her answering forward salvo was equally ineffective, thrown off by the damage to the high sails, but it spat salten spray across the *Empress* and her crew.

"All cannons take aim on her stern! Those who haven't armed, do so—we won't be so lucky again!" A tense but full-volumed shout answered Vidarian's command as crewmembers scurried across the deck.

The *Starless* loomed still closer, weakened but not deterred by the hit to her high mast. Spinning the wheel to starboard, Vidarian turned the *Quest* rapidly on the water, taking advantage of her deep keel to bring her side out of range of the enemy's punishing cannon.

But the fire that he expected never came. Instead, a volley of grapeshot filled the air with a sickening hiss, and pelted in a vicious, stinging rain against the *Empress*'s forward sails, caught not yet furled for battle. Vidarian's stomach sank as their forward momentum fell away.

A comparatively slow ship made slower, the *Quest* now had no chance at flight; Vanderken and his crew would board, it was just a matter of time. Rather than stall the inevitable, Vidarian called Marielle to the wheel and left her to steer. The Rulorat sword sang its freedom from the sheath, and with his free hand Vidarian took up rope from a braided ladder and began to climb the main mast.

When he was halfway up, Vidarian could make out the stalwart form of the enemy captain astride the deck of the *Starless Night*. Vanderken raised his own sword in a salute, and though his grin could not be ascertained with the eyes, it was evident in his voice.

"Ahoy, Captain Rulorat! It's been some time!"

"Not long enough, Vanderken! And 'twill not be until your thrice-damned ship ceases to poison these waters!"

"Now, my boy, what manner of greeting is that for an old chum?" Vanderken's voice grew in volume as the *Starless* continued its inexorable approach.

"Do you see that pennant, Vanderken?" Vidarian shouted, pointing his sword at the banner of Sharli that now flew from the crow's nest. "Would you be so quick to challenge a goddess?"

"Flags and faerie dust, lad!" His laugh carried flat and sharp across the water. "This be Nistra's bosom! Now you just wait right there!"

Moments later, a sickening crash joined the two vessels at the bow, punctuated by musket-fire as the crews exchanged volleys. Enhanced powder or not, it would not be a good fight; by the numbers pouring out of Vanderken's ship, he had, as was his custom, overloaded his berths, and appeared to have roughly a three-to-two ratio on the *Empress*'s crew: hardened murderers, all. Swinging down from the mast, Vidarian ran to the starboard bow, leaping up to the thick rail. Mercilessly he kicked an enemy sailor into the brine as he caught his bearings, and waited for Vanderken to approach.

The captain of the *Starless* styled himself a "real" pirate; he did not hang back behind his crew, but foraged up with them. Men fell on both sides as muskets took their toll on the ranks, but out of custom none touched the region around the two captains.

Finally Vanderken leapt across the brief gap between the two ships' starboard bows, landing hard on the deck of the *Empress*. Vidarian raised his blade and waited, a snarl of disgust on his lips.

Vanderken's sword was a lighter one, and he was quick as a viper with it. Still, Vidarian's defense held, and throughout their first clashing exchanges, neither man gained ground. Vidarian came in high, Vanderken slid the blade away along his own; back and forth they went.

"Tell me, Vanderken—how does one sleep, with infamy like yours?" Though fatigue now warmed his chest, Vidarian paced his breathing so as to seem effortless, baiting Vanderken into expending his own on a tirade.

"In a world so twisted as this, give me infamy over honor," Vanderken said, breathing with each thrust, unfazed by Vidarian's ploy. "Give me infamy," he growled again, and a pulse of dread shot through Vidarian's heart at the pure hate in his voice, "over pandering to the land-maggots. I sleep like a babe—"

When a bass explosion rocked the deck of the *Empress*, Vidarian staggered backward in shock—but Ulweis Vanderken only laughed. "What madness is this?" Vidarian demanded, but the other captain's eyes were on the site of the explosion.

Vidarian had not yet turned away from his opponent, and so saw the look in his eyes when triumph metamorphosed to horror.

It would later be recalled that the burning Eyes of Sharli descended overhead from a bank of clouds that boiled up out of the red sea. A demoness, her eyes rimed with hellfire, had stormed up out of the belly of the *Empress* and unleashed the fury of ten worlds upon the crew of the *Starless Night*—a fury of myth, of universes filled with fire. Brilliant blue flames shot from the pair of golden eyes that seared themselves into the memory of every crewman, igniting the pirate vessel's sails and burning them to ash in seconds. Then the sea around the craft began to boil, and it seemed that the very air caught fire. Men, all who had crewed the *Starless* but none from the *Empress Quest*, found that their clothing combusted and their skin burned. They leapt from the ship, attempting to douse the flames in the sea, but found no mercy there in the bubbling depths. Vidarian remembered only that his sword began to incandesce, pulsing like a living thing, as the enemy captain staggered back from him.

Vanderken ran back to his ship, jaw slack with disbelief, to stand aboard the crumbling bow as the turgid waves rolled up in a burning frenzy and washed him from the world.

In the aftermath, only a single crewman remained from the *Starless*—a midshipman, by the knots on his sleeve. He only had three real teeth, but made up for it in muscle mass, and had survived the firestorm only by having enough sense to douse himself in one of the *Empress*'s fire-fighting barrels rather than pitching himself into the boiling sea. Still, he had taken many burns, and was unconscious.

When Vidarian went to find Ilsut, the ship's healer, he found him carefully but quickly finishing the ties on a sling that bound Marielle's entire right arm, splinted at forearm and upper, to her chest. Vidarian stopped short at the infirmary threshold, stricken. When Ilsut rose, there was no note of accusation in his dark eyes, only purpose, but his hurried nod as he gathered his tools and made for the front of the ship released a wall of guilt to crash through Vidarian's shock.

"Marielle," he said quietly, then stopped, lost again. No use asking how bad the injury was; without doubt, it sealed the only issue of any importance: that she would not be eligible for promotion within the emperor's admiralty, not this year, at least. It was well known that Captain Theravar of the imperial coastrunner *Ardent* intended to retire within six months; Marielle had been favored by the College for the post, had fought long and hard for years. Most of the crew knew that she kept a tiny and expensive scale model of the *Ardent* in her quarters, bought last year when Theravar's coming retirement was announced. But the injury would disqualify her from the—however damnably ceremonial—ritual drills that tested imperial captains.

In her exhaustion—not, Vidarian would not allow himself to think, defeat—her usually precise diction faded into the snarled ship-speak of her humbler youth: "Belay that, Cap'n. The time it could've availed me's long past, so it's naught but empty words."

He knelt, heedless of protocol. "If it is in my power to correct this, after we've returned, you know that I will." He searched her posture for hope, for the spirit that had driven her these many years. For forgiveness.

She would not look at him, and he had known her too long to think it was out of fear. "You did your duty, Captain. I'll do mine. 'Twas my choice setting foot on this ship, knowing what I did."

He moved to try again, mustering a stern argument about acts of heroism and the Naval College, but at that moment Lifan appeared in the doorway. "Sir? The midshipman. He's regained consciousness."

Vidarian looked from his first mate to the windreader. Lifan, hidden away from the fighting, nonetheless was now seeing its aftermath. Though she bore up bravely, she was shaken as any child would be. He stood, thanked her, ruffled her hair affectionately (and took some small relief in the relaxing of her taut shoulders after; the reassured smile—at least he could do that much), and headed for the quarterdeck.

The ship's carpenter had been supplied and dispatched to take care of what mast damage he could with tar and rope, and what crew not assigned to assisting him or other repair work had gathered around Ilsut and Vanderken's midshipman.

"Ye warned them, Cap'n, there be no shame in what they got." This was one of many statements in response to Vidarian's grave demeanor. Little did they know that his concern could be measured less than nothing for Vanderken and his lice-ridden crew.

"Agreed," Vidarian murmured, startling them by lifting his voice for the first time since the *Starless* had gone down. "They should have known the consequences." His eyes rested, not on the poor wretch before them, but on the ladder down into the hold.

"But why would they risk their entire crew to board, Cap'n? It don't make no sense."

"That," Vidarian answered grimly, drawing his sword and resting its tip on the shoulder of the bleary survivor, "is precisely what I intend to find out."

৲৴৲৴৲

Vidarian had hardened himself to the notion of a grueling interrogation, but in the end it was very simple. When Ellara, unasked, had fetched Ariadel, they had no need of so much as rope for restraining. The midshipman began to weep and babble as soon as her cloaked figure appeared in the doorway.

Ellara gave Vidarian a nod, then turned to face the rapidly confessing prisoner. Vidarian offered the priestess his arm and they retreated from the quarterdeck, the sounds of a grown man's sobbing following them in echoes off the wooden walls.

If Ariadel's touch before was fire, her hand on his arm now was a brush of palest smoke. The faint scent of it even seemed to cling to her presence, though he wasn't sure if it was merely his imagination. Her feet barely seemed to touch the deck as she walked, and her skin was a uniform angry red in color. Darker rose marked her cheeks in a persistent flush.

In silence they walked the length of the deck, finally approaching the ladder that led up into the forecastle. When they reached the anteroom, Vidarian led the priestess to a high-backed chair, then moved to close both of the doors. When they were secure, he returned and set about pouring *kava* for both of them. Without being asked, he treated hers liberally with brown sugar and verali cream.

"Are you all right?" he asked quietly, handing her the cup.

She nodded. "I'll be fine." Her voice was not quite a whisper.

Vidarian settled down into a chair opposite hers, fingers laced around his own silver cup. "Then perhaps you can tell me what in the name of all that's holy happened out there."

"I called on Sharli—and she answered."

"I'm afraid that's not good enough, Priestess. I know you are weary, but if my guess is correct, the Vkortha now know our exact position." Memory recalled to him the sensation of burning steel filling his hand, and it hardened his words. "Why did you come abovedeck?"

The priestess's body language conveyed a blush, but with the current state of her skin it was impossible to tell. "Men were breaking into the lower hold," she said, emotion coloring her hoarse voice. "They set off some kind of explosive. I—panicked a little, I'll admit. I called on Sharli. I did not expect her to answer—so forcefully. It was she who ascended the staircase."

"And left your body like this?"

Ariadel nodded. "It will pass within a few days. I experienced this at my initiation rite, much more dramatically than this. Sharli is the Living Flame; we cannot host her in our mortal bodies without some aftereffect."

Vidarian frowned, subdued. He finished his *kava* before answering, letting the warmth fill his stomach. "I have already directed our warrant officer to set a course for the nearest port. We will pick up medical supplies there. I have some here, of course, but none that would treat burns such as yours."

The priestess straightened, wincing as her back thumped hard against the chair. "Captain, you said yourself, the Vkortha know our position. We cannot stop!"

Setting the empty cup on its tray, Vidarian shook his head. "I'm afraid we have no choice. There's only so much the ship's carpenter can do—one of their volleys cracked our aft mast, and we've sustained damage to the hull, not to mention the explosion site. Only the *Empress*'s sound construction prevents her from taking on water even now. We must dock, if only for a little while." He took a deep breath and let it out slowly. "I'm sorry, Priestess."

Ariadel sank down into her chair, staring. "Do not be, Captain. Sharli's will or no, this is on my shoulders—and I have endangered your crew."

Vidarian leaned forward earnestly. "Think not on it, Priestess. My crew does not fear the danger you bring—you've seen it yourself."

She laughed bitterly. "And now they avoid me in the passages, Captain. It will not be the same after this."

"They'll get past it," Vidarian insisted, though his own heart caved with doubt. "We've seen more than you might think." He smiled then, and would have reached to pat her hand out of reflex, but caught himself in time. Instead he stood and gave her a bow, reminding them both of his duty. "The crew of the *Empress Quest* remains at your disposal, priestess. We will see you safely to your destination, I promise you."

CHAPTER FIVE

A RUSE

They sailed through the night and approached Westhill Harbor just as dawn was pooling crimson on the eastern horizon. The crew worked with silent efficiency to bring the *Empress* into port, dropping anchor under Marielle's direction, though Ilsut had ordered her restricted to her quarters. Vidarian selected a dozen crewmembers to accompany him ashore, separated into two groups. One group he intended to return to the *Empress* after the supply run—the other he did not.

As they were making their preparations to disembark, Vidarian stood before the door to Marielle's cabin. He adjusted the boatswain's pipe—captain's gold—around his neck, running his thumb across the engraved *Rulorat* lettering on its throat. Then he knocked.

Marielle opened the door, and a jolt of surprise registered in her eyes, fast fading with her perfunctory nod and salute. "Captain," she said only, and pulled the door further in wordless invitation. The reef charts for Westhill were spread across her cot, but this was the only defiance of neatness. She was, of course, already packed.

He stepped inside and shut the door, then spared a moment to see if she would permit awkward silence between them.

She did. In another officer, such silence might be nervous, searching—a hound seeking approval, fearing reprimand—but Marielle's clear grey stare was predator's patience. Vidarian had only seen a wolf once, a caged creature kept by a wealthy nobleman who had employed the *Quest* on occasion. Even confined, the animal had looked at him just like this.

"I intend to take half of the crew inland," he began, and when she opened her mouth to remind him she'd already been briefed, he raised his hand in a request to continue. "We'll need lumber for the hull repairs, and I aim to be displeased with Westhill's lot."

Marielle's eyebrows lifted. "Westhill has perfectly fine lumber, sir. The coastal hardwood." The tiniest kernel of her old willfulness was there, but only just.

"It may be fine for Westhill, but not for my *Empress*," he said, thumping the nearest bulkhead for emphasis. "I'll demand red teak, what she's built of." She straightened to object again, and he spoke quickly to cut her off. "A week inland, I know, and more than that on return. But there I'll split the land crew again. Half will fetch the lumber and cross coastward to meet you here," he moved to the Westhill chart and indicated a spot back up the coast from their current position. "In two days, I'll return with the other half, and we'll hire passage on the next ship to pass through."

"You, and the priestess," Marielle continued for him, quick on the uptake as usual, though her voice and humor remained low. Then she started. "The *Quest* will sail without you."

Even though it was his own plan, her words made his stomach drop. "Yes," he said. "It will. After I've seen the priestess to Zal'nehara, we'll meet you back at Val Harlon."

Marielle went to the charts on her cot, stirred them, ostensibly reading routes but clearly searching her thoughts. "And doing this you aim to shake the pursuit," she said carefully, her eyes racing with branching speculation.

"That's one reason," he said, and she made a rough noise, a growl in preparation for protest, but he cut her short with a shake of his head. "By turning over command of the *Quest* to you, by returning her to sea with you alone at the helm, you will have a field promotion according to the naval codes. And field captains . . ."

Marielle sucked in her breath, and paled, then flushed. Several things warred on her face—the tight stubbornness of her lips, the outrage in her flared nose—but more than anything, the wide, vulnerable hope in her eyes. The hope of a woman who had given up such frivolous things. He hated it, deeply: what their destinies had done to them. But he was not about to go down without a fight, and neither, ultimately, would she. "Field captains . . . are exempt from qualification drills," she finished for him, with awe and disbelief at her own words.

"The war code," he agreed. It had never been rescinded. Neither, however, had it been invoked in eighty years—since the last of the sea wars, ended when Vidarian's grandfather was a young man.

Marielle was silent for a long moment, her clouded eyes betraying thoughts turned inward. Thinking madly, Vidarian was sure, of a reason he could be wrong.

He laughed, startling her. "This must be the first time I've actually seen you speechless," he said.

"I don't like it," she said, finally.

"There you are," he said. "Back to normal."

"I'm serious, Vidarian," she said. "*Captain*." The hope had faded into worry, and he spared a wistful moment for it, memorizing what it had been like to see her so alight. "You've never been away from this ship so long. Your father was never."

"And it is my family's mandate, my grandfather's action, that binds me now to this task," he said, all levity forgotten. "It does *not* bind the crew. Therefore my duty to protect them, weighed with my duty to fulfill the—" She looked at him sharply, and he skated around the inflammatory term. "The Agreement made by my grandfather," and the outrage faded a touch from her eyes, "demands this course."

She shook her head again, but sighed, and he knew he had won. "Duty," she mused, putting vinegar into the word.

"Mine," he agreed, and removed the golden boatswain's pipe and its chain from his neck. He picked up her hand and pressed the pipe into it, curling her fingers around its precious throat. "And yours."

Marielle looked down at her folded hand with trepidation and wonder. Yet, again, these were short-lived, as her shrewdness took over once more. Her fingers loosened around the pipe. The echo of his father's identical motion ten years ago shot through him like lightning, but Marielle's worried eyes brought him back to himself. "You don't have to do this," she said. "There's no need—"

"I don't have to," he agreed, and closed her fingers around the pipe again. "But it's my decision."

"I thought not to change it," she said simply. "But I will thank you." Her voice was suddenly hoarse, as she brushed the pipe chain with the tips of her fingers, tracing it. Making sure, Vidarian thought, that it was real. "Thank you, sir."

Vidarian drew her into a rough, brief embrace, and she cleared her throat repeatedly, blinking. "We can't escape our destinies," he said, then withdrew, but gripped her firmly by the shoulder. "But we can use what power we have for the benefit of those deserving."

Marielle returned the embrace, her hand steady on his collarbone. "Aye." She lifted the pipe in a little toast. "And may neither of us regret it."

∿∿∿

Abovedeck, a clamor from the main deck drew Vidarian from making a final check of the carpenter's repair plan. The shouts from the crew were concerned, not panicked, and so he did not run, but moved quickly nonetheless for the foremast.

The crew had been loading supplies into the dories for their trip inland. Among the tools had been an ice barrel; Marks was supervising the unpacking of several measures of meat and fish for the land journey, and consolidating their ice to help preserve what remained. Ice, floated down the river from Kara'zul, was easily found in Val Harlon, and they'd taken on a quantity of it to ease the journey through the Outwater.

Ariadel had, beyond any sane explanation, doused herself in the reserved ice awaiting consolidation, and the water that the ice had melted into over the weeks at sea. She was drenched and shivering from top to waist, and was now being swathed in linen run up hurriedly from the hold.

"No accounting for 'em," Calgrath muttered as he passed, shaking his head, "the whims of priestesses." Doutbless a thousand new superstitions would spring up around her latest escapade.

Vidarian went to see to her himself, aiming to find out why in the world she'd dunk herself in ice water, but as he accepted a quickly offered stack of linen from young Lifan, Ariadel spoke first, bringing him up short.

"You're nowhere near as sure of this plan as you'd like them to think," she murmured, teeth chattering, and he looked around rapidly to see if anyone else had heard. "It's all right," she added. "I understand." And her quiet smile, given the impertinence of the observation, was entirely too warming.

≈≈≈

As they disembarked into the dories, Marielle stood at the winch, captain's pipe in hand. Vidarian was sure she was unaware of how tightly she clenched it. At her right hand, Malloray Underbridge, a mute who'd served on the *Quest* since Vidarian's father's days, stood watching the distant harbor nervously, mouthing silent meditation chants. In the twenty-odd years Vidarian had known him he had never once set foot on shore—an odd fellow, but with an uncanny intuition for sea conditions and trade commodities that had kept him aboard on his own terms.

"Fair seas, Captain," Vidarian said as his dory descended toward the water, saluting Marielle. At his accolade, Marielle straightened, saluting in return, and most of the crew couldn't hide their enthusiasm, grinning and returning her salute in kind. Whispered explanations passed through the group for those who looked around, not understanding, and then they took up their own shouted farewells and cat-calls. By the time the small passenger boats touched water, Marielle was shouting commands, her tone daring any who might test her authority, and quick footfalls echoed down from the deck as those left aboard leapt to. And in spite of their downward passage throwing the ship's damage into sharp relief, her side listing in a way that made Vidarian's heart lurch, he smiled as they set off across the harbor.

Chapter Six
A Life Flame

In Westhill, Vidarian made a great show of his dissatisfaction with the local hardwood, oscillating between the genteel apologies of a tradesman who dared not burn bridges in any port and the ravings of a foam-addled seafarer. In the end, he threw up his hands in mock surrender, by turns apologizing to the logging master and haranguing the quality of his product. When they left for the harbor's small livery stable to rent carts for the journey inland, despite the loss of business the loggers seemed relieved to see their backs.

Two men sat in the back of the last cart armed with muskets; they would be marked, no doubt, by passersby, but no more (or so Vidarian hoped) than the average commodity-bearing caravan. To further mask their intentions, they had also taken on a quantity of extra fruit in the carts; true merchantmen, on such a "tedious" mission, would have made the most of it by carrying goods to their inland destination, and so they did.

The priestess sat cloaked beside Vidarian as he drove the leading cart. Her color had improved somewhat, and her eyes looked less sore and watery. By midday, though she remained somewhat subdued, she carried her half of a conversation that helped pass the time (as only so much amusement could be derived from watching the back end of their grey mule).

As the road continued to stretch long before them, the topics grew increasingly familiar. "Priestess," Vidarian said at last, "I really must know. Your, er, display with the ice barrel . . ." Ariadel flushed, opening her mouth for an obvious refutation, and Vidarian reminded her, "You pledged your honesty, for my ears if no other's."

She was silent for a contemplative moment. "It was no esoteric ritual, if that's what you think, though the 'how' of it would likely surprise you." At her abruptly solemn tone he almost regretted the question. Ariadel grew quiet for another uncomfortable stretch, then sighed. "I was trying to Quench myself." She placed a peculiar emphasis on the word, but Vidarian had a shrewd—and stomach-sinking—idea of what she meant.

"Is that even possible?" he asked, finally.

"Supposedly. But I have no idea how to go about doing it. They do not teach us how."

"But why?"

"To throw off the pursuit. It's trained to the signature of my ability—which now brings danger to us all." She grew thoughtful again, and her grim contemplation put an end to conversation for the next several stretches of terrain. At last Vidarian called a halt, and they feasted, though with tense gaiety, on the provisions that comprised their "trade" shipment: foods that did not fare well in ship's storage but would be welcomed further inland. Marks waylaid two portions of the small crew into setting and tending cookfires, and prepared their meal himself. In short order he had fresh fish crackling with butter and garlic on iron skillets and two rounds of creamy white cheese sliced onto soft bread. Fruit juice, nonintoxicating but a treat nonetheless, rounded out the meal.

In due course they were back on the road and Vidarian reflected briefly that land travel would never cease to annoy him. The mule's stubbornly slow pace grew maddening at times, and the surrounding territory, while lush compared to most, seemed dull and lifeless against the endless flow and mysterious depth of the open sea. He spent some time mentally critiquing the landscape, until finally they arrived at their destination.

At a tiny town, really more a trader's waypost than a settlement, the crew halved and parted ways. One cart continued on to collect the promised red teak and trade the rest of their goods further east, while Vidarian, the priestess, and three crewmen stopped at the town. For any natural pursuer it would have been a neat plan, but Ariadel did not seem reassured.

A handful of coin bought them dinner and beds of sweet hay in a farmer's

barn, both cheerfully delivered by a family only too happy to see silver come
into their hands. When captain and crew adjourned to their lodgings armed
with large bowls of ham and pea soup, the farmer's children were gleefully
discussing what they'd purchase at the next coastal faire.

After dinner, the crew divided up the rest of the night into separate
watches. The red-painted barn, though small, boasted a small tack room that
they allocated to the priestess. A few carefully arranged bales of hay ensured
that no one would gain entry to the makeshift safehouse without the knowledge of whomever stood guard beyond the door.

Vidarian took the last watch. In the late evening a storm blew into the
valley, beginning as a squall and gradually increasing in intensity. Having spent
only his early years on land, Vidarian had seen many storms rage across the open
sea, but never one that spent such fury past the coastline. Stinging rain came
down in solid sheets that turned immediately to ice upon striking the ground.
Lightning crackled with strobe-like frequency in the lightless predawn, illumi-
nating the deranged spires and windblown shocks of ice that formed along walls,
doors, windows, and anything that showed itself above the ground.

The old barn creaked in the howling wind, but within all was quiet, and
the structure had been built well—their hay remained dry. Accustomed to
their smaller berths aboard the *Empress*, the crew slept solidly in the comparatively larger space of the barn's loft—but in the tack room a light still shone
when Calgrath woke Vidarian for his watch.

Squinting at the glow beneath the door, Vidarian paced each long wall
of the barn, then came to sit in the pool of golden light. The storm thundered
on and yet the light did not waver, and after two hours Vidarian turned, ven-
turing a glance between the door's hinges.

Inside, sitting on a pile of furs loaned her by the farmer's wife, Ariadel
stared fixedly into a tall candleflame that neither wavered nor consumed the
blackened wick on which it rested. Fascinated by its stillness, Vidarian found
himself staring into the flame as well—and when he came back to himself
with a start, he gave an involuntary jerk of his right arm, thudding it soundly
into the door. Cursing to himself, he stood and continued to peer inside.

The priestess blinked slowly, a dreamer ascending gradually from a deep sleep. Bit by bit she came back to herself, first moving her hands to touch the furs with marked unfamiliarity, then finally standing and squinting myopically at the door. Moments later she stirred again and moved to open it.

"Good evening, Captain," she whispered. Her color had improved yet more and seemed almost entirely back to normal.

"Good morning, Priestess," Vidarian answered, *sotto voce* and abashed by his accidental movement. "I did not mean to disturb you."

She smiled tiredly. "Sometimes one wishes to be disturbed. Please come in, I would not wake the crew."

Still not fully apprised of himself, Vidarian could only nod, then duck inside the tack room at her invitation.

As the door clicked shut the storm receded even further from hearing, muffled by stacked bales of hay that insulated the tack room against noise from beyond the exterior wall. The scent of leather still lingered in the warmer air, although the tack itself had been shut away in storage chests before its many meticulously polished buckles, bits, and cinches could betray the priestess's presence.

Taking a seat on one of the bales, Vidarian squinted in the low light of the candle whose glow had so entranced him from outside the little room. As before, it neither wavered nor dimmed—but up close it was vastly more fascinating. Within the tapered flame he imagined that he could see dragons twisting sinuous in bands of ochre and gold, braided with the image of a phoenix rising with burning wings atop them. The flame danced rhythmically without altering its light, pulsing with such regularity that it achieved an eerie steadiness that seemed to cast no moving shadow.

"It is a life flame," Ariadel murmured, and regarded the little candle with motherly fondness. The flame, which continued its pulsing dance, had moved on to other refrains, now depicting a fiery horse galloping across a field of ever-curling clouds. How he saw these things he did not know, but somehow they emanated from the steady, almost iridescent light.

"It's beautiful," he said quietly, without thinking. He felt more than saw Ariadel blink beside him, awakened slightly from her reverie at the intensity in his words. An apology on his lips, he turned back toward her, but her eyes were shut. With strange fluidity she began an intricate gesture, hands darting to and fro like leaping flames. The candleflame began to twist, and finally at the height of her movement it darted away from its wick, speeding swiftly between her fingers like a fleeing will-o'-wisp.

Ariadel's eyes burned golden as she opened them again. In that moment every image Vidarian had seen dancing through the life flame shone eclipsed by the depth in her dark eyes. Memories, not his own, rushed into his mind—the waiting fury of the Vkortha as a tangible weight on every inch of his skin; a pair of burning eyes searing into his soul from a distance too great to contemplate; a surge of catastrophic power (enough, he somehow knew, to level an entire city); a flickering flame small and vulnerable surrounded by the terrible, gushing sea. Then he returned to himself, reaching at the fleeing memories as a child after dancing butterflies.

Vidarian froze. He had closed his eyes, and when he opened them, he found he had indeed reached—and his hand rested upon the priestess's face. Slowly he registered the smooth, cool skin beneath his thumb, softer still at her neck where his fingers rested, and the silken locks of her hair brushing the back of his palm. Shock coursed like ice through his veins and he stuttered for a moment, darting to withdraw. But Ariadel only smiled, smoke on a sunset horizon, and closed the distance between them.

Her embrace was flame rushing into being where there had only been ember and tinder, but her lips were warm and real when they met his. Vidarian had only a fraction of a moment to reel in shock, and then he was lost again, falling through a world of singing fire.

Ariadel's hair shone in the light of the life flame just before it engulfed them both in sweet darkness, falling down to pool around Vidarian's head as they fell softly onto the pile of furs. The scent of her skin, a peculiar aroma of mingled cinnamon and sandalwood, soared into his senses, revealing a dizzying depth to the tantalizing hints that had come to him before always from a distance. Hesitant but compelled, his hands slid down around her slender waist, drawing her closer. Her teeth flashed white in the sporadic candlelight as she smiled again, and then his eyes slid closed as a rush of ecstasy accompanied her questing lips' discovery of the hollow of his throat.

Moving to meet her, and driven beyond thought, he turned roughly on the furs, smiling.

Then there were two sounds, both so simultaneous as to be forever inseparable in his mind. Ariadel's smoky chuckle, a promise and a challenge at once—and the metallic hiss of his sword, forgotten, sliding loose from its scabbard as he moved.

All hell broke loose.

The storm that raged outside lurched tangibly, air pressure shifting with a nearly audible *pop* as its attention centered on the tiny farm. Vidarian and Ariadel, blinded by the shining light from the Rulorat sword, heard the crash of the two outer barn doors as the storm thundered down on its target. Less than a second later, the unnatural wind and punishing ice found the tack room and ripped away its door with a gut-wrenching creak of twisting metal and the snap of splintering wood.

Rolling to protect the priestess, Vidarian strong-armed the sword back into its place and staggered toward the back corner of the room, Ariadel under his arm. In raged the screaming storm, but it stopped when the light from the sword ceased, and curled like a predator reorienting on the scent of its prey. With a knowledge he did not understand, Vidarian sensed that the storm was not intelligent of itself, but was being driven, at great cost, from far away.

In frozen terror they watched as the spinning wind and frozen rain lashed out systematically, literally combusting the bales of hay stacked up around the back wall. Distant shouts sounded from beyond as the crew woke, but the eye of the storm now rested in the threshold to the tack room, and all beyond was consumed in a shrieking vortex.

The muffled cry of a cat sounded over the wind nearby as the foundling grey kitten darted from cover, seeing its hay bale ripped away into the storm. It staggered, crying piteously, still half asleep and stumbling in the wrong direction—toward the door.

To Vidarian's horror, Ariadel gave a dismayed shout and dove after the creature. He shouted in denial and warning, but it was too late.

The storm struck.

All was darkness, ice, and wind as the vortex leapt at its quarry. Ariadel's hands had just closed around the terrified kitten when the cyclone lifted her from the ground. Her scream came back to Vidarian as he strove with every muscle in his body to run toward the eye of the storm—then bellowed in panicked frustration as it only drove him backward.

And then it was gone. In a single moment the wild gale had fled with its prize, leaving a thundering silence in its wake. Rain—ordinary rain—began to fall outside the barn.

Vidarian's momentum carried him out of the tack room when the resistance of the cyclone disappeared out from under him. There he fell to his knees, landing hard on his upflung wrists and clenching the sodden earth of the barn floor in shock, anguish, and rage.

Dimly Vidarian became aware of the silent eyes of his crew, who gathered around him in a haphazard half circle, questioning fear in their eyes. This alone would not have fazed him, but Ariadel's absence and the accompanying tide of guilt somehow dragged at his very soul. It took a long moment for him to master himself.

Finally he stood, shaking dirt from his hands and water out of his eyes. His haggard voice was soft but implacable.

"Pack the carts. We're going after her."

CHAPTER SEVEN
SEEKING AID

The crew was tense and quiet as they carried out Vidarian's command in the pale light of false-dawn. Every minute that passed itched at him to be on the road, but the storm had left more than significant damage, and he could not in good conscience abandon it to the farmer's repair. Finally, and with reluctance, he again split the crew, leaving behind one of the carts and six men to assist with repairs and then return to Westhill and the *Empress Quest*. To compensate for those repairs that could not be made without the purchase of additional hardware, he left the entire stock of goods from both carts—in the end, the farmer would make out handsomely, and did not complain.

Four men sat in silence on the road east, and three of them did not know where they were going. Neither did they ask.

At a tall sycamore marked along half its length with an ancient lightning scar Vidarian turned the cart onto a narrow trace that led up a steep and rocky hill. After an hour punctuated by the crackle of rocks that rolled away in the cart's wake, lush grapevines began to fill the fields around them as they passed from wild lands into tame. Now and then they caught sight of a female worker toiling among the trellises, but none offered a greeting.

They crested the hill and a sprawling but symmetrical structure of white stone came into view, mostly composed of columned terraces open to the air. Women moved among the simple courtyards and passed in and out of the buildings, but no one acknowledged the cart that trundled into their midst. The banner of Sharli snapped in the wind over the tallest column.

Swinging down from the cart, Vidarian handed the reins to Calgrath and strode toward the center building, passing undaunted through its towering supports. There, however, he stopped—he had no idea where to go from here.

Long ago he had learned of this settlement of the fire priestesses, but only as a speck on a map.

More women passed through this central hall, most wearing the grey raiment of novices. They passed him a few veiled glances, but their eyes darted away when he tried to catch them. Finally he addressed them all, "I must speak with a priestess on behalf of a Daughter of Sharli. She is in great danger." Tension sharpened his words, but it was only with the strictest discipline that he refrained from simply grabbing one of the novices and shaking them into cooperation.

He did not know when they appeared, or how long they had been watching, but there were three burgundy-robed women standing in the colonnaded threshold to one of the other buildings. They stared at him evenly and he noticed that the passing novices now gave him a wide berth. A very wide berth.

Clearing his throat self-consciously, he said, "I come to you on behalf of Priestess Ariadel Windhammer. She took passage with my ship under the authority of the Priestess Endera. This morning she was abducted by the enemy she fled, and even now is in their custody. I seek your help."

"A clever ploy for a bandit, sir, even if you do carry the names of two of our sisters." The priestess furthest to the right, shorter than the other two, eyed him coolly. Fury rose, but he schooled it, lifting a hand to mimic the gesture he had seen Ariadel perform to summon her life flame. As his hands moved from memory he ground down on the abrupt convulsion in his heart, the freshened recollection burning guilt into his mind anew.

He felt nothing, but when he completed the gesture the three priestesses drew back as if pulled by a single string. They stared, and he did not know whether they were aghast or merely disgusted.

Finally one spoke, her voice quick and dangerously nonchalant. "Where did you learn that?"

"I saw it performed the night before Ariadel was taken. I have a very good memory."

She frowned. "Apparently so. Come." With that, and no alteration in her expression, she turned, sweeping down the hallway like a ship at full sail. Vidarian hastened to follow.

The priestess's heels echoed on the marble floor as they traversed a narrow hallway. At her raised hand, the other two gave identical demure nods and turned off at a crossway, disappearing down the passages. After some thirty feet, along which the decorations that filled occasional niches in the walls grew increasingly ornate, they came to a door that swung open under the attention of a grey-robed novice.

Tall and golden-haired, the priestess turned intensely blue eyes on Vidarian as she took a seat before a heavy ebony desk. "Now then," she said quietly. "What can we do to aid you in your quest to return my Sister?"

"You know her?" Vidarian asked abruptly, surprised to be taken at his word so easily now.

"There are fewer full Sharlin priestesses than you might think. I do know of Ariadel, and the gesture you performed was her sign."

"I see." He scrutinized the priestess, but found no strategy. "I need passage to the High Temple at Kara'zul."

Her demeanor slipped. "What?"

"Passage, I said. To Kara'zul. I must speak with Endera."

"That is impossible. Only the inducted are permitted to travel to the High Temple." At his visible umbrage, her brow furrowed. "I myself have been there only once." When Vidarian did not waver, the priestess spoke again, folding her hands on the desk with earnestness. "I wish to help you, truly, but what you ask is not within my power."

"Then who should I seek?"

She stared at him for a long moment, then sighed. "If you travel to the foot of the Mountains of Sher'azar, where Kara'zul lies beyond, you will find another conclave of our Order."

"Sher'azar . . . those mountains are weeks away." He spoke mostly to himself, a horrible discouragement sinking down around his shoulders, but she answered.

"Luck is with you in that much. Your crew must stay here, but there is another way for you to go, if you are strong enough." A glint of speculation shone in her eyes, and it reminded him painfully of Ariadel.

"Show me."

She smiled. "Go to your crew and tell them of your journey. I will bring the rest to you."

~~~

When Vidarian returned to the cart he saw the crew in a new light. It was apparent that, throughout his passage in the halls of the fire priestesses, they had not spoken. Each sat slumped, eyes not quite focused, and he recognized their pain as his own. He cursed himself for not realizing that the crew might also blame themselves for not protecting Ariadel.

Breaking into a trot, he closed the gap between himself and the cart and swung up onto the driver's bench. Clasping Calgrath's shoulder, he shook the men from their introspection.

"The priestesses have agreed to help us," he began, and they brightened, "but I must ask you to stay here. They have some way of giving me passage to Kara'zul, but only on the condition that you remain. I cannot ask it of you . . ." He trailed off, looking at them.

Calgrath glanced at the other two, then settled his eyes back on his captain. "We'll be here, sir." With that, he reached up to clasp Vidarian's shoulder briefly, but firmly. The others nodded.

Vidarian was about to offer his thanks when all three of the other men suddenly gasped. Two of them reached for weapons. Expecting the worst, Vidarian turned.

Passing through a large archway came a trio of creatures, filing one at a time, that were straight out of a storybook. A very lethal storybook—one of those where the children get eaten at the end.

Their forequarters were of a goshawk, if a goshawk could be the size of a horse—complete with white and navy feathers and slightly unhinged-looking red eyes. The hindquarters were heavily built, something like a mountain lion's, but with claws that did not retract and which dug divots into the packed earth of the courtyard as they walked. Massive wings shifted with each supple movement and their tufted ears flicked to and fro with alertness.

Gryphons. The holy books said that each of the goddesses kept them, but he'd never quite believed it. Now he understood the statues that decorated nearly every elemental shrine he had visited before. None of them did the creatures justice.

While he was still gawking, the first of the three captured his gaze with burning red eyes. Then there was a voice in his head, coppery like the taste of fresh metal: // *My, my, Captain. You look as if you've swallowed a fish sideways.* //

It was too much. It was too gods-be-damned much. Vidarian, who had ridden three hurricanes and safely navigated Dead Man's Hook four times without breaking a sweat, fell over in a dead faint.

He woke to the sensation of being gently rocked in the embrace of a soft hammock. A faint creak as of braided hemp on wooden beams vouched for this illusion, and he could almost hear the rush of the sea. Vidarian opened his eyes to the sight of a soaring sky spreading overhead in every direction.

But the rhythmic pulse that vibrated in the air was not the rush of waves against a rocky coast.

As he looked around, bleary-eyed, Vidarian found that he rested in a large basket. The contraption sloped upward all around him, and the rim was just above his eyes. Further up still, three gryphons beat strongly and regularly at the air with long speckled wings, one to either side of him and one— smaller than the other two—directly before. It took him a long moment to calculate how high up they probably were.

One of the gryphons, a long-necked fellow to his right, must have seen Vidarian's bulging eyes. // *Don't look down,* // he warned, and this mind's voice was like salt on bread, sharp but humble. // *It's a little startling if you haven't flown before.* //

Vidarian stiffened as the creature's voice echoed in his mind. For once, the grief, restlessness, and guilt he had borne since Ariadel's capture worked for him; his anger forged a forced acceptance of the situation. A talking gryphon. It really wasn't that bad.

"My men!" Vidarian shouted finally, finding that he had to work even to hear himself above the beating of the gryphons' wings. "I remember—er—collapsing . . ." Fainting. He hadn't *really* fainted, had he?

// *You did indeed, Captain.* // This from the gryphon to his left, her voice female like the first, though with no resemblance whatever to a human female's voice he couldn't say how he was sure. Her voice called up the warmth of a hickory-fueled hearth in winter, spiced and soothing. // *We explained to the men that we had given you a traveling draught to ease your comfort in the air, and that it had acted faster than we expected. Fortunately, they believed us.* // Vidarian felt a flush heating his cheeks. Likely the men knew exactly what had happened, but forgave him. As he moved further into the waking world, he found himself able to cope with a strange situation made much stranger.

"In the stories, you speak like men," Vidarian shouted over the wind. The gryphon to his right clacked his beak, a sound like timber cracking. Cocking his large head to one side with catlike pupils flaring, he somehow looked surprised.

// *What, with our voices?* // The feathers all along the creature's long neck fanned outward and he released a trilling call that deafened Vidarian momentarily. It sounded like warbling laughter. // *Speaking telepathically is not something easily explained in a children's book. But it is said once that we did speak your tongue, long ago. All things come full circle; perhaps we will speak again someday.* //

Vidarian hunkered back down in the basket and pulled his coat shut against the wind. As he scooted toward the back of the basket to redistribute its weight, he found that it carried built-in wicker bins, three of which were tied securely and a fourth that was only loosely fixed. Curious, he peered inside, and found that it contained a smaller basket covered with white linen cloth.

// *Help yourself,* // the gryphon to his left offered, catching sight of his movements with her sharp eyes.

Vidarian needed no further invitation, discovering an abrupt wave of intense hunger that washed darkness across his vision. Within he found a waxed and stoppered bottle of a thick golden wine, two rounds of hard-crusted bread (curiously tangy, he found upon tearing one open and taking a bite), and equal portions of dried beef and fresh green grapes. Pausing every now and then as the basket gave a lurch and temporarily obliterated his appetite (// *Sorry, breakage in the wind currents,* // came quick apologies), over the next hour he made himself a simple but satisfying meal of the provisions.

Stomach full and heart empty, he finally allowed his weariness to overcome him. Though not knowing how in the lilting movements of the basket, he slept.

⁓⁓⁓

For the second time Vidarian woke in the basket's embrace, but this time it was discomfort that roused him. The gryphons were rapidly descending, and as they neared the earth he found an alarming pressure building up in his head.

// *We're landing,* // the forward gryphon announced, turning his head to look back on the passenger. // *Move your jaw, it will loose the pressure in your ears.* // Vidarian did as he was told and found to his relief that, after a slightly worrisome *pop!*, the pain did recede. This process repeated itself perhaps three times before the mountain below hove into view.

The gryphons' great wings tore at the clouds as they descended, sending tendrils of thick moisture spiraling away in their wake. Directly below, golden-capped spires began to appear, and they sparkled in the mist.

"Is this Kara'zul?" he shouted.

// *No,* // the gryphon to his right answered. // *It is Sher'azar Temple. We cannot take you directly to Kara'zul; you will have to speak with the gatekeeper here.* // As he spoke, the gryphon landed in tandem with the other two, setting the basket down lightly on the mosaic-tiled ground. On legs that did not quite want to work properly, Vidarian managed to lever himself out of the basket, and landed weakly.

// *Here we must leave you,* // the front gryphon said, giving a bow of his beak. // *We have tidings to bring to the high priestess.* //

"Then I thank you most sincerely for your aid," Vidarian said, giving a bow of his own, and knowing little else what to do. "If I can ever be of service to you, please let me know of it."

// *We will keep it in mind,* // the right gryphon answered, with a twinkle in his eye. Then the leading gryphon gave a nod and the three creatures leapt once more into the air. The wind from their wings beat strongly down upon Vidarian and he squinted as he watched them ascend. Within moments they had disappeared back into the clouds.

Vidarian peered intently at the handful of tiny buildings that comprised the Temple at Sher'azar. Built in black lacquered hardwood, the structures echoed those of the lightning-scar settlement priestesses, reaching up into the slate-grey sky like the remnants of kindling in a smoldering fire. None were quite the same height.

Like the previous settlement, all was stonily silent—but this one was apparently unpopulated. Though the etched clay pots and their occupants, a variety of strange (and probably dangerous) plants, showed signs of recent and dutiful tending, no creature, human or otherwise, gave a sign of their existence here.

As time dragged on Vidarian grew increasingly restless, finally forcing himself to sit on a large spur of rock that climbed up out of the ground. Some interminable minutes later, the steady but painfully slow sound of hoofbeats began to echo from further down the foothill to which the Temple clung.

Vidarian stood and waited long enough for his legs to start stiffening in the damp air before a covered cart arrived, drawn by a grey donkey. Its driver was a shadowed figure wearing one of the now familiar burgundy robes.

"Greetings," Vidarian called, raising his hand. "I come seeking the Gate-keeper of Sher'azar."

"Then I'm afraid you've come at the wrong time," answered a dulcet voice from inside the hood of the burgundy robe. "The gatekeeper is not here."

"Not here?" Vidarian asked, startled out of protocol. "Where is she? This is a matter of most urgency."

"She has gone Down to teach children at a neighboring village," the priestess answered with peculiar emphasis as she pulled the cart to a stop. Tossing back her hood, she unveiled a rather startling mass of deep red curls that bounced across her shoulders as if thankful for freedom. Her pale green eyes turned upward as she gave voice to a strange, warbling chant.

A smattering of hooded figures began to materialize out of the mist, many of them carrying baskets partially loaded with mountain vegetables or wild mushrooms. They gathered around the cart.

"We will help you if we can," the redheaded priestess offered, a less than reassuring smile on her thin lips. She remained in the cart.

Vidarian stared at her, wondering where to begin. "A trio of gryphons brought me to your Temple . . ."

"Gryphons brought you here?" she asked, looking at him slantwise. "Strange, we had no word from them, and they did not remain to introduce you?" She clucked her tongue.

"They claimed urgent business with the high priestess," Vidarian frowned, brow furrowing.

"Ah, and so you seek the Gatekeeper," his erstwhile hostess smiled, folding her hands around the cart reins. "I'm afraid that in her absence, your only option would be to ascend the mountain yourself. And by our law, we cannot offer you more than a token assistance with such an undertaking."

At her words the other followers of Sharli exchanged a few surreptitious glances. More of them were smiling more than Vidarian liked, but all he could do was forge ahead.

"Very well then. I will gratefully accept any assistance you can render." He decided on forthrightness, which seemed to inexplicably miff the priestesses slightly.

"Come, then," the one on the cart said, with abrupt coolness. "We are permitted to trade with you for supplies."

ᴧᴧᴧ

He had very little coin on him, but the attendants accepted what Vidarian did carry with his gratitude. They did not offer a mount, but supplied him with a rather disturbingly small quantity of food in a canvas sack along with a firebox and a very basic assortment of medical supplies. Then all of the priestesses gathered to see him off, bowing with synchronized solemnity. Without preamble he started off along the ascending mountain trail, but he caught a flash of white teeth as the priestesses turned back to their chores. He hoped he had imagined their smiling mouths, and all disappeared into burgundy velvet and mist before he could decide one way or the other.

The mountain loomed before him, indistinct in the mist. Drawing in a deep breath, he filled his lungs with the pine-laced scent of the thick air, then started up the rocky slope.

Time gradually lost its cohesion, punctuated only by the heightened rush of blood in his veins. He repeatedly steered his imagination away from thoughts about the fanciful forms of torture a telepathic race might visit on a captive.

He did not know precisely where he was going, but the priestesses had offered only a single word in response to numerous queries: "Up." Presumably the High Temple was at the pinnacle of Sher'azar Peak itself, lost somewhere in the maddening fog that engulfed the mountain range. The muscles of his legs and arms began to grow stiff in the clammy air, but he grit his teeth and forged on up one craggy pass after another.

Only when he first began to hallucinate did he stop to rest. The slender demi-peaks that reached up off of the mountain began to take the shape of hazy hooded figures, shadowed against the mist. Their invisible eyes seemed to reach right to his bones.

Blinking rapidly, he turned at the next spur leading off the trail and sat gingerly on an outcropping of blue slate. But the shadows still watched, and after a few moments he spurred himself on again, unable to stand their scrutiny while sitting still.

Driven by that new discomfort, he passed a ghostly night climbing the mountain. The unending mist made sunset unclear; he only became aware of it when there was so little light that he stumbled on the forbidding terrain. At last he found his legs would carry him no further; the air had grown cold and thin in the heights. Dizzied from lack of air, he made a poor excuse for a camp, did not bother with a fire, and set himself down in a shallow hole dug from the gravelly floor. He tried not to compare it to a grave.

The darkness that shrouded the mountain came at last to drape itself across his mind, and he slept.

∿∿∿

The pale grey light of dawn did not wake him. Only when the sun began to burn through the mist, falling like liquid flame through the morning fog, did Vidarian stir. He struggled upward in his pit of a bed, blinked bleary-eyed at the rising sun, and prepared to force his aching muscles once more into movement.

A flicker of motion from the eye of the sun gave him pause.

Before he had time to stand, a figure separated itself from the crimson sphere that slowly flooded the morning with scarlet light. Her hair burned with wild abandon down the length of her back, seeming to take its color from the blood of the sun itself, and her skin in the painfully bright light was whiter than the finest porcelain. Sharp blades of sunlight, now streaking down across the mountain, gave the illusion of elfin slenderness to her burgundy-robed form and sheltered her feet from the indignity of making contact with the cold, wet earth. In the tepid twilight her hands glowed golden at her sides.

In a moment the fiery vision was gone and in its place stood a woman of indeterminate age and build. Her hair was indeed red, and gloriously so, but when separated from the sun her entire form seemed to dim into mortality. The smile that lit her features when she caught sight of him, however, reminded him of Ariadel. Presumably they instructed all fire priestesses in the art of smiling to dwarf the breaking dawn.

"Well, hello there," she said, and there was a strange hollow quality to her voice as it echoed against the stone mountainside. "You certainly look a sight."

Vidarian scrambled in the gravel, surprise making his sore muscles move faster than they might have otherwise. "Er, good morning, Priestess . . . ?"

She smiled again. Her voice was like crystallized honey—strong and hard but sweet and bright at once, as if just on the verge of bursting into song. "My name is not important now. I was simply out on a . . . morning constitutional, you might say, and was surprised to see a Son of Nistra this far up our mountain."

"S-son of Nistra?" Vidarian echoed, unsure that he'd heard her correctly.

"Well, yes, of course," the priestess answered, pursing her lips and folding her arms across her chest. "You have the mark of Nistra all over you. Didn't you know that, boy?"

Miffed at her overfamiliar tone, but unable to argue, he only shook his head. She sighed in heavy exasperation, but did not drop her smile; if anything, it widened.

"It's no matter. Tell me, what do you want here on the Great Mountain of Sharli?" The title she emphasized grandly, as a jester would of a king who thought too much of himself. Vidarian had never heard the name of the fire goddess used so lightly, and this strange priestess intrigued him. She took a seat beside him on the shale and he found himself drawn into telling his story—for once not begrudging the time that slipped away while he did so.

When he had finished, she drew him back into a retelling of the spell cast on the sun emeralds.

"Do you remember, dear Vidarian, if the priestess stopped for breath when enchanting the two stones?" She looked at him intently, but, as before, there was a smile hidden beneath her seriousness.

Vidarian thought deeply, trying to call the memory back to his mind. "No," he said at last, "I'm almost certain she didn't. There was only that strange glow, and then both stones were changed."

"Interesting," the priestess smiled. "Very interesting. Endera is out of practice."

Vidarian tried not to gawk. "And—why would you say that, my lady?"

The priestess only broadened her smile. "If I were you, I should find those emeralds. They're quite valuable, you know. As for answers, you ask for too many, when you know them yourself."

At length she stood and brushed off her robes. Vidarian spoke hastily as she turned to go.

"Lady, I must know. Who are you, who are so—wise?"

Her eyes were alive with secret mischief as she looked back over her shoulder, voice fading as she walked off into the mist. "The gryphons called me Ele'cherath of old. The seridi, my children, who have also been called so many different names, called me San'vidara. But for myself, I call me—"

CHAPTER EIGHT

BEYOND THE CONTRACT

Vidarian woke, gasping desperately yet finding no comfort in the air that rushed into his lungs. It was thin and cold, sending spangles of black across his vision as he attempted to focus on the blinding glare of the sun that beat down into his eyes. Thrown so suddenly from consciousness to darkness and back again, his body could not keep up, yet from the depths of his soul he clung to the striking sensation of a vast, pulsing rhythm that seemed to come from all around.

Gradually sounds began to separate from the pulsing beat—a flurry of rapid, excited whispers.

Finally his eyes focused, but he blinked again, not quite accepting what he saw. Leaning over him with an expression he guessed to be concern was a sleek face with a narrow nose and a line of golden dots painted above each eyebrow. The eyes below were a warm, almost molten gold, exotically tilted.

"Ah," his watcher murmured, with a tiny tap to her nose, "he wakes."

At her words the whispers that surrounded them increased in velocity and volume, though in his dazed state Vidarian could not make out any individual words. Shaking his head, he sat up.

There were fewer whisperers than he had initially thought, but the small handful of priestesses that crowded around him drew back as he moved. Only one among them did not.

"Priestess," he acknowledged, then winced as pain lanced through his skull, awakened by his own voice.

"Captain Rulorat," Endera answered, her half-lidded eyes evincing no sympathy for his suffering. "My priestesses found you out cold halfway down the mountain, sprawled on the rocks. Care to explain?"

"I think one of your priestesses knocked me out," he answered testily, rubbing at his left temple.

"That would be impossible," Endera answered, folding her ceremonially robed arms. "There were no priestesses on your side of the mountain all night."

"Perhaps you can be a bit more specific," the first priestess said gently, placing a hand between his shoulder blades. It was warm. "Did she give you a name?"

"I think she called herself . . . San'vidara," Vidarian said, eyes half closed as he attempted to clear his vision. He was looking at the first priestess just long enough to see her eyes do what a human's never would—the pupils rapidly shrunk and flared, pinning like an eagle's. All around him the whispers grew to a furor.

Vidarian turned swiftly to demand what was going on, but found his neck suddenly up against the edge of a dazzlingly shining knife. Endera's eyes were burning.

"So help me, Vidarian, if you dare to mock me at this time and place . . ." her growling tone promised the torture of a thousand deaths. Slow ones.

"I'm sure I don't know what you're talking about, Priestess," Vidarian grated, being very careful not to move.

"It would explain his appearance, Endera," the golden-decorated priestess murmured, her voice half an octave lower than it had been, with a harmony like tolling bells. "Among other things."

Vidarian looked desperately at his strange-eyed supporter. "She said the seridi called her that. And that the gryphons called her . . . Ella . . . Ele'chertoth. Or something like that."

// He speaks the truth, // a new voice rumbled in all of their minds, and the priestesses drew back again. Even Endera lowered her blade. // Even if he had somehow learned the Seridan name for Sharli, the name Ele'cherath is protected among the scholars of gryphonkind. // The speaker stepped forward, a gryphon more massive than any of the three he'd seen before. She was tall and muscular, colored like a goshawk but with an array of golden designs painted on her wings. Fiery red eyes settled like burning coals upon Vidarian. // She gave you *her other names, those that we call her by, because to hear her True Name would unmake you,* // she explained, with a soft tone that nonetheless gripped his heart with ice. // *Our goddess is ever one to toy with our own mortal makings, but still you are lucky to be alive.* // The stunned and frightened looks of the younger priestesses confirmed the gryphoness's statement.

"I trust your judgment, as always, Thalnarra," Endera answered, but kept one hand on the knife and looked as if she'd rather have it in Vidarian's gizzard. Or somewhere worse. But she only sighed, then gestured to two of the other human priestesses. "This will bear some explaining. Bring him."

The two priestesses closed in around Vidarian and helped him to his feet, not unkindly. They then marched him down a hall that carried a faint aroma of smoke and honey, barely perceptible but daunting to his spirit nonetheless.

At length they passed through a marble hall, but none of the priestesses showed any signs of slowing. At the end of the hall in either direction sat a huge white marble altar topped by a massive gold chalice, squat and crowned with a circle of bright fire. Even with the lengths of cold marble between them, Vidarian could swear he felt heat on his skin.

"Are those . . . ?" Vidarian trailed off, staring wide-eyed at the chalices.

"Yes," Endera answered shortly, continuing her brisk walk ahead of them and not turning her head. "Those are the Living Flames of Sharli."

Never in his life did Vidarian think he would see the Flames, revered by all followers of Sharli, no matter how meek. Even as they passed, he caught sight of elaborately robed priestesses attending the twisting flames, their garments in the characteristic wine red but rimmed at cuffs, hem, and collar with white ribbon. The Flames had not gone out in twelve hundred years, and likely longer—twelve hundred years merely marked the point at which the priestesshood began to keep count, nearly four dynasties ago.

Beyond the marble hall was a door, plain by comparison but carved of fine heavy ironwood. A young acolyte garbed in ashen grey rushed to open the door before Endera's sweeping feet, and then they were all inside.

"Now then," Endera began, settling down at her desk. Her eyes were clear as they looked up at Vidarian. "You've spoken with our goddess. It seems that she wishes you to pursue this quest."

"I intend to rescue Ariadel, Priestess, no matter what it takes," Vidarian managed, taking a step forward ahead of his attendants.

"Mm," the priestess murmured, sliding open the top drawer to her desk and withdrawing a sheet of slick ivory parchment. "If it is the will of Sharli, we will certainly assist you. Even now my priestesses are sending for gryphons to carry you as far as you will go."

"Sh-Sharli did instruct me to do one other thing," Vidarian began, then plowed ahead before Endera's abruptly sharpening eyes could stop him. "She told me to retrieve from you the sun emeralds. She seemed to think they would be my key in locating Ariadel."

For a fire priestess, Endera could pull off an incredible icy glare. Straightening as he would against a torrential wind, Vidarian steeled himself for the worst. In the end, though, Endera only reached once more into her drawer and withdrew a black leather pouch. It clinked softly on the desk when she dropped it.

"Sit down, Captain," Endera said, so sharply that Vidarian did as he was told before even thinking about it. The priestess glanced up for a moment and the two other priestesses bowed out of the room. When the door clicked shut, Endera spoke again. "You're here now to give me a detailed report of your encounter with our goddess." When he did not answer, she continued, but her tone slanted upward warningly. "The goddess comes to us in many forms, and, rather than waste her time in speaking, delivers her word on many matters through nuance of her appearance and slightest gesture. You are to recall to me as much as you possibly can." Suddenly Vidarian became aware of how absolutely strained Endera was—he conjectured that he must have been the first of the uninitiated to give such a report. Maybe even the first man.

Endera glanced up from her parchment, lifting her pen from the paper and making that small gesture seem the greatest weighty annoyance. "You had better get started, Vidarian. I don't think you have much time to spare."

The priestess grilled him until his head swam with fatigue, pursuing points on the tiniest possible detail yet telling him to skip entire sections of their dialogue. Finally he had described it all to her satisfaction, right up to a detailed account of the drowning sensation that immediately preceded his waking.

Endera abruptly dropped her pen, splattering black ink across the neatly lettered page. She did not move to pick it up. "You felt—what?"

Vidarian's brow furrowed. "I felt as though I was drowning—swimming through a sea, yet all was too thin for me to breathe. I gasped."

"You were blue when we found you," Endera said, retrieving the pen and absently sliding it back into its case. "But we thought it was from the cold." She did not speak again, but stared for a long time into the tiny flame that topped the ornate oil lamp to one side of her desk. Finally she looked back up at him, golden eyes dark with tense confusion. "She's kindled you," she said, then turned her head back to the flame, "but not to her own fire."

Silence gaped wide between them as Vidarian stared at her in confusion. "I take it that's unusual?"

Endera glared at him, then returned her gaze to the candle, saying nothing.

"She said I was a Son of Nistra," Vidarian thought aloud, and the priestess returned her burning gaze to him with alacrity.

"That you are, Captain. In more ways than you even know. Sharli has kindled—or, the Nistrans would call it awakened—in you the water magic of Nistra. We did not know she would ever do such a thing . . . though obviously it is possible." Restlessly the priestess stood, the hem of her robes brushing the slate-tiled floor.

"Priestess," Vidarian said abruptly, realizing something. "If I am kindled, or awakened, or what-have-you . . . do I have a life flame?"

Endera blinked. "No, certainly not. You—" she paused and sighed, closing her eyes for a moment. "There is much more information—theory if you will—to it than this, but what the Nistrans have that we do not is called the Sense. They sense the presence of living things in their vicinity, and further away when trained, through an ability to home in on the rhythm of the Sea that abides in all living things."

"A rhythm. I heard a rhythm, when I woke—I felt it all around me." He listened for it again and found it as it had been, pulsing softly in the background. If he let his mind wander, he imagined that he could feel the presence of every priestess in the temple, their ripples reaching him as those from stones dropped into still water.

"Yes, that's it." The priestess sighed, settling back into her chair. "You hardly have time for an ecclesiastical education, but two things I can and must tell you: The first is that water magic is just as complex as fire magic, but it is substantively different. Water, along with earth, forms a side of energy called Substantive energy. Fire and air are on the balancing side of Ephemeral energy. Water works through manipulating the tiniest pieces of water that live everywhere—in the air, in your body, in the very ground. Fire, conversely, can act on these pieces, but of itself has no material property. This is what will differentiate your magic from anything I could possibly tell you about ours; water I only understand in theory, not in practice."

Vidarian nodded slowly, wrapping his mind around the concept. "And the other thing?"

The priestess leaned across her desk, boring into his presence with her own. To his fledgling Sense she suddenly flared up into a towering flame. "What you now wield is more dangerous than any sword, any spear, or indeed any physical weapon you could possibly imagine. It is imperative that you understand this. The ripples that you can create by moving water will reverberate throughout the entire world, and as their ripples pass outward, they can potentially grow in size and cause catastrophic effects. As one new to the craft your own mind will limit you from doing most damage, but you *must* be aware of your potential."

Then, like a candle snuffed, she dwindled to all his perception and fell back against the soft leather cushion of her chair. Vidarian only stared, an insidious chill seeping through his body.

"Ordinarily you would have the guidance of a Nistran priestess," Endera muttered, gazing off toward the door. "I can only assume that Sharli gave you this gift—and understand that it is a great gift indeed—so that you could use your Sense to amplify the effect of the sun emeralds and locate Ariadel."

"Why?" Vidarian blurted, hands moving to grip the arms of his chair convulsively. His heart rebelled against the question, but he asked, "Why is Ariadel so important that your goddess herself would intervene through a simple sailor?"

At this Endera raised a hand to her temple, her half-closed eyes going again to the still flame of the oil lamp. Vidarian did not know if she did this out of a need to focus on her Element or out of a simple desire not to look at him, but the unwavering light did seem to calm her.

"Sharli told us many months ago that Ariadel Windhammer would be the most influential priestess to grace our world since the Third Age."

Vidarian stared, trying to count the thousands of years that that implied, and failing. Endera glanced up at him, a flash in her eyes condemning him for everything from birth to breathing, but she said, "Well, that's not exactly what she said. She appeared to us as a glowing beacon with eyes of two typhoons centered with cyclones, a burning elderberry bush in her left hand, and a silver truncheon in her left."

Vidarian's throat was too dry to allow for a good splutter, but he coughed. A sharp glance from the priestess warned him not to question her authority. He didn't. Instead, he moved to pick up the leather pouch that rested atop the desk. Thumbing it over in his fingers, he slipped the sun emeralds out of their nest and into the palm of his hand.

They were as beautiful as he remembered. One now seemed to shudder with the rhythm that pulsed within it, a storm roiling within the small gem, but the other . . .

The other emerald still bore its dancing flame, brighter now to his sight . . . and as it rested against his hand he felt a resonance of energy between himself and the stone. Sharli had been right—they were tied together. And the rhythmic waves that pulsed out of the stone, out of the air, and out of Vidarian himself had never been so strong to him. They reverberated throughout his awareness. Unthinking, he raised the emerald, and suddenly the resonant waves circled into completion. Through the morass of pulsing energy some buried intuition took the three points—his location, what he could only assume was Ariadel's, and the emerald's, though it was so close to him—and told him exactly where they all rested in relationship to each other. The result was a beacon so bright in his mind that he could almost see it with his mortal eyes.

Quickly he slipped the stones back into their pouch, banishing the vision, and stood. Endera slid to her feet as well, looking at him in dark-faced confusion. He only held up the leather bag in a slightly quaking hand.

"I know where she is."

The priestess stared at him long and hard for a moment. "You know that this is beyond our contract," Endera said, her voice for once candid and subdued. Vidarian did not answer. The priestess only nodded, after a moment, then said simply, "I am gratified to know you are the man I thought you might be." With that, she led the way back to the temple entrance.

CHAPTER NINE

GRYPHONS

Once again Vidarian was borne into the sky by a trio of gryphons, but this time he was awake, and each of the gryphons bore a pattern of gold painting on their wings. The patterns danced as they flew, tessellating back and forth from images of leaping fire to stars that spangled across the white feathers.

Vidarian sat toward the front of the carry-basket, Ariadel's emerald lifted high in his left hand. With his eyes closed he explored his new Sense, trying to focus and nurture it as quickly as he could. Now and then he experienced an intense urge to do more than simply take in the "surroundings" painted before him by his new ability—an urge to *move* the ripples that pulsed in his mind. Determinedly he shoved these aside, keeping his metaphysical hands behind his back, and the sweat that beaded along his forehead with the effort grew icy cold in the high-altitude winds.

In remarkably short order the basket began to descend, and he remembered to work his jaw as pressure began to mount in his ears. The gryphons dropped swiftly, at times seeming to plunge almost vertically downward, and Vidarian wondered every few hundred feet if his stomach had been left behind among the clouds.

They landed in the courtyard of Sher'azar Temple, and such was the control of these gryphons that they made his previous landing at the mountain's foot seem a child's first stumbling walk. As the great creatures removed their harnesses he recognized the leader as Thalnarra—and if his guess was right, the rapid flare-and-pin of her pupils only very thinly disguised a smoldering anger. He followed her blazing gaze to a collection of three priestesses that stood hesitantly at one of the many temple archways.

Finally one of them approached, reluctance emanating from her body language. "Thalnarra," she said, bowing, "It has been—quite some time since you visited us here . . ." Then she caught sight of Vidarian and inhaled sharply. "*You . . .*"

// *Priestess Alshandra,* // Thalnarra growled, punctuating each of her words with biting anger. // *May I introduce Captain Vidarian Rulorat, whom our goddess delivered to the Temple of Kara'zul.* //

"Sharli . . ." The priestess backed away a step, her eyes going wide. "We thought . . ."

// *You thought she would kill him,* // Thalnarra finished for her, sitting down on the gravel and coiling her tail snakelike about her feet. // *You sent him up the mountain* at night *knowing that the goddess permits no mortal uninitiated to see dawn on Kara'zul Peak.* //

"W-we thought he was an interloper—"

// *You did not* think, *girl, at all.* // Thalnarra's mental voice rose to a crackling thunder and Vidarian winced at the sudden pain in his head. // *Gryphons bore him to you, yet you did not send any of your messengers after them. The temple was unattended or they would have spoken with you themselves. Have you any idea who this man is?* //

The priestess did not answer, and Thalnarra pounded relentlessly on, each of her words more forceful than the last. // *He is the sole assigned protector and sole remaining hope of Ariadel Windhammer, if we ever do see her again since her fall into Vkorthan hands.* //

It was too much for the chastened priestess, and she broke into tears. "Thalnarra, please don't send me to . . ."

// *Oh, do shut up, girl.* // The gryphoness sighed, lifting her beak and giving a tiny disgusted shake of wing feathers that glittered golden in the pale sunlight. // *I will be reporting the misbehavior of the priestesses here to the high temple, and they will be responsible for you. Perhaps they will send* you *up the mountain to see what the Dawn Goddess thinks of your actions. In the meantime, I have escorted the captain to Sher'azar to see that he has the proper equipment for his journey. I will be accompanying him on his quest and both of us will need proper provisions.* //

Vidarian started at her words, but could not argue—and strangely enough, all of the priestesses of Sher'azar were suddenly extremely cooperative.

~~~

That evening they were back in the air again, Thalnarra leading with two hand (claw?)-picked gryphons flanking the harnessed basket. Unlike Vidarian's recent carriers, Thalnarra's companions this time bore no gold on their wings—they were uninitiated into the rites of the fire priestesses, and as a result greatly deferred to her as a matter of course. She seemed to encourage this behavior.

The basket was considerably heavier this time, as well. Packed in with provisions of food for all parties (the gryphons planned to hunt, but Vidarian learned to his surprise that they preferred an assortment of supplementary foods that aided in health and meditation) was a tight packet of medical supplies, a strange navigational unit intended for air use, and, most interestingly, a small chest of carefully packed magical implements. Tucked into canvas pockets on two sides of the chest was a pair of leather-bound books, each no longer than his hand and roughly half as thick. The cover of one was a deep blue, the other a dark burgundy. After the gryphons had settled into a comfortable altitude, Vidarian weighed one book in each hand, looking between them with a mixture of trepidation and intense curiosity.

Both books had the exact same number of pages—a fact that he verified by checking the last carefully numbered page of each. Setting aside the burgundy volume, Vidarian opened the other and began to gingerly thumb through it. He paused when he reached a richly illuminated page that described a fist-sized translucent globe identical to one that he had seen in the chest.

Setting the book aside after marking it with an attached blue ribbon, he flipped the lid of the chest open again. Nestled into a bed of narrow wood shavings was a pale blue globe, translucent and dotted with an intricate array of identically deep pinholes, that confirmed his suspicions. It lay alongside a narrow box of dark wood that he promptly used to support the reopened blue leather book.

A richly calligraphed diagram marked out the uses and significances of each set of holes on the globe. Following its footnotes, he observed that the pinholes were arrayed in groups of five, most often depicting a diamond shape with a single pinhole in the center. When he had studied the page for several minutes, he felt confident enough to very carefully place his fingers in specific points around the object and lift it from its nest.

Nothing happened, which was good. Vidarian consciously let out his breath, becoming aware that at some point in the procedure he had forgotten to do so. What the book specified next was clear but daunting: that somehow a Nistran should apply their Sense *through* the sphere, using it, he supposed, as a sort of lens. This would lead to greater focus of the user's ability.

After he had held the globe long enough to make his awkwardly bent fingers complain, Vidarian—following the logic that if he wasn't meant to use it, it wouldn't be in the chest—decided to try it out. He closed his eyes and held the sphere at arm's length in front of him.

As the book had recommended, he took a deep breath and then exhaled slowly. As he did so he imagined that every bit of his breath was going through the sphere, flowing around its perfect shape and sounding off of its pinholes as through finger-holes in a flute.

It took nearly long enough for Vidarian to assume that he lacked the skill to activate it, but, just as he was running out of breath, the sphere began to resonate.

Unlike the ripples that other living creatures generated to his newfound Sense, the rings that came off of the sphere harmonized with Vidarian's own, which he only then realized that he even recognized—his mind automatically filtered them out. There was a *pop!*, more felt than heard, and suddenly his own rings—his own pattern—had expanded immensely.

He didn't have long to enjoy it, though, because at that exact instant his vehicle began to fall out of the sky.

The plummeting (quite naturally, he thought) jolted him out of his experiment with the sphere, and he threw it unceremoniously back into the chest and occupied himself with hanging on for dear life.

Gradually the craft evened out in the air, but Thalnarra was practically molting with anger. Her head snapped around and she looked Vidarian full in the face, still pulling the basket and maintaining her wing-speed.

Absently he realized that he didn't know her neck was quite so agile—it was disturbing in a way, but less so than her angrily widened eyes.

// *What in the True Names of all that's holy did you think you were doing?* // Her telepathic voice thundered in his head and he strangled down the distinct urge to hide under the cargo.

"I was following an exercise in the Book of Nistra—"

// *You sent out a "welcome, please make yourself at home!" beacon to anyone with a lick of Sense in a two-hundred-mile radius! And doing exactly what you did, unannounced, would have Quenched a lesser priestess than I!* //

Vidarian blinked. "I didn't know anything about Quenching . . ."

// *Then perhaps you shouldn't be meddling about with the Book of Nistra. I suppose you looked up the amplification sphere in it without even reading the basics of Nistran magic, much less the Five Magics and how they interact?* // Her thick wings beat violently at the air as she grew increasingly incensed, causing the basket to rock unsettlingly.

"I thought—"

// *Maybe you had better start at the beginning,* // she said acidly, then turned her beak back forward, feather-tufted ears swiveling away from Vidarian as if to pointedly deny his existence. Trying to make as little sound as possible, he withdrew the Book of Nistra and closed the little chest, going so far as to latch it securely before settling back to read—this time from page one.

An insidious sense of futility crept over Vidarian as he toiled through the book. At intervals he pulled out Ariadel's emerald to assure they were still on course—but with the gryphons' sharp eyes for navigation, they always were, and it was mostly an excuse for him to stop reading. But every return to the neatly lettered pages was more daunting, and in the end he gave it up, choosing instead to stare vacantly across the cloud-traced sky.

// *I apologize for snapping at you.* // Thalnarra's clipped words jolted Vidarian out of an unintentional reverie, and he jumped.

"No harm done." He smiled weakly, peering up at the lead gryphon.

Although she continued to face forward, her ears had swiveled back to catch his movements and speech.

// Not by me, I hope. You do realize that what you did was tremendously dangerous? //

"I think so. But I still couldn't find anything in the book about Quenching."

// It would have been in the Book of Sharli. But I can tell you. // Several moments passed, punctuated by the steady beat of the gryphons' wings, before Thalnarra spoke again. *// The Five Magics are arrayed in opposition and balance, //* she began, her tone taking on a lecturing hint. *// There are a number of . . . classifications, shall we say, between them, but the most important for you to know is the difference between what we call Substantive magics and Ephemeral magics. Earth and water are Substantive; air and fire are Ephemeral. That is why the greatest danger for you is to apply your new ability to manipulate Nistra's gift to "physically" touch the world—because water is Substantive, anything you touch in it will reverberate throughout the entire universe. On a universal scale this is insignificant, but locally it can have dramatic detrimental effect. The danger of an Ephemeral magic user is different, because we cannot actually move any of the elements, only apply energy to them, which is not quite the same thing. Moving for us is much more difficult than it is for you, and much more complex—but it is very easy for a beginning fire priestess to push the balance of energy within her, and this can be dangerous in a variety of ways. //*

"You mentioned five magics—what is the fifth?" The whole of it made sense to him, but Vidarian wanted to know everything before he began drawing parallels in his mind.

// We call the fifth element aether, and it is really more theoretical than actual, from a magical perspective at least, because we have no one who can manipulate it. But it is in a third class of magic called Subtractive, whereas all the other four are considered Additive. Try what we may, the very nature of Substantive and Ephemeral magics both dictates that we cannot actually destroy substance or energy—only manipulate it. Aether has the power to destroy. //

"Can it also create?" A dry, humming click sounded in Vidarian's mind, and he gathered from the faint rush of emotion that followed it that Thalnarra was chuckling.

// Clever. Yes, in theory, aether can create. But we assume that its basic nature is to destroy, the same way that an Ephemeral's basic nature is to generate energy—so to create is probably much more difficult than destroying. Creation is the domain of the gods. //

"What is it that the Vkortha do? Where does that magic fit in?"

Thalnarra's tone grew dark. *// The Vkortha do not practice magic. They are telepaths, and telekinetic—we do not consider these as part of the magical hierarchy. The way I am speaking to you is telepathic, and among gryphonkind it is considered mundane. There is some dispute, given the Vkorthan's recent activity, as to whether the old books should be changed to include their . . . activities. But we know so little about them, which is one of the reasons Priestess Windhammer was assigned to study them— we believe that their "magic" is actually a clever use of the mundane telepathy in conjugation with certain tools. //* After a moment, she added, *// We are not altogether certain what those tools are. //*

Again they passed a length of time in silence, with Vidarian wondering, not for the first time, just what he'd gotten himself into. The thought that perhaps he was the one to solve it, since he knew nothing of the details and was therefore theoretically undaunted, was cold consolation.

The group rested by night, with the gryphons angling downward in the red twilight once they sighted a clearing appropriate for a safe landing. Each night one of the gryphons disappeared into the darkness and returned one or more hours later dragging a fresh kill. Thalnarra took her turn in this, and in each case Vidarian joined in their dinner—though he found that he still preferred his meat cooked.

During their brief meals he gradually came to know the other two gryphons that had volunteered to escort him. They were brothers—brown-plumaged and long-legged harrier gryphons whose loyalty to Thalnarra bordered on outright fanaticism. Their body language and sharp eyes reflected a spaniel-like demeanor whenever she so much as spoke one of their names. It was almost disturbing.

The older brother, Kaltak, took to telling Vidarian stories of the lairs and hunting grounds of the Cherath'kettu'ssa, or "children of Ele'cherath" as they referred to themselves. A friendly rivalry existed between Sharli's two gryphon subspecies, and both agreed that it was probably well that the harriers had little interest in the goshawks' territory, since their own was more than large enough.

Perhaps unsurprisingly, Kaltak (with the occasional side note provided by his brother) painted a portrait of a very warlike society—or, at least a society that would be warlike if not carefully mediated by the fire priestesses, called Shamans in their home. Each gryphon underwent a maturation rite before being accepted into the pride as an adult, and these two were in Thalnarra's service for a full preparatory year. Ishrak, though two seasons younger than Kaltak, had passed a test that allowed him to enter training in tandem with the older gryphon. In another species this would have incited cockiness, but Ishrak seemed to have nothing but respect for his older brother. Vidarian knew of few societies save those of pirates and merchants on the high seas, and the gryphons' intricacies fascinated him. He listened avidly to their tales of adventure and lair life, sometimes understanding little about the details but gaining volumes of new regard for gryphon culture. Even had he accepted the existence of gryphons before he had seen one, "culture" was not a word that would have occurred to him even at the bottom of the deepest wine bottle. That disbelieving self, so unwittingly narrow in experience, seemed more than a lifetime away.

By night he found himself guarded by three balls of feathers and fur. When the gryphons curled up to sleep (and, birdlike, they grew tired as soon as the light faded), their wings hid any leonine portions of their body almost entirely from view, and the long, stiff feathers that ran along the back of their necks plumed upward as they buried their beaks between heavily muscled shoulder blades. One of them snored, and he wasn't sure which.

Perhaps reminded by his companions' fluffy nighttime presence, he found his mind wandering to what had become of Ariadel's kitten. What could the Vkortha possibly make of it? Had they killed it out of hand? Inevitably his thoughts would venture into dark territory, and he heaved at them halfheartedly before at last settling into uneasy sleep.

◠◠◠

The monotony of a blinding sun cast the basket in harsh, jagged shadows day after day and made the journey stretch into one long hypnotic noon. The pattern broke only once, causing Vidarian to start out of a bleary nap (one taken, as they had been for days, with the Book of Nistra open before him), when the gryphons began to angle downward in the sky—not at sunset, but with the sky still glaringly bright overhead.

"Priestess Thalnarra?" Vidarian mumbled, tucking the book back into his pocket and rubbing his eyes.

// *We, or I should say* they, *can take you no further,* she answered, casting an obliquely apologetic glance over her shoulder. *We approach Vkortha territory.* //

"How can you tell?"

One of the gryphoness's feathered ears slanted down at a sharp angle in his direction. // *Listen. Feel. You will Sense it.* //

He complied, carefully, but nearly before he had even been able to close his eyes, Vidarian became uncomfortably aware of a buzzing vibration that lingered in his mind. It grew steadily even as the party descended, as if they were passing into a great bank of fog, but the world to his mortal eyes remained disconcertingly mundane.

On the ground the woods were preternaturally silent. Whenever the gryphons landed a hush of the smaller forest creatures followed in their wake, but always there had been the ambient noise of distant activity. Not so, here. Either nothing lived in this forest, or if it did, it was being very careful to maintain an illusion of absence.

Under Thalnarra's supervision, Vidarian helped the gryphons separate provisions and particular supplies into a set of leather pouches that locked cunningly into brackets along the brothers' harnesses. Thalnarra, though, made no move to collect the special herbs that Vidarian had come to recognize as exclusive to her use.

"Shall I help you pack, Priestess?" he asked, when at last the brothers were completing final preparations and there was little left to be done. Thalnarra's scarlet eyes pierced through his poorly veiled question.

// *I intend to stay with you, Captain, for as long as I can.* // She did not say more, but instead turned to the other gryphons, who abruptly stood at attention. Vidarian heard nothing, but by the narrowing and flaring of the creatures' pupils, they were engrossed in a deep discussion. He turned away so as not to intrude even upon their expressions.

A heavy weight on his shoulder—one that, he noticed, bore a set of five-inch talons—surprised him out of his quiet contemplation. The claw was surprisingly warm—almost hot beneath the clean, dry skin. Vidarian turned slowly.

Ishrak's large golden eyes focused intently on Vidarian's for a long moment. Finally he uttered a strange, piercing call, and said, // *Charnak; vikktu ari lashuul.* // Then, as swiftly as he had come, he turned and paced away with casual, measured steps. Neither of the two gryphons looked back before they took to the air, the wind from their wings throwing leaves and dust in all directions.

When they were out of sight, Vidarian turned to see Thalnarra inspecting him with the tilted head and raised cheek-feathers that he had come to recognize as bemusement.

// *I believe that would be the first time that a human mind has heard those words. You should feel honored.* // Despite the amusement in her words, it was apparent that the gryphoness was quite serious.

"I do," Vidarian said, watching Thalnarra carefully and folding his hands behind his back.

// *It means, "be resolved; victory will find you." It is the traditional parting phrase for a company of gryphons departing for war.* //

Vidarian thought this over for a long moment, then nodded. "That's what we're doing, isn't it?"

Thalnarra did not answer, but her feathers, mantling up behind her neck as she sat down and gazed into the impenetrably dark forest to the west, spoke for her.

CHAPTER TEN

QUENCHED

The buzzing hum continued to increase as they trekked further into the forest, rising into a palpable sensation of itching at the back of the brain. Frequently Vidarian caught himself shaking his head, a futile but reflexive response to the unnerving itch.

At length the forest gave way to a rugged, wind-blasted coastline. When they stumbled out of the trees and into the dubious grey light of the open shore, there was no warning—the trees, hung heavily with parasitic moss and vines, had blocked out any view no matter how close it was. Cold, sleet-fingered wind lashed at the tree line, whipping up out of the sea like the angry swats of a petulant cat.

Vidarian stared out over the open water, squinting at the hazy horizon.

// *This confirms what we suspected but could not ascertain,* // Thalnarra said, feathers rippling in the constant wind as she too squinted out over the waves. Her voice in his mind was not loud, a calm non sequitur in the maddening combination of thundering waves and buzzing Presence. // *The Vkortha are on an island, or, if not an island, a peninsula whose bridge they have managed to hide from view.* //

"An island?" Vidarian shouted, struggling to make himself heard. "How are we going to get to it?" Thalnarra cast him an unruffled glance.

// *The flight basket is watertight. The ride won't be pleasant, but we can make it.* //

"Make it to where?" He tried not to sound too alarmed.

// *We'll see, won't we?* //

～～～

There was no help for it. Vidarian trudged back into the dense forest, working to manage his dread at the notion of sailing literally blind into the unknown. He realized for the first time his dependency on the usual navigational implements—charts, compasses, sextants, and the few precious little charms that made the vast openness of the sea and sky at least somewhat manageable.

The thought of navigational tools made him pause. There was that strange tubular tool packed in with the magical implements, an air navigator—could it be used to guide them? At that point Vidarian would have clung to any hope of a useful instrument with ferocity. He asked Thalnarra about it as they wove their way through the tangled vines and rushes that seemed to have grown back in duplicate force since they had last passed through.

// *It would work,* // she answered, giving a nod of her beak as she leapt over a fallen log. // *It's not ideal, but I can recalibrate it to the coast and we can, at the least, have some idea of where we are in relationship to land.* //

That gave them a way back, if and when they needed it, which was enough for Vidarian. He plowed through the foliage with renewed vigor.

᷍ ᷍ ᷍

Although he had not considered it before, the seaworthiness of the gryphons' basket became immediately apparent as Vidarian and Thalnarra slid it out onto the rocky sand. Vidarian wondered if perhaps its boatlike construction had subconsciously comforted him on that first harrowing ride.

Catching sight of his expression, Thalnarra nodded to his thoughts. // *Rather than reinvent the wheel, so to speak, we based the baskets off of the design of a small boat. What slides through the water also slides through the air. It works in our favor all the more, now.* // Without waiting for assistance, the tall gryphoness braced both foreclaws solidly on the basket's "hull" and gave a tremendous shove. The vessel slid wetly across the grey foam and slime that marked the waterline, and then it was afloat. Vidarian hopped in quickly as the tide took hold.

Before launch Vidarian had loaded a pair of long, supple branches into the basket. He now grabbed the first of these and used it as a poor but effective pole. Once he felt confidence in the method, he looked around, wondering where Thalnarra could possibly fit.

But she was already high above him, feathers twitching constantly to battle the erratic wind. // *Take your bearing, Captain—I will follow the craft.* // She held the recalibrated air navigator in one claw, having detached it from its place hooked to her chest strap.

Pulling in the pole and relying on the tide to wash them out, Vidarian carefully extracted Ariadel's emerald from a pouch around his neck. For a brief moment he closed his eyes, focusing on the faint, flickering presence of the emerald and the distant fluttering that called to the stone, far past the horizon. Swallowing a flood of emotion as he noted both the increasing strength of the emerald and what seemed to be a decrease in Ariadel's "signal," her true life flame, he tucked the stone back into its nest and lifted his branch-pole unerringly south-by-southwest. Thalnarra gave a quick answering cry from overhead and angled away in that direction. Vidarian roughly thrust the branch back into the water, guiding his erstwhile craft toward the towering bank of dark clouds that marked their destination.

⌇⌇⌇

The first attack came by night, when the clouds overhead became menacing shadows that blotted out the stars and the sea was an expanse of cold, shifting mountains of glass that stretched into forever. Vidarian and Thalnarra, caught between the two, soldiered on against the onslaught of wind and wave, but at times it seemed they made no progress, and twice Vidarian swore that the shifting water was actually pushing them backward toward the shore.

Vidarian had poled his craft across the angry waves throughout the night, eventually reversing it to use the leafy end as a makeshift oar, but no dawn showed on the horizon. His muscles were reaching their utter limits—he had thought this perhaps a dozen times in the past several hours, but now he knew with a sallow dread overtaking his stomach that he was rapidly losing ground to fatigue.

He was just about to call a halt when Thalnarra gave voice to a chilling hawklike cry overhead. // *Stay!* // The single word flung itself into Vidarian's mind and took several moments to percolate, after which he shifted his weight and began fighting not to move onward but to keep the basket-boat in the same place. Thalnarra darted forward and upward, disappearing into the cloud cover.

Whether he succeeded he did not know, but Thalnarra appeared overhead before he could so much as wonder where she had gone. Her wings twitched in a rapid pattern as she kept herself hovering in place over the basket.

// *Throw me the amplifier!* // She placed a strange emphasis on the last word, and Vidarian knew what she meant. He moved to the chest, dropping the oar to the basket's wet deck and trusting the gryphoness to keep pace with the now-moving vessel. After fishing inside the opened wooden container for a moment or so, he froze; what was Thalnarra going to do with the sphere, and how in the world was he going to throw it to her? But the priestess's sharp eyes caught his hesitation and she let out another shriek, this one impatient and an inarguable demand. Vidarian picked up the sphere.

He hesitated again as he hefted the solid weight of the globe. // *Just throw it!* // Thalnarra's sharp words triggered the movement of his hand more than Vidarian's own will did. He wound up and slung the globe up into the air with as much force as he could manage.

It wasn't a good throw, but, with a stunning display of agility, Thalnarra dropped like a gull and snatched the globe out of the air. The sharp, ringing *clack* of her formidable talons against the glass of the amplifier carried faintly over the howling wind.

No sooner had Thalnarra touched the sphere than a wave of energy pulsed outward from her, intensely hot and carrying with it the faint but pungent odor of astringent smoke. Vidarian could see it with his eyes—a bright, blinding circle of red shot out across the waves. But the ring did not disappear into the distance as he thought it would. It stopped perhaps six gryphon-lengths away before pulsing back toward the center and simultaneously shooting up into a half-dome in the air.

The wind died away. Vidarian found himself acutely aware of Thalnarra's presence, from the steady beating of her wings overhead to the thump of her heartbeat. But the waves beyond the circle grew indistinct, as if seen in a dream.

"What did you do?" he called, voice echoing in the abrupt quiet.

// *Shielded us from the Vkortha,* // came the answer, and the gryphoness sounded very, very tired. // *It won't last for long.* // She dropped the amplifier back into the basket and Vidarian tucked it into his sash absently.

"Why now?"

// *Because we're passing out of the storm—it's a barrier around their island. I can see the break in the clouds from here.* //

The swift, cold water carried them toward the break so quickly that by the time Thalnarra completed her sentence they were breaking into a patch of open sky. Vidarian staggered forward as the water itself grew abruptly still, nearly pulling the oar from his hands. He stared blankly over the opaque, glossy water that seemed to have no depth as it reflected a sky that had no clouds. It took several moments for him to realize that palpable in the air was another stillness, this one strange: Thalnarra's mind, over the course of his time with her, had developed a certain "static"; he found that he could sense when she was nearby. No more—she hovered on the wind, wings beating regularly to keep her aloft, but the presence of her mind was far astray.

Then—

// *Wait . . . I'm losing it . . . brace yourself—* //

"For what?" he shouted, then winced at the booming volume of his own voice in the silence; he was too long accustomed to the thunder of the waves. But Thalnarra was gone.

～～～

Stars spangled in front of Vidarian's vision as if he'd taken a massive blow to the head. A strange whiteness clouded his eyes, and he blinked rapidly, raising arms that did their best not to respond.

"Vidarian, I'm so sorry."

A shape clothed in golden silk gradually resolved to his left. Endera was seated next to him in a silver-chased mahogany chair. Her large green eyes were tight with grief and sympathy.

"Priestess?" Speaking sent lances of pain through his dry throat and caused his head to spin.

"Ssh, don't speak. You are safely returned to the temple now and in the hands of the Goddess." Her hand on his shoulder was cool. He shivered.

"Ariadel—" Vidarian choked out her name, hoping it was recognizable. Endera's brow contorted and she looked away. Her voice came as though from a great distance.

"Lost. She was lost. And before we even sent you from the Temple. We couldn't call you back in time, and when our forces could finally reach you, you were caught in a Vkorthan mind-trap. Their *silisva* had you ensnared in—"

"Their what?" Each word seemed to cost him more, but the priestess's words hammered him. Ariadel was dead? Loss, profound and blinding, swept through his veins like black oil in a stream.

Endera paused and looked at him, hard. "The *silisva*. Surely you remember."

Anger sparked somewhere deep within him; it fluttered like a moth, but grew wings of flame. Though his throat felt filled with broken glass, he spat at the priestess, "You said . . . knew nothing about the Vkortha. You said *Ariadel* told you nothing . . . to protect . . . Temple." Grinding out Ariadel's name set him back, but only for half a second, and at last he broke through the agony in his throat; the pain faded to numbness and he felt strength returning to his arms in a haphazard rush. He wrenched himself upright and took in the strange white walls that enclosed the small room. At first his mind boggled at the absence of any door—but then he blinked, and it was there, with the memory that it always had been. He turned in the bed, pulling cotton sheets into disarray, and threw himself at Endera, who leapt back like a doe. There was panic in her eyes.

"This isn't right," he said, advancing on legs that were at once strong and in the next instant weak as water. "None of this . . ." he winced as his vision lurched, "is right." Staggering sideways, he swept the silver-chased chair onto the floor. It clattered as it hit. "Sharli's colors are gold, not silver. No temple room would miss both a window and a candle." He lifted his gaze to Endera, who was backing up slowly. "Your eyes are not green." As he stared at the priestess, her eyes widened—and began to change color. They slid from green to turquoise to blue, and then through purple—but Vidarian had already turned away. He charged at the bare wall with a primal scream ripping from his lungs.

∿∿∿

The ground swept away under his feet and he almost stumbled—but Vidarian Rulorat had never so much as placed a foot wrong aboard ship, and would not do so now.

The waves of the An'durin, green and deep, rocked the *Empress Quest* as her captain gazed out over the cloudless waters. It was an unnatural sea, they said—the An'durin suffered no living creature within it, save one, and so its waters were clear as autumn air. Shifting white sandbars were visible hundreds of feet below the glassy surface.

There was something he was supposed to remember . . .

Vidarian shook his head. An item left at port, perhaps. Some trinket his mother had asked for. He could find her another; ports dotted the shores of An'durinvale like gulls on a pier. He could not turn the *Empress* around now, with the wind so full in her sails and the sky so ripe for conquest.

In the distance a pair of wings soared just above the horizon, shadows on the salt-chased air. A gryphon?

A smile parted Vidarian's cracked lips at that. The sour salten breeze dried his teeth. A passing sailor saw his expression and paused, smiling hesitantly back with a question in his eyes, but the captain only shook his head and gestured the man onto his duties. Thoughts of gryphons indeed! Next he would be thinking of mermaids; gryphons were creatures of myth. He squinted to locate the creature in the air again—surely a wayward albatross—but it was gone.

Absently Vidarian pulled a brass spotting scope from his coat pocket and trained it on the horizon. He squinted—the waves had grown, tossing the ship to and fro on the swells. Thinking that it would pass, he continued to peer through the glass, but the waves continued to rise. Frowning, he re-pocketed the scope, just in time to see the first churning foam froth white off the *Empress*'s port bow.

A Rulorat did not stagger, but Vidarian took a decisive step backward as the sole occupant of the An'durin Sea surfaced not two lengths from his ship, whipping the waters to a frenzy in her wake.

An'du, they called her—the sea was named after the great green whale that lurked in her depths. The top of the creature was white as the sand, lending her invisibility from above; three times as long as the *Empress Quest*, An'du had three sets of long, tapering fins speckled with white against slick moss-green skin. *I remember you!* The words whispered in Vidarian's mind, soft and strangely feminine. As she rose titanic from the sea An'du rolled to one side, fixing an eye the size of a dinner plate on the *Empress* and her cap-tain. Phalanged tendrils of translucent gold flesh, kelplike camouflage from some long-forgotten home sea, trailed from her fins and spine, slipping above the water's surface as her huge torso slid sideways in the water. The great eye dilated, black rising against deep brown, and then pinned, sending a thrill of alarm down Vidarian's spine. There were legends about An'du—that the deadness of her sea was not her making, but man's, and she cultivated vengeance in her heart so black that it could kill with a single thought. But the sharpness in her one visible eye was not directed at him, focused instead at some point over his shoulder.

They do not know whom they trifle with, calling up your memory of me, she said, and Vidarian's head spun, not at the danger in her tone but at a sudden dis-tortion of what seemed the very world around him, which bowed like a glass fishbowl. *They think to trap you here! But then they think that all are as ignorant of their secrets as the priestesshood. . . . I do remember you.* Then with one mighty push of her broad tail, she was gone—leaving behind only a voice that lin-gered painfully on Vidarian's thoughts—

And you must remember as well . . .

And he did. Visions of a lightning-cracked sea flashed before his eyes, weirdly juxtaposed on the serene waves of the An'durin. He clutched his head and screamed as images flooded his brain—a pocked crystal orb on a bed of velvet, a gold-chased mahogany chair beneath an alabaster window, a slender white hand slipping into darkness . . .

Blinded, he lurched across the deck, leaping over the bow as he reached it and flinging out his arms to embrace the green waters. The piercing cry of a raptor, far too loud to be an albatross, screamed over his head, melding with the song of a breaching whale that thundered in his skull—

CHAPTER ELEVEN

KINDLING

He fell, long and long. The expected assault of the cold sea never came. He was a boy, standing at his father's side; he was a man, weeping at the empty bower of his mother; he was a captain, leading a battle-quickened crew aboard a black pirate vessel.

He was a man, holding in his arms a creature whose soul burned with white fire.

Suddenly his feet were back on the unstable but unshakably real surface of the gryphon basket, which had taken on an alarming amount of water. The real world engulfed him; every detail shouted its existence to his baffled senses. Only Thalnarra's triumphant shriek overhead brought him back into control, as she swooped low enough over his head to raise a wind that sent the falling rain blasting back onto the sea.

She did not speak, but arrowed off to the northwest, disappearing back into the storm. Magic glowed red at the tips of her talons, and she still looked near to exhaustion, but her wings took on a stronger beat when Vidarian waved to acknowledge her dive.

His time in the Vkortha's enforced trance had pushed him back out into the stormy whirlpool beyond the enemy's lair, but with a surge of adrenaline fueling his fury he fought his way back into their sacred circle.

This time, they were waiting for him.

Six figures robed in black stood in a semicircle just inside the perimeter of the cyclone that protected their domain. Their casual display of yet another intimidating magic made his heart skip; slippered feet rested easily on the still surface of the too-glassy water. His mind reeled, ready to battle another dream, but then the waves shifted, baring thin columns of ice that gave the lie to their illusion. Water magic? His own new sensitivity surged up, longing to study how they'd frozen the sea—but he did not need the sun emerald to know that Ariadel lay beyond them, fighting for consciousness—fighting to keep her life.

The attention of the Vkortha was fractured, but enough rested on Vidarian to make the six figures his entire world. Nothing they could have done would shift his gaze. But Ariadel's voice, hoarse with fatigue even as it spoke in his mind, could.

Vidarian, you have to get out of here . . . they're trying to get one last piece of information from me, or else I would be dead. More they can reap from your mind, and Thalnarra's—they search for her still, though her cloak has thrown them off! The web of their magic is everywhere . . . everywhere. . . . His mind spun again—he had not known that Ariadel could speak telepathically. But he worked to get beyond his shock and concentrate on her words—the last of which, and the insanity that touched it, percolated deeply enough to make his very soul quake. *You must go, now!*

"You know I can't do that," he said aloud, trusting Ariadel to hear the words of his mind even as he stared at the still immobile figures of the Vkortha before him. The priestess, mad with fear and fatigue, continued to object—and Vidarian knew that the Vkortha were listening.

As they listened, and as they sent their minds questing outward into the churning sky for Thalnarra, Vidarian moved his hands behind him, slowly.

When his searching fingers found their targets, he was not slow. With one hand he drew his sword from its sheath, steel against steel singing even over the roar of the storm that surrounded them. As one the Vkortha stepped back, focusing the full weight of their formidable awareness on him as the clean steel—fireborne and rife with the spirit of Vidarian's ancestors—drew their magics like a magnet. As he had suspected, they'd trained their magics to strike any fire spirit that manifested nearby, the better to bring down Thalnarra the moment her shield slipped—not expecting that Vidarian's sword could provide a false target.

A wall of flame roared up around the edge of the Vkorthan island; Thalnarra had seen her opening. It would burn Ariadel—if it had a chance to get there.

Even as Thalnarra's defenses surged up around them, Vidarian sent his own awareness into the Rulorat sword. The torrential life force inside him, the storm that the sun emerald had only hinted at, poured down his arm and into the blade, becoming it. To his awakened senses, a coil of crashing water energy wreathed the weapon from pommel to tip. The burning light they now displaced flared as if living and angry, and Vidarian's chest threatened to collapse in on itself as the energies warred—he fought now, not just against the drilling eyes of the Vkortha, but to stay conscious under the weight of his own magic.

A second force welled up in him, something he could only call his own will, embodied. His teeth clenched, the bones of his grip went white around the sword, sparks flashed in his vision—and the energies obeyed him. Like chastened hounds, they suddenly bent to his mastery, weaving together, sealing the sword into a thing of living energy.

A cry of triumph and rage clawed free from his throat, and he was throwing himself from the basket before he realized it, into the embrace of the waves. Even as his feet tumbled toward the familiar shifting surface and the depths beyond, he snarled, a pure wordless denial of the forces claiming his body—and they listened. The waves stiffened, solidified—and when his boots met them, they held him, propelled him toward his enemies.

Another leap and he closed the gap. The sword with its woven energies met the enemy mage's defenses, crashing against them like waves breaking over ice. And like waves, the energies came rebounding back at Vidarian, pushing him backward. But his momentum gave him the advantage, and the Vkortha *folded* under the blade with an unearthly wail, its barriers collapsing and its body dropping into the sea.

The Vkortha dissolved into chaos. The five remaining turned and fled, each in a different direction, the seas freezing before them, waves sent rising up behind them in panicked last defenses. None made any effort to assist the others, and they were rapidly scattering over the sea and island.

From the sky, Thalnarra screamed a challenge and fell upon the one nearest her, bringing it down in a torrent of flame. But Vidarian knew they could not chase down the three remaining—one, at least, would escape, to warn its fellows and bring a renewed attack. Without thinking, he brought forth the etched orb of the amplifier from his sash. He raised it to his forehead, closed his eyes, and *pushed*.

A wave of energy pulsed out from man and amplifier, leaving a path of momentary but profound silence in its wake. All life stilled for the brief second of its passing. The Vkortha between it and the island wailed their death-cries as the magic found them distracted, unprotected, and utterly unable to defend themselves. Behind him Vidarian felt Thalnarra raise up her own magic to shield herself from the onslaught, and withstand it—but what happened beyond the line of Vkortha was strange.

The wave found Ariadel, bound only by magic that was quickly dissolving around her but unable to avoid the crashing pulse of water energy. It cascaded down over her, and the light within her soul went out.

Time slowed to a crawl. Amid the roar of the diminishing storm that raged around the island, Vidarian felt the stone in his breast pocket go cold. In that very instant, when despair would have taken him, the fire that lived within that rare stone leapt into Vidarian's heart—and found tinder there.

Vidarian fell to his knees in the waterlogged basket, his will sundered by the fire that roared up in his spirit. The sword in his hand began to glow, then incandesce. Just at the moment when he thought the flames would consume him—and when he would go willingly to their opiate embrace—an eagle's shape dropped out of the sky (. . . *too big to be an albatross* . . .) and dove down upon him. Thalnarra's aura covered his own and soothed his depleted spirit.

She stayed with him as they struggled to the shore of the island. There was no sign of the Vkortha; the ones that had survived the blast of the amplifier had fled. Absent the terrible storm, the island was quite mundane: white beaches dotted with brush and palm stretched to the east and west. And to the north, a crumpled figure lay still on the sand.

Weak in body and mind, Vidarian staggered across the sand, his feet sinking in dull thuds as the beach fought his passing. When he reached Ariadel's fallen body, he dropped to his knees and reached to turn her toward him. Blood flowed renewed in a strangled heart when he saw that she still breathed.

But there was accusation in those tormented eyes—eyes that had so long struggled against madness, and now had their last bastion taken from them. Gone was the mysterious beauty he had met so long ago, and in its place was a creature of shadow and a mind that did not recognize him.

He whispered her name, but she could not hear it. Helplessness turned rapidly to anger—the last of his energy was not spent. In a fury he turned his gaze to the sky itself, and throughout the core of his being screamed as he had not known he could: *HOW COULD THIS HAPPEN?*

But there, in the heart of his rage, a spark jumped from the inconstant flames that had taken hold in his soul. It flickered, jumped, landed—and found tinder.

Golden light roared up in Ariadel's eyes, and consciousness returned with them. Thalnarra, silent so long, hissed audibly behind them and rushed forward, spreading a wing over the once-broken priestess and extending her magic to feed the burgeoning new flame there—magic that Vidarian could now sense.

The sun moved far in the sky as they sat silently on the beach recouping their strength. Gradually warmth returned to their bodies, and Vidarian settled down into the sand, trying to make some sense of the energy that now swept without rhyme or reason through his body. A sudden sound—an angry "Rrrawl!"—distracted him momentarily from observing the turmoil inside his spirit.

The gangly kitten, looking even more emaciated than usual with its fur slicked down from the rain and sea spray, clawed its way out from under a broken plank, where it had apparently been nesting since the capture. The look in Ariadel's exhausted eyes said that she had not expected to see the little creature again. Gingerly and silently she picked the tiny cat up; even sitting where he was, Vidarian could smell the tinge of garbage and old fish oil that clung to the wet fur. Even as his nose wrinkled, he smiled, an expression that quickly faded when a surge of flashing colors swam across his mind again.

The magics there were arguing. Fire and water did not easily coexist. But it was a manageable struggle—in the scope of recent events, it was almost comforting.

When Ariadel spoke at last it was with a voice choked by disuse. "You— Quenched me. How?" Vidarian stared at her for a long moment, wondering how to answer.

Thalnarra, settled next to them with her wings spread out under the sun like a vulture, took up the answer without opening her eyes. // *He had the amplifier and your fire was already low—the Vkortha had worn you down, the better to sense attacking fire magics. As for Vidarian—//* one red eye revealed itself in a narrow slit between her heavy eyelids, // *I have matched him to another of our prophesies, though I thought not to live to see this one: the warrior of fire and sea.* //

Ariadel blinked dully, though with obvious recognition, as the kitten squirmed in her arms. "The Tesseract? Then . . . that would . . ."

// *One revelation at a time, my dear.* // Amusement colored Thalnarra's voice, obliquely reassuring Vidarian despite the irksome nature of her words. // *He is a Kindler—and that is enough for him to know for now.* //

"And then . . . where can we go now? We can make a boat from what remains of the Vkortha settlement here . . . but the last of them have surely gone elsewhere, and they will not take this defeat well." Ariadel frowned, still struggling against the fragility of her body but gaining in cogency rapidly.

Thalnarra did not answer and Vidarian pulled himself slowly to his feet. He looked out over the calm, ordinary waters as they lapped against the shore. The sky was a deep sapphire blue as day made its steady journey toward evening—and where it met the sea could not be told for certain, so similar in shade was the distant horizon. Brushing sand from his beard, he turned back toward gryphon and priestess and folded his arms. "For now," he said, "I think we go home. I have a matter of sun rubies to settle."

PART TWO

RUBIES

CHAPTER TWELVE

DEEPER THAN YOU KNOW

Vidarian Rulorat's hands rested with soft confidence on the lacquered prow of the *Stormswift*, a sleek black ship with the banner of Sher'azar snapping from its highest mast. A gilt bronze weathervane overhead creaked with movement as the vast sea, incarnadine in the twilight, rippled with a change in the wind. The waters were as mesmerizing as they had been for Vidarian on the day he first remembered watching the waves. No matter where he was in the world, the water was his constant: one mother, one mistress, one life. She was eternal.

Vidarian? The sudden voice in his mind snapped him out of contemplation of the sunset reflections below. *She's starting. You might want to see this.*

Try as he might, Vidarian couldn't quite suppress a start when Ariadel spoke in his mind. He'd gotten used to Thalnarra's telepathy perhaps more easily because she never spoke with a physical voice. That, and she didn't speak *inside* his head the way Ariadel did.

In the rush of adrenaline that came with their recent standoff with the Vkortha council and the shock that followed, no one had noticed that, beyond being dehydrated and shaken, Ariadel had taken a strong blow to the side of the face and suffered a broken jaw. When cooler realization had set in and the fire faded from her veins, the lower right part of her face had started to swell, and soon she had joined Thalnarra in silence, if by a more painful route.

When Vidarian turned to walk quickly to the *Stormswift's* cabin, another banner caught his eye—the white torch insignia of the Sher'azar Healers floated from the crow's nest of the smaller ship that brushed sides with the greater black corsair. Sher'azar's reach was long—when their ordeal was over,

Thalnarra stretched her mind to contact her fellows on the shore, who in turn relayed swift messages to the Fire Temple. Within three days the black ship that now bore them had appeared on the horizon, and two days later they met up with the smaller *Greyvale* in the northern waters off Val Harlon.

The *Greyvale* was a stout, stable rig with an expansive array of wide, square masts and a low waterline. She had three decks, though her aft quarter combined those three into a single chamber for a gryphon healing station where the creatures' instinctive dislike of closed-in spaces could be mitigated. Right now it was full of ballast: huge bales of straw weighted down with lead, the former of which could either be thrown overboard or broken open and spread across the deck for a warm makeshift den. Thalnarra had declined the comforts of this hideaway in favor of a sleeping nest atop the main deck of the *Stormswift*, ostensibly because she preferred the cool sea air, but in reality to spare the healers the trouble of breaking open straw bales that they would then have to discard later as unsanitary. That, and having a fire magess in the back hold of a ship atop a bunch of kindling was probably not the healers' idea of safety and sanity.

Inside the forecastle of the *Stormswift* Vidarian caught an odd medley of scents: the faint sweet nut-spice of Thalnarra's feathers, varnish from the dark wood paneling the walls, and an odd, grassy aroma that he couldn't identify. Thalnarra's tail thumped sedately on the deck just ahead of him, curled out from the threshold to the captain's cabin. Quiet nods met him as he entered the cabin's anteroom—the doorway into the cabin proper was open, and Ariadel perched on the edge of the captain's bed, bracketed by the captain herself (a burgundy-uniformed fire magess) and an adjunct healer from the *Greyvale*.

The strange smell seemed to be coming from a platter of crushed plant material that rested on a steel tray to one side of the bed. The healer, a vastly wrinkled woman with grey hair and nimble fingers, held a linen poultice of the stuff to Ariadel's jaw.

It's cactus, Ariadel thought at him, and she smiled, then immediately winced, from her perch. There was no separation of her thought from his— it was as if he'd thought it himself, only he had no idea what a "cactus" was.

She realized this, too. *It's a plant from the plains-desert south of the Windsmouth range*, they thought together. *By the ruins?* (This time it was actually his thought.) *Even past the ruins*, came the answering thought. *Far, far south.* That would explain why he'd never seen it before—it must be tremendously rare. The volcanic Windsmouth Mountains were beyond treacherous—some said they had swallowed up entire civilizations. And a series of skeletal reef-islands that confounded even the most learned navigator barred access to the southern continent by sea. Naturally it was the fascination of every dreamer and dusty-nosed archivist north of Cheropolis, and many more to the south.

The healer had rolled up her sleeves—apparently the strange green pulp wasn't the only act in the show tonight.

Vidarian felt an abrupt tightening in his chest, a sensation he had come to recognize as the precursor to someone wielding elemental energies in his immediate vicinity. Strange green lights that his eyes told him he saw but he knew had no real "light" of their own danced out from the healer's fingertips, ribbons of energy that filled the air with a refreshing crispness, almost like the scent of pine needles. The ribbons were joined by bands of blue, red, and gold so quickly that Vidarian was not able to identify any of the matching changes in the air, though he knew they were there, and a strange harmony thundered in his ears.

Then, suddenly, all of the energies were one, and they flickered out of his sight. Vidarian staggered and leaned into the doorjamb—it felt like something was crawling under his skin, swimming just below the reach of his consciousness. A sickening coppery taste filled his mouth.

All at once it was over; the healer was folding her sleeves back down and Ariadel was carefully testing the mobility of her healed jaw.

// *Fish go down straight, not sideways,* // Thalnarra offered helpfully.

Vidarian felt his eyes bulge further. "What?"

// *Nothing. You look like you're having a bit of trouble there. Remember to breathe.* //

"Right," was all he could manage, around concentrating on pulling air into his lungs.

// *It gets easier the more you see it. What did you sense?* // The gryphoness's piercing red eyes sharpened on him, their pupils pinning and flaring briefly.

"Like something . . . crawling . . ." He rubbed compulsively at his forearm.

// *So you can feel it.* // There was distinct satisfaction in Thalnarra's voice. // *Some only experience a ringing in their ears, or a paling of the energy-light.* //

"No, I felt it, all right." Belatedly he remembered his manners and turned to the healer. "Thank you, Mender, for your help."

The old woman smiled, baring a set of surprisingly white, strong teeth. "It's an honor to make y'r acquaintance, er—sir—"

"Just Vidarian, please, Mender," Vidarian said quickly. The healer only smiled and bowed out of the room.

You should let them say it, Ariadel chided with Vidarian's mind. *They are getting the chance of a lifetime, to meet the Tesseract.* The word had rapidly become a trigger for cold chills up Vidarian's spine. *I just don't think any good can come of spreading big titles around. . . .*

"No good can come of trying to hide what you are, either," Ariadel said, testing out the flexibility of her jaw.

// *She speaks true,* // Thalnarra addressed all of them, then tilted her head to fix Vidarian with a scarlet eye that once more flashed light and dark with her scrutiny.

// *How can you do what you must if you are balked by a mere word?* //

"And what must I do?" He couldn't quite keep the impatience out of his voice, having lost count of how many times he'd asked the same question.

But this time Thalnarra answered, black pupils flaring to fill her eyes.

// *Change the world, of course.* //

At midafternoon the following day they made port in Val Harlon to bid farewell to the *Stormswift* and board a lighter rivergoing craft. Val Harlon was unrivaled in splendor, as always—its white filigreed arches gleamed in the sun, visible far from the shore. Even at this distance it was possible to make out the strange famed sculptures that perched atop the spires—shaped like a human, but completely feathered, and winged like a gryphon. Fishing "farms" spread out in narrow fingers to either side of the channels that led to and from the port, crisscrossed with floating walkways woven from white reed.

The *Sunstar*, yet another Sher'azar-commissioned vessel, sat alarmingly low in the green water, its black hull set with thick glass in portholes that looked out no more than a handspan above the river's surface. She was sleek and narrow, which meant for smaller sleeping quarters, but to Vidarian the sight of her trim deck and precise three-cornered sails more than made up for the inconvenience. He also didn't spend much time below, in the first place.

The river fascinated. Vidarian had never liked rivers; even on the largest ones, the land crowded in too closely, and the calmer land waters gave berth to indolent but deadly creatures; somehow that combination struck Vidarian as cosmically wrong. Now, though, he sensed how the water changed; he felt it in his veins. Though thinner and tamer, the water here was of a purer source, absent the salt that gave the sea her body and wildness—it was clean and alive. Even the lush greenery that drank the river's essence from the shore pulsed with the presence of water itself, flavoring the very air. Vidarian spent many hours each day simply sitting in the shade of the mainsail, drinking in the new flavors of the elemental energy around him. He would return below only for meals and to sleep.

Though small, the *Sunstar* boasted more amenities than the *Stormswift*, being something of a luxury vessel and never intended for the abrasive salten sea. Vidarian grudgingly admitted that a few of her fittings outshone the *Quest*, and a small handful, such as the clever mirrored light fixtures that spun to distribute tension but never tilted, he memorized for adaptation onto his family's ship. If he could have discerned it, he would eagerly have learned what allowed the *Sunstar* to boast such elegant interiors while remaining as light and fleet as a sailfish on the water.

Vidarian spent two days perched at the bow of the small river-ship before the smooth separation of the green waters before the knifelike prow began to wane in its wonder. The other occupants of the small vessel had left him to his peace, perhaps wisely recognizing his need for quiet with the magics at war within him, but on their third day on the river, Thalnarra came and sat next to him, her muscles shifting with the gently swaying deck.

"How did she do it?" Vidarian asked, without turning his head to look at the gryphoness. Thalnarra chuckled.

// *You refer to the fish incident,* // she said, as if that was any explanation, but she continued before he could contradict her. // *Healers maintain an internal balance of all four elements, at least insofar as we can tell. To tell you the truth, I don't know if anyone completely understands it. It is an ability that they display from an early age, and it is instinctive.* //

"Why did it keelhaul me like that?" Vidarian folded his arms and consciously smoothed the scowl from his expression as he turned to regard Thalnarra, leaning against the carved, upswept "flames" that formed the *Sunstar*'s bow.

// *Only because you've never seen it before, while Kindled. Exposure to Healing strikes us all differently. Most air magicians smell it; water magicians hear it; fire magicians see it; earth magicians taste it.* //

Vidarian's brow furrowed. "But . . . I'm almost certain I *felt* it, crawling around . . ." He rubbed his hands on his shirtsleeves, trying to shake the memory of the strange sensation from his fingertips. The gryphoness did not answer, though she flicked a momentary scarlet glance at him before returning her focus to the parting river below. Vidarian clenched his teeth. He had come to conclude that not all magicians had such a flare for the dramatic—just the Fire ones. "Who feels it, Thalnarra?"

// *We have records of magicians from long ago—centuries upon centuries ago, as far as we can reckon—that could "feel" Healing.* // The feathered tip of her tail flicked against her ankles. // *They were called PrimeAdepts, and they were masters of all four elements.* //

"Am I going to be a . . . PrimeAdept?" Vidarian swallowed. He was having a hard enough time with two elements in his blood; what would it be like with four?

Thalnarra gave a purring chuckle, the feathers on her throat rippling, that set him at ease. // *Not likely. For one thing, all of the PrimeAdepts were gryphons.* // She fixed him with a superior stare for a moment, and he met it, though his survival brain clamored against facing down that primal predator regard. Her amusement rippled in his mind, not unkind, and she again turned her head back toward the water. // *And for another,* // she continued, // *we do not think there remains enough magic in the world to support a PrimeAdept.* //

"There was more magic, before?" The question was obvious, and somehow Vidarian felt that he knew the answer in his bones, in his blood, but he needed it spoken.

// *Oh, yes. There was a time when most creatures had magic . . . and when humans and gryphons were quite outnumbered by other sentients on this planet. And further back, in the Age of the PrimeAdepts, magic was everywhere.* // Thalnarra twitched one tufted ear, her pupils contracting and flaring, her mind some-when else.

"What happened?"

// *Get me that fish,* // Thalnarra said abruptly.

"What?" Pulled from his imaginings, Vidarian looked down into the river.

// *Get. Me. That fish.* // She gestured down into the ship's wake with a talon; a small school of silver fish swam alongside, staying just ahead of the rolling water. Still trying to figure out when he had missed the turn in their conversation, Vidarian reached down to take a fishing pole from the hooks suspended below the rail. // *Not that way,* // Thalnarra corrected. Even more confused, Vidarian stared at the fish. They were starting to separate from the ship, would disappear in moments.

He almost realized Thalnarra's intent too late. Then, as the last fish started to change its course, he reached out with his senses.

Coolness flooded his mind as he made metaphysical contact with the river. All of the life he had sensed before roared up before him—the reeds as they whisked past on the shore, the slimy moss that covered the stones on the bank, the flat lily pads with their pointed orange blossoms . . . and the silver fish, each as long as his forearm. He found the nearest fish with his mind and then crept forward into the rushing water just in front of it. Then, not entirely knowing what he was doing, he *pulled.*

The fish flipped out of the water, or rather, the water flipped upward and took the creature with it. As it sailed high in the air and then began to fall, the still-moving ship coursed to meet it, and Thalnarra caught it neatly in her beak. Two twitches of her throat and it was gone. // *Very good,* // she said, and Vidarian did not know if she praised him or the fish.

"Don't mention it," he said anyway. Thalnarra answered his question as if uninterrupted by the snack.

// *We do not know for certain what changed,* // she said, // *whether it was of "our" doing or whether the world simply began to lose its magic. We do believe that some of the continuing loss is population-related. Our populations—and, more specifically, your human populations—continue to rise, but the amount of magical ability doled out to both our species seems to remain the same. Therefore we have fewer magic-workers, and those few we have are not as strong as magicians of old.* //

"But I thought the goddesses gave magic."

Thalnarra nodded. // *They do, and at the beginning of the history of the great Temples as we know them today, magicians turned to the elemental goddesses and asked them to renew their magical abilities. To a certain extent, the goddesses answered, and so the priestesshoods were born. Some would say that it is Ele'cherath's will that magic should dwindle, or that we do not act on her will enough and so she slowly withdraws her blessing from us. The fact is no one really knows.* //

It was all getting a little too philosophical. "What am I supposed to do?"

The gryphoness tilted her head, eyeing him. // *I told you. Change the world.* //

"But you didn't say how."

Thalnarra sighed and returned her gaze to the river. Her pupils started to contract and flare again for several moments before stopping suddenly. // *The Tesseract is prophesied to seal the Great Gate,* // she said, still not looking at him. // *The Gate of the PrimeAdepts.* //

"Oh," he said. "What happens after that?"

// *We don't know.* //

CHAPTER THIRTEEN

THE LUSTROUS PEARL

The following day, the water changed color slightly, growing less green. By midafternoon the watch called out a sighting—Moorport was on the horizon. At this, Ariadel, looking considerably less sun-touched than Vidarian for her time spent below, clattered joyfully up to the top deck. She smiled as she squinted into the sunlight.

"You're in fine feather," Vidarian said, chuckling at her gaiety.

"Moorport is my favorite stop," she said, beaming at him despite his gentle jibe. "Come, I'll show you."

Ariadel's excitement, Vidarian was later forced to admit, was fairly justified. She led him to a stately establishment far enough away from the river to shed its scent but close enough to be within easy walking distance of the port. A sign hung over the door proclaimed it the Inn of the Lustrous Pearl.

Within was a paradise in miniature. Strange plants with leaves and flowers that Vidarian could not name filled a small conservatory just inside the tall front doors, and tiny birds twittered from the trees that arched slender branches over a cobbled path that led to the inn itself.

Either Ariadel had sent word ahead, or the proprietors of the Pearl were ready for custom at any time of the day; neither would have particularly surprised Vidarian. As soon as they stepped inside the warmly lit entryway, a pair of smiling women, strikingly beautiful with dark hair and eyes, took Vidarian in hand and led him down the left corridor—Ariadel accompanied another pair to the right, flashing a wicked smile at his alarmed expression. She wiggled her fingertips at him before disappearing around a corner.

After a couple of right-angle turns, the wood-paneled hallway opened up into a small, comfortable chamber lit with lamps of frosted golden glass, each easily as large as Vidarian's head. Spaced between the lamps, covering every inch of wall space, were beveled wooden racks—and in the racks, row on row of gleaming glass bottles, all identically shaped but no two of the same color. In the center of the room was a padded leather table flanked by a pair of cedar cabinets.

The two women separated, neither having spoken. The first went to peruse the bottles, while the second began removing Vidarian's clothes, after briefly introducing herself as Orchid. He jumped as she tugged gently at his coat, but she only smiled again. "Come now," she said, and though her voice was low, it was courteously businesslike. "You must remove your clothes for massage." She glanced over at her partner. "He looks tense." They shared a grin, and the second girl nodded, moving to another section of racks and selecting a series of bottles.

Vidarian managed to keep some parts of his anatomy from going completely red by the time all of his clothes were off, but it was a struggle. The first attendant wrapped a warm, fluffy towel from one of the cedar cabinets around his waist before guiding him to the table. She made a move as if to help him climb atop it, but he gently slipped away from her grasp and levered himself up on his own.

The leather was cool against his chest, but not uncomfortable. The clink of glass from behind him indicated that the second attendant had made her selections, and shortly Vidarian heard her slippered feet pad across to the table.

"First a lotion," one of them said—he thought it was Orchid, but wasn't sure. Both of them had exotic accents, something like the intonation of the islanders in the northwest tropics, but not precisely. He puzzled over the lilt and emphasis of their words until a touch of liquid coolness in the center of his back made him tense involuntarily. There was a smile in the attendant's words. "You are with Lady Ariadel. She has asked her usual therapy for you." A sharp, cool scent filled Vidarian's nostrils as the girl worked the lotion into his back muscles. The vapors were remarkably refreshing, seeming to clear the clutter from his mind.

"What is that?" he asked, impressed.

"The scent is from the oil of crushed laurel-wood and cedar bark. We blend it with a salve made from dustneedle leaves and pods." Vidarian was racking his memories for anything like what she'd described, and had come up with nothing when a sudden spreading warmth between his shoulder blades blurred any future thoughts traveling through his head. "A warmed almond oil," Orchid offered, and he could hear the smile in her voice. She added, without being asked, "Sandalwood, lavender, and mayweed."

Time blurred for a spell as Orchid expertly transitioned from spreading the sweet, heady oil to a deep-tissue massage. Her surprisingly strong fingers found pockets of tension he was fairly sure he'd been carrying around for several years, and the abrupt, heated release was almost painful. Then the gentle orange warmth of the lanterns took hold of Vidarian's senses, briefly becoming his world.

His thoughts drifted, as they were wont to do since the battle with Vanderken, toward his ship and his crew. A pang of longing and guilt echoed in his chest, an itch to be back upon his own deck that no magic, however remarkable, could suppress. There was pride there, a glowing ember of pleasure at how Marielle would now receive her own long-overdue captainship, but he'd sailed for so long that the daily tasks of life at sea sprang upon his unconscious mind—was the sailcloth sound? Had they taken on enough vegetable to keep Ilsut appeased for the crew's health? Little Lifan, when should she be sent to a true windreader for apprenticeship? Like little gnats they surfaced, and one by one he forced himself to let them go, to trust in Marielle and the crew to see themselves safely home. At length, he ran out of worries, and his mind bobbed as on a gentle sea. Almost, he heard a soft voice singing a strange and wordless song.

When he came back to himself, Orchid was doing something rather remarkable involving her thumbs and the balls of his feet—it sent little prickles of sensation jolting up his spine. Despite the sleepy haze he'd drifted into earlier, he suddenly felt quite awake and energized.

Orchid seemed to sense his return to full consciousness. Her quiet voice was pitched for his ears only, a tone that said she was describing plant leaves, or linseed oil. "You must be careful with priestesses," she pressed deeply just above his heel with her thumbs. Vidarian's heart picked up speed, and not from the pressure. "They are rarely what they claim, and even more rarely what they seem to be. You know this, I am sure, good sir, but you have been with Lady Ariadel long, and your air together is one of shared pain that binds. Take care it does not bind you too closely."

Vidarian would have spoken at that, for an objection rolled up like a blue squall in his chest, but Orchid twisted his foot in a way that sent thin lances of white energy up his calf—hardly unpleasant, but utterly disabling. Lights flashed across his eyes, and Orchid was still speaking as she moved to his other foot, with a smile as though she were commenting on his reaction. "Lady Ariadel is long a friend of this inn, we have known her family for generations. But there are secrets that the priestesshood keeps from her. Never confuse her for them."

Quelled, he said, finally, pitching his voice to wonder, as though he were asking about her technique: "How do you know so much of the priestesshood?"

"They do not have a monopoly on secret knowledge," she said, a careless murmur that said she was discussing the weather, a cloth shipment. "You have energy of a kind I have never seen, sir Vidarian. Your task will be as great, of this I have no doubt. Look to yourself for answers, and trust not what you hear." She raised her voice. "Prepare a robe, please."

Orchid's assistant padded lightly across the room and was promptly at his shoulder, ready to help him to his feet and into a plush cotton robe.

Orchid appeared in front of him just as he settled the robe across his shoulders. Something glistened on each of her index fingers, and she reached up to massage his temples with them. The sharp, clean scent of lavender filled his nostrils, and he took a deeper breath almost without meaning to. "Remember always," she said, rhythmically as if in harmless ritual benediction, "the gifts you carry will bring many to desire your friendship. But that friendship is your own gift, to be delivered to those most deserving. And the world is wide and full of secrets." As if to complete her anointing, Orchid brushed one thumb across his forehead, and smiled, the intentness of her eyes sealing the words they had exchanged into silence. She and the assistant stepped back and bowed gracefully, still smiling, palms flat on their thighs. Vidarian fought the impulse to return the bow as they smoothly straightened. Orchid gestured, and her assistant nodded, then turned to lead him down another hallway.

In his haze of physical relaxation and mental brooding it was difficult to recall what directions they'd taken before, but if his suspicion was correct, the inn was huge—Orchid's young assistant, still unnamed, led him further in toward its center through another series of wood-paneled hallways, one of which opened up suddenly into a misty atrium.

Ariadel awaited them there, stretched like an indolent goddess across a satin-upholstered lounging chair. Her eyes roved up and down Vidarian's body as he approached. The assistant did not quite bow quickly enough to mask her smile.

When the young masseuse had taken her leave, and Vidarian had settled gingerly into another lounging chair next to Ariadel's, the fire priestess spoke. "You had Orchid? Oo." Catlike envy twinkled briefly in her lazy gaze, and her voice lowered to a conspiratorial whisper. "She's my favorite."

Vidarian searched her eyes for any hint of hidden intent, but found none, and grabbed at random for something to say. "I didn't catch her assistant's name. . . ." He craned his neck to look back up the wood-paneled passageway.

"She probably didn't have one."

"What?"

"I mean, she has a *name*, of course, but she probably doesn't have a flower-name yet. They only get those after they've completed training. The assistants are all trainees."

"I see." He consciously smoothed his furrowed brow. "Do you come here often?" As he spoke, Vidarian took in his new surroundings, eyes roaming to absorb the tall, waxy-leafed trees, spreading ferns, twittering little birds, and strange hanging decanters that issued forth steady streams of white mist.

"I try to stop in every time I come up this route. They're very kind, and adjust their schedules to accommodate me when they can." Ariadel was picking delicately at a silver platter of strange pink-orange fruit. After a moment she selected a thin slice and began to nibble at one end, away from the slim green rind. Between bites (which by her ecstatic eye-closing she thoroughly enjoyed), she said, "It makes the rest of the journey quite a bit more tolerable."

Vidarian lifted his eyes from the fruit platter, one hand hovering over it. "Rest of the journey?"

Ariadel wrinkled her nose. "It's by verali. Smelly creatures. I never liked them."

CHAPTER FOURTEEN
UP THE MOUNTAIN

Priestesses had a fondness for heights that continually baffled Vidarian. The climb to Sher'azar was steep, blasted by wind and sun alike, and treacherous. Thalnarra had parted with them at the mountain's base, and as they watched her climb into the sky, wings angled and embracing the wind, Vidarian got a glimmering suspicion as to why all of the great temples perched like rock gulls on barely accessible mountaintops. If what Thalnarra had said about the origins of magic was right . . . he wondered if the priestesses that inhabited the temples now knew they had been meant for gryphon perches and not human habitation.

This trip up a treacherous mountain, at least, bore stark and comforting contrast to Vidarian's lone trek up the unforgiving crags of Sher'azar. Though the wind bit, the warmth of their verali mounts and the soft shrouds of black wool given to them at the mountain's base kept them both warm and protected from the howl of Sher'azar's persistent winter.

The verali themselves seemed agreeable enough: lanky creatures with exceptionally long necks and legs. Their curled wool—black for Vidarian's, a kind of mottled rust-and-ochre for Ariadel's—had a strong smell to it, not entirely unpleasant, but carried by oil from their skin, and as such it clung to any who handled them for days after. It was the smell of them that Ariadel claimed drove her mad. Between being saddled with a verali and having to leave her kitten at the Gatehouse (Endera, it seemed, was allergic to cats and would not permit them on temple grounds), Ariadel had worked up a fine head of ire, and Vidarian kept as clear a berth as he could without drawing attention to his distance. Irrational Ariadel had been about that kitten from the very beginning, but Vidarian had to admit that leaving it behind hadn't been easy—the thing had made such a terrible fuss, seeming to know even before Ariadel did that it would not be coming with them.

When they stopped to make camp halfway up the peak, with the wind intensifying and threatening ice, the sun had already sunk low beyond the foothills, leaving only a smudge of ruddy light to carry its eulogy. When Vidarian slung himself down from the saddle, jolts of forgotten feeling speared his legs, and he reached for his mount to steady himself.

Something, he was never quite sure what, guided his hand to one side, away from the hold he normally took on the pack's open flap. Startled anew by his sudden lack of control over his hands, he was about to stretch out his legs to make sure no other muscles were failing when he caught the glint of something small and metallic out of the corner of his eye.

There, tucked into a fold of the pack, rested a tiny glinting spider, gold of body, its ten legs balancing it cozily on a network of gossamer stretched across the parted leather. Vidarian's sharp breath of surprise brought Ariadel to his shoulder, and when she saw what the pack contained, she let out a little cry of astonishment.

"These spiders were prized by the priestesshood decades ago," she said, a flush high on her cheeks, all thought of verali or abandoned kittens forgotten. "We haven't seen one in all that time, and they were rare long before my mother was born. Endera will be ecstatic."

"What do you want to do with it?" Vidarian eyed the spider, unsettled by its returning ten-eyed unblinking gaze.

Ariadel's forehead wrinkled as she considered the creature. "We can't leave it in there. One jolt and it'd be done for." With a little turn that scraped gravel under her feet, she turned to her verali and dug into its packs. After a moment of rummaging she came up with a sheet of the thick, fragrant parchment the priestesses used as a kind of quick-flaming incense; when burned, it would go up in a rush of bright flame all at once, leaving behind only a column of richly scented smoke.

With deft fingers Ariadel began folding the parchment into a small but secure little box. "The acolytes used to practice at making paper figures," she explained. "This won't be paradise, but it'll do." She'd left one side of the box open and held it widely ajar as she returned to Vidarian's side.

The spider lifted its two front legs as her shadow crossed its vision, but otherwise did not move, not even when Ariadel, exquisitely careful, brought the box around behind it and scooped it, plus a good portion of web, gently into the paper box. She shut the lid by tucking its flap into one of the intricate folds, then cupped the box between her hands as though it were the warm egg of some precious bird.

But another occupant of the pack had been disturbed by the tearing of the gossamer web. It skittered across the back of the pack, tiny clawed feet clinging delicately to the leather. Vidarian took an involuntary step back as its motion caught his eye. "I think you're going to need another of those boxes."

Ariadel rushed back to the pack, still cradling the paper box with fingertips touching it as little as possible. "Another one?" Her voice was dry with incredulity.

The second spider, as far as Vidarian could tell, was identical to the first, glittering gold body and tiny black eyes. "Looks like it. Is that lucky?"

Ariadel cast him a look that made him feel quite the cabin boy, but superstitions had never been his forte. "Not particularly." She frowned. "Just very strange." But she made another box, and it went next to the first, tucked with a cushioning nest of underclothing into the emptied case for their firebox. By the faraway look in her eyes Vidarian knew she was still contemplating the spiders as they set about making camp—Ariadel with the fire and cooking, Vidarian seeing to the verali.

It was the first night that they had spent together, truly alone, since the farmhouse and the storm. That quiet realization set in with the fading of the sky and the appearance of the first bright stars. Three moons brightened the sky, enough to show them both to each other clearly even without the golden light of the fire.

"Did you always want to be a ship captain?" Her soft voice barely rose above the crackling of the fire as it consumed the dark, pitchy wood that was all that was available on the mountain.

Vidarian stared into its quiet light a long moment before he answered. "I wasn't supposed to be," he admitted finally. "The *Quest* was my father's ship, my grandfathers'. . . . They won her from the first Emperor." He thought again of his ship, his crew, and here his feet further from the sea than they'd been in years. "I was born on her. But Relarion, my brother, was supposed to be her captain. He died when I was young."

Concern wrinkled her forehead, and something more—a fear and a hesitancy. But she said only, "I'm sorry."

He lifted his hands to the fire's warmth, shaking his head. "You never let go of a pain like that, but it's an old one. I became the captain I thought my father wanted from Rel."

Ariadel smiled, a soft smile of quiet wonder and unfamiliarity. "We never had a ship, but . . . my family always thought that I was special," her head tilted with shyness, "destined for something."

His hand moved of its own and brushed her arm with the back of his fingers. "You are."

Her eyebrows lifted a heartbeat before her laugh, high and sudden, but then her fingertips, cool with the night, were on the back of his neck, pulling. Vidarian moved to her with a quiet rush, filled his hands with her hair, drawing their faces closer, and when they met it was with electricity, searing memory and completion that shot straight down to his bones. His hands traversed the slender column of her neck, rested on her shoulders, thumbs tracing slim collarbones, before he opened his eyes again.

"This was where we left off," Ariadel breathed, and her heart was a wild rhythm beneath his hands.

"Then it's a good place to pick up," he said, and her arms tightened at his back, drawing them closer again, sliding to guide him to parts of her that were soft as summer waters, firm and smooth beneath his weathered hands. As their faces met again something dropped inside him, and every sensation doubled. When his hand slid down her arm the sweet rush of warmth was in his mind as in hers, felt as she felt, and when she drew quick breath, the same headiness quickened his pulse. *That's very interesting*, she breathed, in his thoughts. And pick up they did.

Vidarian woke, gasping.

They had made camp in the lee of a rocky prominence, a pocket in the stone sheltered from the wind. Here it seemed full night, but a red glow that just touched the stony path outside whispered of the oncoming dawn. Vidarian's eyes sought it out of reflex, reaching for light as he drew in a deep breath to still his pounding heart.

There, resolving with the slowly grown morning, was the curve of a slender foot disappearing beneath folds of velvet.

The red-haired priestess he had met on his first journey up the mountain stared coldly down at him for a long moment, then turned and left the niche opening. Her footsteps made no sound.

The command in her stare had been unmistakable, and Vidarian swallowed a groan as he levered himself up from the blankets. He moved carefully and watched Ariadel as he did so, but she did not stir.

The priestess stood facing the dawn, pupils reduced to pinpricks and rendering her golden eyes all the more unworldly. There was no sign of the splendor of images that had surrounded the goddess at their first meeting; only, for several long moments, her stony silence.

"I miscalculated," she said at last, and Vidarian tried to wrap his mind around that thought. The perpetual winds of Kara'zul seemed to rise at the sound of her voice. "We have all miscalculated. And now the hour is late." Her eyes remained fixed on the rising sun, a steady gaze that would have burned the eyes of a human in moments. "You should die for what you bring into this world. I should have killed you, last you came here. I only want you to know that."

No protocol that Vidarian had ever learned dealt with apologizing to an angry goddess. "If I have angered you, my—"

"Leave my mountain quickly," she said. "You cannot anger me. But you are mine no more."

Chapter Fifteen

VKORTHA REVEALED

In the morning Ariadel was as subdued as Vidarian felt, and he resolved then to mention the appearance of the fire goddess to no one. There had been no symbols for Endera to mine, and indeed no message for any but himself. As they packed in wordless cooperation, he wondered if somehow Ariadel suspected that the goddess had visited, and spent the remainder of the morning puzzling over how she could know, or, if she did, why she remained silent.

But Ariadel's mood seemed to lift as they closed in on the temple by midday, and Vidarian listened with genuine interest as she described the history of the various parts of the architecture and the paved road that led to it. It was a much finer way of approaching the temple, he decided, than being carried in unconscious.

Their welcome, too, differed night and day from his first visit. Acolytes stood waiting for them at the temple doors, panels of carved red ironwood that stood three times a man's height. One of them took the verali, leading them off to an outbuilding as soon as Ariadel had taken the paper spider boxes from the packs. She carried them gingerly and led the way through the temple doors.

"I'll need to see Endera right away." She turned apologetically to Vidarian. "But they'll have prepared quarters for us both."

"We have," the remaining acolyte said, and her eyes were round and blue and large as she addressed Vidarian. "Lady Endera has prepared a private banquet in honor of your arrival, my lord—"

"It's Captain."

"—my lord Captain," the acolyte corrected with a deep bow of apology, and Vidarian swallowed a sigh. "If you'll be so kind as to follow me, I can escort you to our bathing house, and your quarters."

Vidarian lowered beseeching eyebrows at Ariadel, but she only lifted the spider boxes gently in encouragement. "Some hot water would do us both good," she said. "I'll see you at dinner, Captain."

"All right." He surrendered with lifted hands. "Lead the way."

By the time he was seated at the alabaster banquet table, Vidarian was glad indeed of the temple's opulent bathhouse, though he could swear he still detected a hint of verali musk on his skin. Perhaps Ariadel was right about the smelly creatures. He found himself smiling as he thought of her reclining at the Lustrous Pearl, and mastered his features with conscious effort.

Endera joined them some time after Ariadel arrived, accompanied, rather to Vidarian's surprise, by Thalnarra. Despite the presence of the huge gryphoness, the four of them were dwarfed by the high-ceilinged banquet hall and vast alabaster dining table, and their voices echoed. The two golden spiders had been invited as well, it seemed—each occupied a mesh terrarium filled with thick green-leafed branches.

"Welcome, Captain," Endera said, bringing her hands together in a gesture of goodwill before she sat at the head of the table. "You return to us an invaluable treasure." She touched Ariadel's arm gently, and Ariadel gave a demure bow of her head, but Vidarian did not miss how her eyes searched Endera's expression beneath lowered eyelashes. Vidarian himself had not known what to expect from the Sher'azar priestess, now that he was . . . what he was. But he allowed himself a measure of cautious relief that Endera's demeanor toward him had not changed.

"As agreed," he said, watching her. "A Rulorat does not fail a contract."

"Indeed not." Endera's teeth glowed in the candlelight with her smile. She lifted a hand, and a pair of robed acolytes entered, one moving to turn over each diner's teacup and the other filling them with a pale steaming drink from a silver urn. When the first had turned over all of the cups, she lifted the cover from a porcelain bowl set between them, revealing a heap of wine-red sun cherries, and bowed out of the room with the tea carrier.

Vidarian lifted his tea to stop himself from gaping at the fruit. He had never seen more than a handful of them in the same place in his life, and knew none who had. Endera plucked about that many from the bowl with a set of silver tongs and proceeded to spoon a frothy sugared cream over them with staggering familiarity. He waited until Ariadel had taken a portion before setting down the tea and selecting his own, resisting the urge to put a price on each thumb-sized fruit that hit his plate.

The flavor was extraordinary, as it always was. The summer intensity and gentle sweetness of them took him back to nearly forgotten early childhood, when his mother had strong-armed his father into purchasing three of them for his birthday. And, he had to admit, the cream balanced their vivid tartness perfectly.

"No one," he said at last, "has really explained to me just what the Tesseract is."

Thalnarra's crushed-paper chuckle brought the hair on the back of his neck up, much as he should have been used to it by now. The gryphoness had been watching the cherry bowl dwindle with what Vidarian assumed was a mild curiosity, but at Vidarian's question she reached across the table and, with surprising delicacy, lifted a cherry between two hooked claws.

// The Tesseract seals the Great Gate, // she said, as she had on the *Sunstar,* // because he bridges Substantive and Ephemeral magics. // With a disregard for fabric that made Endera stiffen ever so slightly, Thalnarra pierced the cherry and proceeded to draw a diagram on one of the table's cloth napkins. The juice stained the white fabric scarlet, and she doled it out with gentle claw pressure until a diamond shape emerged. // Air, // she indicated the top corner of the diamond with a droplet of juice, // Earth, // the bottom, // Fire, // the left, // Water, // the right. // And this is you. // She rent the cherry deeply then, drawing a stream between the left and right points of the blurry diagram. // Centuries ago, the Great Gate was closed, but as the years pass the influence of what lay behind it grows. You represent that change, and have the power to seal the gate. //

The emptiness in the center of the diagram, crossed by "him," somehow turned Vidarian's guts to water. "What's in the middle, there?"

"It is theoretical," Endera still looked slightly sour for the ruining of her napkin. "Referred to as 'void,' and described in some connection to telepathic abilities, and other magics since lost."

"The other elements have goddesses," Vidarian blinked against a moment of lightheadedness. "Who is the goddess of the void?"

Ariadel laughed, and her merriment was a flash of silver in Vidarian's thoughts. "There is no goddess of chaos." She twinkled with mirth, visibly lingering over the absurdity of Vidarian's suggestion—and clearly unaware, as Vidarian was not, of Endera's hands subtly clenched around her teacup. He met her eyes, only briefly, and the grip eased, smoothly, as though without thought.

Vidarian cleared his throat, then took up his tea and sipped it. One of his eyebrows leapt up in curiosity toward Endera before he could quite help himself. The tea was delicate but unsophisticated, surely no prize leaf from the surrounding mountains for which the temple was so renowned—and yet both Endera and Ariadel tipped their cups carefully, as though it were priceless.

"Simplicity, my dear Vidarian," Endera said only. "We are but a simple priestesshood."

"And what does this simple priestesshood want of me, Endera? For I suspect all this—" he took in the hall with a swept hand "—is not merely trapping for the delivery of my sun rubies."

The priestess smiled. She tapped her knuckles lightly on the table, and the acolytes returned, bearing covered platters that trailed wisps of curling steam. Seeming by chance, but surely it wasn't, the acolytes lifted the silver covers in order: Thalnarra, Endera, Ariadel, and finally Vidarian. Beneath was an artfully arranged spiral of sliced meat—runnerbird, he thought, in a light herbed oil.

"We merely wish to advise you," Endera said, as they picked up forks, "to prevent you from making, shall we say, avoidable mistakes."

"Such as?" Vidarian asked, scooping up and eating a polite forkful of the sliced meat. And then dropping the fork with a clatter he saw but did not hear, as unbelievable spice roared up to close his throat and even his ears as he coughed instinctively—managing only with the aid of years of diplomatic drilling to avoid spraying meat and sauce all over the table. His eyes filled with water and the room vanished into heat and color.

"Lambwillow tea," Endera was saying, when his ears finally cleared enough. "It has certain pepper-amplifying properties."

"We drink it so often, I'd forgotten," Ariadel was apologizing, and her own cheeks were flushed, whether with an echo of his pain or mere abashedness, he wasn't sure. *Truly, I'd have warned you*, she insisted in his mind, and he thought forgiveness at her, but wasn't sure if their connection worked that way.

"These 'avoidable mistakes,'" Vidarian began.

The doors to the dining room banged open, an admirable feat for such large panels of wood, and what stepped across the threshold threw Vidarian to his feet before he quite knew what he was doing. His sword, brought for ceremony, sang from its sheath, then, exposed, leapt with energy—fire and water, this time his own.

"So it's true," the first hooded figure said, throwing back her black velvet headpiece to reveal blonde curls and piercing grey eyes. "He is the Tesseract—and you've kept him from us, Endera." The look she—Vkortha? Priestess?—turned on Vidarian made his stomach turn: fervent. Mad.

Endera, too, was on her feet, standing in Thalnarra's path, which seemed altogether unwise. The gryphoness had summoned a halo of blinding fire energy, visible now to Vidarian's kindled sight, but without this, her pinning eyes and near-vertically stiffened feathers told any wise prey animal to find another acre as far away as possible. "This was not our agreement, Aleha." Endera's voice was tightly controlled, pitched low to avert gryphon murder.

It didn't work. // *Your* agreement? // Thalnarra thundered, and reared, flaring her wings in spite of the closed space. One of the spider terrariums was caught by an outflung primary and clattered to the floor, its spider sent scuttling from the room.

Endera, Aleha, and her still-hooded attendant fell back toward the door, and only Vidarian's voice stopped Thalnarra from leaping upon them: "Explain yourself, Endera. Quickly." As they moved, his swordpoint remained trained on the Vkortha who had spoken. In the dance of fire and water about the blade, crackles of energy snapped between his aura and Thalnarra's.

"There are no Vkortha. These women are Nistran priestesses, envoys from Zal'nehara," Endera said.

"No. We serve the Starhunter now, Endera," Aleha said.

Endera spun, her eyes wide. "Madness!" she hissed, and in spite of her betrayal, the sheer alarm in her voice chilled Vidarian's spine. Aleha's eyes were wild, ecstatic.

In the chaos, Thalnarra's voice was acrid smoke in Vidarian's mind alone. // *I knew nothing of this. Endera has made a fatal error. I am making arrangements. Their minds slip from mine like fishguts,* //—the last in frustrated disbelief.

"They'll not have Ariadel, I don't give a damn the reasons why," Vidarian began.

"Your mistake, Vidarian, is in thinking she is half so valuable to us as you are," Endera murmured, and Ariadel choked—her thoughts radiated confusion, heartache, fury. "And you'll not abandon her here, we both know it."

"No," Ariadel said, her voice distant, numb. "He won't."

// *This is a deep betrayal, Endera.* // The word "betrayal" had a cloud of thoughts connected to it, smoky tendrils of a complex language altogether inhuman.

"I am sorry, Thalnarra."

// *You have no idea yet how sorry.* //

Ariadel looked across the table at him.

Vidarian, the name was a whisper in his mind, a quickening of his being. "*Run.*" They breathed the command together.

Vidarian leapt across the table, and Thalnarra let out a deafening shriek that nearly stopped his heart. Thalnarra, Aleha, and the other Vkorthan priestess staggered away from the door, and Vidarian and Ariadel fled through, Thalnarra quick on their heels. Ariadel grabbed Vidarian's hand and led him at a run through the maze of temple passageways; Endera's voice echoed behind them, a command to her acolytes: "*Control this situation!*"

When they emerged at last on the ground floor of the temple and staggered out onto the stone courtyard, two pairs of familiar golden-painted wings were waiting. "Kaltak! Ishrak!" Vidarian shouted.

The two brothers, harnessed again to the little "flying boat" (as Vidarian had come to think of it), parted their beaks in welcome, feathers rousing—but they clacked shut again and smoothed, all business, when Thalnarra roared out onto the courtyard behind them. The acolyte who had harnessed the two harrier gryphons started babbling at Thalnarra in confusion when she saw the gryphon priestess's flaming aura and battle-raised feathers, and Thalnarra curtly ordered her back into the temple, lifting her own lead harness with her claws and climbing into it by herself.

// *We meet again, brother!* // Kaltak welcomed cheerfully, oblivious to his commanding officer and the acolyte.

The acolyte fled, shouting, back into the temple, just meeting Endera and the two Vkorthans as they emerged.

// *Up,* // Thalnarra barked, and the three gryphons leapt into the air, leaving Ariadel and Vidarian to scramble into the craft behind them. In moments, they were aloft. // *Shield yourselves,* // Thalnarra warned, and auras of fire leapt up around Kaltak, Ishrak, and Ariadel. Vidarian clumsily followed suit, but his blended energy made things difficult—the water pulled at the fire, which snapped back at the water. The strange buzzing he'd felt over the Vkorthan island filled his mind again, and that strange murmur, the wordless song that brought to mind Aleha's wild eyes.

You're doing well, Ariadel encouraged, and he worked to focus words back at her: *Where are we going?*

"To sea," she shouted, and Thalnarra cried a piercing agreement. "To Val Harlon, and the *Quest*. To my father."

CHAPTER SIXTEEN
CALL ME RUBY

The steep and winding tracks of Sher'azar dwindled in moments of arrow-swift gryphon flight. Robed figures boiled up out of the temple as the mountain dropped away beneath them, and when the two so-called Vkorthans emerged, they raised their arms, and immediately the air chilled around the airborne craft. But Endera, now mouse-sized with distance, pulled their arms back down, pointing and shouting an objection, and the chill dissipated.

// *You're no good to her dead.* // Thalnarra spoke his thought, but in her voice it was with pungent irony, and more of that predatory focus that made the small mammal inside his brain want to find cover.

Below, the twisting river marked their path to Val Harlon, perched on the horizon and marked by the sparkle of the western sea and the sun that arced slowly toward it as late afternoon advanced into evening. The two younger gryphons flew unevenly, even to Vidarian's ill-practiced eye, but Thalnarra's determined, angry wingbeats kept them from voicing any question, at least where their passengers could hear. Feather-tipped ears flicked back toward them now and then with what could have been speculation or silent conversation with their leader.

"I should have known Endera was capable of this," Ariadel said, breaking him out of his contemplation of gryphon and skyview. "But I didn't." Her eyes and her voice were full of hopelessness that cut at his heart, and he shifted carefully in the basket to wrap an arm around her.

"This whole business blew off course long ago," he said. "If I'd had my father's business sense, I'd have seen Endera was angling to betray us." A laugh escaped him, hard and bitter, and Ariadel squinted askance. "Marielle," he said, battling a surge of guilt and the flash of anger that came with it. "She said fire priestesses were trouble, before all this started."

"Well, they are," Ariadel said, all lightness, but her fists clenched and unclenched for just a moment.

"There are many in your family?"

"No, actually," she said, surprising him. "I'm the first in several generations."

"But I thought—" he began, but stiffened when she gasped, staring fixedly at his neck. "What—?"

"Hold still!" Her hand darted out to brush his collarbone, then came back, curled. She cupped it with her other hand, and when she parted her fingers just enough for him to see, a tiny golden spider skittered across her curved palms.

"Not another one," he said, beginning to be unnverved by the whole thing, in spite of considerably more shocking recent events.

"No, it's the same one," Ariadel said, motioning with her elbow for him to dig through the craft's storage crates for something to keep it in. "Thalnarra knocked over its enclosure, and it must have jumped onto you when we escaped." He suppressed a shiver at the thought.

He found an oiled packet of string, but Ariadel vetoed it with a shake of her head. A tiny traveling tinderbox passed muster, and she gingerly emptied the spider into it, then tucked the box into a pocket of her robe. He didn't bother asking what in the world they were going to do with it on ship.

"My parents came from air and earth families," she said, picking up the earlier, spider-free thread. "'Windhammer' is a conjugate name. I have an aunt four generations back who was a fire priestess, but no one since."

"Your family from air and earth," he said, "mine from fire and water. Trouble, the lot of it."

She laughed, and said, "My father will like you."

"Your father," he said, remembering her instructions to Thalnarra. "Why are we going to see him? And where?"

"The Selturians, and he can help you," she said. "He's a magus. An Air monk."

"What?" Vidarian was stunned. "I've only read about them. I thought they were all gone." A male element-wielder . . .

"He's one of the last. The priesthood doesn't like to admit he exists."

Ariadel smiled sadly and seemed about to say more, but Thalnarra called out from ahead.

// *Angling down.* // With her words she sent a dizzyingly sharp mental image—via gryphon-enhanced eye—of the shoreline, just now coming into view. They squinted against the sun, and what Vidarian caught sight of made his gut clench with anger.

"Is that what I think it is?" he shouted up to Thalnarra.

// *Yes. They've surrounded your ship.* // Another mental picture, impossibly detailed from this distance: the *Quest*, Marielle at the port bow, her sword arm raised angrily—while the knife-prowed messenger craft of the fire temple hedged the ship in from all sides. // *I doubt they intend to let you board.* //

"She'll not steal my ship from me—" Vidarian snarled, a white rage bubbling up in him now. Elemental priestess or not, Endera had gone too far.

"Not that I disagree," Ariadel murmured, in a tone he'd begun to recognize meant she was trying to defuse a situation that she recognized as unreasonable, "but at the moment we have a question of resources. Not even the five of us can succeed against so many ships and priestesses—if we try, they'll have us back on the mountain by nightfall."

// *She's right,* // Thalnarra said, breaking over his immediate argument like a drenching tide. // *You must focus on what you need, not what you want.* //

"We need to get to sea," Ariadel said, again her voice calm, persuasive. "We don't necessarily need the *Quest*—yet."

In his fury, Vidarian couldn't mask a flash of recognition as he caught sight of another ship on the edge of the harbor.

"What's that?" Ariadel followed his sightline, raising a hand to shield her eyes from the sun. "You know that ship?"

"I might," he prevaricated. "It's been a long time."

"Thalnarra, can you land us close to the harbor but outside the city?"

// *There's an inlet north of the harbor—we can take you to the shore there.* //

As one, the gryphons banked, tipping their right wings down while their lefts went up, catching the wind coming in off the ocean. The flying craft tilted sharply and Vidarian and Ariadel scrambled for purchase; soon they were angling around the southeastern edge of the city, turning northwest.

The broad loop would keep them out of eyesight of Endera's messenger ships, and perhaps buy them a little time before discovery.

They landed in a long clearing flanked by a stand of coastal pine and then the shore beyond. Vidarian thought that Thalnarra would remain and see them to their destination, but she didn't move.

// *We must go to our flight at once,* // she said, her mind still clenched with thought and anger as it had been since Kara'zul. // *There's much I must discuss regarding our alliance with the priesteshood.* //

"Thalnarra—" Ariadel began.

// *This is beyond your reach, Priestess,* // Thalnarra said, and an apologetic softness only just took the sting out of her words, but Ariadel lowered her head, chastened. // *Endera does not yet know what she's set in motion. But I suspect neither do you two.* // Some of her old humor was back at this last, and Vidarian managed a brief smile.

"*Charnak; vikktu ari lashuul,*" Vidarian said, and Kaltak let out a trilling whoop of approval.

Thalnarra's voice was warmer, but still guarded. // *Your memory proves excellent again.* // She reared back and stretched her wings, then folded them again. // *I could wish we would not need that particular blessing, but fear that we shall.* //

// *And we extend it to you also.* // Ishrak, smallest of the three creatures and usually quietest, gave this solemnly, and the other two nodded, an odd expression from beaked faces.

// *Good luck to you. We will meet again soon, goddess willing.* // Thalnarra's voice, Vidarian realized, was comforting, like a crackling fire in autumn. He would miss it.

They stepped back as the three gryphons first shook out their feathers—beginning with the tips of their beaks and extending all the way to the plumes at the ends of their leonine tails—and then began to beat their wings in preparation for taking to the air. Ariadel and Vidarian watched, taking in the wonder of powerful muscle and feather, until they completed a tight upward spiral and disappeared over the trees to the southeast.

As they watched from the north shore of the harbor, Val Harlon went about its business with tranquil ordinariness. Ships passed in and out of the harbor, queued for inspectors, were shuttled in and out of drydock. The dull thud of carpenters' hammers echoed off the shoreline here, where the soundest trees had long ago been cut back for ship lumber.

Vidarian knew some of the ships, but none sufficient for the kind of favor they needed: a sea journey across the Outwater. Grudgingly, he told Ariadel as much.

"What was that ship you recognized? Out on the harbor's edge?"

"It's called the *Viere d'Inar*," he said, knowing the name itself would mean nothing to her.

"Is that Velinese?"

"Yes," he said, impressed. "It means 'the crown of the sea.'"

"Rather ostentatious."

"It comes by the name honestly."

Ariadel squinted at him. "What aren't you wanting to say?"

Vidarian drew in a deep breath and held it, then exhaled fast. "It's a Sea Kingdom ship. A close ally of my family's."

"Then we should speak with the captain!"

"It might not be so simple." Gods, this was tortuous. But better, he decided finally, to have it all out at once. "Her name is Roana. Years ago, her mother and my parents thought that she and I should marry to cement a business alliance."

Ariadel blinked. "Oh."

Vidarian soldiered on. "She's the West Sea Queen now, after her mother." Ariadel's eyes widened even as he felt a pang at the words—Rhiannon had died when they were teenagers in some sort of duel. "Once she became the Sea Queen so young, a business alliance became far beneath her station."

"Isn't it dangerous for her to be here?"

"Probably. But the Sea Kingdoms are peculiar. If she were to show weakness, a fear of a particular port, no matter how reasonable, she could be challenged and even overthrown."

Ariadel looked out over the water, to the far side of the harbor and the

Viere. It was a large ship—half again larger than the *Quest*, truly a queen of the waves. Strong and formidable, even in the Outwater. He saw Ariadel making these calculations, eyeing the other ships in the harbor, turning at last to face him again. "I think we should ask her. I don't think we have a choice."

"We can't afford to linger in the city," he said, "but I can at least look around in the shipyard. Could be there are other friends here."

"We have little to bargain with," she reminded him, and he nodded. "This could be fortune."

"Or more ill luck," he agreed glumly, ire still tickling the back of his eyes whenever he caught sight of the *Quest*, so close and yet impossibly out of reach.

∿∿∿

The shipyard of Val Harlon was run by an old ship's carpenter known to the Rulorats—he'd even repaired the *Quest* a time or two. Stimson Allanmark seemed to have been crushed by the weight of the sun over his years, and had handled so much tar it now marked a permanent dappling on his hands and forearms. His beard, knotted with sea air, gave him a perpetually put-upon expression that made it difficult to tell when he was being friendly.

"Vidarian, my boy," he greeted them, first bowing to Ariadel with polite correctness (and no more), then reaching to shake Vidarian's hand. "Nistra's gift to see you again. I wondered where you were, with the *Quest* anchored aught. Never seen you apart."

"Strange times, my friend," Vidarian said, and Stimson's thick eyebrows knit with agreement.

"Strange indeed," he agreed, voice husky with seriousness. "Scuttlebutt is you've had some trouble with the fire priestesses. Beggin' your pardon, my lady," he gave another proper nod to Ariadel, though with an eyebrow inched in curiosity at Vidarian.

"There is a disagreement," Vidarian agreed. With the knife ships blocking in his own, there was little point in arguing.

"You Rulorats and your mucking about." Stimson chuffed. "I hope you can resolve it before you get an Imperial inquisitor's attention."

"I'm working to address it presently," he said. "But at the moment, what we need is a ship and an exit—outside the temple's sight."

Stimson grunted, then turned and waved a gnarled and tar-stained paw for them to follow. "We should discuss this in my office."

"You have an office?" The words escaped Vidarian before he could stop them, and Stimson turned back for just a moment, giving him a look that asked if it were entirely necessary for him to be quite so thick. Vidarian cleared his throat and motioned Ariadel to follow.

The yardmaster's "office" was the belly of a permanently drydocked galleon, a retired Imperial war-queen. Stimson led them through a heavy salvaged door that had been fit into a massive patched fissure in the hull. He hauled the door open, and before Vidarian's eyes could adjust, the yardmaster's voice carried a smile with his greeting: "Well, here's one might be able to help."

The shadow of the familiar leather cap over inimitable riot of red curls came into view first, and Vidarian braced himself as he crossed the threshold.

For a moment it was like seeing a ghost. The bold figure perched on a supply barrel—white swordsman's shirt and black leather vest, longsword and main gauche at hips, black linen trousers disappearing into embroidered leather boots—was direct out of his childhood. Roana, from the mantle of red curls to her sardonic, challenging smile, was the spitting image of her mother as Vidarian had known her, sun-gilt and utterly unstoppable. The tattoos that curled around her neck and hands, indeed most visible patches of skin, were different ones, but they were in the same places.

"Queen Roana, I take it," Ariadel glided in front of Vidarian, all smoky diplomacy. "I am Priestess Ariadel Windhammer. Vidarian has told me much about you."

"Call me Ruby." She winked aggressively as she stood to greet them, and Vidarian saw his life becoming more difficult.

"Queen Ruby." Ariadel was unfazed. "Mr. Allanmark suggested you might be able to assist us with passage from Val Harlon."

Ruby's widening smile, all faux-innocence and teeth, was aimed at Ariadel but intended for Vidarian. "But Priestess, the harbor just happens to be full of temple knife-ships. Surely one would bear you hence at far gentler expense?"

Her feint scored; Ariadel colored.

Vidarian stepped forward to join Ariadel, deliberately placing himself with inappropriate closeness. "We're looking for passage to the Selturians. The temple is not especially well disposed toward us, nor we them, at the moment. A simple misunderstanding surely soon corrected."

"Surely," Ruby repeated, still smiling at Ariadel. "And until then, you're a renegade fire priestess. Fascinating." No seafarer sympathized with a follower of Sharli, as a general rule, but Ruby was far too canny a captain herself to let herself be won over by a religious vendetta. "And a liability."

Flashbacks of his original deal with Endera disoriented him for half a moment, but he didn't hesitate to use exactly what had turned that conversation, hoping the tiny chime of guilt in his conscience wouldn't percolate into his voice. "I am owed a pair of sun rubies by a high priestess," Vidarian said, and Ruby's eyes darkened with surprise and greed. "When our disagreement is resolved, they are contract-bound to deliver. I assume you'd have a natural interest."

Ruby covered her avarice adroitly, but not before Vidarian could make it out, and she conceded his point with a genteel wave of her hand. "For the pair—"

"For one," Vidarian interrupted.

Ruby laughed and extended her hand. "For you, Vidarian—of course. One sun ruby, passage for two to the Selturian Islands. My ship, as it happens, stands ready to depart." Not without trepidation, Vidarian shook the proffered hand, altogether too aware of his situation. Whereas he had demanded collateral from Endera, Roana knew that her resources were too powerful and vast to even think of worrying whether Vidarian would repay his debt. With a gallant sweep, she released her hand and spun in theatrical invitation toward the back of Allanmark's "office." Vidarian and Ariadel squinted, and just barely made out the upper edge of a concealed door further masked by a wall of stacked crates.

While they calculated where it must go—down into the earth, below the harbor—Ruby laughed again, a sound like a pennant snapping in the wind.

"You thought we'd come in through the front door?"

CHAPTER SEVENTEEN

NULLS

The tunnel that wound from Allanmark's door down beneath the pier was highly illegal, and therefore spared the inconvenience of safety inspections. Twice in their journey out of the city they took side tunnels that detoured around muddy cave-ins, and by the time they emerged, Vidarian and Ariadel found their hands covered with silty muck from the cave wall. Ruby, of course, was spotless.

From this promontory over the north side of the harbor, a precarious stairway of small granite slabs marked a track down to the water, where one of the *Viere*'s shallow prams waited to ferry them aboard. Vidarian thought he recognized the old sailor who saluted them aboard the craft and wordlessly launched it, but couldn't summon a name. To buy time and forestall awkwardness, he turned to point out to Ariadel the gallant ship that grew larger with their approach, a shadow rising out of the sunset-stained harbor waters.

To know the *Viere d'Inar* was to know love and envy and terror all at once, a storm of rapture that clenched the heart of any seafarer who knew boot from tail. She was a spectacular frigate-built brigantine, tall sails like the arched wings of a gull fit to split the sky, sleek and truly unreasonably fast for a ship her age and tonnage. And she was a city—thirty-two guns and over a hundred and fifty souls, if he remembered right. The emperor might boast larger ships in tamer eastern seas, but here in the west with its wild ocean and labyrinth reefs, the *Viere* was queen of all she surveyed. There would never be any ship for Vidarian save his *Empress*, but only a fool would doubt the *Viere*'s primacy.

As the pram drew closer, two sailors high above manned the davits, dropping its hook lines in unison with powerful strokes on the winch. Their sailor shipped his oars just in time to fasten the hooks, and they rose into the air, all with the swift efficiency of a machine. Ruby affected a stern expression appropriate for a captain surveying her sailors, but the glint in her eye betrayed her pleasure at this small demonstration of the *Viere*'s superior performance.

Vidarian was close enough to Ariadel to feel her rapidly indrawn breath as they ascended the rail, bringing the full bustle and scurry of the ship into view. With night coming on, cabin boys trotted briskly across the deck to light rows of ship's lanterns. Even this mundane task was elevated on the *Viere*—the boys (and one girl) used antique glow-poles dating back before the Sea Wars. Vidarian had only ever seen one in operation, and here Ruby had four. The ball of fire-magicked glass at the end of the elaborately worked iron rod would ignite a wick but nothing else—not even flesh or powder.

As they stepped onto the deck, a burly man wearing the knots of a first mate strode purposefully toward them. He wore little ornament, likely needing only his vast size to intimidate; the deep lines etched into his face were hereditary rather than marks of age.

"You look familiar," Vidarian said, before he could manage pleasantries. The man grinned, wide mouth parting like a riven hull.

"This is Galon, my first mate," Ruby said. "You knew his father, Remi."

Vidarian turned toward her in surprise. "Old Remi had a son?" The man had been a sea dog if there ever was one—veteran of multiple wars, hardened further by a yearslong feud that had devoured most all his blood kin. He turned back to Galon and offered his hand. "Vidarian Rulorat, captain of the *Empress Quest*."

"Two sons!" Galon said, taking Vidarian's hand inside a massive paw, and indeed his deep voice was an echo from Vidarian's childhood. "And a daughter. Though my sibs're land-crawlers, all. A merchant and a scribe."

"I'm pleased to hear of the Aldani clan's thriving," Vidarian said, and Galon's grateful smile betrayed some of the gentle giant behind the hardened mariner.

Ariadel shifted beside him, and before Vidarian could make a belated introduction, Ruby sailed in.

"And this is Priestess Ariadel Windhammer, of Sher'azar. We'll be escorting her and Captain Rulorat to the Selturians."

"Around the horn?" Galon chirped, surprised. Ruby smiled, and Galon only shrugged, then returned her smile and bowed himself out. "Adventure awaits, then. I'll see us launched, it won't be but a moment. Vadri's been working on the mizzen, so I'll have to pry him off."

"Tell him to check the aft hold," Ruby said. "It should keep him busy for a few days." When Galon saluted—a casual thing, more parody than military precision—and turned aft, shouting commands to the crew, Ruby explained, "Our ship's carpenter is a little zealous. Fantastic in a bind, requires a little managing otherwise." She smiled, turning to watch the accelerated motion of the crew as they moved to set the *Viere* on course. "Shall I show you to our guest quarters?"

A genteel request it was not, entirely—without waiting for them to agree, Ruby turned aft and set off in long stride, leaving them to hop to or be left in the scuttle. They crossed the *Viere* as fish swimming upstream, traversing the long deck—twice the length of the *Quest*—before reaching the capstan. Beyond it and the towering mizzenmast lay the large and heavily carved aftcastle, and there a cabin boy—scruffy, redheaded, likely a cousin of Ruby's—scrambled to haul open the ponderous oak door that led inside.

Vidarian had assumed Ruby was exaggerating when she mentioned "guest quarters," but she hadn't been. A childhood memory of the *Viere* gave him a rough understanding of its layout—he'd spent six weeks aboard this ship in exchange for training that had, among other things, cemented the goodwill between his parents and the West Sea Queen—and the quarters he and Ariadel were assigned had been Ruby's while her mother still lived. The captain's quarters occupied the many-portholed stern of the ship, ornately worked inside and out, and flanking the carpeted hallway that led to them were two other large (by ship standards) chambers, one for the first mate and one, it seemed, for the captain's guests.

Ruby shouldered open the heavy door while still managing a flourish, and invited them in with a sweep of her hand. Ariadel stepped inside and Vidarian followed, swept in a memory. Himself, an awkward fourteen made more awkward by knowledge of his parents' intent for Ruby and he; the Sea Queen's daughter, sprawled on the deck of this cabin with her then-frizzy head of copper curls obscuring the book open across her palms. The furniture had changed, but the pale celadon rug, expensive silk from the Qui Empire, was the same.

Ariadel turned toward the door, where Ruby leaned against the jamb. "We thank you for your hospitality, your majesty."

Ruby, who had never been called "majesty" in Vidarian's hearing, grinned. "You've paid handsomely for it. Or you will." There were teeth, but no threats, in her smile. "We'll be under way presently, and I'm for the launch. A pleasant rest to you both, and be welcome on our Lady Crown."

While Vidarian set to inspecting the contents of the satchels they'd salvaged from the gryphon's little craft, Ariadel moved toward the small shelf of books set into the aft bulkhead like a moth toward light. A narrow bar of polished brass kept each shelf from losing its contents with the ship's movement, and it took a bit of maneuvering for her to extract a small cloth-bound volume. The books, too, Vidarian remembered from his youth—largely texts written about the Sea Kingdoms by outsiders. Queen Rhiannon had wanted her daughter to know what was said of their way of life by landers.

The leather satchels proved disappointing: a few days' rations for the two of them, a fire kit and flat traveler's pan, and a map. No magical artifacts this time. Likely Thalnarra had learned from the last trip and hidden them away.

A whisper of movement as he set the second satchel beside the bed was his only warning.

Something struck the side of his head, hard—the heavy blow sent him reeling with spots across his vision. He spun, sword flying from its sheath, but staggered into the port bulkhead with a crash. Ariadel stood with feet braced, her hands, still wrapped around a book, glowing with elemental energy that sang the sword into life. Clenching the hilt, he wrapped his own energies into it, turning to face one corner of the room and then another, baffled—he and Ariadel were alone. The crash had brought shouts from above, and thundering footsteps echoed down from the deck.

The unseen enemy struck again, darkening the world for precious seconds. The blow left dizziness behind it and he faltered, seeing three Ariadels and lowering his sword for fear of accidentally striking any of them. He raised his arms to protect his head, blade flat against his neck as he crouched, half in defense, half in fear that if he remained upright the vertigo would take him.

A whisper in his mind—*this is quite a mess, isn't it?* Words quite unlike Ariadel, and the voice wasn't the same—

The door exploded inward, and his heart leapt to face another attack, but it was Ruby, her face a storm of fury, Galon and another crewman close behind. Her own sword was drawn, the longsword that had belonged to her mother, and it too incandesced in the light of Ariadel's life flame. She spared a glance for it, surprised, but returned her attention to the attacker. Vidarian expected confusion, but when she saw that the room was empty, she only snarled again.

Another blow, this one to his calf, and he fell to the side. Ruby leapt over him like a cat, a glittering chain and pendant in her left hand. She threw it forward, around nothingness, and suddenly a man was there, gasping as she yanked the chain taut around his neck. In the swing of her right arm came the longsword, its blade a flash of cold metal across his exposed throat, cutting clear through half his neck, withdrawn only after the sickening thud of its impact with bone.

The Sea Queen, taut as a belled sail, straightened with a snarl of disgust, wiping the blade on the man's tattered shirt. His limbs spasmed with death, but an equal measure of her raised lip was for the blood spilling across the expensive carpet, not his suffering.

Vidarian lifted himself to his knees, and regretted it. Ariadel rushed to him as he swayed, the fire wreathing her hands dimming to a warm glow. The book she'd been clutching, a treatise on Sea Kingdom culture, thudded softly to the carpet. As adrenaline faded from his veins, the full extent of the attack's force was beginning to register, and Vidarian blinked against a pounding in his skull that brought waves of darkness with each pulse.

Beside them, Ruby was turning the head of the dead assassin with the flat of her blade. "A null," she said, deftly moving the tip of the blade under her pendant and twisting it free. She turned to Galon, her voice promising a soon-arriving storm. "Find out how he snuck aboard." And then to the crewman, "And clean up this mess." Both saluted and rushed from the room, grim and intent, leaving Ruby to smolder.

"Will you put him on your skin?" Ariadel asked, and if there was nervousness in her voice, she worked well to mask it.

Ruby lifted an eyebrow at Ariadel's acknowledgment of their custom, and the fingers of her right hand, marked with an old tattoo—left for the death of her first enemy—flexed around the sword. Her answer was a spit of disgust. "A man who never existed deserves no honor mark when he dies. He'll not touch me." She turned away from the body to face them in full. "You'll sleep in my quarters tonight." Ariadel started to object, but Ruby lifted a hand. "Someone was intent enough on killing you to sneak aboard the most dangerous ship in these waters. It would dishonor the West Sea Kingdom if you were to arrive at your destination dead."

CHAPTER EIGHTEEN
WILD MAGIC

The ship's doctor, after a thorough examination that brought Vidarian into full awareness of the extent of his bruises, declared him unlikely to die. Night now was under way in full, and they'd wrapped his head in bandages before burying him in the thick featherbeds and embroidered coverlets of Ruby's bed. The sheets smelled faintly of cedar and cinnamon, and though there was easily room enough for two, Ariadel insisted on sleeping in a hammock strung in front of the door. Vidarian found it all rather ridiculous but was in no condition to complain, and, with the assistance of a bitter draught administered by the ship's doctor, fell into a deep sleep as soon as the lights were out.

Ah, here we are again. A voice. Soothing, almost. Familiar, almost.

The soft rush of the sea against strong ship-beam was a deep comfort after their days on land. But the sound was distant, because he was floating, reaching out into the sea itself. It should have been cold, but it wasn't—the fire of life that lived within it sang through him, from the tiniest creatures too small for the eye to see, all the way to the ship-sized whales who fed upon them. Their warmth was his warmth, and the sea was filled with bright consciousness, here between water and fire.

So curious. It's refreshing after all this time. I enjoy your mind.

The voice pulled at him, stopping him from reaching further. Annoyance, mild—he wanted to find the boundaries of this place. *Ariadel?* he thought, and her name filled him with sudden confusion. Who was he? They were on a ship. Where was the ship? Where was Ariadel?

Oh, that? That's very inconvenient. Let me fix it.

And the soft, warm presence that had—ever since the Vkorthan island—seemed just beyond his reach, but comfortingly near, was abruptly gone.

You're too good for her, you know.

～～～

He woke in a cold sweat, throwing back the opulent bedclothes with a wrench that set his head pounding. A sense of dread threaded with panic crept through him unlike any he'd experienced in his adult life. Strange nightmare . . .

A rustle from across the cabin. "Ariadel?" he whispered. She was a deep sleeper, but something had awakened both of them; there was more rustling of sheets, and then her feet thudding against the carpeted deck. Her hand was cool against his forehead, and she bent over him, concerned eyes meeting his.

It was just a nightmare. But—*Can you hear me?* he thought.

Ariadel's eyes continued to search his, looking for further sign of his injury. No thought came back to him.

Hoarsely, he whispered again, "Think something at me," and her eyes sharpened with worry. A wrinkle between her eyebrows, for a moment—then her eyes widened.

"You couldn't . . . hear that?" her voice trembled, ever so slightly.

He shook his head.

In the dim light, her eyes glistened with water, and her hand clenched beside his head. Then she blinked them clear. "The blow to your head," she said, and then coughed, grief closing her throat. "The nulls are a scourge," she choked, anger burning through her pain. "They have no magic of their own, so they attack those of us who do."

"Why couldn't we see him?" He knew he was asking a simple question to avoid telling her about the dream—that someone, another woman, had spoken in his mind and taken away their bond. Guilt welled up inside him, and he shivered involuntarily.

She took his shiver for a chill, and crept under the covers with him, sliding an arm carefully around his shoulders. He sighed at her warmth, coiling an arm around her waist, even as his bruises and head twinged. "They have no elemental nature," she said, and pulled the covers higher around them. "It's an aberration—all sentient creatures, save them, have some elemental nature, even if it is faint. Most people have a balance of the elements—it's an imbalance that allows us to wield magic. But nulls have none at all. We don't consciously see elemental nature, but our subconscious mind processes it, and without it, a person becomes all but invisible to us."

"That pendant Ruby had—"

"Fire magic," she said, and without their link he couldn't quite tell whether there was a touch of anger beneath the words or not. "It imbues the wearer with a small amount of fire energy. She's dealt with nulls before."

Like a child, he didn't want to sleep, fearing a return to the strange dreams, but fatigue, pain, and warmth conspired against him, pulling him down into unconsciousness again. Ariadel shifted, gently settling her arms more tightly around him, and he closed his eyes, surrendering—for now—to sleep.

Stepping onto the main deck the next morning was like staggering out of a tavern with a roaring hangover. The light assaulted his eyes, pounding the back of his head like an iron anchor, and Vidarian staggered half a step. Ariadel's arm, linked around his as if he were an old man, tightened, keeping him upright.

The journey to the bow, where several sailors told them Ruby kept an eye on their course, was a long one at such a slow pace. The busy bustle of the ship—brass being polished, sail repaired, rope knotted—was a homey comfort, even as it was a reminder that this was not Vidarian's ship and these were not his crew. He knew that Marielle would steer them steady, but the sense of wrongness at being away from his ship was a constant companion, and some primitive, superstitious part of his mind blamed all their recent misfortunes upon it.

Just as they caught sight of Ruby, perched like a gull on the tip of the bow,

Ariadel gasped. At first, Vidarian thought it was at the young girl standing next to the captain, her arms full of a glass bowl with a writhing sea witch inside, but then he felt the coil of elemental energy—water, of course—wreathed around Ruby's body and outstretched arm. Below, the sea was a frothing, joyous tumult, propelling the *Viere* forward with unnatural speed.

Ariadel's frustration radiated out at him even without a telepathic link, and her mouth was twisted with disgust. "She's a rogue," she muttered, aghast. "That magic is raw and untrained! She should be remanded to the Nistrans!"

"The Sea Kingdoms do not answer to land authority," Vidarian said quietly, turning his head to make sure none of the crew had heard her. "Not even the priestesshoods."

His words only enflamed her ire, but she caught his pointed glances and kept it silent.

As they closed on Ruby and the dark-haired girl Vidarian took to be her windreader, Vidarian noted with a sinking feeling the familiar dried-blood color of the sea witch inside the glass bowl. The girl bowed herself away without a word, arms wrapped protectively around glass, water, and octopus.

"I see you keep to the old rites," Vidarian said, not quite keeping the weary resignation out of his voice.

Ruby snorted, still looking out over the waves, her first acknowledgment of their arrival. "You know full well a wise captain keeps the rites of her crew, and no more. Galon called for the sea witch after the attempt on your life." She turned, then, and leapt down onto the deck, her boots thudding hollowly on the damp wood. In liquid coils the sea energy wrapped itself back into her body and disappeared, and with it, their unnatural speed dropped away.

Ariadel seethed beside him, and Vidarian spoke to stay ahead of her. "What's your decision, then?"

"I will call a Conclave. Not in a decade has there been an assassination attempt aboard this ship." The tightness with which she emphasized 'decade' had Vidarian calculating backward. Rhiannon had been killed just over a decade ago. Surely she hadn't been assassinated? He searched Ruby's face for a hint of the answer, but she gave none.

"And turn us away from the Selturians, and my father? I must object," Ariadel said, and Vidarian hoped Ruby hadn't noticed her clenched fists.

"I'm sorry, Priestess," Ruby said, "but I'm quite resolved."

"By Sea Kingdom law, you owe me the right of resolution by individual combat," Ariadel said.

"Ariadel—" Vidarian began, his head managing to swim and pound simultaneously, but Ruby took no notice.

"I would," Ruby said, unruffled, "if landers were due the rights of sailors, which they are not."

"I am the mate of one of your allies, and so due his rights." Now Vidarian choked—wondering if Ariadel knew what she was claiming (the lander equivalent of marriage!), and then wondering if he wanted to know. The coughing fit that seized him brought blinding bouts of head pain with it.

Ruby, for her part, raised an eyebrow, smiling laconically at Vidarian's discomfort, and conceded with a genteel nod of her head. "Terms?"

"Staves."

"Swords."

Ariadel glared. "Magic."

"Enough," Vidarian managed, and their heads snapped toward him like unruly vipers. He glared back through a pounding head. "You both know full well you can't engage in public battle on these decks." He turned to Ruby. "However you fought, it would come to magic, and she could burn down this ship—I've seen it." And to Ariadel, "And even if you won without killing us all, you'd have an even bigger problem, because the crew would either kill you or declare you captain."

Thwarted wrath emanated from each, either of which would have been intimidating alone. Only the pulsing of his head gave him impatience enough to hold his ground. Ruby was quicker on the uptake, visibly smoothing.

"He's correct, of course," she said, all royal diplomacy again. "But I assume that you play Archtower?"

Ariadel stiffened, feeling for an insult. "Gevalle," she said, not quite a question.

"The Velinese name," Ruby agreed. It was a war game played with pieces of carved stone on a kind of grid. Vidarian had never once in their many games managed to defeat Ruby when they were children, a fact that she doubtless needled him with now. "I have a board in my quarters."

"Very well," Ariadel said. "One game."

After she stepped across the threshold, Ruby raised an eyebrow, then shut the door in his face. He squawked an objection, but Ruby's muffled reply was command-voiced: "You are dismissed, sir!"

They crossed the ship in silence. There was no diplomatic way to search either woman for weapons before they entered Ruby's quarters together, more was the pity. Vidarian opened the door for them, expressing his disapproval with an abrupt wave of mock gentility, but Ariadel did not acknowledge it, and Ruby replied with an exaggerated curtsy that was no doubt perfect Alturian Imperial form.

He gritted his teeth, then regretted it as pain flashed in front of his eyes. *And you are enjoying this far too much*, he thought at the door.

I like her, came the foreign thought, its voice growing more familiar, and his vision swam. Knives of anxiety swept up his spine in successive cold chills, and he looked around wildly.

Who are you? he thought, reaching out with his mind. But the voice, if it did have a presence at all, danced outside his reach. For a moment, before it left entirely, he sensed a giddy amusement, as of a malevolent child who torments an animal. Sudden rage flooded through him, beating back the pounding in his head, and only the sound of Galon moving in the adjacent quarters reminded him to contain himself.

Was he going mad? Had the initial link to Ariadel, forged by the fire goddess, cracked open his mind like an oyster shell, and now other thoughts leaked in? Were such things even possible?

There was no sound from behind the captain's door, and so he retreated up the passageway and exited into the sunlight. The aftcastle was largely untended this hour of the morning, though men and women moved in the rigging, scurrying to answer the commands called out by the second mate from the wheel ahead. Vidarian climbed the narrow ladder and ascended the top deck to look out over the stern, the blue waves, and the wake left behind from their swift passage.

Watching the rushing water, he was aware as he had never before been of the tremendous energy that surged around the ship. It seemed such a small and inconsequential thing, this creation of wood and tar and sail, to have the audacity to brave the ocean. Down, down went the water, deeper than his ability to perceive with eye or Sense. Not for the first time in his life, but for the first time in a great many years, he was in awe of Nistra, lady of the waters.

One little element, a voice whispered, *who plays with her little ship toys, and loves that you love her. You're too good for* her, *too.*

The chill seized him again, and he forced himself not to turn, knowing he would find no one. But this time, he wasn't alone in hearing it: around the ship, the waves crept higher, and the ocean sang dissonance to his senses, and anger. Inside his mind, the voice laughed, again with the strange edge that lifted the hairs on the back of his neck—but it mercifully retreated, and the waves calmed again.

Two hours later, Ariadel and Ruby emerged from the aftcastle, and to the sinking of his stomach, both looked entirely too satisfied for his well-being. Vidarian had no desire to witness a pirate Conclave, even though it might be, as Ruby claimed, the safest place in the sea.

Ruby walked to capstan and placed one booted foot upon it, calling out to the crew. "We remain on course," she said, and a chorus of "Aye, Captain" answered from the deck.

CHAPTER NINETEEN

LORD WINDHAMMER

Ariadel's victory was short-lived. She might have won a game of Archtower, but now there was Maladar's Horn to contend with.

Vidarian had passed around the horn twice, and only twice. The *Quest* was shallow-drafted enough to manage the great winding Karlis River, if ever he had need to access the eastern sea, now that the Imperial locks were in operation. Most ships used it to bypass the horn if they could, and the reasons why were looming on the horizon: anvil-headed clouds, dark as a betrayer's heart, and a cold wind that drove them toward the knife-reefed coast.

A good speed would carry them around the arm of the perpetual storm. From the wheel, Ruby was calling out the trimming of the mainsail, and the *Viere* made crisp progress through waters just beginning to turn dark. As Vidarian and Ariadel watched the sunset-stained water from the bow, the wind fell out from under them. After a rattle of rigging settling back against the poles, all was silent, save the distant boom of thunder that echoed across the wave-plain from dim flashes in the bellies of the thunderheads.

The *Viere* continued to make slow progress through the waves, tacking against a nonexistent wind. Ariadel looked askance at Vidarian. "A silence before the storm," he said. "You'd better go below. Make sure everything— and I mean everything—is tied down securely." She nodded, then moved toward him. He wrapped his arms around her tightly for a moment, chin resting on her hair, and then she turned for the forecastle, moving quickly while the deck was still steady.

As she crossed, she exchanged nods with Ruby, who advanced toward the bow, having turned the wheel over to Galon. He still had not figured out what had so securely settled their feud.

She lifted a brass telescope and looked out at the distant storm, answering his unasked question. "We'll go in with the storm jib as far as we can," Ruby said, all levity for once gone from her demeanor. "I may require your assistance, at the worst." She gestured down at the water, and a chill stole over Vidarian as he took her meaning. It was one thing to play at magicking a handful of riverwater, and quite another to attempt taming a storm. Ruby seized his shoulder and smiled. "Just follow my lead."

He managed half a smile. "Aye, Captain."

The wind picked them up then, cold and ominous. The sails snapped taut against their trim restraint, and the ship lurched forward into newly agitated waves. "Reef main and hoist storm jib!" Ruby shouted, turning away from the bow and striding for the wheel. "All hands check harness to jackline! Look sharp!"

Men and women scrambled for their posts. From the bow, Vidarian tested the security of the jackline anchored there and extending back to the stern. A series of metal hooks guided the line over the forecastle, and he checked each as well as he moved down the deck. Below on the gundeck, three young sailors were moving to secure and check the cannon, and Vidarian joined them in hauling and tying rope. Above, rain began to drum the deck.

The thunder was echoing closer as they sailed into the reach of the storm, and the ship pitched to steeper and steeper angles, testing the cannon-lines. Wind lifted the rigging, howling through the sails, and at last on one great pitch to port, the sea broke over the rails, coursing over the spar deck in a rush that sank his stomach before cascading down the ladders and onto their heads.

Vidarian had worked his way to midships at this point, and stood with the ladders and capstan just before him to stern. Ruby's voice came down from overhead: "Heave to! Get me in front of that—!" Vidarian had not heard that word in over a decade: a particularly creative bedroom maneuver unmentionable in polite company.

Despite the pitching of the ship, the cannon were secure, and none too soon with the full wrath of the storm upon them. Vidarian looked with dread at the dripping ladder, then took courage between his teeth and mounted up it.

Abovedeck the world was in chaos. The thunderheads bore down on them from above, blackening the sky. Lanterns had been lit across the ship, bolstering the thin light from beyond the storm at the horizons, where, somewhere, the moon still shone. Vidarian staggered under the assault of rain and wind to fix his harness to the swinging jackline.

The ship tilted down a swell nose-first at a speed and angle that gripped Vidarian's stomach with vertigo. He took hold of his lifeline with both hands as his boots lifted off the deck—only for a split second, but the crash as they bottomed out, the long bowsprit ahead knifing through saltwater, knocked hardened sailors to the deck across the entire ship. The sea came pouring over the gunwales, drenching the decks and everyone on them.

"Cast drogue!" Ruby shouted over the din, and the command was relayed to the quarterdeck, where hands rushed to toss a series of linked heavy buoys overboard to snake across the undulating swells. As the drogue line snapped taut, the ship steadied for a few precious moments. Vidarian fought to join Ruby at the wheel.

"It's driving us into the reef!" he yelled, sputtering as torrential rainwater streamed down his face, and pointed out across the bow. The ship now angled to port, running from the storm but straight into the murderous embrace of the knife-reefs, the glistening tips of which surged into view in the lee of the swells.

"I realize," Ruby said dryly, an impressive feat, "this is that 'worst' I was talking about." She eyed the bow, and for the first time, Vidarian realized that she was humming. It was a low sea shanty, old and familiar, but her voice imbued it with strange energy, and a great strength poured out from her through the base of the ship. She paused in her humming long enough to shout, "Bare poles! All hands to lifelines! This is it!"

Vidarian saluted, one hand on the jackline, and hauled himself along it toward the bow. It was a long fight, and for every step forward he lost three more to the pitching deck and howling winds. At last he was climbing the ladder to the forecastle deck, clinging to the rail against what seemed the worst of the storm.

From here the black glittering spines of the horn's reef were far too close for comfort. Knowing his duty, though not how it would be accomplished, he thrust his awareness down into the turbulent sea.

The shock of the ocean's cold presence stunned him for several long moments. This was not the peaceful sea of the northern empire, but an angry, wild place that had nothing but hostility for the minds of men. It stalked around him with patient curiosity, and he knew that his death would be but an afterthought in its power. *Beloved Nistra*, he thought, *my life has been yours, and my fathers' lives before me.*

And then, unequivocally, a presence was there. It restrained the angry ocean with the gentle absolution of a woman's touch on the neck of a snarling guard dog. But there was curiosity in the presence, too, and an unfathomable depth unlike any he had ever experienced. *Show me*, came the impression, clear as tropic waters, but wordless, an assault of a thousand images and sensations.

He opened himself fully to the ocean, as he had only in dreams before. It coursed into him, became him, subsumed him. There was no Vidarian, only the current, without constraint or barrier. He was cold and strong, full and relentless. With the slightest movement, he reached to turn the ship away from the reef, and from his distant body felt the deck move beneath his feet.

Deep within him, fighting within that distant body, was dissonance—something not cold and substantive but bright and ephemeral, light but untouchable, electric and hot. And from the heart of this dissonance came a snarling voice: *He isn't yours! He's MINE!*

A sensation of distaste, sulfurous, wafted at him from the presence in the sea. It turned from him, and with it, he lost his grip on the ocean currents. They pulled him down into darkness, and it would have been without hope, save that, even as he descended, he saw the bowsprit ahead emerging into early morning sunlight, out of the grasp of the terrible storm. Behind them curved Maladar's Horn, and he collapsed to the deck, exhausted.

The curl of land that encircled the Selturian Islands protected them from the wrath of land or sea. This spur of mainland in the southwest corner of the Alturian Empire was technically held by the emperor, but it was a wild place, full of strange creatures that had no love of humankind. The Selturians were sparsely populated despite their tropical weather—it was simply too much trouble to reach them by any means, save perhaps flight.

Vidarian woke with the warmth of sunlight slowly drying his soaked clothes and hair. Gulls cried overhead, approaching curiously from the islands to inspect the ship for scraps of food. He struggled upright, first to a sitting position and finally pulling himself to his feet. Dizziness hammered at his head, the night and storm and ocean reawakening the ache in his still-battered skull.

When he staggered down the ladder, Ruby was waiting, looking tired but cheerful.

"You did well," Ruby said, "if a little impetuously. They'll have felt you in the wastes, I'd wager."

"Better than in the deeps," he said, and she laughed, with a gesture of concession. He shaded his eyes and looked out over the water. The three green Selturians surrounded them. They were close enough for him to catch sight of the strange furred animals that swung between the trees.

"I've had a pram prepared," Ruby said. "You and Ariadel may set off when ready. I've given the crew leave to explore the islands if they'd like, but most are interested in sleep."

When he made his way to the boathook, Ariadel was waiting, looking across to the islands. Her skin was pale and her eyes sunken—she'd likely fared no better than he in the aftcastle. He helped her into the pram, and two men at the winches lowered them down into the water. Vidarian took up the oars himself, pushing them away from the steep sides of the *Viere* and settling in to row. Between strokes, he asked, "How long has it been since you saw your father?"

"Years," Ariadel said. "The islands are so remote."

"And his occupation not—encouraged."

She shook her head, surprising him. "There's little reason for interchange between the priesureshood and the rare elemental monks. Their magics are just so different. Men," she paused, and smiled gently, "most of them, anyway, cannot wield the greater magics. You'll see."

In a few minutes he was helping her from the boat and onto the sand,

and then pushing the little craft above the tideline. Ariadel had directed him where to land, and by the time he had shipped the oars and set the pram aright, a modestly dressed figure awaited them at the tree line beyond the sand.

Ariadel set off toward the figure, and Vidarian was surprised to find nervous energy swirling in his gut. What was that Ariadel had said about "mates" to Ruby? He realized he had no idea what Velinese wedding or courtship customs were. But confidence, perhaps, could overcome. He advanced up the beach, taking care to keep Ariadel beside him, and approached the figure, which turned out to be an elderly man with age-spotted skin and hair that had most likely once been black, like Ariadel's.

"Lord Windhammer, I presume," Vidarian extended his hand, and caught Ariadel's flinch out of the corner of his eye.

The older man's smile was sad as he took Vidarian's hand and clasped it briefly. "It's been quite some time since I bore that name," he said. "It's Aldous Windfell, the name of my birth." He turned to Ariadel, who embraced him warmly, but gingerly. "How is your mother?"

"It's some years since I saw her," Ariadel admitted, returning to Vidarian's side. "She's been off on another of her collection trips, and—well, you know how she is about time."

Aldous smiled, and his eyes disappeared beneath folds of wrinkled skin. "I do indeed." He made a motion with one hand. "Her goddess, or mine, or yours," the hint of another smile turned his tone, "protect her. But we can discuss this later. You will be exhausted after your night at sea," he said. "We have a number of guest cottages. Sleep now. We'll speak again in the evening. I am sure there's much to discuss."

○○○

Collapsing on the deck of the *Viere* didn't quite constitute "sleep" so much as "lack of consciousness," and Vidarian was too exhausted to argue with Aldous's prescription of true rest. He and Ariadel fell into their beds, and when they woke, sunset colored the peaceful sky beyond the cottage's window. Ariadel's movement woke him, and once she realized he was awake, she rose and lit a peculiar blown-glass sphere designed, it would seem, to respond to the touch of life flame.

"Your father didn't seem surprised to see us," Vidarian said, finding rest had returned coherent thoughts to his head. He hoped he hadn't said anything too unforgivable yesterday.

"He is Air," she said, as if this explained everything. "I don't think they know the word 'surprise.'"

Vidarian wanted to quiz her further about her father to avoid another misstep, but knew that they must not linger. Continually he felt the pull of the *Quest*, and the knowledge that the longer he stayed away from her, the greater her danger from overzealous priestesses.

This island, one of three that bore the name Selturian, was small but ample enough for a large, airy plantation house, three guest cottages, a thorough vegetable garden, and several acres of jungle besides. Silent young men and women tended the gardens and the goats that provided sustenance for Aldous and themselves; plain-clothed as they were, Vidarian would not have recognized them for apprentices without Ariadel's telling him so.

In the main house a simple but luxurious spread of goat cheese, tree nuts, and tropical fruit was laid out, and both Vidarian and Ariadel found themselves ravenous. Aldous sat with them, shelling and slowly eating a few nuts for politeness' sake, but his gaze was distant and his thought clearly elsewhere. Finally, he turned to Vidarian.

"So," he said, a gentle humor seemed constant in his voice, "you're the Tesseract, then?"

Vidarian paused, a dark-juiced berry halfway to his mouth. He looked across at Ariadel and was somewhat gratified to note she seemed surprised by his abruptness also.

Aldous laughed softly. "We do little but research, here," he said, "and the winds of destiny flow freely about you." He gestured to Vidarian's neck, where the small crystal whistle, given him by the priestess at Siane's Eye, still hung on its silver chain, all but forgotten. "That is the Breath of Siane, is it not?" When Vidarian nodded, Aldous smiled. "May I?"

Vidarian looped the chain free from his neck and passed the little whistle over to Aldous.

"You didn't tell me you carried an artifact," Ariadel said, her tone dangerously light and neutral.

"You didn't ask," he said, and Aldous smiled again, his eyes still on the whistle.

The older man turned the whistle over in his hands, sending light reflecting across its crystal surface. Then, he breathed across it, an odd tone emanating from his chest that made the hair on the back of Vidarian's neck stand up. The whistle glowed and seemed to hold the man's breath within and around it, a spiral of air that hummed like the rim of a crystal goblet touched with water.

"It's quite beautiful," Aldous murmured, then passed it back to Vidarian. "But what you need are the storm sapphires."

Vidarian put the silver chain back on and tucked the whistle into his shirt. "Storm . . . sapphires?"

"Well, yes, if you're to journey to the gate between worlds." Aldous speared a slice of burgundy-colored citrus with a fork and proceeded to eat it slowly.

"The Great Gate?" Ariadel managed around a mouthful of goat cheese. "I thought that was just a legend."

Aldous smiled again. Vidarian was coming to dread that expression. "Much knowledge is lost to the priestesshoods, my dear, including the closing of the gate some two thousand years ago. When they do acknowledge it, the priestesshoods hold that the Tesseract should seal it shut."

"Legends said the gate must not be opened," Ariadel agreed, though irritation edged her voice. "That it should let chaos into the world." At her words, something sent a chill up Vidarian's neck again, but neither of the other two seemed to notice.

"Chaos, yes. Change," Aldous said, brushing crumbs from his fingers. "And those who hold power rightly fear change." He looked up at Vidarian, his eyes grey with age but missing no sharpness. "You should be on your way."

Ariadel all but squawked. "But—I've only just brought him here. I thought you might—"

"There's little time to lose," Aldous said, addressing them both. "Little time, I'm afraid. And this coming from an Air master." He rose, pushing his chair back behind him with a soft scud across the slate floor. "Ariadel, if you wouldn't mind, in my study is a book that will help us. Mayene will know which one—our collected learnings on the Great Gate."

Ariadel stood and nodded, looking between them intently for a moment, then leaving to find Mayene.

The old man lifted a hand wizened like dried ginger to point the way out of the hall. When Ariadel had quite left their hearing, he set off slowly, speaking without turning. "You must be worthy of her, Vidarian," Aldous said, his gaze going distant like the air priestess's had at Siane's Eye, what seemed so long ago. "Be worthy of her," he said, and smiled, "or I'll break your knees."

CHAPTER TWENTY

THE JEWEL OF HIS HEART

A whistle from the island's watchtower split the air the next morning. As Vidarian and Aridel emerged from the tiny guest cottage, eyes bloodshot from a night spent scrutinizing Aldous's books, they caught sight of what the watch had seen: three gryphons, flying in ragged formation in from the east. As they drew closer, the cause of their ragged flight became apparent: the lead gryphon flew irregularly, and the two that followed were forced to rush ahead or backwing alternately to keep up. When they came upon the island, their wings stretched outward in a long glide, and they fell to earth quickly in the heavy tropical air.

The three banked together in a wide curve as they came in to land, and now their differences were clear. In the lead was Thalnarra, her feathers battered and thin; she was missing a primary on her right wing, among other things. The gryphon back and to her left was bizarre, unlike anything Vidarian had seen in statues or paintings, much less live and real: it had a long, triangular head and an even longer beak with a hooked tip and a huge flap of loose skin below the lower jaw, like a fishing bird. Its neck, too, was long and crooked, and its broad rectangular wings were longer than Thalnarra's, though its body was smaller. The third gryphon was strange as well, with huge sapphire-blue eyes against snowy white feathers and a compact black-tipped beak; the feathers at the end of its leonine tail forked in a swallow-tail, beginning with white feathers that gave way to slender black ones, matched also on the tips of its otherwise white wings.

They landed on the sand several yards from the cottages, but the wind of their passing rattled the fronds at the top of the tall trees. The landing was not graceful; the strange fisher-bird-gryphon seemed unaccustomed to landing on solid ground, and Thalnarra stumbled as she touched the ground, favoring a wounded foreleg. Vidarian and Ariadel exchanged a look, not quite believing what they were seeing, and ran for the three creatures. As they did so, Ariadel turned to call for medical supplies, sending three of the apprentices scrambling for the large house.

Thalnarra's breath was labored when they reached her, and close inspection revealed her condition to be even worse than it had seemed from afar. Numerous open cuts wept fluid sluggishly across her body from five-taloned slashes on her shoulders and hindquarters. They'd been treated at some point, for they ran clean, but the flight had broken them open again. She had more body feathers missing, and those that remained were tattered and drab.

"What on earth happened to you?" Ariadel asked, then turned to the other gryphons in apology. "Be welcome, friends, to the Selturian Islands and the home of my father, Aldous Windfell."

// *We are in need of friends,* // Thalnarra said. // *Though my battle, for now, is won.* //

The white gryphon with the large eyes and pointed face spoke with a voice like a low flute. // *It was ritual combat. Her people use the old gryphon law to resolve disagreements.* //

// *Being an old tradition, hurr,* // the fisher-gryphon agreed, his voice like drifting kelp, peaceful and remote. He shook his head, sending his chin flap flopping, and lifted his feathers, from the white and grey stripes of his face to his blue-black wing-feathers.

// *But it was won,* // Thalnarra said, exhaustion in her voice, and a steely insistence, rebutting the disapproval of the other two. // *The gryphons of the fire clans stand with us. It will take some time to gather them, but gather they will, and our allies.* // She indicated the other two with the tip of her beak, and they nodded each in turn—water and air, Vidarian realized.

"Stand with 'us'?" Vidarian said, turning to gesture to the three apprentices who now emerged from the main house with armfuls of bandages and a crate of medicines.

// *With you, of course,* // Thalnarra eyed him dangerously, // *against the priestesshood.* //

The cottage was quiet when Vidarian returned to it, looking for Ariadel, who had fled while he helped see to Thalnarra's wounds. He called out her name, but there was no answer, and he expected to find the building empty when he pushed open the door.

He found her crumpled on the floor, the embroidered robe loaned her by one of the apprentices pooling around her. Her breath came with a rattle of emotion, and she sniffed as she turned toward the door to look at him, her face streaked with tears. In her lap was the gangly kitten, half grown, and before it occurred to him to wonder how in the world it had gotten there, Vidarian thought perhaps it was dead, and this the cause of her distress. But the kitten, lying on its back, rolled over with easy agility and pushed its face at Ariadel's hand, demanding attention.

"How—?" Vidarian managed, rushing to Ariadel and kneeling. She pointed across the floor, where the small tinderbox that she had used for the golden spider, before their flight to the Selturians, lay open and empty. Vidarian looked at it blankly. "What? I don't understand," he said.

Ariadel stroked the kitten's head, then leaned close to look into its eyes. Something passed between them—and then the kitten disappeared. Vidarian gasped, leaning closer, and Ariadel lifted her hand. Perched upon it, balanced delicately on the tips of its feet, was the spider.

"How is this possible?" he whispered, head swimming.

"She's a shapechanger," Ariadel said, and laughed softly, incredulously, a sob half mixed with it. She reached out with her free hand to slide a leather journal open to a marked page across the carpet to Vidarian. He picked it up; the page was labeled "Snowmelt," and held sketches of a white horse, some of them fancifully rendered, the horse's rear end replaced by a sinuous fish tail. Ariadel turned her hand, and the spider skittered, then vanished, replaced once more with the kitten.

"What is this?" Vidarian asked, turning a page. "And why does it trouble you so?" He reached out to touch her shoulder, and she leaned into him.

"My great-great-great-grandmother had a horse named Snowmelt," she said. "She was the last fire priestess in our family, until me. As a girl I loved the stories of Snowmelt, her devoted horse—there were stories that he wasn't just a horse, but a shapechanger, able to turn into a great cat and protect her. We always assumed they were just stories."

"It's remarkable," he said, reaching out to let the cat sniff his hand. It did, then turned up its nose at him. "But why does it affect you so?"

"Everything's changing," she said, and blinked back tears again, composing herself. "The gryphons declaring war against the priestesshood. Shapechangers returning to the world. New magics are coming, many of them strange and dangerous." She stopped again, breathing deeply. Something in her tone made him think of the strange voices he'd heard, and he thought of confessing them, but she went on. ". . . And I . . . I'm afraid I . . ."

He wrapped his arms around her, careful not to upset the kitten, and rested his chin on her shoulder, waiting.

She shook her head, swallowing. "It's nothing. It's just overwhelming, that's all." She coughed, clearing her throat, and stiffened in his embrace ever so slightly. "None of us know what's coming. I fear for all of us."

Aldous had treated the gryphons' arrival with as much nonchalance as he had his daughter's, and now he sent them off again with equal gentle authority. The gryphons, he said, and their intention to aid Vidarian's cause, meant that the hour was truly grown late.

"I wish you strength," the older man said to Vidarian, seriousness in his pale eyes. "If our studies are accurate, you are even now encountering some strange things, indeed." His weighty gaze searched Vidarian's, and then he patted his shoulders with both hands like a father would a son. "But you'll bear up under them. You must." Vidarian longed to ask him about the voices, and the severing of his telepathic bond with Ariadel—but in his features saw the father of the woman he loved, and dared not.

On their second day on the island Ruby had joined them, availing herself cheerfully of the hospitality of Aldous's house. Now, though, they were to separate, and Vidarian saw her off from the sandy beach.

"You're off in search of more booty, I understand," she said, grinning at him from the shadow of a rather absurd feathered hat. "I should think you'd be satisfied with what you had, you greedy git."

"Are we ever?" he asked, for once not finding her ceaseless ribbing grating to his nerves, and realized with surprise that he'd miss the *Viere* as well. Her solid decks had stood them well around the horn. "You've executed your part of our bargain. I regret that I cannot pay you yet."

She tutted in response. "My business is in Val Harlon, as it was before we departed. We'll meet you there, and I'm sure your friends will have helped sort out this little misunderstanding with the fire priestesses by then." Ruby indicated the gryphons with a gesture of her chin. When she'd seen them for the first time, her eyes had widened, a shadow full of dread and memory passing behind them—but it was gone, fled behind her customary mask of an easy smile, before he could inquire.

"You'll be for the horn again, then," Vidarian said, guilt welling up that he would not be there to assist them.

"Tish. We've sailed it before. I got you here, I can certainly get my own ship back."

"At Val Harlon, then," he said, offering his hand.

She took it, and pulled him into a rough, brotherly embrace. "Val Harlon. Take care you're not late."

Aldous, despite his unruffled demeanor toward them, had never worked with gryphons before. They had no carrying boat, but the older air monk had closeted himself away with the white gryphon, called Altair, to discuss their shared magic at incomprehensible detail. That left Ariadel, Vidarian, Thalnarra, and the fisher-gryphon, called Arikaree, to improvise one.

They started with a yawl, a small sailboat decommissioned from a larger sailing vessel kept by Aldous and the small community. With its mast removed, it was larger and considerably less unnerving than a dinghy or pram, but still small enough for its weight not to tax the gryphons overly. Still, it was heavier than the lighter craft built for flight, and so, after fitting it with harness and rope—a light, strong kind made of silk here on the islands—they provisioned it sparingly. The flight path east to An'durin, the great inland sea along the Karlis River, should take them over forests plentiful with game, and the gryphons were confident of their ability to hunt along the way.

At length, and as they were prepared to depart, Aldous and Altair emerged from the former's study, still chattering but more conscious now of those around them. Vidarian was impressed that they'd managed to reckon the time on their own, until he saw an apprentice emerge behind them and exchange a nod with Ariadel.

Ariadel's departure from her father was not without a few tears, and it pulled at Vidarian's heart to separate them so quickly after so long and perilous a journey. The few days on the islands had been a respite, not just for the warm sun and clear air, but from the strange voice that spoke to him as well. The presence in the ocean still nagged at him: he would swear that the one who spoke to him during the storm first was Nistra. But the second— the one that had invaded his thoughts so many times now? Had the magic in his mind grown wild, developed a personality of its own? It certainly seemed capable of it.

The kitten, now, was inseparable from Ariadel, and looked quite pleased with itself. Either natural maturation or its time as a spider had favored it: it was sleeker, seemed not quite so desperate for food, though it still ate its own body weight daily, it seemed. Aldous had exclaimed with wonder the first time Ariadel had shown him its trick of shapechanging, and inspected it closely; Thalnarra had also been impressed, but more reservedly.

The gryphoness, the largest of the three if he didn't count the fisher-gryphon's overlong neck and head, had benefited from the attentions of the field healer that lived here on Aldous's island. The man's talent was small, but made a difference: her cuts were not quite so vivid, and would hold together in flight this time.

As the apprentices helped Thalnarra and the other two gryphons into their harnesses, the gryphons spread their massive wings, testing flexibility and the strength of their harnesses. Finding both satisfactory, they sat back on their haunches, waiting for Vidarian and Ariadel to board.

"I thank you for your hospitality and invaluable advice," Vidarian said, clasping Aldous by hand and elbow in a formal Imperial gesture learned from his father. "I know little of such things as fate, but knowing what we know now, I should think our course doomed without either."

Aldous chuckled, shaking his head. "I suspect you would have found your way, if indeed fate is involved, as I suspect she is. Thank you for bringing a little sunshine to an old man's island retreat. And remember," he smiled broadly, magnanimous as the gentle tropic wind, "what I said about the knees."

"Of course, sir," Vidarian agreed, and stepped back hastily to the craft where Ariadel waited, perched on its newly padded center seat. He vaulted into the craft beside her and sat, reaching for the rope ties they'd fixed to the craft's sides to help keep them from pitching out. The craft Vidarian had ridden before had no such precaution, but he wasn't about to replicate that particular design if he could avoid it.

As soon as Aldous and his apprentices stepped back to the tree line to give them clearing, the gryphons began to beat their wings, each giving two to stretch the muscles before leaping into the air and laying about with earnest. The craft lifted steadly, its counterweights balancing as intended, and they rose steadily into the air.

The island, its house, and its inhabitants dwindled rapidly as the gryphons circled higher. Whitecaps on the waves crashed against the shore, and soon they could see the other two islands, one north and one east, bare of inhabitation it would seem from here. Far below, the *Viere d'Inar* angled toward the northern coast, and Maladar's Horn with its ever-present storm. He wished them better luck with it, and watched the ship move through the waters for as long as he could, until they passed through a layer of clouds and mist that obscured the world below.

An'du, the great whale of the inland sea, was the last known possessor of the storm sapphires. How they would find her, much less convince her to relinquish them, he had little idea—and he had two days in the air to figure it out.

CHAPTER TWENTY-ONE

THE BATTLE
FOR THE QUEST

Distances were strange by air, but on a map he knew the An'duril to be as far east as Val Harlon was west, but only a third as far north. The gryphons rode prevailing winds from the sea and so flew strongly, tracing the edge of the Windsmouth Mountains. By day, the trees rushed by below, so regular as to be hypnotic, and by night they dipped beneath the canopy to take shelter and sleep. Not only would it have exhausted the gryphons to fly through the night, it would have been dangerous as well: after sunset, their heads seemed to nod unwillingly with sleep, some deep drive urging them to roost.

At noon on the second day the trees thinned out below into a meadow, and then into a sparse grassland as they arrowed northeast. A glint on the horizon was the Karlis River, and it widened toward late afternoon into the glittering expanse of the An'durin. By sunset, the whole of the inland sea dominated their horizon, and distantly, at its far northern shore, was the shadow of the An'durinvale, the dark forest that half-wreathed it.

The gryphons dropped altitude as they drew nearer to the expanse of water, turned to dark glass by the sun sinking below the skyline behind them.

They made camp, foraging for fallen wood and grass for a fire, the five of them silenced by the presence they knew waited in the water. The gryphons tore the earth, digging shallow sleeping holes and lining them with grasses before they flew off to hunt. Vidarian and Ariadel made a cold supper out of provisions from the yawl, and were preparing the night's campfire when the gryphons returned. When Ariadel moved to light the fire, Thalnarra stopped her.

// He should be exploring the other half of his abilities, // she said, and Ariadel looked at Vidarian, then nodded.

Vidarian regarded the pile of grass and branches for some time before he reached out with the smaller, brighter sense within him, the erratic one that snapped and snarled as it could against his water sense. In attacking the water within him, as it did perpetually, it turned and lashed out at his own essence, and without quite realizing what he was doing he snarled back at it as he would a dog. It quailed, dipping in what he would swear was apology, and cooperated as he reached out to the stacked sticks. It seized upon them hungrily, and flames leapt up with alarming quickness. As the light and heat flared, something, too, flared inside him, opening, and for a moment every detail of his surroundings was revealed in instant clarity, as if he were more awake than he'd ever been in his life. Then the fire crept back inside of him, coiling, to bicker with his water sense again, and the feeling faded.

// A little rough, but well done, // Thalnarra said sleepily, settling into her bed of grass. Vidarian and Ariadel followed suit, climbing under blankets they'd spread across more of the ubiquitous summer-burned vegetation.

Yes, well done, a voice whispered in his head, half giggling. His arms clenched involuntarily around Ariadel, who looked up at him in sleepy askance, but he forced himself to smile and shake his head, relaxing. She closed her eyes, but as Vidarian looked out over the still waters of the An'durin, spangled over with stars and dark heavens, it was some time before he closed his.

∿∿∿

They woke to thin light and cold air, a heavy fog that had obscured the sun and drenched the world in white mist. The fog stopped a spare handspan from the surface of the An'durin, as if some unearthly force kept it from touching the water and what lay beneath. All was quiet.

"We're going to have to go out on the water, to talk to her," Vidarian said, though none too keen on the idea of piloting a mastless yawl on such a large body of water. The gryphons, with the exception of Arikaree, didn't like it, either; the pelican-gryphon tested the water with his claws, then proceeded to wade in and swim, buoyant as a gigantic duck. Thalnarra watched from the shore, and Altair took to the sky; his long, sharp wings allowed him to hover effortlessly high over the water.

They unloaded the yawl of all its cargo and took supple branches from a young tree, heavy with leaves on their ends, to use as makeshift paddles. The pebbled shore made launching the yawl a simple exercise, and soon they were paddling laboriously for deeper water. While they launched, a wind picked up, swirling from Altair's tiny form high above them; a slow cyclone spun mist away from the surface of the lake in a cone that met his glowing claws at its pinnacle.

Just as the silt-lined sandbar disappeared beneath them, dropping into cloudy depths, An'du appeared.

For a split second she was a shadow beneath them, and then she was breaking the surface. For Vidarian it was a dizzying memory—the massive whale, easily six times the length of their small craft, was exactly as he had pictured her in his vision at the Vkorthan island.

She rotated in the water, her movements turning the yawl as well. In a moment her massive head was at the prow.

Your presence, An'du said, and by their reactions Vidarian saw that Ariadel heard her also—not as gryphons spoke, from a respectful mind distance, but straight inside their heads. *I know you. Please, come closer.*

"Vidarian—" Ariadel began, but Vidarian was already leaning out across the water.

An'du's great eye rolled toward them as she turned on her side, then gave a powerful pulse of her tail to lift her great anvil-shaped head out of the water. *Don't be afraid*, she said, as Vidarian drew back into the boat. *We are rarely quite what we seem.*

When her nose touched his outstretched hand—slick and suppler than the finest leather—she vanished.

Thrashing suddenly in the water was—impossibly—a woman. Her skin was mottled green, a shadow of what An'du's had been, and, as she writhed, it became clear that her whale body remained below her waist, though much diminished in size, complete with broad white tail and frond-like camouflage.

Her head broke the surface, followed by her body, as her powerful tail propelled her up to "stand" above the water. Her hair—a deep green—clung to her face, and as she brushed it from her eyes, she laughed, high and full. She spun in a circle, arms akimbo. Vidarian looked away from her bared chest, though it didn't seem entirely necessary: the skin there was covered with pale mottling, but otherwise smooth, without human feature. When she swam toward the yawl, her size became clearer: she was easily half again the size of a normal woman, and would have towered over Vidarian if they stood side by side.

"It has been centuries," she said, brushing hair away from her face and opening her eyes, "since I have known my true shape." An'du's eyes were inhumanly large and without whites, filled instead with deep brown iris and pupil. She smiled at Vidarian and Ariadel, then held the expression, as if testing it.

Vidarian looked at Ariadel, but she only shook her head, as astonished as he. "We came to ask you about the storm sapphires," he said, stunned into the obvious.

Her smile brightened, savvy. "Of course you would. And I will give them to you, for your coming signals the long-delayed awakening of my people. You have no idea how long we have waited."

"How many are you?" he asked, before he could help it. "And where?"

"Many," she said, her smile dwindling at last into seriousness. "And through all the oceans of the world. But the tale is long, and you haven't time." She dropped down into the water then, and dove. Seconds later, there was a pulse from below the water that rocked the boat again—and An'du was a whale once more. She continued to dive, disappearing from their sight, but in three breaths was returning again, and, as before, when she lifted her head from the water near Vidarian, she became the half-human creature again.

An'du gagged, and Vidarian reached toward her out of reflex, tipping the yawl, but she recovered on her own, spitting out two large blue stones. She touched them to the water, and they shuddered in her hands—deep within, they echoed with lightning and swirled with cloud.

Vidarian held out his hand, but An'du shook her head, closing her hands over the blue stones. "When you depart, so too will my ability to hold this shape, until the gate is reopened."

"Reopened?" he said in surprise, exchanging a look of confusion with Ariadel.

An'du flicked her tail, sending a ripple through the water. "There are two paths," she said. "In one, you seal the gate; in the other, you reopen it. You must know the consequences of each."

"And you can—become yourself—if I'm here . . . or if the gate is open. But I can't—"

"Certainly not," An'du agreed, dipping below the water for a moment and surfacing again. "You can't remain here. But part of you can." She traced the surface of one of the sapphires with a fingertip, and lightning echoed beneath it.

Vidarian's hand went to the pouch at his side. It stayed there, not removing either of the stones that lay inside. He looked at Ariadel.

"It seems a fair bargain," she offered, still clearly subdued by the thought of opening the gate, and An'du smiled.

"The stone will be destroyed upon my death," he said. "I think it only fair to warn you."

"I only need it until the gate is opened," she said. "If you should do so, the awakening will begin, and I will even return it to you, if you wish."

"No," he said, and drew the emerald from his pouch. His heart quickened as he touched it, a tremor of recognition pulsing through his senses. "I give it to you in trade. I've trusted you in my darkest hour, and need all the allies I can get."

They exchanged the stones, and as the sapphires fell into his hands, it was with a great weight, and he struggled to regain his balance. Overhead, Altair cried out, a piercing cry that cut the air, and the sky darkened.

"You must control them," An'du warned. "Especially when they're near the sun rubies. The gate must be opened with both, but they will not be content to be near each other."

Vidarian sat back in the yawl, wrapping his hands around the stones and extending his senses over them. They pulled him in like a funnel cloud, and he fought for control, gripping them in his mind. The sky lightened, reluctantly, and the cold bite that had hung in the air eased. Deep inside him, from within the braided core of his elemental senses, something tested the power of the sapphires, and exulted.

"I wish you luck," An'du said seriously, rolling the emerald between her fingers in a way that made Vidarian shiver and turn back to her. In the early morning light, her dark eyes cast down and bathed in the light of the emerald, she was strikingly beautiful, if equally alien. "You will have enemies, change-bringer, that will not end with the gate's opening—or sealing. Allies you need, and you will have, but the powerful have the most to lose, and so will resist what you bring with all their strength." Her hands closed around the emerald, dousing her face with shadow. "Luck, indeed, for all of us."

ﾉﾚﾚﾚ

When they returned to shore with the sapphires, Arikaree, after stepping away from them long enough to shake the water from his feathers and fur, approached Vidarian, his eyes fixed on the blue stones. Vidarian's hold on them felt like pulling a sail filled with the wind; he was not fatigued yet, but he would be. And so when the pelican-gryphon extended his foreclaw, palm open, Vidarian tipped the stones onto it with a measure of relief.

The gryphon inspected the stones for some time. Within, miniature clouds roiled, and the occasional soft peal of thunder even caused them to shudder. // *A storm is being a bridge, hurr,* // he said, touching a talon to the surface of the stone. The electricity within it shot from the bottom of the stone to the tip of his claw. // *The lightning, hurr—the storm being meeting of sea and fire, the lightning a lance between earth and sky. Bridge for gate-opening, bridge for change-bringing.* //

"Thalnarra," Vidarian said, "An'du said that the Tesseract *opens* the gate—not seals it."

The gryphoness made a dry clicking noise in her throat, a sound of dissatisfaction that wasn't quite a growl.

// *There are—conflicting prophesies,* // Altair said.

Vidarian felt his eyebrows lifting.

// *According to some prophesies, the Tesseract seals the Great Gate, solidifying the choice made by the PrimeAdepts centuries ago. In others, he opens the gate, bringing its old powers back into the world.* // The gryphon's large blue eye turned toward Vidarian, pinning. // *A modern theory indicates that the Tesseract chooses the world's destiny.* //

// *But in either event,* // Thalnarra said, her tone not conceding an inch, // *your path, and ours, takes us to the gate.* //

It seemed too great a simplification for so great a decision, but a look in Thalnarra's eye told him now wasn't the time to press for detail. "An'du said that I would need the rubies as well," Vidarian said.

"Which means Val Harlon," Ariadel finished. "And the *Quest.*"

// *We are strong mages, all of us, but not enough to stand up to all that Endera will bring, if she chooses,* // Thalnarra rumbled.

"I can't imagine this would come to violence," Ariadel protested.

Thalnarra turned to look at her, red eyes pinning, but she said nothing.

"Ruby will be docked there," Vidarian said, talking between them. "If we fly quickly, she won't have waited long."

They hauled the yawl from the An'durin and prepared it for flight once more. As the gryphons were stretching their wings in preparation for the flight, Thalnarra said, // *The fastest route to Val Harlon by air takes us over Cheropolis, and an assortment of outlying villages.* //

// *We must ascend,* // Altair said, his flutelike voice surprising after Thalnarra's intense but familiar one. // *In the higher altitudes I will protect you with a shield of air. We can breathe there, but you cannot.* //

And indeed, while the beginning of their trip took them at a familiar height over hills and forests, as they drew closer to human-inhabited roads, the gryphons angled upward in the sky. The ground dwindled further beneath them, and Vidarian, who had become accustomed to the lower altitudes, found himself dizzied all over again as the landmarks grew smaller and smaller. His ears crackled with pain, and Ariadel motioned him to move his jaw—they made a midday snack of nuts and goat cheese from the Selturians for an excuse. As Altair had predicted, the air grew thin and harder to breathe. His lungs worked gamely, but it was as if the air simply was not there. When the gryphon's shield closed around them, muffling and enriching the air, it was a relief, and a however-illusory sense of security against the heights.

As if buoyed by the higher altitudes, or perhaps an unexpressed air of urgency, the gryphons flew quickly west, and crossed the distance in a mere three and a half days, rising earlier and flying deeper toward night. Only when their wingbeats began to falter did they move to descend; Altair, who seemed to handle the upper altitudes more easily than his partners, looked as though he alone could have gone much longer.

At midday on the fourth day, the spires of Val Harlon crept over the horizon, five points like talons on a gryphon's foreclaw reaching into the sky. And by midafternoon they were descending, spiraling toward the shielding forest that had cloaked the gryphons from view the first time Vidarian and Ariadel had landed here, fleeing the might of Sher'azar.

But to Vidarian's surprise, they did not curve toward the sheltering forest. As they drew closer to the ground, it became increasingly apparent that the gryphons intended to land on the docks themselves, bearing toward the long arm of an empty pier adjacent to the *Empress Quest*. Further out, at the mouth of the wide bay that sheltered Val Harlon from the wild outer sea, the *Viere d'Inar* stood vigilant.

"Thalnarra!" Vidarian shouted. "Where are you going?"

// *The time for subterfuge is ended,* // she said, and the finality with which she rested on the last word sent a chill down Vidarian's spine. // *Our separation from humanity was half our culture and half yours. I demanded from my flight a dissolution of our alliance with the priesthood, and with it ends our exclusive contact with them.* //

// *The air flights stand with our fire brethren in this,* // Altair added, his voice even softer than usual, a subtle (or perhaps Thalnarra would have said "passive aggressive") dig at the larger gryphon's increasingly heated words. // *We do not wish to alarm the smaller villages, whose mythology has grown against gryphonkind, but it will begin here in the cities.* //

Vidarian was learning not to ask what "it" was. *Changebringer,* he thought acidly, if only to cover his trepidation.

As they dropped toward the ground, the gryphons' wings fanning outward to brake and glide, the dockworkers raised their hands to shade their eyes and point, then turned and shouted. Men and women alike stood, stunned—some turned and fled, seized by fear, while others ran toward the water, summoned by the spectacle.

Perhaps thinking to protect her, the priestesses had moved the *Quest* to the inner harbor. There was little traffic from other ships here, and the gryphons glided to a landing on the empty adjacent pier.

Vidarian's family ship was covered with fire priestesses. Almost all his crew had been removed. They'd been gone so long, certainly many would have taken berths on other ships. But Marielle stood at the bow beside Endera, her hands in irons. His first mate and the priestess were exchanging heated words, indecipherable at this distance, though by the jerking of Marielle's chained hands they clearly concerned two too-familiar black-cloaked figures that stood behind Endera.

The priestesses held torches each alive with an unnatural light, their life-essences burning in the clear light of day. The hair stood up on the back of Vidarian's neck as he counted how many coated his ship, each armed with flame. He helped Ariadel out of the yawl, and together they unharnessed the gryphons. The crowd that had gathered was growing larger, but none dared approach within fifty feet of wing, beak, or talon.

The three creatures stretched and folded their wings, and Thalnarra nodded to Vidarian. He turned toward the city, advancing up the pier, and in short order they were drawing near the *Quest*'s mooring.

"Come no closer, Vidarian!" Endera called when they approached hearing distance. "We will negotiate the terms of your ship's return from here!" An unearthly, malicious sound like low thunder vibrated the air around them, and Vidarian realized that Thalnarra was growling.

// *Peace, sister,* // Altair murmured, but his entreaty only heightened her ire.

"My air brother, I welcome you to Val Harlon—and wish it were under better circumstances!" Endera shouted to him.

// *He is not your brother,* // Thalnarra said, and the growl in her throat was dwarfed by the force in her mind's voice: a raw ferocity crackling in her mind, and a fierce satisfaction. // *And I am not your Sister. Our bond with the priestess-hood is ended, Endera, over your rash choice.* // She punctuated this with a piercing cry, rearing back on her hind legs and hooking a talon in the direction of the two black-cloaked figures that stood behind Endera.

"These are water Sisters—" Endera began, turning.

// *Indeed they are not, hrrr!* // Arikaree objected, radiating affront, his dark feathers rousing. // *They are being known to no ocean!* // His words, like Thalnarra's, were oddly weighted, carrying swirls of thought for which Vidarian's language had no words, and Altair turned to him in surprise. // *Yes, hurr,* // the fisher-gryphon affirmed, with a dip of his long beak. // *You are feeling it also. A madness!* //

"The temple cannot sanction this action!" Ariadel shouted, and in her voice Vidarian heard how it taxed her to contradict her mentor.

"I act alone!" Endera agreed, her own voice strident and shrill. "But for the good of us all, as you well know, my student! The priestesses you see here are loyal to me!"

Ariadel colored at the reprimand, but her jaw was firm. A heated retort died on her lips, though, when they all heard familiar boot-heels smartly crossing the dock behind them. In a moment, Ruby was at their side, her sword unsheathed and raised. She lifted it in an ironic salute to the *Quest*, and then back toward land, at the rowdy crew that raised their voices in a raucous cheer as she acknowledged them. The tip of the sword swung low and dangerous as she rewarded their acclaim with a theatrical bow.

"Impeccable timing," Vidarian said quietly, and Ruby only grinned, wolfish.

"It was looking a bit dodgy," she said, gesturing with the tip of her sword at the *Quest*.

The priestesses aboard grew visibly nervous at the cheers of Ruby's crew. Their flames flickered, then roared higher, licking dangerously close to the ship's rigging.

"Your choices are your own," Endera called to the gryphons, deliberately ignoring the pirates. "History will doubtless condemn me for a villain—"

"Then perhaps you should reconsider your action!" Ruby shouted, lifting her longsword. The crew cheered again, eliciting more uneasiness from the priestesses.

"As much as I appreciate your assistance," Vidarian murmured, "do take care they don't torch my ship."

A scuffle broke out atop the deck, and by the time Vidarian realized what was happening, Marielle was being hustled from the deck, shouting obscenities at the cloaked figures. One of them strode toward the rail, reaching a hand toward Vidarian. Her hood fell back, baring the same blonde hair and grey eyes he'd seen at Sher'azar.

"Tesseract!" she shouted. "Fortune be upon you! Even now you draw close to our most exalted lady—"

The gryphons mantled at the tone in her voice and the weird energy that rose around her as she reached toward him.

Curious . . . the voice purred inside his mind.

"I sense her!" the grey-eyed priestess exulted, an hysterical wildness in her voice. "She is near!"

Both black-robed priestesses raised their arms, and in the strange energy that emanated out from them, the flames atop the torches that covered the *Empress Quest* roared lurid blue.

Chaos broke out aboard the *Quest*. Priestesses cried out as their own life flames leapt from their hands, wild and out of control. The flames, unearthly blue, crawled and writhed like living animals, and swept across the deck faster than if it had been doused in oil. Endera fought the flames, managing to douse her own, but only barely managing to rescue some of her acolytes from theirs. The freed priestesses ran down the gangplank, while others still on the deck leapt into the sea. Endera, abandoned, turned back toward the black-cloaked priestesses, shouting over the roar of the flames, "What is the meaning of this? Do you abandon yet another vow?" The blonde priestess hissed, an inhuman sound, and flung out a hand, releasing a wave of energy that knocked Endera to the deck.

Ariadel ran to meet Endera, lifting her hands to fight the flames aboard the ship. Thalnarra and the two other gryphons leapt away from Vidarian and Ruby, taking flight to wage their own war against the strange blue fire.

But their best efforts, Vidarian knew, might be enough only to save a few lives. Not the *Quest*, which even now, to his numb horror, was engulfed with ravenous fire.

Something ripped loose in Vidarian. In his anguish and fury, he relinquished control of himself to the power that simmered beneath his skin.

Pure vengeance, a celestial retribution that had consumed stars and entire planets, poured through his veins, and this world and even the universe beyond ceased to exist save for these two creatures, which deserved death and suffering through their every fiber.

His arms moved without his will, reaching toward the priestesses. They cried out in ecstasy, shouting for their goddess, babbling how they had waited, how they had been devoted.

He knew what it was to pluck a galaxy from the sky and swallow it whole. This was what he unleashed upon the cloaked figures: a nothingness that unmade them, ate them away from their cores to their skins, leaving nothing, not even a smoking circle where they had stood. He felt bone and sinew give way before him, marrow and muscle, as their screams of devotion turned to horror and fear.

Last to vanish were their thoughts, which lingered in the air like an echo in a ravine, and at last faded from a wordless cry of despair to a ringing silence. The flames rushed to fill the gap where they had stood, no longer blue, but a deadly and more familiar red.

In that moment of exultation, when the Vkortha had been reduced to nothingness, Vidarian seized back control of himself, gasping. He looked up and saw the burning tops of the *Quest*, the falling rigging, the skeletal main and mizzen blackened with ash and fire—

Ruby was suddenly there, hauling on his arm, dragging him away from the inferno. He turned back to her and saw his own anguish reflected there in her eyes. Tears streamed down her face—whether for his grief or from the searing smoke, he couldn't know. "She's gone, 'Darian," she shouted over the blasting heat, calling him by the childhood name his sister had used. He hadn't heard it since her death. "And you won't help anyone going down with her! Not like this!"

Vidarian staggered backward, pulled from the falling wreckage, but could not tear his eyes away from his family's legacy listing over, consumed by fire, groaning like an animal as one of the holds gave way and it tilted into the harbor. The main snapped, its base eaten by flame, and Vidarian's heart broke with it. He cried out, a wail lost in the roar of the fire, and threw a hand back toward it.

The main yard high overhead gave way with a sickening crack, and Vidarian stared up at it, numb. Ruby pushed him out of the way, throwing out her arms. The rent edge of the yard caught her in the side, its splintered and blackened end disappearing a handsbreadth into her flesh, so fast that it took her breath away midway through the start of a scream of pain.

Vidarian dove after her as she fell to the planks. A span of wood as long as his arm protruded from her side, and her legs spasmed helplessly as her body realized its trauma. He reached toward her, and her cry of pain was not from his touch, but it stopped him nonetheless. Gritting his teeth, he reached out with his senses, wrapping the projectile in elemental energy, and searing through the top of it, leaving it to fall away from her.

Debris from the ship continued to fall around them, splashing into the sea and crashing onto the deck. The *Empress Quest* was an alien thing, a burning demon from a nightmare, not the ship his great-grandfathers had sailed. Ruby gasped again, and Vidarian looped one arm beneath her shoulders and the other beneath her knees, then staggered to his feet and ran up the pier.

Ash burned his lungs as he cleared the radius of the burning ship and fell to his knees, taking as much of the jolt with his legs and body as he could. Ruby groaned and lost consciousness, her head lolling. He lowered her to the ground, supporting her neck with one hand.

"Healer!" he bellowed, scrubbing water from his eyes with an ash-stained sleeve. "Fetch a healer!"

PART THREE
SAPPHIRES

CHAPTER TWENTY-TWO

UNEASY PEACE

The hospital at Val Harlon, adjacent to the three-partnered Collegia of Herbmastery, Mindcraft, and Healing, might be dwarfed by the great Healing Center and Imperial University far to the east in the Imperial City, but it was one of the oldest and largest institutions of its kind. Consequently there were few cities in the known world quite so recommendable for sustaining a serious injury in.

The Imperial healers had devised ways of prolonging the life of a man or woman into long centuries. Some—Vidarian's family among them, and the emperor himself—considered the practice unnatural, but so honed was the healers' art in their time that the merchant princes of the Imperial City were known to surpass a thousand years in their lifespans. It was said that a merchant princess died when she chose, regardless of the desires of the goddesses.

But some things were beyond the long reach even of an imperial healer.

Vidarian and Ariadel, half asleep, leapt to their feet as the door to Ruby's chamber opened. Madwen, the senior surgeon, shook her head wearily as she emerged. She walked to them and clasped one of their hands in each of her own, then patted Vidarian on the shoulder.

She sank wearily into the faded velvet divan to the right of the chamber door. Ariadel gave Vidarian's hand a squeeze, then pressed him down into the opposite divan before moving to prepare tea for the three of them.

"I've seen my share of traumatic injuries," the surgeon began, dabbing the faint sheen of sweat on her forehead with her sleeve, "but this is one of the strangest. It's severe, certainly—fatal within minutes had she sustained it at sea. But it should have been well within our arts to repair, here on land."

Ariadel returned with the tea, a dark and bitter brew laced heavily with lemon and honey, and pressed a mug into Marwen's hands, then Vidarian's, before she took her seat beside him. The little shapeshifter, as was its wont lately, perched on her shoulder in its golden spider form. The healers either didn't notice it or were polite enough not to comment.

"But she will survive?" Vidarian passed the hot mug between his hands, soaking in its heat.

"I believe so." Marwen sipped on her tea, then winced and blew across its surface. "I've applied a poultice that will heal her slowly over time, perhaps four months. The injury resists healing energy, and even if it didn't, to heal it all at once using her own energy or mine would cause her body such a shock as to be potentially fatal." Her voice was calm, academic—but as she finished, it lilted slightly upward in an unasked question.

"What is it?" Ariadel asked, lacing her fingers around her mug.

Marwen blew across the tea again in an exasperated sigh. "This energy, what's resisting my efforts," she said, then looked crosswise at Vidarian, "I think it comes from you."

Vidarian coughed, sending searing liquid up his sinuses. It wasn't bad enough, then, that his lack of control had caused Ruby's injury in the first place?

All things and their antithesis, the increasingly present voice in his head whispered.

"I'd like to allow my colleague to examine you, if you'd permit," Marwen said, a faint frown filling a much-traveled crease in her forehead.

"Of course," Vidarian murmured, numb.

Marwen took a long pull on her tea, then dipped her head in an apologetic nod. "I sent word an hour ago, hoping you would agree," she admitted.

They finished their tea in silence, and as Ariadel rose to clear the mugs, a knock on the anteroom door preceded the entrance of a mindcrafter. Marwen and Vidarian rose also now, to greet the visitor. Her face was lined, but faintly, and her black hair sparsely streaked with white, but her irises were the dense indigo of a newborn child's. Although she wore the deep blue robes of the Collegia, they were strategically disheveled, and warm rather than imposing.

"This is Anise, grandmaster mindcrafter," Marwen said, and Anise smiled a gentle greeting. "Her work is known throughout the continent by mindcrafters and healers alike. Anise," she turned between them, "the fire priestess Ariadel, and Captain Vidarian Rulorat—the Tesseract."

Anise clasped their hands warmly, one after the other. "A great pleasure," she said, lingering to look deeply into their eyes. Vidarian had never met a grandmaster of mindcraft before. He wasn't entirely sure what to make of her—what she was seeing, with each of those deep looks, and whether the reassurance that flushed through him when she did so was of his own making or hers.

"Ours also," Vidarian said, to be polite. "We're extremely grateful for Marwen's assistance with Ruby."

"Her injury is grave," Anise said. She turned toward Ruby's room, regarding the door as if she could see through it. Could she? "She sleeps. Her heart aches for you."

"You can read her thoughts from here?" Ariadel asked. Vidarian was somewhat gratified that she seemed to know no more about this level of mindcraft than he.

Anise turned back, smiling gently. "Not her innermost thoughts—only those she sends out to the world. No more than you would know simply by looking into her eyes."

Vidarian wanted to know what *she* saw, then, looking into their eyes—but what he asked was: "And during your examination?"

Her features smoothed into a clinical calm confidence. "It will not take long, and for the purpose Marwen has described, I will not enter your mind itself so much as read the energies coming from it." Ariadel and Vidarian exchanged a look of mutual incomprehension, and she continued, "We have found that wielders of elemental magic relay that energy from their minds, on an ambient level, even when they aren't actively using their ability. As your heart beats, as you breathe, so your elemental ability is pulsing and 'breathing,' and is as much a part of you as your heart or your lungs. I will read this energy only; you would know if I were to go further into your mind."

Vidarian nodded his agreement, and she softly motioned for him to take a seat on the divan.

As Vidarian sat, Anise took a seat beside him, smiling reassurance. She lifted her hands, then paused, and raised her palms to either side of Vidarian's head only when he again nodded his agreement. With her hands spread close to each of his ears, she closed her eyes.

Vidarian felt nothing, but Anise's eyebrows lifted, then came together thoughtfully. She leaned forward ever so slightly, as if searching.

And if she finds what she seeks, what then? he heard, the soft voice insidious and close.

Anise's eyes snapped open immediately, and with a sharpness that left no doubt in Vidarian's mind what had recalled her. Her eyes—intense with the fullness of her skill and power behind them—bore into his, and as he stared back an emptiness quivered in his stomach, as though the force in her eyes were the tip of a glacier far deeper than he could possibly comprehend.

But then she blinked and lowered her hands, drawing back from him. She was quiet for a moment, closing her eyes with her palms on her knees, and neither Ariadel nor Vidarian exhaled until she reopened them and spoke.

"Your mind's energy is, of course, like none seen in my lifetime," Anise said, and the slight hesitation in her tone said that she was reassuring herself of this as much as them. "There is a duality, and between the duality, a gulf great enough to transverse worlds." At this thought her eyes unfocused slightly, but she remastered herself after a moment. "It is this gulf that draws the energy from your friend."

Ariadel gasped softly. "His nature—impedes her healing?" The thought of it closed viselike around his heart.

"Yes and no," Anise said, her voice warm with sympathy. "In its moment, his energy held her. In fact, her life is at this moment bound to his presence, and likely will be until her healing is complete." She let that sink in, and silence fell between them until she filled it again. "The emanations I feel from her match the rhythm of this dualistic balance. To disrupt it now would almost certainly be fatal."

Vidarian breathed deeply. "So . . . she took a blow meant for me, and my mere presence has sealed her injury."

"For good and ill," Marwen said, and Anise nodded. "We have no idea what her fate would have been had she taken the blow alone."

"And when she wakes, your friend will surely tell you she would take the same action again, and wish for the past not to chain your thoughts," Anise said, placing a light hand on Vidarian's shoulder. Her eyes were serious and inscrutable again. "The four goddesses know your mind to be weighed enough already."

Four? the voice laughed.

∿∿∿

As they left the hospital, navigating Val Harlon's narrow cobbled streets on the way to the inn that Endera had arranged for them—the priestess had fallen over herself to accommodate their physical needs in the wake of the *Quest*'s destruction, providing for Ruby's surgery as well as their room and board—Ariadel grew quiet. The closer they came to the inn, the tighter her silence, until Vidarian feared to interrupt it. He searched his memory, wondering what he'd done.

When they reached their room, a sequestered corner chamber with a thick door that closed out any possible listeners, she suddenly dissolved into a baffling sequence of emotion: tears were the simplest part, colored here and there by a laugh (some of which were genuinely mirthful and some which were not), and finally anger that burned away into frustration, and more tears.

He had no idea what to do, and so as it started he took her hand, and was swallowed by confused relief when she turned to sob into his shoulder. Whatever he had done, apparently it wasn't completely unredeemable. The shapeshifter, unsettled by Ariadel's emotion, skittered across her shoulder and onto his. He tried very hard not to shake it off in a shiver of revulsion, but it transformed into its less unsettling kitten shape, hissed once, then leapt off his shoulder to run under the bed.

"Curse you," Ariadel sniffed, just when he was beginning to think he was almost in the clear. She pulled away and moved to sit on the bed, gesturing him to follow. "I never cried so much in my life. I've been through elemental trials you couldn't imagine. I—well, never mind. With you it's every other day."

He settled beside her gingerly, still searching for what brought this on.

Women, the voice whispered. *They're crazy.* Then another of its wild, unsettling giggles. He directed a stream of maliciousness in its direction, which seemed to amuse it, but it dwindled from his consciousness, returning back wherever it went.

"The Tesseract was prophesied to lose the jewel of his heart," she said. "And I thought—"

A dozen things clicked into place. "You thought it meant Ruby," he said softly.

"Well," she sniffed, "before I met her, I thought it was me." She laughed, but tears welled again to her eyes, and he wrapped an arm around her, sailing his own storm of emotion: dominant among it a kind of agony at what she had been putting herself through. "She told me she loved you only as a brother," she said, blinking, "that she had loved a lander in the south for years, an artist, even though it was forbidden by her status."

Vidarian laughed suddenly, bittersweet warmth loosening the pressure on his chest. Ariadel craned her neck to look up at him. "She never told me that," he said. "Poor thing. She never wanted to be Sea Queen, you know."

Ariadel blinked, tears beading on her eyelashes like tiny crystals. Vidarian bent to kiss her forehead.

"She was her mother's only daughter," he said. "When we were children, she wanted to run away from the *Viere* to a farm in the south."

The absurdity of the thought surprised a laugh out of Ariadel, and he smiled. "A *farm?*" she repeated, incredulous. "Ruby?"

"She had a fascination with growing vegetables and animals," he said. "When you live a life on ship, they do seem rather magical." Her childhood laughter flooded his mind in a memory, and his smile turned rueful. "I'm not sure she ever told anyone else about that. We are all called by our destinies."

"That's all very well," she said crossly. "But if Ruby isn't it, things don't look so good for me." Bravery gave her words their sharp lightness, but Vidarian could hear the fear beneath, even while truth swept him like an ocean wind.

"It was the *Quest*," he whispered, dread and grief and certainty seeping through him again at the thought of the ship, now a pile of ash and ruin in the harbor. "My fine lady." The tide that swept him carried despair with it, a kind he had never known in his life. There was no doubt in his mind what the prophesy meant, nor that it was true—as disgusted as he was by the concept of prophesy in general.

Ariadel snorted wetly, but she wrapped her arms around him, holding him tightly for a long moment that said she understood. Vidarian leaned into her strength, just for that moment. "A ship," she whispered back finally, then ran her fingers through his hair before bringing a hand down to gently trace his cheek. "Is that supposed to make me feel better?"

The next morning, Endera hosted them at a breakfast in the city. A sumptuous spread of delicacies prepared by one of the finest chefs in Val Harlon lay between them, but no one moved to touch the food.

"I wish for peace between us," Endera began, when it became clear that no pretense would be tolerated. "And you cannot deny your need for assistance, even now. Would you turn away an ally?"

Vidarian stiffened at the echo of his own words to An'du, wondering, for a scant moment, how far Endera's reach truly was. But there was no knowing sharpness in her eyes; it was coincidence only. "I have allies."

"Incomplete ones, as you well know," Endera replied relentlessly. "I am no weak meddler, Vidarian, to pull your strings, but you must understand your importance. And you must understand what I will do to protect the world that I know."

"Do you truly think you know this world, Endera?"

"Never in its totality. But more than most." At this she reached for an arrangement of artfully sliced fruit, but she only moved it to a plate. She leaned forward slightly. "You have no quarrel with me. I set you on this path, but it unlocked a potential that was not only latent but inevitable in you."

"You destroyed my ship." He kept a tight rein on his temper, but the words threatened to pull fire from his veins.

"You know my sorrow for that is great," Endera said, and Vidarian was surprised by the genuine weariness in her voice. "As well as for Ruby's injury. I know that neither of these are reconcilable. Yet you also know that they were unintended."

"How is it not intent, when you lure me repeatedly into the hands of madwomen?"

"They are what you have always been told," she said, and his blood boiled anew. "Wielders of a new and dangerous form of magic, a hybrid of energies not seen for thousands of years."

"And you thought you could control them."

"Not control," she corrected. "Open channels to. Understand, perhaps. But all this is now quite thoroughly moot. I knew them, once. But the women you killed were none that I knew."

Vidarian could not quite suppress a shiver as his memory of the blonde priestess's death shadowed his mind.

"And speaking of moot," she continued, a sharpness creeping back into her voice. "So too is your pretense for rejecting my offer. I have something you need." She reached into the pouch at her side, and released onto the table two stones identical to the sun emeralds save for their vivid red hue. They glowed even more than the emeralds had, shining like tiny suns beside the silver platters of pastry and fruit.

"Horses," Ariadel said, and Vidarian looked up in surprise. "The priesesshood has them, and it's the least you can do to ease our journey."

Endera bridled at Ariadel's tone, but she only stared at her younger colleague for a long moment; sensing, Vidarian knew, as he did, the completeness of the bridge burned between them, and Ariadel's still raw sense of betrayal. "Horses," she agreed. "Two."

"Three," Ariadel corrected. "Mountain breeds. And three verali. All awaiting us at the Invesh Pass."

"For peace," Endera said, extending her hand across the table. "And what advice—I will not say guidance—the fire priesesshood may provide you."

Vidarian watched her for a long moment, then turned to Ariadel, who inclined her head. He took Endera's hand, and she exhaled as they touched, a vulnerable relief in her eyes. In that moment she seemed aged far beyond her already long years. When she released her grip, she set his hand down atop the sun rubies, which flared with warmth to his touch.

The thrum in the pouch at his side was the response of the storm sapphires, and his mental grip tightened around them. They subsided only after several moments of resistance.

"Do you know, Vidarian, which path you will take, at the gate?" Endera asked. The look Ariadel gave her at these words was another blend of anger and surprise.

"With respect, and peace," Vidarian said carefully, looking up from the stones only when he was sure of his control over them, "I can't take your advice on that any longer. My counsel is my own."

CHAPTER TWENTY-THREE

THE GRASP OF CHAOS

O n their fifth day in Val Harlon, Vidarian and Ariadel woke in good spirits. Ruby was at last showing signs of mending, and of a return to her old self. Being in one place for more than two days straight had settled Vidarian's mind, which over the last several weeks had grown nervous and brittle. Anise, whether summoned by Marwen or her own intuition, visited him often at Ruby's bedside. The mind, she said, could not be healed as could the flesh, but it could be shaped in one direction or another.

They stepped into the morning sunlight under a clear sky that gave credence to their enlivened spirits. Ariadel insisted that they detour through the west end market before making their way to the hospital—Ruby should be feeling well enough for a more substantial breakfast than the nutritious but flavorless fare insisted upon by the healers.

Val Harlon's famous west end market was a riot of colors, sounds, and aromas. Fruit vendors plied passersby with sliced delicacies in an impossible array of colors, while bakers and tenders of traveling carts of meat pies needed to rely only on the wafting rich scents of freshly baked bread and savory sauces that drew custom straight to them.

One particularly busy purveyor of mushroom and venison pastries tempted them, but they resisted, gathering up a modest basket of cinnamon buns, white melon, royal tangerines, and fresh *kava* sealed hot in a porcelain jar. Vidarian, who had sampled *kava* from the far southern continent alongside the strange *kava*-strength teas of the Qui Empire, had to admit that Val Harlon's distinct variety of the peppery and potent *kava* bark was among the best in the world, smooth and palatable to even the most finicky of connoisseurs.

While they were haggling over a tiny burlap sack of cinnamon sugar, an ornate carriage pulled by a huge black gelding rattled over the cobbles along-side them. The horse caught Vidarian's attention first: he was huge, and had a faint iridescence to his coat and a canniness of eye that brought to mind the winged steeds of the Alorean Sky Knights, protectors of the emperor. Surely no mere merchant, however wealthy, could boast an animal descended from that rare and coveted lineage, but the likeness was striking.

An elaborately coiffed head appeared from the window of the carriage, and as soon as Ariadel had handed over a pair of coins for the sugar, a slim white hand followed it and beckoned them closer. "Sir, madam, if I may a moment?"

Vidarian and Ariadel approached the carriage cautiously. Carts and wheelbarrows flowed around it, their operators grumbling under their breath but none daring to challenge the vehicle that blocked their way. Val Harloners were rarely so given to politeness, and it prickled the back of Vidarian's neck to see it.

The woman inside the carriage, her grey eyes hawk-sharp, was dressed to match both carriage and coiffure, in expensive black brocade with silver piping. Her precise smile conveyed her relief at speaking equal-to-equal in the market's morass of banality. "Lord Tesseract," she began, and was on to the next before Vidarian could correct her, "I am Oneira Ehrenfar. I represent the Fourth Mercantile, and speak also on behalf of the greater Alorean Greater Import Company. The senior partner in Val Harlon wishes to extend an invitation to you both," she nodded to Ariadel, and Vidarian didn't like the superior way she assumed Vidarian's prominence between the two of them.

Fourth Mercantile. Alorean Greater Imports. Vidarian flexed his diplomatic muscles, attempting to hide his distaste. "Certainly the desires of such a friend to the empire are of great interest to us," he said, pitching his tone carefully flat to convey his own superiority, even as he hated doing so, "and we would be glad to arrange a meeting at the partner's convenient time."

"Now, actually, is quite his convenience." Her eyes lost no sharpness, making no concession for the abruptness of the request—which should have been embarrassing. Dangerous territory.

Vidarian worked again to stifle his irritation. "We are just now en route to visit a good friend in hospital. Surely the Company's business is not so desperately urgent?"

"All business is urgent," Oneira replied, "the Company's more so, for those who make real decisions, as I'm sure you understand, Lord Tesseract. Your friend, 'Queen' Roana," her mild disgust at Ruby's title danced a careful edge of offense, "surely requires her rest. I can arrange to deliver your gifts, and perhaps you could call on her this afternoon, after our conversation? The senior partner is a busy man."

Even without his ship—as the Company surely knew—Vidarian had too many friends and allies at the mercy of the Company's controls over ports and harbors to risk their ire unnecessarily.

"We will be glad to take you up on your kind offer, then." He sighed.

"Excellent," Oneira said, and rapped on the roof of the carriage. When a footman scrambled down the polished brass ladder at the aft side of the vehicle, she waved him to take the basket from Vidarian and gave instructions on where to take it, including the building and room where Ruby was housed, without prompting. She smiled, looking down into the basket, adding, "and do pick up a few delicacies on our behalf. Salted morels, marmalade, and olive tapenade from Bertram's." Vidarian calculated as the footman bowed and took his leave; the quality and price of the additions were both a show of power (as well a reprimand of Vidarian's taste in gifts, if he wanted one) and a bribe. He fumed behind the bared teeth of a gracious smile, and they mounted up at her invitation into the carriage.

The inside of the carriage was as ornate as its exterior, gleaming with oiled leather and polished brass. Another rap on the roof from their erstwhile hostess, and they were on their way. Being beholden to wheels, their conveyance was no smooth sail, but some mechanism involving oiled springs made it the gentlest carriage ride Vidarian had ever experienced.

He was unsurprised when they turned toward Val Harlon's wealthiest Point Ista district, but he did lift an eyebrow when they turned up a long drive flanked by mounted guards. Three more checkpoints were between them and their destination, as it turned out; any escape would be with their host's cooperation, it would seem.

They stepped down from the carriage onto tightly fitted paving stones that marked a circle around exquisitely manicured gardens of perfectly clipped green and blue grass. The manor itself was, for its splendor, certainly over a century old, of the antique colonnaded type, but upgraded with modern brass lanterns and window-fittings. When they were shown into the foyer, Vidarian took a deep breath, expecting a long wait, but their abductor led them directly up an imposing grand staircase of white marble.

At the end of a long carpeted hallway at the top of the stairs was a heavily carved pair of mahogany doors attended by precisely uniformed guards in red wool and glittering brass buttons. The polish hid a functional edge—a familiar wear on chain-wrapped sword hilts, coats cut for movement as well as aesthetic, precise-fit vambraces. The guards recognized Oneira and opened the door for her immediately; Vidarian moved her status upward in his loose estimate.

The senior partner sat behind a massive desk flanked by ceiling-high windows and velvet curtains all intended to cast both light and awe upon whomever entered through the mahogany doors. Bright eastern sunlight cast the partner as a silhouette, but as their eyes adjusted, he revealed himself to be eerily identical to the few other Alorean Import partners Vidarian had ever met. Cosmetic differences aside—he had black hair and blue eyes, unlike the others—all of the so-called merchant princes of the Company had the same uncanny features, flawless and vibrant youth with none of its innocence, purchased duly from those healers who cared more for coin than mending. There was no telling how old this particular company man was, though to achieve the rank of senior partner his years numbered almost certainly over three hundred.

And whatever their status, they didn't rate the partner standing up to greet them. Oneira waved them to a pair of brocade-cushioned chairs worked with gold leaf where they weren't covered with imported silk. And possibly, Vidarian thought sourly, beneath where they were. He walked Ariadel to her seat and bowed over her hand when she was seated, brushing his lips across her fingers with just enough impropriety to tease a disapproving frown out of their host. Be damned if he wasn't going to get some satisfaction out of this.

"So," he said as he took his seat. "What can we do for you, partner . . . ?"

"Senior Partner Justinian Veritas, overseer of the Fourth Mercantile and the Greater Alorean Import Company's voice in Val Harlon," Oneira said, standing at the man's shoulder.

Justinian smiled thinly. "We thank you for making it here on such short notice. Oneira is my second, and the future representative of the Company here in Val Harlon."

"You know that will never happen," Ariadel addressed their escort for the first time, and she stiffened ever so slightly. "They need you here because of the power of the priestesshoods, but any partner naming a woman as his heir would be committing political suicide. And none of the partners are especially interested in dying."

"As I'm sure you understand, Mr. Rulorat," Justinian said, addressing Vidarian as if Ariadel had not spoken, certainly knowing how it caused Vidarian's hands to clench at his sides, "our dealings can be pleasant or unpleasant, and I will ultimately leave the choice between up to you." Justinian folded his hands together and rested his elbows on the desk. His gaze was sharp with intelligence but carefully casual. "To be quite honest, I think the Company's interest in you is ill considered at best. But if you truly know our ways as well as you'd have my junior colleague believe, you also know that my orders come from the top. I'd just as soon avoid any unpleasantness."

"'Unpleasantness' would be an interesting way of describing your company's control over ports my family has needed to survive for over a century," Vidarian said.

Justinian gave a small wave of his hand, somewhere between a concession and a dismissal. "We are a force across the five seas, this is true, and the responsibilities that come with such power are significant."

"What I meant to say was," Vidarian consciously unclenched his hands and folded them on his lap, "I really don't have any interest in working or cooperating with you."

"All business," Justinian said softly, "is in knowing the interests of your partners," his eyes lifted, piercing blue with the light coming through the window behind him, "and of your competitors."

"What you call 'competitors' we call 'enemies,'" Vidarian said, meeting the partner's stare unflinchingly.

Justinian looked down first, but only to nudge a packet of paper across the desk with a slim fingertip. "I understand full well that you have no natural inclination toward us, but I also understand you to be a rational man. A businessman."

Vidarian reached across the desk and slid the paper packet toward himself, catching it with his other hand as it slid off the desk entirely. He opened it, but kept his eyes on Justinian, lowering them to the papers only when he could read them at a downward glance. But as his eyes passed over the words it became harder to keep his head up—and clear. As anger—and, he would admit only under duress, a bit of fear—thrilled in his veins, the storm sapphires in his waist pouch rumbled a response. He closed his eyes for a moment, willing them and himself to stillness. When he opened them, he said, "You don't have the authority to do this."

"Oh, we do," Justinian said, with an almost-boredom that set Vidarian's veins to bubbling again. "You've been in the west too long, Lord Tesseract. The Company is now quite strong with the emperor, and with the imperial city. You realize, then, why I don't find your cooperation a particularly challenging objective."

He passed the packet to Ariadel numbly. The company, for whatever reasons known only to them, wanted to hole him up in the imperial city, far away from the sea or the gate. The princely commission for his "service" in the city would have intrigued him six months ago, but only irritated him now. And the dispatches, which by all accounts looked absolutely real, also commissioned the imperial army in enforcing his compliance if necessary. "Why bother warning me?" he asked, finally.

"As I told you," Justinian said, "I find this all rather unnecessary and poorly thought-out. What I do object to is any besmirching of the Company's name from your however-fruitless resistance." He tilted his head, squinting at Vidarian. "You *do* intend to resist, do you not?"

"I don't intend to cooperate with you or anyone else merely for the sake of doing so."

He sighed theatrically. "And I suppose you also can't be bought."

"Not by you."

"How unpleasant," Justinian said, and took a carved geode from atop a stack of documents. He rapped hard on the desk, which echoed hollowly. One of the guards from outside opened the door. "Andrews. Please escort our guests back to the city. We've fulfilled the requests of the partners."

∫∿∿

The beds at the inn were now familiar, from plush mattress and featherbed to the lavender oil that scented their sheets, and as Vidarian sank into theirs, it was the first genuine moment of comfort he'd had since that morning. The candle beside the bed flickered out—Ariadel's doing, and not by hand, something he was only beginning to become accustomed to—and she, as usual, was asleep in moments, leaving him to stare up into the darkness.

The curtains over the room's large window hadn't been closed. He thought about getting up to draw them shut, but as he moved his arm with the thought, Ariadel shifted in her sleep, murmuring. Settling his arm again, he shifted gingerly, then shut his eyes, reaching for sleep.

It was to no avail. The light of the stars winking through the far window should have been negligible, but it seemed to cut right through his eyelids. Aimless thoughts tumbled in his brain, worries half coherent and half not, until finally he opened his eyes again, if only to banish them. The window and its light were still there, insistent.

Gradually, his eyes blurred, and the stars blurred with them. They drew together and began to spiral gently. He blinked, then rubbed his eyes, but the pattern persisted. Slowly, but steadily, the swirl drew itself into the shape of a woman, reclining in midair, clothed in tendrils of darkness that covered not nearly enough of her light-drawn skin. He flushed, and shook his head, but to no avail.

"Go away," he said finally, glancing at Ariadel out of fear of waking her. She didn't stir.

The figure drew closer, still lying in midair. When she spoke, it was a soft voice echoing across a great distance. He fought down the flare of recognition that lit in his soul when he saw her. This was the creature that had lived in his mind for so long, it seemed, now made manifest at last. "Where do you think you are?" she asked, floating sedately. She did a lazy barrel roll in the air, her hair fanning out in a graceful arc as though it were underwater.

Vidarian blinked. "I'm sleeping," he said. For a split second his vision doubled dizzyingly, and he saw two realities: himself, sitting up in bed, facing the floating woman; and himself, one arm looped around Ariadel, sleeping soundly.

"Correctamundo," she said, rolling again until her feet were pointed toward the ground, then twisting lightly back into a standing position.

"What are you?" he asked, and she laughed, as some part of him knew she would.

Her face—just her face, leaving neck and all below in place—turned upside down.

"What do you think I am?" she asked, in his voice. Hearing his own voice echoed back to him, in addition to sending a chill through his body, made him realize he'd asked his question the same way—as a statement.

"You're the goddess of chaos."

"*Chaos*," she flared, her head spinning back upright as she advanced on the bed, eyes inhumanly large and filled with livid white light. It was a whiteness of absence, a whiteness of between-being, a whiteness of nonexistence. Her fingers spidered over the footboard, fingertips hooked into gleaming claws. "That's what they call it," she said softly. "I bring them balance, and they call me *chaos*. Chaos goddess, *star hunter*." The name rang recognition again through his very core.

"They call you retribution," he said, fixing his eyes on her, much though his brain willed him to look away.

"Rich men call me retribution," she agreed. "Poor men call me justice." Straightening, she raised her arms in front of her, hands balled into fists, halos of empty white light fluorescing around her body. Her voice dropped into an eerie, inhuman hollowness. "And what is retribution, but a return? All things," the voice dwindled to a soft hiss, "and their antithesis." She lifted off her feet again, the light dwindling around her, and floated toward the bed. Her right eye flashed red while her left burned blue. "At the heart of all things living is a wildness, a chaos, a not-being. I am the sea and I am the fire, and we are what's in between. And you, dear Vidarian, will set me free."

Fear and stubbornness gripped him in iron fists that pulled apart from his center. "You don't know what I'll do."

"Don't I?" She leaned close, whispering as if imparting a secret. "I'm a goddess." The word carried power, like the language of the gryphons; it was more than merely what met his ears.

He held firm. "I've met goddesses."

"But not," she whispered again, sidling close, her scent like lightning, "like me." She pushed herself away from him, floating toward the window. "I can do bad things to you, Vidarian. *Bad things.* You should do what I want."

"I'm not afraid of you." Strangely, he was fairly certain it was true. What more was there left to be afraid of? Should he fear her? The empire? The Alorean Import Company?

She looked down at the bed, into the reality where Ariadel slept beside him, and smiled.

A snarl leapt into his throat, a threat onto the tip of his lips. But she blew into his face, a cold wind that sucked the breath from his chest.

"See you later, alligator."

CHAPTER TWENTY-FOUR

INVAEL

H
ands on his shoulders threw him into gasping wakefulness. Instinctively he rolled out of their grasp, blocking Ariadel's body with his own.

"*Vidarian*," Endera whispered sharply, and he swam out of sleep and into his senses. Ariadel moved underneath him, squawking groggily, and he twisted, sitting up and facing Endera.

Her shadowed form gradually resolved from the silhouette of the Starhunter supplied by his sleep-addled brain and into the weary and worried golden eyes of the fire priestess. "I apologize for waking you," she said, in a tone that was certainly no apology, "but you must leave the city immediately."

Ariadel had awakened quietly and now sat up in bed, frowning at Endera, but there was fear and respect in her eyes. She had not, and perhaps would never, recovered from the personal betrayal of her mentor's manipulation, but she knew, as Vidarian did, a survival order when she heard one. "The Company," she said only.

Endera nodded. "I don't know what you told them," she addressed Vidarian sternly, "but the guard is moving as we speak."

"We have to get to Ruby," Vidarian said.

"Out of the question," Endera replied.

"She'll die," Ariadel said, an entreaty and a warning in her voice.

Endera looked at them for two long moments. "Fine," she said. "But hurry, both of you."

They hadn't much in the way of possessions to begin with; Vidarian had purchased a new pair of boots more suited to their current land travel, but the rest of all his worldly holdings had burned with the *Quest*. In moments they were dressed, packed, and descending the inn's outer stairs into the cold night and the black carriage that awaited on the cobbles.

"Thalnarra, Altair, and Arikaree are waiting at the north field," Endera said, as the carriage rattled toward the west hospital. Ariadel shivered, and as Vidarian moved to wrap an arm around her for warmth, Endera pulled a thick black verali fleece–lined wool cloak from a satchel at her side and handed it across to Ariadel. She produced another for Vidarian. "For the altitudes," she said, and Ariadel reluctantly accepted the gift. Vidarian did the same. "There will be more supplies for you at the waystation on the southern border." Her voice was strained, and Vidarian knew it to be with the pain of being so distrusted by Ariadel. Vidarian's distrust she no doubt took in stride, but some part of her conscience still railed, it would seem.

They tossed the cloaks across their shoulders as they stepped down onto the street outside the hospital. At the door were two cloaked fire apprentices who stood ready with baskets of supplies. They climbed aboard the carriage, clinging to the outside rails like footmen, as Viadarian and Ariadel rushed inside.

Ruby was awake and waiting for them.

"You have to take me to my ship, Vidarian," she said, imperious even while half healed. "I can't die on land. You know that."

Vidarian walked straight to her, slid one arm under her legs and the other behind her shoulders, and lifted. He spoke while carefully maneuvering her out the door that Ariadel held open. "We can't go to your ship, Ruby. I'm sorry. And you're not going to die."

Ruby twitched in his arms, but wasn't strong enough to seize her own fate. "Please, Vidarian," she said, turning her face toward him. Her face was hollow with the trauma of her healing, her eyes and cheeks sunken, if not deeply. Her entreaty, so far from the imperious Sea Queen who had commanded them mere weeks ago, tore at his heart. "You know you'd be out to sea if you had a choice," she whispered fiercely.

"I'm sorry," he said again, heartsick but willing courage into his steps as he carried her out to the carriage.

Once again the vehicle was clattering through the night, and Endera took them out to the open field behind the north dock, where they had landed so long ago. Ruby took one look at the flying craft—a proper one, this time, and no makeshift pram—and started thrashing again.

"I'm not riding in that thing," she declared, a bit of her old fire back, even if it was out of panic.

"You are," Vidarian murmured, watching the apprentices leap adroitly down from the carriage to load their supplies. When they finished, Vidarian took a step toward the craft, causing Ruby to struggle again. He almost lost his grip on her, and staggered. When he regained his balance, he shook her just hard enough to get her attention. Or, it was supposed to be. She ignored him and continued to thrash. Vidarian reached out with his water Sense and *pushed* at her, again gently, and this time she grew still as soon as the ripple passed over her.

"I don't like gryphons," she said quietly, though her eyes went to the tufted ears that flickered toward them at her words. Her face only hardened. It was an odd statement from someone with a gryphon's face entirely covering her right shoulder, unless you knew Sea Kingdom rites. Vidarian had never asked her where the gryphon had come from; usually the tattoos were symbolic, but the white gryphon on her shoulder was much too lifelike.

"They're hardly all the same," was all he could think to say, though even as he did so he realized he knew only five of them at all well.

Ruby didn't struggle again, but said only, "You'll wish we'd sailed." Then she closed her eyes.

Vidarian lifted her up and over the rim of the craft, handing her gently into the waiting arms of the two apprentices who had loaded the supplies. They worked silently and efficiently, settling her into a padded and blanket-covered gurney directly on the deck.

As soon as they finished, the apprentices hopped lightly out, making way. Vidarian held out a hand to Ariadel and helped her up the portable wooden stepladder, then over the rim and into the craft. He lost no time in following her, and even as he was throwing a leg over the edge, the apprentices were moving to clear the stepladder away in preparation for takeoff.

Endera approached the basket, pausing only when one of the gryphons threw out a wing, stretching, to block her path. None of the three acknowledged her presence. "Your horses and supplies await at the Invesh Pass, as requested." She rested a hard stare on Ariadel for a moment. When she found no response there, she turned to Vidarian and started to say something, then shook her head. "Safe travels," she said only, and stepped back, leaving plenty of room for outstretched wings.

In addition to being larger, this craft boasted padded leather seats and an admirable use of space reminiscent of a well-kept ship. A simple galley set into the pointed aft held all of their food supplies and a tiny cast iron cookstove mounted on sea-swing-like gimbals. Benches of polished wood and leather cushions with woven silk safety harnesses provided seating for nine, though Vidarian wondered how three gryphons could carry so many. A clear area just behind the bow provided enough space for Ruby's nest, while cabinets set to port and starboard carried a familiar array of navigational equipment, as well as a few additional tools Vidarian guessed were associated with altitude measurement. He wondered, briefly, how so much development could have been done for these crafts—enough of it was all too familiar, but much had been custom created specifically for flight. There were stories . . . Once again he was forced to assess sea stories and mythology, wondering what was exaggeration or fairy tale, and what was lost knowledge—but then they were lifting into the sky.

As the gryphons exchanged a series of chirps and calls that Vidarian had come to realize were some kind of takeoff preparation signals, he noticed that his safety harness had an expansion belt. If he moved these two clips—yes—it seemed to be designed to allow a rider to stand up from one of the benches. As he adjusted the harness, then stood and took hold of a brass handgrip mounted in the side of the craft seemingly for this purpose, Ariadel reached out in alarm.

"Vidarian—" she said.

// It's quite safe, // Altair murmured, his voice like fresh-broken mint leaves in their minds. The craft lurched gently as the gryphons broke into a lope, headed for the cliff, but Altair's tone was conversational. // This is one of the safest crafts in the air fleets—from the days of the skyships. A treasure lent our cause by my people. // Just as he finished speaking, the three gryphons threw out their wings in perfect synch—and leapt out over the cliff. Vidarian's contemplation of Altair's casual reference to "skyships" was swallowed by the sudden view of the glittering sea hundreds of feet below them.

The craft itself dropped, pulling a startled shout from Vidarian and Ariadel both, and suddenly they were seeing the undersides of the three gryphons—the chains and braided silk bindings that held the craft to the gryphons' harnesses played out on pulleys, pulled by gravity.

// A more efficient suspension system, // Altair explained, apology coloring his words. // I should have warned you. The longer bindings allow us to maneuver with much greater agility than other styles of flying craft. // Even as his heart hammered, Vidarian could see that this was true—the three gryphons now each had a much greater range of motion for their wings and bodies.

The gryphons climbed, their wings stroking strong and even. Wisps of cloud tore past their wings, beaks, and the sides of the craft—Vidarian reached out once to touch one, marveling as it broke across his fingers like steam from a teapot, leaving cold moisture in its wake.

As they broke above the last layer of harbor mist, the night sky opened huge over their heads, studded with stars. On the eastern horizon behind them, the sun now crept skyward, staining the distant land—flat farm fields precise with rows of crops—with brilliant orange and gold, a pool of liquid fire. Directly below, the lights of Val Harlon flickered against the still dark hours of morning, glimmering through breaks in the clouds.

When he wasn't in fear for his life, Vidarian observed, flying like this was actually rather beautiful. He and Ariadel exchanged a shared smile of wonder; she hadn't stood, but leaned out over the edge of the craft from her seat. Ruby, however, had not moved.

"Ruby, we're—" he began.

"Don't tell me," she said, her eyes shut and mouth creased in a frown. "I don't want to know."

"Suit yourself," he said, and returned his eyes to the remarkable panorama of city and coast below. Seemingly tiny waves crashed against the rocks south of the city, and the sea, which melted into darkness to the west, arced gently below them as the gryphons marked out a gradual curve in the sky, turning south. "Thalnarra," he called, looking up and to port where she flew. One red eye tilted down at him for a moment, an ear swiveling in inqiry. "Does this craft have a name?"

Mirth lent a cinnamon spice to her thoughts. // *I thought you would have seen the markings on the bow. She's called* Destiny. //

"Of course she is," he said, and sat back down.

~~~

For five days they watched the sky in all directions for signs of pursuit. Logically speaking, it would take any Sky Knights—even assuming the Company's claims of such an alliance were legitimate—more than a week of fast flying to reach Val Harlon even from the closest outpost. But after so many surprises they weren't willing to leave anything to chance.

// *Arikaree has great mind-strength,* // Thalnarra assured them. The gryphon could reach out with his mind for leagues in either direction, detecting the presence, if not the precision, of any thoughts near them.

// *Hurr,* // the pelican-gryphon agreed. // *None be following us, yet.* // Even still, Vidarian couldn't help scanning the skies with the brass sighting glass every few hours.

Two days into the journey, Ruby roused enough to sit up and look out at the afternoon sky. Her healing was clearly progressing—she complained with greater fervor every day as she downed the bitter draughts prescribed by the healers—but her expression as she gazed out at the sky was bleak. One night, after they'd made camp, Arikaree walked up to her as she stared out at the western sea.

They stood looking at each other for a long time—the gryphon's eyes pinned and his head tilted at intervals, and Ruby's expression changed every few moments. It took Vidarian several moments of surreptitious observation before he realized that they must be speaking to each other—and that apparently Ruby knew how to speak mind-to-mind with a gryphon without also speaking out loud. More mysteries—but as Ruby's attitude lightened considerably after that night, he didn't pursue them.

On the fourth day, the great southern Windsmouth Mountains rose up before them, and on the fifth day, they dominated the horizon. The weather turned, also, and they huddled under the fleece and wool cloaks Endera had provided as the twisting arm of a miniature blizzard washed snow across the craft. Altair, at the front flight position, deflected the worst of the stinging snow away from them, but this did little to warm the air. When they began to descend, gliding toward the glowing tower that marked the watchpost at the Invesh Pass, it was with relief.

The rugged guards at the watchpost had less welcome news, however. Their supplies were present as promised—three fine horses and twice as many verali, three to carry the gryphon's flying craft and three to bear their gear—but rather than providing shelter for the night, the guards suggested—strongly—that they ride immediately through the pass.

At the far side of the pass, they were told, was another traveler, and even with the gryphons' protection augmenting their own abilities, another set of eyes and hands would be most welcome. Especially if, as the Invesh guards claimed, the traveler had been this way more than once before.

// *And a storm is coming,* // Altair said, lifting his beak to the air and testing it with his tongue. The guards agreed, and after a warm meal of mutton stew, sent them on their way.

The gryphons, for their part, were as at home on the ground as in the air, though they clearly preferred the loftier vantages of the heights, and a slight tenseness in their bodies hinted at their increased alertness. Each bore a ball of light—deep red for Thalnarra's, blue-white for Altair's, glowing green for Arikaree's—that led them through the deepening dark and the shadow of the mountains. Ruby took to her saddle bravely, but was exhausted by the end of their short ride through the pass; relief shone clear on her face as they emerged from the towering mountain walls.

On this side of the pass was a break in the mountains, and a dark clearing. The guards had established an unmanned waypoint for travelers, and here, as promised, was the sleeping figure of the man who traveled the pass also. A line of verali and one horse stood sleeping at a rough hitching post at the camp's edge. The man's fire, banked, glowed softly and illuminated his shadowed form, and they moved quietly, though in exhaustion, to make a cold camp. The gryphons dug shallow sleeping pits in a loose triangle around the humans, and, after picketing and watering the verali and horses, they slept.

〜〜〜

Dawn at the pass came slowly, with pale light inching over the eastern mountains to brighten the thin and ever-present fog. Even at this low altitude the wash of meager daylight made the world seem dim and half asleep.

The intoxicating smell of brewing *kava*, rather than the advancing light, pulled them from their bedrolls.

Kneeling near the fire and tending the *kava* pot was the stranger who had been sleeping when they'd arrived at the waypoint. By day, his string of verali proved to be weighed down with sacks of—if their stamped labels were to be believed—*kava*, imported from across the entire continent.

He looked up when they rose blearily from their blankets and waved them closer. *Kava* alone hadn't stirred Vidarian from sleep in years, but by its strange and complex aroma, this was no ordinary brew.

"A personal favorite," the man said, rising from the fire and nudging a small woven sack with a proprietary toe. His voice, eyes, and hair were dark like the *kava*, thick with some accent Vidarian couldn't quite place. He extended his hand, and Vidarian clasped it. "Luc Medicka, *kava* collector."

"Vidarian Rulorat," he introduced himself, and held a hand out to Ariadel, "and Priestess Ariadel Windhammer." Luc took her hand and bowed over it, a brief motion that spoke of foreign custom rather than flirtation. Nonetheless, the slightest heat edged Vidarian's voice. "Collector? You're traveling a long way with that collection."

The man followed Vidarian's gesture with his eyes, and waved his hands dismissively at the loaded verali. "A modest shipment. My clients pay handsomely for these strains of *kava* on the southern continent. To be honest, their tastes are rather ordinary."

"The southern continent?" Ariadel repeated, skeptical. "The mountains have closed passage for nearly a century."

"For caravans, yes," Luc agreed. "If you know the way, there are cave systems that still connect to the continent."

// *Quite dangerous ones,* // Thalnarra rumbled, and Luc turned to her in surprise. If he'd never seen a gryphon before, he didn't show it; his eyebrows arched higher for just a moment, but soon he was bowing in greeting.

"This is Thalnarra," Vidarian said. "The others are Altair and Arikaree."

"Northern gryphons," Luc said, and Thalnarra's tufted ears flicked forward in surprise. "I've met your kin, though rarely, on the southern continent—if they can be said to be kin."

// *They are,* // Altair agreed, approaching and giving Luc a nod of his beak, a strange gesture that the man again took in stride. // *If distant ones. A forest people.* //

"Brilliant colors, their feathers, like you wouldn't believe," Luc said, then gave a dip of his head in apology. "Not that yours aren't, of course."

// *Of course,* // Altair said dryly.

Luc turned to Vidarian, and at first it seemed to be in an attempt to change the subject. "You radiate, if it is not rude to say, sir, a most peculiar energy."

All three gryphon heads swiveled toward the man at this, and Ariadel smiled curiously. "You're quite perceptive," she said, her tone lifting upward in a question.

Luc bowed again, a habit it would seem, then bent to pour *kava* for the three of them—as he was pouring, Ruby approached sleepily, and they exchanged introductions. Quick, soft gestures of his hands inquired as to their tastes for sugar and verali cream; Vidarian and Ariadel took both, while Luc and Ruby kept theirs black. Luc gave Ruby a proprietary smile of approval at this.

When they sat around the fire with their cups, Luc spoke again. "There is a word in Ishmanti: *invael.* It means truth's antithesis. The opposite of truth. Not a falsehood, which is a sliding-aside of truth, a dodging of truth with truth at its core, but a direct negation of the very fundamental nature of truth itself, the heart of truth. The antitruth that devours true things, that spreads into the world and undoes what truth we forge."

"Like the Starhunter." Thalnarra's hackles raised as Vidarian said this, and Ariadel turned to him in puzzlement, but Luc was unfazed.

"Yes, the Starhunter is *invael*. But she is also truth. She is truth and its antithesis. She is the differentiator." He turned toward Vidarian. "She is choice." He took a long draw on his *kava*, pausing as if in meditation as he savored it. "And that, sir, is what emanates from you."

CHAPTER TWENTY-FIVE

ALL RETURNS
TO LIQUID

"Y ou'll find all manner of strange characters in these mountains," Luc said, as their horses picked their way over a particularly intricate length of trail. The beasts were smart, thank Nistra—Endera must have known they would need to be for this territory. Vidarian's horse, according to the labeling on his gear, was called Feluhim, another Ishmanti word that he didn't know, but Luc, being from that sun-blasted place, did: it meant loyal son, but most often was used for horses, strangely. "We're on the fringe of civilized places. My father used to say, if a man lives where no others will, there's a reason why, in the man and the place."

After the waypoint, they had moved again into the mountains, where they gauged the passage of time more by the phases of their hunger than by the light, which was fickle and pale. Steep walls rose to either side of them, and twice they had to detour around rockslides, adding hours to their days. The gryphons made ready use of their claws and talons in scaling rocks and boulders, but the horses needed clearer trails lest they risk slips and broken legs. High overhead, the perpetual storm that hung over the Windsmouth was their constant companion, now and then casting down a thick blanket of snow that further obscured the ground. The everstorm, as it was called by the Invesh guards, was what kept the gryphons from bearing them south by air—it was massive, beyond Altair's ability to tame, and extended so far to the north and south that any gryphon that had ever attempted to fly over it had never been seen again. All this the gryphons did not admit easily, and the storm was one of the few things Vidarian had ever seen the creatures universally respect.

And so they picked their way through the mountains by foot, holing up in caves when the storm grew fiercest. On their fifth morning in the mountains, they reached a split in the trail. One path descended—according to their maps, it traced a route to the southeast by way of descending altitudes. The other path led higher into the mountains.

"And here we part," Luc said, "for your path is stranger than mine." He smiled jauntily at this. They had not disclosed their final destination, nor their intent, but he'd seemed to divine something of both without being told. "Your journey leads up," he said, and pointed to the trail that wound up the mountain. "There is a waypoint, the last known to the empire, at the top. I believe it's kept by water priestesses," he nodded to Arikaree, who returned the gesture with some diffident surprise. "There ends my knowledge." He clasped each of their elbows in turn, the parting gesture of the Ishmanti—Vidarian knew it from etiquette books, but had never experienced it. "I hope that we meet again. I'd like to know what lies beyond that mountain."

"We hope to tell you," Vidarian said.

"If you ever find yourself in the west sea, ask for me," Ruby said, as she clasped Luc's elbow—clearly comfortable with the gesture in a way that obliquely irked (but didn't surprise) Vidarian. "I don't know how we'll get by without your brew every morning." Now that she was on solid ground, Ruby seemed to be recovering more every day, though the presence of the poultice at her side kept them from forgetting her injury.

"I'd be honored to trade with the famous fleets of the West Sea Queen!" Luc exulted, and Ruby colored with satisfaction. The two had taken to rising earlier than the rest of the party, and Luc seemed to take particular pleasure in introducing Ruby to the various blends he kept with him, including those housed in vials Vidarian knew he didn't share with the rest of them. A developed palate, he claimed, was needed to appreciate them. He removed one of these from his wide-sleeved multicolored coat and presented it to Ruby with both hands. "You must take this as a token of my goodwill for our future business," he said.

Ruby accepted the glass with reverence, turning it over in her hands and watching the flakes of bark rotate within. "No, you mustn't," she demurred, then squinted more closely at the vial. Her breath quickened ever so slightly. "Is this—?"

Luc winked, then stepped back and gave a sweeping bow to the three of them. "Farewell, friends," he said, then turned to mount his horse, a rugged roan that had fared better in the mountains than the taller horses Endera had provided. It seemed to eat anything, including the daily mouthful of *kava* bark fed it by its master. Luc clicked his tongue at the string of verali that bore his goods, and started down the long trail.

They ascended the mountain slowly, stopping frequently to water the horses. The air grew thin as it had when the gryphons had flown high over Cheropolis; Vidarian had never climbed a mountain so high.

By midday, another of the mountains' heavy weather patterns began to move in, an arm reaching down from the everstorm. A familiar chill settled wetly into the air, and by late afternoon snow was falling in earnest, thick clumps of it that piled on their shoulders and quickly began to accumulate on the trail.

A thin light high above them at first seemed a mirage, but proved otherwise as they drew closer to it. The storm thickened and thinned by turns, obscuring the light, but as they reached a plateau on the trail they suddenly found themselves faced with a tower of stacked slate. A glittering limestone monument was thickly engraved with the emblem of the northern water priestesses.

"What is a water priestess doing so far from sea or river?" Ariadel asked, shaking snow from her hood.

// *We are being surrounded by water,* // Arikaree pointed out, snapping at a particularly large clump of snow as it spiraled toward the ground in front of him. // *Water is having many domains, and each be holding a secret of elements.* //

// *This branch of the everstorm is perpetual,* // Altair added. // *It is a peculiarity of the Windsmouth. A relic, some say, of the long magic days.* //

"PrimeAdepts," Vidarian said, and Altair made a soft clicking noise in his throat, a gryphonic note of assent.

They banged on the heavy door to the tower, and shortly were answered by a short woman clothed in teal velvet. She waded out into the knee-high snow and led them to another door in the side of the mountain, which proved to be a warm and comfortable barn carved out of the stone. The verali and horses huddled inside without much prompting, and were soon settled with water and warm bran mashes.

The tower itself was considerably more spacious than it seemed from the outside. In a large vaulted receiving room at the base there was more than enough room for the gryphons, and after accepting an evaporation treatment from Thalnarra, each of them curled up on the plush carpets while the water priestess prepared tea.

Her name was Ilisia, and she was very strange. Twice she called Ariadel by the wrong name, despite polite correction, and during their short visit she seemed to forget what she was doing midtask at least four times.

// *We go into the mountain,* // Arikaree said. Ilisia seemed to be able to keep track of his words a bit better than the rest of them.

"Ah, yes," she said, her eyes disappearing into the wrinkles of her face as she smiled. "You will open the dragonspine. They've been speaking of it."

"Who?" Vidarian asked, but Ilisia only smiled as if he'd said something in another language she didn't understand.

"What is it you study here?" Ariadel asked finally, when any logistical questions proved impossible—and this, as it were, opened the floodgates.

"Study, study," she said, as if repeating a child's rhyme. "We study inevitability." Her eyes went vague, and for a moment she closed them in ecstasy. When she opened them, there was neither white nor pupil, but a glassy blue-green as of the western sea in summer. Something churned with recognition in Vidarian's blood, and her voice pounded between his ears: "The world passes away," she said, hollow and full all at once, "knowledge fades, runs together. The world is connected, streams like invisible water—our minds melt together, carried by waves, all thoughts become one—all returns to liquid."

The route through the mountain, Ilisia insisted, was not up, but down. She seemed to have some trouble keeping track of opposites—up and down, left and right, living and dead—which wasn't the best for endowing her proclamation with confidence. But up was the everstorm, and that, at least, was indisputable.

After they loaded and pulled the reluctant horses and verali from the warmth of the mountain stable, Ilisia led them behind the tower. There, a gigantic pair of stone doors were set directly into the slate wall that the tower's materials had been carved from. By its position, it seemed that the tower existed to guard this entrance, but, to Vidarian's surprise, Ilisia pulled the doors open without ceremony. A small, cold breeze wafted up from the opening, which revealed a dirt path that spiraled down into darkness.

A thin howl echoed through the mountains; a wolf calling its brothers and sisters in celebration of a kill. But Thalnarra's hackles lifted at the sound, and Vidarian turned to her. "What was that?"

// *A wolf, only,* // she said, though her hackles remained up. // *Surely no concern to us. Though you should mind the meat-creatures.* // The image in her mind of a "meat-creature" was an amalgam of horse, cow, and verali, and he was unsettled again at the reminder that she likely considered Feluhim a snack candidate at best. He had no special love of horses, himself (though he certainly preferred them to verali), but the thought of eating the tall dark horse that he fed bits of dried apple to every morning turned his stomach.

"Down you go," Ilisia said cheerfully, then turned and shuffled through the snow back toward the tower without another word. The horses, however, were not convinced by her cheer, and balked at the mouth of the trail. Altair stalked behind them and hissed, but this only worsened matters, eliciting a shriek of fear and anger from Ruby's horse that further spooked the other two. Finally, Ariadel pulled the head of each horse, one by one, down to her eye level and rubbed between its eyes, murmuring. The little shapeshifter skittered out from her hood and changed into the kitten, leaping onto Ruby's horse and purring. This was enough, at last, to convince them—and none too soon, for all three snow-sodden gryphons were looking increasingly carnivorous by the minute.

Ooh, it's dark down there, the Starhunter whispered just as they crossed the threshold, and Vidarian shivered in spite of himself. He'd learned by now that her absence was always more ominous than her presence, and that if she vanished from his mind, it was only to await a more opportune time to disturb him. The shiver, and his wave of anger at her, rippled through his mind and heart, where it resonated off of the rubies and sapphires. Their answering swing of energy was wilder this time, stronger, and he fought to throttle them down.

He didn't realize he'd been holding his breath until a wave of dizziness made him gasp. A thin bead of sweat crept down around his left eye, and he shook his head.

"That was her, wasn't it?" Ariadel asked quietly, walking beside him. The stone tunnel gave a hollow echo to her words, carrying them ahead and down. Behind her, the still-nervous Feluhim jerked on his lead, and she turned to soothe him, while Vidarian's heart skipped a beat as a thousand very bad ways to explain the Starhunter flickered through his mind: *She's a voice in my head, I see her in my dreams, she doesn't like you very much. . . .*

So honest, though. The Starhunter giggled. *Don't you want to be honest?*

"Yes," he said instead, through clenched teeth.

"How . . . does she speak to you?" Her voice was strained, but he recognized a thin line of determination between her eyebrows.

"Like you used to" would be another wrong answer, and it made the Starhunter chuckle again. "Invasively," he said. "Annoyingly. She—says confusing things."

"Like what?" was an obvious question, and he cursed himself for walking into it. Then he wondered why the thought of describing all of it terrified him so.

Maybe Lord Tesseract Vidarian Rulorat is not so noble as he wants everyone to believe.

"She makes you angry," Ariadel offered, rescuing him from repeating things he didn't want to voice. He realized she was trying to understand, had striven to accept the existence of something she had always been told—by people she trusted—was impossible.

Vidarian nodded. And now that they were discussing the goddess riding in his brain—"Thalnarra," he said, sweating again as he forced his voice to a controlled tone. "You and Endera knew about the Starhunter. Why hide it from everyone else? From Ariadel, from me?"

Altair clicked his beak in disapproval, a sound like bone cracking that made the horses jump again as it echoed. But Thalnarra's voice was nonchalant. // *Mysteries and layers of the priesthood, you'll have to ask Endera, not me. Gryphons have known of the Starhunter since she was locked behind the gate.* //

"But gryphons mistrust humans with a great deal of knowledge," Ariadel argued, and the bitterness in her voice refuted any reply before it could be spoken. Thalnarra gave none.

They descended the cave trail in silence, the gryphons' spheres of light racing forward and back to light their way.

Hours were difficult to count down here, as they had been above, and the slow spirals of the trail added to the hypnotic lull. Vidarian would have walked directly into the sudden wall that loomed up in front of them, his thoughts far from his body, were it not for Arikaree's rough squawk of warning.

This set of stone doors, like the walls around them, were sandstone, the slate having been left behind long ago. The gryphons' colored lights cast everything in a dull orange hue, but the rock itself was a dull yellow, thick with dust that obscured the detailed carvings that covered every inch of the doors' surface. But the sinuous path that they described could be little else.

"A dragon's spine," Ariadel said, reaching out to brush dust from the door. It gave way in a powdery flutter that made her cough, baring an intricately carved scale like that of a giant fish.

The rubies and sapphires had been humming in Vidarian's mind, and as he brought them from their pouches at his waist, they flared so brightly that he nearly dropped them. Ariadel shielded her eyes beside him, and he squinted as he raised them to the doors.

He drew his hands back as if burned when a shudder rippled through the stone, but it came from the doors only, and so, after a quick look back at the gryphons for agreement, he touched the stones together again. A triangle of energy loomed up before his senses: earth from the doors, earth from all around them, fire and water from the rubies and sapphires. "It needs air," he realized, and reached for the crystal whistle at his neck—

// Fool, you'll kill us all, using that down here, // Altair hissed, and Vidarian tried to mask how the gryphon's warning stung. He dropped his hand, and Altair added his own energy to the pattern on the door.

That's four, but you need one more . . . the Starhunter whispered. Vidarian's stomach dropped—

And the doors opened.

They stood and watched the opening, breathless, but in spite of the infusion of magic needed to open the passage, there was no revelation beyond the threshold—only another trail, this one leading upward. The horses didn't balk this time, and seemed only too pleased to begin climbing rather than descending.

The path up to the surface was shallow and broad; the spiraling path beyond the spine must have brought them down from much of what they'd climbed over the past many days. At long last, they stepped into sunlight—not the bone-rattling cold of the everstorm, but long-missed sunlight, streaming down from a vaulting blue sky. Trees, vivid green and lush, lined the edges of the clearing at the cave's entrance. Pockets of snow dotted the ground and the trees, giving evidence that they hadn't entirely escaped the weather, but for now, at least, the sky was clear.

They waited until everyone had emerged from the cave to attack.

Feluhim screamed—no gentle warning, this, but a shriek of total herbivore terror that rattled Vidarian to his bones. Wolves—creatures he had read of but never seen—poured out of the forest from all sides of the clearing, lunging toward them.

Thalnarra and Altair loosed battle cries in answer to the horses' screams of fear, and leaped over them, taking to the air just long enough to flare their wings and dive upon the wolves. Arikaree, no raptor, reached out with his senses, an arm of water so strong and pure that it stunned Vidarian to see—and then he plunged it into the nearest wolf, extinguishing the flame at its heart without so much as slowing down. The wolf dropped, dead, and its companions wailed in grief and fury.

The wolves split immediately into groups, most harrowing the two gryphons that reared and slashed, while pairs of them darted in toward the horses and humans. Vidarian's sword sang from its sheath, marking a deadly arc in the air that gave them pause, and as he fed it with his mind, it incandesced, a flowing flame that rushed hungrily for their life-energies. Behind Ariadel, Ruby moved to draw her sword also, and managed it, though not without a grunt of pain.

A strange whisper, wordless or incoherent, a language Vidarian couldn't understand, rippled through the wolves, and he shook his head, sure it was an illusion.

Oh, how interesting, the Starhunter observed, and in his mind she was casually eating while they battled for their lives, something that filled his head with the scent of melted butter. *They weren't like this when I was here before.*

He snarled at her, in thought only, but fear and curiosity beneath it made him wonder what part of this could be new to a goddess. And what *were* these things?

The more they whispered, the more he thought he could almost understand them, and even as another wolf leapt into his blade, only to be impaled at the shoulder, words with their lunges came clear: *Ours, ours! Ours, curseyou. Curseyou!* Ariadel lifted her hands beside him, and the next wolf that leapt up to take advantage of his bound sword cried out in agony as its fur burst into flame.

One of the verali had collapsed under a pile of wolves and lay thrashing on the ground, but at least ten dead wolves joined it in repose, and suddenly the rest decided with one mind to abandon the fight. They turned and fled into the woods, yelping, howling, their minds whispering those strange mad epithets.

Abruptly all was silent in the clearing, save for their labored breath. The fallen verali was now quite thoroughly dead and still.

Thalnarra lowered her great head to scrape blood from her beak on a patch of snow. She left a vivid red smear across the slush, and when she lifted her head again to look at Vidarian her beak glittered wet-black. // *I don't like to kill them.* // In the hearth-warmth of her voice was a thread of guilt and unhappiness like fouled meat. // *They're thinking creatures, intelligent,* // she said, giving an agitated shake of her neck-feathers.

// *But they wouldn't listen,* // Altair said, a deep sadness in his voice that cut like ice. // *Our languages have drifted.* //

233

"You know what these are?" Vidarian said, moving to one of the wolves to clean his blade on its pelt, then thinking better of it and using snow instead.

// Sightwolves, // Thalnarra said, lifting her head to look back at the cliff that loomed behind them, and the Windsmouth beyond it. // We're on the other side now. //

Chapter Twenty-Six
Sacrifice Gate

Though exhausted to the bone from the trek through the mountains followed by the sightwolf onslaught, they couldn't bear to sleep in the clearing, littered as it was with blood. Aided by the gryphons' massive claws, they were able to dig a trench for the dead wolves and lone verali, then trek into the forest. According to Ilisia's maps, these woods formed an arc around the edge of the mountains, and at their far side was a stone outpost, centuries old, but it should be strong enough to house the horses and verali for a few days.

The horses, smelling wolf, first refused to enter the forest, and had to be persuaded by growls from the impatient gryphons. There had been little meat through the snowy mountains, and Vidarian knew that Thalnarra would have far preferred to eat the beasts than herd them, but he'd convinced her that they were needed for the return journey. He found his eyes lingering on the gryphons' beaks and claws with renewed respect; it was one thing to realize in the abstract what they were capable of, and another entirely to have its evidence now burned into his memory.

Their shadowed trek beneath the trees—ancient, brooding conifers of a type he'd never seen before—was an insensate exhaustion blur punctuated by flashes of eyes in the dark. Some of these, he was sure, were figments of the imagination, anxiety-constructs—but some, he was equally sure, were not.

The forest's shadows had deepened toward true night when they finally emerged from the other side. A cool wind brought the scent of fresh water to their noses, and the blue twilight spilling across verdant hills rolling before them had a strange, tranquil loveliness. The hills flattened in the southern distance into a great plain, while the mountains curved to the west, ending distantly in what appeared to be coastal cliffs. And here at the edge of the forest, to their great relief, was the promised outpost: a small house of stacked stone, much neglected, and a sounder stone barn. With so many trees nearby it was odd that the barn wasn't made of wood, but they didn't question the small blessing: if it had been, it would certainly have deteriorated beyond use long before their arrival.

Even the gryphons' steps were faltering by the time they unloaded the verali. They arranged themselves in front of the stone barn to sleep while Vidarian, Ariadel, and Ruby unrolled their bedding in the space between. The night forest behind them was alive with the howls and yelps of a wild place's survival dance, and as sleep took them, Vidarian tried to remind himself that nothing here could be foolish enough to attack a sleeping gryphon.

In the morning, Ariadel didn't rise with the sun as she had every day that Vidarian had known her—brief though that time might be. Vidarian rose quietly, trying not to wake her, and found his way to the nearby river for the first morning wash he'd had in some time that hadn't involved snow. The water was cold, but restored him to full wakefulness, along with awareness of a number of stretched and sore muscles.

Ruby had risen before him, and crouched beside a fire she'd made by the river, tending a kettle. She was scrutinizing the metal pot so intently that she jumped when Vidarian laid a hand on her shoulder.

A flash of irritation followed her embarrassment at having been surprised, and she answered the question in his eyes hotly. "The temperature has to be precise," she said.

"Your exclusive *kava*?" he said. "Better not let any tyros such as myself near it."

"It's really no fault of mine that you have a peasant's palate," she huffed.

"I'm just glad to see you're feeling better," he replied. Sincerity was one of the few ways to defuse her ire.

Ruby eyed him, but stretched the arm closest to her injury, showing a greater range of movement than she'd had a few days ago. His comment had the desired effect: it mollified her enough to share the *kava*. He coaxed a few fat fish out of the river with water magic and cooked them with fire while she brewed the bark—be damned if this whole Tesseract business wasn't going to have some silver lining—and they made a very decent camp breakfast of it.

When Ariadel didn't rise by the time the gryphons returned from their morning hunt—nearly too fat to fly, Altair accused the other two; they'd taken two medium-sized deer—Vidarian started to worry, and went to rouse her.

The kitten, which had ridden for most of the journey in its more portable spider form, slept curled across her neck, as if huddled there for warmth. But when Vidarian moved to touch Ariadel's shoulder, he was taken aback by the worried intelligence in the creature's very awake and alert eyes. *It knows*, the Starhunter said softly. She'd been silent since the wolf attack, and seemed strangely thoughtful now. *My creatures know things.*

Ariadel's face and hands were both pale, and Vidarian rejected his immediate fear, but it refused to subside entirely. He'd seen this kind of pallor before, in his childhood. . . .

It's what's inside her, the Starhunter whispered, *warring against itself. Wind meets hammer!*

Vidarian's stomach dropped. "No . . ." he whispered. But his new senses showed her accusation to be true. If he closed his eyes, her dominant fire nature rose up before him—but beneath it, in her blood, twined the energies of her parents: implacable earth and volatile wind, now turned against each other. He realized, with an echo of the terrible fear that had haunted his childhood, how the visiting priestess had known with a single look the nature of the disease that took his brothers.

Ask her, the Starhunter insisted, with a callous titter, *if she has any brothers or sisters.*

But he knew the answer.

Ask!

He took her hands and massaged them in his own, willing warmth back into her frighteningly cold fingers. "Ariadel," he said, and she made a soft noise, her face contorting. Her pallor and reflexive grimace threw him back twenty years—his mother, a dried husk from grief, standing at the bedside of

Relarion, his oldest brother. He was ten years old. . . . "Ariadel," he forced himself to urge again, hoarse. "Do you have . . ." his voice rasped and he swallowed. ". . . brothers or sisters?"

"No," she said, confusion wrinkling her brow. She cleared her throat, but it was a weak sound. "I—my parents had two children, before I was born. They—didn't survive."

"They got sick," he said quietly.

Her chin tipped down once in the shadow of a nod. "Blood plague," she whispered.

Ruby's indrawn breath behind them lifted his head. She stood, her arms wrapped around herself, a handful of emotions warring on her face. He knew that expression well; the Rulorats had parted from their Sea Kingdom brethren to support the Alorean Emperor seven generations ago, but seventy years ago Vidarian's great-grandfather had further parted from sea custom by marrying a fire woman. The rigid Sea Kingdom rites weren't always so practical, but the stricture against interelemental marriage centered around a single purpose: avoiding the specter of blood plague.

The disease came on suddenly and usually took children, but cases had been documented in adults as old as thirty years of age. When Vidarian had turned thirty, three years ago, and survived, a peace had come over his mother. On her deathbed two years ago she said that she could die happy, knowing she wouldn't lose him as she had his brothers.

Ariadel was twenty-eight.

Jealous, jealous elements, the Starhunter whispered. *How they fight when I'm not around. . . .*

A cold chill penetrated the heat of Vidarian's grief. "What are you saying?" he said softly, ignoring the confused looks that Ariadel and Ruby turned on him.

You know what I'm saying, she laughed coldly. *Set me free, and she lives.*

Vidarian lifted his voice. "When was the first case of blood plague recorded?"

"It's ancient," Ruby said, her tone dismissing the question. "Two thousand years."

Has it been that long? the voice mused. *Man, time flies.*

"Two thousand years ago," Vidarian said, willing strength from his hands into Ariadel's as he tightened his grasp, "they shut the Starhunter behind the gate."

∿∿∿

After wrapping Ariadel in every blanket they could find, and convincing Thalnarra to use a small amount of fire magic in a persistent spell to keep her warm, Ruby and Vidarian loaded the flying craft in silence. On the far side of the river was the start of a grassy plain, and Ruby, no longer hiding her facility with water magic, walked across the surface of the river to collect fodder for the horses from the other side. Arikaree complimented her on her technique, but her only reply was a flush that could have been pleasure or anger, and seemed probably both.

Vidarian wasn't convinced that the sightwolves wouldn't find some way to break into the old barn, but they could only fortify it minimally with the available materials and hope for the best. The horses and verali, for their part, seemed content and relieved to be housed and not traveling. By early afternoon all was prepared, and they were taking to the air.

The gryphons lifted with a will after their respite through the mountains, and Ariadel occupied Ruby's previous place at the bow. It seemed odd that they had never flown the craft without one of them being incapacitated, and an ill omen for a ship named *Destiny*. Vidarian's mother had been a superstitious keeper of sea adages, and in spite of his rational inclinations otherwise, at such times it was as if a small voice inside him whispered fear, caution, just-you-wait.

Ruby came to stand next to him at the stern, taking an interest in the ingenious galley hardware as he had on their first journey. Now that she had let go of her stubbornness regarding the gryphons (she even seemed to be developing a hesitant kinship with Arikaree), she was discovering the wonder of the altitudes.

"It's a bit like being at sea," she observed, looking down over the clouds. "You can almost imagine it's fog over the water."

Vidarian blinked, shaking off the malaise of superstition—a construct, he knew, to distract him from the fast-approaching choice he would make, and how Ariadel's fate tied into it. "I suppose it is," he said, following her gaze. The clouds were thin here and whipped by beneath them, catching on the craft and splitting around it. A moment later, the sky opened up beneath them, clear, and their breath caught simultaneously. At the involuntary leap in his heart, the storm sapphires rumbled from the pouch at his side, answered immediately by a growl from the sun rubies. He closed his eyes, stretching control around them—an act that was becoming increasingly difficult the longer they stayed in his possession. Exhaustion, mental and emotional, tugged at him, and the stones seemed to realize his weakness and surge up in response.

"They're exhausting you," Ruby said, pointing at the pouch.

Vidarian looked at her closely, wondering if he'd been unwittingly projecting his thoughts, but then realized they must have been written across his face. He nodded, moving forward and sitting down on one of the leather benches.

Ruby took a seat beside him, a thoughtful expression on her face. "If you gave the rubies to me, would they harass you so much?"

He blinked again, surprised. And again he searched her eyes for motivation, even as he felt a pang of regret for doing so. There was only a friend's concern in her eyes. "I'm not sure," he said, opening the pouch. He reached inside slowly, touching the stones one at a time, and withdrew one of those that pulsed warm to his fingers. "Keeping them in separate packs doesn't seem to help." Carefully, he extended his hand, holding it out to her.

Ruby accepted the stone with equal care, cradling it between her two cupped palms. She looked back at him and raised an eyebrow. "Any better?" When he shook his head ruefully, she grimaced and turned her attention back to the stone. As she pressed it between her palms, her eyes lit with surprise at its warmth, and she lifted it to the light, staring into it. "What *are* these things?"

"I've wondered that," he said, drawing one of the storm sapphires from the pouch and resting it on his palm. By far the sapphires were the most volatile of the three types of elemental stone he'd seen firsthand. Physically they were identical in size to the rubies, but to his mind they felt "bigger," as if they had more space inside them, however that was possible. "If they opened the mountain, and can open or close the gate, they must be keys of some sort, but it's related to their energy patterns, not anything physical."

She snorted. "You sound like a priestess."

"Or a gryphon," he agreed, and she gave him a sharp look.

"Your sun emerald," she said, before he could pursue the look, "the one you left with An'du." Ruby's eyes had looked fit to pop out of her head when they'd told her, in the hospital, about their trip to the An'durin. "You said that it was bound to you, somehow." He nodded cautiously, and she continued, "Could you bind this one to me?"

The swirl of his thoughts echoed through the storm sapphire, which flashed with ricochets of internal lightning.

"It's going to be mine anyway," she said lightly, mimicking avarice. Then her voice lowered with seriousness. "And if it were bound to me, I suspect I could control it. You're going to need all the mind-strength you can get for what's coming, I'll wager."

"I've only seen it done once," he warned, "and I hadn't any sense at all at the time."

Ruby laughed, a sudden shock of brightness in what had been a dark journey. "As if you do now."

Vidarian punched her knee, then regretted it, as the sapphire echoed with a new round of thunder. "You know what I mean." He looked at the sapphire in his hand, attempting to fathom its nature anew, aware of the headache that was growing in the back of his head as he reached with his mind to control it. They were becoming more frequent. "I could try," he said at last.

She passed the ruby back to him, and he slipped the sapphire back into its place in the pouch. He lifted the ruby, looking through it and to Ruby herself beyond it, then stretched his senses into the stone. As it was warm to the touch, so it was warm to his mind—alive with a flickering energy that perpetually sought . . . something. He felt a sudden urge to touch Ruby's hand, but knew that Endera had not done so when she'd bound the emerald to him, and so he worked to keep his free hand at his side. He reached through the stone with his senses until he encountered Ruby's energy—a familiar tumbling roar, an ever-moving pattern of the living sea that lived just beneath her skin.

Carefully, he curved his own sense, siphoning a piece of that roiling pattern back toward himself, and into the stone. It surged into it, and Ruby gasped, closing her eyes—feeling, he was sure, the dropping of her heart that he had felt when Endera bound him to the sun emerald. For a moment he was gripped with a terror that he wouldn't be able to stop the transfer of her essence into the stone, that it might take all of her—but the stone seemed to "know" how much it should contain, and released her of its own accord.

When Ruby opened her eyes, an echo of the ruby's energy glowed in her pupils, and he knew it was done.

The craft shuddered, and both of them reached for the support rails, riding out the sudden movement.

// VIDARIAN, // Thalnarra barked, and as he looked forward Vidarian saw that the disruption had come from her agitatedly beating wings. // Tell me you didn't just do what I think you did. //

"We were discussing it for the last several minutes," he said, stung. "I thought gryphons had superb hearing."

// This flying business is not as easy as it must look from back there, // she snapped. // I was focusing. //

"It's fine," Vidarian said hotly. In fact, it was better than fine. He passed the stone back to Ruby, who looked at it with renewed wonder. Now that it was bound to her, it did seem to be paying more attention to her than to the sapphires, if rocks could be said to have attention. "Isn't it?"

// By luck only, // Thalnarra growled. // Binding magics can go awry more easily than you can imagine. And you knew nothing about that stone! Some elemental stones are extremely dangerous. //

// He is being the Tesseract, // Arikaree offered, though the hesitancy in his voice said that he, too, questioned the wisdom of what Vidarian and Ruby had just done.

// You're all going to be the death of me. //

CHAPTER TWENTY-SEVEN
GRYPHON WAR

"**W**hether or not we're the death of you," Vidarian said, "I want to know how we hold Ariadel's fate."

The sudden wave of sympathy that emanated from the gryphons caught in his throat. It was a sudden sensation of soft wings enclosing him, and for a long moment he wanted to sink into their strength. That desperate yearning opened the crevasse of reality before his feet; he wanted to unmake the last several weeks, to do anything if it would mean her illness could be averted.

// *Her condition is grave,* // Altair said.

"I'm told," Vidarian said, forcing air past the lump in his throat, "that she can be cured by the opening of the gate."

If Thalnarra's irregular wingbeat had disrupted the craft, the surprised pitching of all three of them nearly threw Ruby and Vidarian out of it entirely. They grasped for handholds, and Ariadel murmured in her sleep as the craft slewed first to one side, then the other.

"I really wish you wouldn't do that," Ruby said between clenched teeth. He wasn't sure who she meant—probably all of them.

Once they recovered their flight pattern, all of the gryphons spoke at once: // *Who told you this?* // from Thalnarra, // *When did this happen?* // from Altair, and // *It is deceiving, would tell you so,* // from Arikaree.

"I think you know," Vidarian said.

// *The Starhunter,* // Thalnarra said, and in her voice it was an epithet. // *Have you learned so little, to listen to her? She has no domain of her own, and preys upon those of the four true goddesses. What else would she tell you?* //

Nothing the goddess could have said would refute this, but her laugh, full of satisfaction, sealed its answer in Vidarian's heart.

"She knows I would do anything to deny her what she wants," Vidarian said, his heart sunken, "except this." He looked across the craft to where Ariadel slept fitfully, her face pale and body hunched in for warmth even beneath Thalnarra's warmth spell.

// *Don't you think you owe it to her to ask if she would have you open the gate?* // Thalnarra said, a hot anger simmering beneath the smoke of her voice. *Betrayal*, her thoughts whispered, with that cloud of concepts that lingered beyond human language.

Vidarian looked again at Ariadel. Did he know what her answer would be? "I—"

Ruby cried out behind him, stopping his thoughts. When he turned, she was pointing aft behind them, to the north.

There against the mountains, a dark cloud was rising, too fast and dense to be weather. As it spread out and came closer, tiny wings could be discerned on each particle. The sheer number of them set his stomach ill at ease.

"Gryphons?" Vidarian asked.

// *No,* // Altair said.

// *Horses,* // Thalnarra said. // *Winged horses, and riders.* //

"Sky knights!" Ruby breathed, turning to Vidarian. "From the empire? What are they doing here?"

"There was a disagreement," Vidarian began, and Ruby's eyes widened with incredulity—which was something, coming from a renegade warleader whose people had been fighting the empire for over a century.

// *And coming over mountains,* // Arikaree added. Vidarian realized he was right—they hadn't taken the dragonspine tunnel, but had come up and over the mountain range. It shouldn't have been possible.

But the bottom line was: "Then they'll be exhausted." He turned to each of the gryphons. "Can you fly higher?"

In response, they angled their wings again, gradually ascending.

"Make them work for it," he said grimly.

The knights closed like an inexorable slow tide.

// *They're carrying healers!* // Altair exclaimed. The gryphons' ability to see details of their pursuers long before Ruby or Vidarian could hope to was an advantage, but it was hard not to be unsettled by it. // *They must be feeding energy to the horses—that's what's keeping them going.* //

// *I've heard it done, but it's reckless,* // Thalnarra agreed. // *With that endurance and one of the remaining relics of Siane, they could have opened the ever-storm. The Company must mean to do anything to stop you. What exactly did you say to them?* //

Everyone kept asking that, Vidarian thought irritatedly. As if saying something could cause an entity so large to empty its coffers trying to detain you. Or stop it from doing so.

His spirit sank within him as he took in their sheer numbers. They were close enough now for a human to count, not just a gryphon. Three flights closed on them—an entire wing, if his dull memory of imperial air organization held true; close to fifty horses and riders. And they couldn't have come from the imperial city—not this fast. Which meant they were bordermen, accustomed to rough conditions. Dangerous and hungry.

"I have to talk to them," he said, and the three gryphons at once sent him a pulse of surprise and unhappiness. They were *afraid*, he realized, with a shock like ice water. On even footing, a gryphon wouldn't fear even a flight of Sky Knights—but here, harnessed to the flying craft, they were vulnerable themselves, to say nothing of the wingless passengers. "We're too far from the ground," he argued. "They could knock all of us down. If I can talk them into landing, we have a chance."

// *Their intentions are not peaceful,* // Altair warned, and Thalnarra and Arikaree radiated agreement.

"You can read that from their thoughts?" Ruby asked, surprised; an edge of her previous suspicion toward gryphons had returned to her voice.

// *The horses,* // Thalnarra said. // *We can smell their readiness. The riders encourage them for battle.* //

How exciting! the Starhunter whispered. Vidarian managed to ignore her. "I have to try," he said only. The gryphons were not pleased, but also not arguing. Vidarian's ears were popping as they continued to ascend. The knights' horses were following, but slowly. Gradually, the gryphons leveled off, allowing the knights to catch up.

When the group drew close, one of their number split off and approached, guiding his horse up within a few wing-lengths of the port bow. It was not the commander; she was still flanked by a chevron of knights in the center of the wing, distinctive by the gold pauldrons at her shoulders and the glimmering purple iridescence of the coat and feathers of the royal she rode.

Their approacher rode a young beast—a grey, its feathers still banded. His armor was provincial, not standard to the imperial city, confirming Vidarian's suspicion that they'd sent a border wing. He signaled his mount to hover, which it did with a toss of its head and feathered tail, and lifted his visor.

"Second Vadron Illinsvar, Imperial Sky Knights, Hawkstorm Wing." When he named the wing, the knights behind Illinsvar lifted their lances and gave low shouts that were picked up by the rest. The lieutenant smiled slightly and Vidarian cursed to himself. A young, stupid cowherd with ambitions. Fantastic. He was eyeing the gryphons with speculation and excitement.

// *He doesn't know we're intelligent,* // Thalnarra growled in his mind alone, anger and satisfaction coloring her words. // *Don't enlighten him.* //

"Greetings, Captain," Vidarian called, intentionally mistaking his rank to puff his ego. "How can we assist you?"

"The Hawkstorm wing is dispatched to escort one Vidarian Rulorat to the imperial city. If you are he, I am instructed to take you into custody."

"I'm afraid we can't agree to that," Vidarian said. "Perhaps we could discuss this on the ground?"

"To allow you to land would be allowing you further progress toward the gate," the knight said, with another irritating half-smile. Thalnarra fixed his horse with one sharp red eye, and Vidarian knew only he and the horse heard the word // *Snack* // she directed at it. The beast tossed its head, backwinging, and Thalnarra clicked her beak at it. The knight snarled. "You should control those creatures!"

"I apologize," Vidarian called. "They're just impossible sometimes." He directed unhelpful thoughts at Thalnarra.

"We are instructed first to negotiate with you and seek a peaceful solution," Illinsvar said. "But my orders are clear: we are to detain you by any means necessary. No living knight is permitted to allow you to reach the gate." The way he emphasized "living" made Vidarian's skin crawl.

"Why?" Vidarian called. "What are they afraid I'll do?"

The knight pulled back on the reins of his mount, which tossed its head and snorted in response, backwinging. "Why should the empire—"

"You mean the Company!"

"—allow one man to decide the fate of millions?"

He doesn't know, the Starhunter whispered. *Leave the poor toy alone.*

"This from you?" Vidarian muttered.

"Will you come peacefully?" the knight called, lowering his lance. The others along the forward line behind him followed suit, facing the *Destiny* with an arc of knife points. Illinsvar kneed his mount, and it hovered closer to the flying craft, bringing the tip of his lance closer to Arikaree's flank.

Thalnarra hissed, and the horse's mane and tail burst into flame. The creature shrieked in unison with its rider's angry shout, and the knights behind them wasted only a moment on raw shock before charging forward.

// *Climb!* // Thalnarra shouted, and the three gryphons immediately angled their wings and began ascending. Thalnarra herself aimed upward at the sharpest angle, and the craft tipped steeply. Ruby and Vidarian scrambled for safety holds, and as he did so Vidarian leaned forward across the craft to check the safety straps around Ariadel. For a blessing, they held, and though Ariadel's forehead creased and she murmured uncomfortably in her sleep, she was not otherwise disrupted.

Arrows were hissing around them as the gryphons rose higher in the air. In the commotion among the knights—acrid smoke still rose from beneath them, with the scent of burning horsehair, and the panicked screams of the inflicted animal—they'd gained several lengths on their pursuers in altitude, but not clearance. The gryphons were strong, but the knights had the advantage in both encumbrance and number. Soon, Vidarian knew, their breath would begin to labor at this pace.

"You have to get me to their commander!" he shouted. "They won't fight without her!"

// We can't maneuver the craft so close to her, // Thalnarra argued, then released a shriek and a lance of searing fire as a knight passed beneath them, firing a bow up at her. She twisted, catlike, in the air, and snatched the arrow, breaking it in half between her talons before it could touch her, and the craft lurched sickeningly with her movement. *// I can't move in this bloody thing! //* she cursed.

// There is a way, // Altair said, *// if you have the heart for it. //*

"Tell us!" Vidarian shouted, untying a ballast bag from the craft's side and slinging it down at the pursuing knights.

// The craft can be maintained by two gryphons, // Altair said, and Vidarian's stomach plummeted as he realized what the gryphon was suggesting. *// With the aid of the Breath of Siane, I can carry you to the knight-commander. //*

// Madness! // Thalnarra barked.

// No, // Altair said with icy calm. *// Madness was lighting that beast's hair on fire within range of their lances. //*

// Only an air-brained— // Thalnarra began.

"I'll do it!" Vidarian shouted, pulling the whistle from his shirt and clenching it in his fist. "What do we do?"

By way of answer, Altair twisted in the air, and, to Vidarian's horror (and Ruby's, by her cry of shock), sliced through the primary harness strap that bound him to the craft. The craft tilted sideways for a split second, but then the riven strap slithered through a set of rings in the rigging below, caught, and swung the craft to the right. Arikaree gave a squawk of surprise as they slid into place before him—the craft itself now rested between him and Thalnarra. They slowed, but mostly out of surprise.

Thalnarra snarled something menacing and incomprehensible at Altair.

Altair ignored her and shouted to Vidarian. *// Jump! //*

"He's got to be kidding," Ruby breathed.

"He's not," Vidarian said, knowing it through his core. He took a deep breath, unhooked his safety harness, and vaulted over the side of the craft.

He fell, and instinctively spread his arms and legs. The craft disappeared over his head, and below him ranged the clouds, astonishingly lovely, and the advancing Sky Knights in their formations.

// *Blow the whistle!* // the gryphon shouted, breaking him out of his astonishment.

Vidarian blew into the crystal whistle, a long breath that echoed in his ears, in his blood, in his skin. A gale swept through him, and out of reflex he tried to shape the energy, but it flowed through him like wind itself, slipping through his fingers unmoved. Altair *caught* the energy, wrapping himself around it and dancing with it, teasing it into going where he wanted.

// *Beautiful,* // the gryphon whispered, and then, as an afterthought, it seemed, juggled Vidarian into the reach of the wind's grasp. They stopped falling, and Vidarian arced in a curve, "flying" as if of his own volition just above Altair's wings. He drifted downward, featherlike, until he was touching the gryphon's back, taking a hold on the thick feathers at the base of his neck. The sphere of energy that surrounded them, allowing Altair unnatural strength in the air, was the clearest and most exhilarating Vidarian had ever breathed.

Then he looked down. The ground was *awfully* far away. . . .

// *Try not to think about it,* // Altair advised. Vidarian nodded numbly.

"We need to distract them!" he shouted over the roar of the wind, and Altair sent a wave of agreement.

// *This will be a little dodgy,* // Altair warned, then dove before Vidarian had a chance to answer.

They plummeted through the knights, who had stopped advancing when they saw Vidarian leap from the craft, and Vidarian's heart flew into his throat. Altair, loose, had unnerved the knights, indicated by their raised lances—but Altair, diving, claws outstretched, utterly scattered them. Feathers, horseflesh, and plated armor slid past them, and as their sphere of Air passed through, knights fell to either side in its wake. One was unhorsed, and plummeted, screaming—his horse dove after him, and they disappeared together into the clouds.

Then they were below the formations, and the sky opened up beneath them. Far below, the ground was green and wreathed with rivers, bizarrely peaceful, wisps of white cloud streaking by Altair's wings. He backwinged, slowing, and gravity flattened Vidarian against the gryphon's back. Then Altair folded one wing entirely, rolling sideways in the air. Vidarian clung for his life, his grip tight around the thick feather-shafts, knowing the sphere of air would adhere him to Altair but hardly trusting it.

The gryphon's wings opened again as they came to the side of the amassed knights, which as a group had reoriented upon them as the greater danger—and Vidarian as their instructed target. Altair whistled, and the sphere of energy seized around them again, and lifted them. His wings rowed the air, and they shot up above the knights; Altair extended a claw as they passed, tearing open the flank of a black horse that screamed in response and fell away from the group, its wings faltering.

Now they were above the group, again, and as Vidarian looked down over Altair's strongly pumping right wing he saw that the gryphon had positioned them squarely over the commander. This was it. For a split second his mind reeled at the sight of something few westerners had ever seen: a Sky Knight commander and her royal mount, its black coat glittering with signature iridescence, its feathered wings, crest, and tail bright with fierce health. The creature's body dwarfed the commander, who was no small woman—it was easily a quarter again the size of the other horses.

// *Remember that you must control the beast once you're upon it!* // Altair shouted. The "hand" supporting Vidarian suddenly fell away, and Vidarian was plummeting toward the horse and rider.

The commander and the knights surrounding her were looking up as Vidarian fell toward them, their swords and lances raised. Vidarian bent himself to one side, turning in the air, getting his feet underneath him—and only just managed to swerve to one side of the commander's arcing sword. An arm of wind whistled by his head, and the commander shouted as her sword was struck from her grasp, her wrist snapping back painfully in an attempt to retain it. The weapon spun through the air, disappearing below them.

Vidarian fell heavily onto the rear of the horse, which shrieked and kicked in response to his weight. He threw his arms around the commander's waist, grappling with her for the reins. Her armored elbow came up in a defensive maneuver and nearly knocked him senseless, and then she was swiveling in the saddle to bring her other fist around in a punishing strike. He managed to dodge that one, but was quickly losing his balance.

Around them, the other knights were shouting, and she shouted something back at them, then dug her heels into the horse. It leapt forward in response, and she shouted another command, sending it into a dive. Her practiced legs clamped around the beast's barrel, but Vidarian felt himself lifted out of the saddle, and grabbed the nearest object to hand—the commander's helmet.

She jerked her head, and the helmet came free, leaving him hanging in midair as she clung like a barnacle to the horse's back and directed it to roll beneath her. Horse and rider spun to one side, and Vidarian curled into a fetal position in the air to protect himself from the flashing hooves that now lashed out at him.

An aquiline shriek, and Altair swooped by him, white feathers a blur. Then he flared his wings, rising beneath Vidarian, supporting him with the shield of air.

Vidarian had just started to breathe again when the grip of the energy sphere began to falter.

A flash of strength blew Vidarian away from Altair, and then he was falling again, striking the gryphon's back—and the sphere went out entirely.

He fell onto Altair's back again, and the gryphon squawked with frustration as Vidarian's weight bore them steadily toward the ground. His wings labored, but only for a few fruitless moments—he was simply not strong enough to bear a full-grown man on his back.

Above them, the knights were rallying, and one group of them followed Vidarian and Altair while another broke off to pursue the craft. Vidarian gave a yell of despair, for the moment thinking more of Ruby and Ariadel, helpless in the craft, than of his own dire predicament.

They were falling relentlessly. Altair held out his wings, but only in token—fearful, Vidarian knew, that if he fully extended his wings, their combined weight would snap them, sending them both into a deadly spiral toward the ground. Vidarian pulled the whistle from where it flapped beside his head on its strand, and blew it, but to no response, its power spent.

// *Hold on!* // Altair shouted, somewhat extraneously, Vidarian thought. But then he was squashing his own impulse to ask if they were about to die. Instead he did as he was told, gripping Altair's neck-feathers tightly again.

Overhead, a scream—an animal one, as it turned out. Half of a black wing dropped past them, followed by a spray of blood—and a plummeting horse and rider. The cut was clean, a precise cut from a sword. Ruby, it would seem, was not entirely helpless in the craft above. Even under the circumstances, the thought was comforting.

The ground swooped closer below them. Altair was drawing his wings and limbs closer to his body now, controlling their fall, angling them forward. The tops of trees came clear beneath them, deadly arms reaching up to catch them, and not kindly.

// *BRACE YOURSELF!* // Altair's voice thundered in Vidarian's mind, uncontrolled, and as they whipped past the first branches of the tall trees, the gryphon let loose a blast of raw air energy, pushing toward the ground, cushioning them.

They crashed into the undergrowth, slowed by the expanding radius of Air, but hardly stopped. Branches whipped past Vidarian's face, tearing at his skin, and then the ground hit them, knocking the wind from his chest and blackening his vision.

All was still.

Distantly, the cries of the battle above them raged on, while Vidarian grasped for consciousness. Some lengths away, something crashed to the ground—a Sky Knight, and a dead one, he hoped. Beside him, Altair was struggling to his feet, and gave a high and piercing scream of pain as he did so.

Vidarian's vision came back slowly, and he moved each of his hands and feet, groaning as he did so, but with relief when they moved as he asked them to. "Altair?" he gasped, his breath still not recovered.

// *Right wing,* // the gryphon mumbled. // *Broken, I think.* //

Something else crashed into the forest some distance from them, this time to the left.

They began to realize slowly that there were too many cries in the air. Horses couldn't make those noises—and there were only two gryphons.

Vidarian looked up slowly.

High overhead, framed by the gap they'd made in the brush with their fall, a battle was raging in the air.

The flying craft was angling toward the ground, forgotten. Above it, at least twenty gryphons were diving upon the knights, slashing with beaks and claws, wreaking havoc in the sky.

// Thalnarra's pride, // Altair said in wonder, relief drowning out pain.

CHAPTER TWENTY-EIGHT
BLOOD PLAGUE

They stared at the sky, transfixed, as the gryphons darted in among the knights, falling upon them from above like stooping hawks. It was unlike anything Vidarian had ever seen. The gryphons writhed in the air like fighting cats, but swooped and spiraled like falcons, building momentum with powerful wingstrokes in order to bring their tearing claws down upon the knights. For their part, each horse and rider had the advantage of mass on the gryphons—and their lances and swords here and there found marks in gryphon flesh.

But for each hit the knights scored, the gryphons took three more—and in spite of the lieutenant's bold "death before retreat" claim, the commander evidently thought differently, and called a retreat when a third of her riders had fallen and only two gryphons had been injured. In spite of their violence, Vidarian almost pitied them when the gryphons moved to give chase to the fleeing riders—but one of the gryphons gave a screeching command, and those pursuing fell back with the group.

The gryphons above had moved into a circling perimeter when a rustling thump some distance away drew Vidarian and Altair's attention back to the ground. Altair started to move, then cried out in pain as his wounded wing convulsed. "Stay here," Vidarian said, and foraged through the brush.

The presence of the gate pulled on his mind. The storm sapphires, since they had crashed into the brush, had been a constant dull roar of activity, pulling the energy of the gate toward them. A rolling susurrus filled his thoughts but he blinked past it, bearing down with his will. But they were close, and the stones yearned to fulfill their function, whatever it might be.

He came upon the *Destiny* in an open meadow, where it had landed and now tilted to one side. Ruby was outside the craft unharnessing Thalnarra and Arikaree with one hand. Her other hand was at her side, where it staunched blood around the poultice—her wound had reopened in the action. Vidarian leapt over the knee-high grasses and ran toward them, taking Ruby's place in the unharnessing. She gave a gasp of relief when she saw him.

"We saw you go down," she said, looking him over for damage.

"I'm fine, but Altair is injured," he said. "He thinks his right wing is broken." With the gryphons unharnessed, he leaned over the rim of the flight craft, checking Ariadel's safety straps and blankets. Her eyes fluttered open, and his heart leapt, but moments later she closed them again, sound asleep.

// We are watching Ariadel, // Arikaree said. Vidarian turned to him and started forward when he saw the blood seeping sluggishly from a shallow wound at the pelican-gryphon's shoulder, but Arikaree waved him away with a gesture of his long beak. // He be needing you more now. Be taking medical kit from craft. // Vidarian followed his instructions and fished a leather satchel of medical supplies from the Destiny.

// Show me, // Thalnarra said, shaking out her feathers. Vidarian looked at Ruby, who nodded agreement, and Vidarian foraged back through the grass toward Altair, following the trail of flattened foliage he'd left moments before.

When Thalnarra caught sight of where Altair crouched, his wing crumpled at his side, she surged ahead of Vidarian and began inspecting the other gryphon. She crouched at each of his sides and moved her talons over him, looking but not touching. Both of their eyes pinned and flared in silent conversation.

// Now who's crazy? // Thalnarra said, probably for Vidarian's benefit, and for a second Vidarian was swallowed in the traumatic memory of their fall from the sky. He gave a shake of his head and opened the medical satchel.

Under Thalnarra's guidance, Vidarian gave Altair a dried pod of some vegetable from the satchel that within moments had the gryphon disoriented and relaxed. They maneuvered his broken wing into a proper fold with only the occasional yelp of pain—loudest when they moved the large bone between his wrist and shoulder back into alignment. As painful as it was to have broken that bone, Thalnarra seemed relieved—the more delicate pair of bones at the leading edge of his wing, she said, would have created a much more serious break.

At length they splinted the now-straightened broken bone with a cut sapling, then folded Altair's wing against his body and bound it there with lengths of silk bandage. When they were done, he hadn't yet recovered from the dried pod medicine, so Thalnarra waited with him in the forest while Vidarian returned to the downed craft.

When he came upon the meadow, he found not just one pelican-gryphon waiting there, but a goodly portion of Thalnarra's pride—including Kaltak and Ishrak. The rest of the gryphons were goshawk-type—it was startlingly like seeing a dozen Thalnarras until their minute differences became clear—and so the brothers stuck out with their brown feathers and long feathered legs.

The two young gryphons bounded up to Vidarian as soon as he crossed into the meadow. They clearly had been cleaning themselves up, but the remnants of blood shone red-black on their talons and beaks. Vidarian had seen them with fresh-killed prey before, but never with the heightened blood of battle, their ruffs puffed out, their eyes flashing. He wondered how much of the blood on their talons was human, and decided he'd rather not know.

// *Greetings, brother!* // Kaltak chirped, his tufted ears flicked forward in happy excitement.

"Good to see you, my friend," Vidarian said, holding out his hand for Kaltak to press his beak to in greeting. The smooth, curved killing instrument felt familiar now, and Vidarian realized how much his life had changed. His gaze drifted to the other gryphons, shocked again at how very much like Thalnarra they looked—though, if it was possible to be sure at this distance, none of them seemed to have her red eyes. But in form and size they were as similar to her as the brothers were to each other.

They weren't always like that, the Starhunter whispered. *Everything has come so far apart. Separated. Boxes, little boxes . . .* She started humming an extremely annoying tune, and Vidarian tried to block her out.

// *Ishrak has had his first battle!* // Kaltak said, and the younger brother dipped his head in acknowledgment. // *We aren't Thalnarra's pride, but she allowed us to join them for Ishrak's sake, and on account of us knowing you.* // The young gryphon was practically garrulous, his energy clearly excited by the action they'd seen.

"Congratulations," Vidarian told Ishrak, not sure what else to say.

The smaller brother's cheek-feathers puffed out in shy pleasure. // *We should return to our duties,* // he said. // *They're clearing the field and setting up a camp.* // Kaltak looked disappointed but couldn't argue, and the brothers turned back to their tasks.

It was no mean thing, it turned out, to support an entire pride of gryphons, even for a largely under-hunted wild area that had known no gryphons for some time, perhaps even centuries. To Vidarian's horror, they proceeded to eat the slain horses, though mercifully not within sight of the camp. The riders they buried, those that they could find—after a quick calculation Vidarian was quite sure that more still lay fallen. He wasn't much for prayer, but considering that she'd been instrumental in saving his life, he said a brief blessing for the knights to their air goddess, Siane.

Much good she did them, the Starhunter chuckled.

As if you're doing better, he thought viciously at her, even as he berated himself for letting her get to him.

That's hardly my fault, she said, and the hurt in her voice seemed oddly genuine, if—as all things seemed to be with her—fleeting. *They locked me back here. How am I supposed to do anyone any good? I can hardly think with these irksome bird-people everywhere.*

Though she'd been given to exaggeration, such a specific fabrication tugged at his mind as unlikely. *There are gryphons back there?* But surely Thalnarra would not oppose the gate opening if she knew there were gryphons trapped . . .

Not gryphons! she snapped. *Then I might have had some conversation. Just . . . well, look!*

She seized his mind, and Vidarian abruptly found himself somewhere else.

It was dark, and the darkness receded into infinity, a shadow that came from nowhere. Surrounding them, just out of reach, were glimmering presences, fascinating little lights. He found himself reaching toward them, stretching himself, expanding.

No, no, a voice said crossly. *This!*

And there they were, thousands of them, millions! Uncountable faces, bodies, almost human—but covered with feathers.

See! Bird-people! What are you calling them now . . .

Their faces were haunted, tortured. Some of them seemed to see him, others did not. A collective murmur rose up from them, and when those nearest caught sight of him, the murmur increased into a roar.

Oh, great, the Starhunter sighed. *You'd better go back.*

And then he was back, the sounds of the meadow sudden in his ears, the smell of the earth, the warmth of the sun on his skin, chased by a moist forest breeze.

Back in his own mind, he also realized what he'd seen, if indeed it was real. Statues of winged humans littered Val Harlon, beaks on their faces where noses and mouths should be, their hair wrought in fanciful plumes that stood up from their foreheads like crests. Could the world have forgotten an entire people?

Thalnarra stepped into the meadow, holding back a branch with her beak so that Altair could gingerly follow. He winced as he stepped into the sunlit meadow, his eyes still wide from the pain medicine.

The world hadn't forgotten, Vidarian realized. Humans had.

He reached out with his Sense as easily as he would have with his hand, but this reached much farther, brushed up against Thalnarra's presence at the meadow's edge. She flared up instinctively, a shield of fire energy lifting around her, ready for attack. Vidarian was already walking toward her, but stopped a stone's throw away.

"Tell me about the bird-people, Thalnarra," he said. "Tell me what else the gryphons know and have kept from us."

Her aura dimmed as she took in his question, then dropped entirely, metaphysical arms falling to her sides.

// *They made a decision,* // she said, and Vidarian already disliked where this was going. // *Centuries ago. When the gate was closed, they went in before the Starhunter—all of them. It was the only way to trick her inside.* //

"And they're still there."

// Presumably they would be. Though what would be left . . . //

"How many, Thalnarra?"

// Two million, we believe, // she said, the words pulled from her.

Sounds about right. Though some of them aren't right in the head, the Starhunter giggled. *Maybe they count for halves? In that case it's only one million.*

"And they suffer."

// No one knows that. //

"I can *hear* them, Thalnarra!"

The gryphoness bridled, undaunted. *// Would you undo their sacrifice? All that they gave to win peace in our world? //*

"A peace in which the strong prey upon the weak, and power is relegated to a chosen few."

// She fills your head with lies! //

"So far," Vidarian said, "I don't think she's lied to me yet."

"Vidarian," Ruby was calling—and the edge in her voice quickened Vidarian's pulse. He ran toward the *Destiny*, where Ruby bent over the rim of the craft. Within, Ariadel was trembling, her skin sickeningly pale. "She's fading," Ruby said, pain lacing her voice. "It takes them so fast. I'm sorry, Vidarian."

His jaw tightened. "I need to get to the gate." He looked up at Ruby, and she nodded, wordless.

They emptied the craft of all its contents save Ariadel and her blankets, lightening it enough to lift between them like a large gurney. Vidarian buckled his sword at his side, stowed in the craft for flight. While they worked, the gryphons were circled in intense conference of some kind, a passionate one punctuated often by clacking beaks and flared wings. When Ruby and Vidarian lifted the craft, Vidarian pointed them toward the east, where the sapphires told him the gate waited. He expected Thalnarra to follow, expected the burst of renewed fury that was sure to come with her—but the gryphons only watched him, and when they did follow, it was at a distance, peaceful but ominous.

CHAPTER TWENTY-NINE

GATE OF STORMS

A t the forest's edge the trees thinned and disappeared entirely into a golden plain that ran in undulating hills to the horizon. This stand of trees was deceptively small, large for a small human standing inside it, but a pocket seen from the air—one that had grown up around the ancient stones of the Great Gate.

The wild land that had grown up here in centuries of civilization's absence had consumed almost everything save the gate. Stacked sandstone originally shaped flat and precise had been worn down by wind and rain at all its edges, and dry sun-loving creepers wrapped its base to the height of Vidarian's eye. The gate itself—an empty thing, a frame only—extended thrice the height of a gryphon, and was twice as wide. The remnants of stone foundations littered the ground a respectful distance away, and the ground at their feet was once paved with clay bricks, but few remained to fight the invading grasses.

Vidarian and Ruby carried Ariadel to the gate's threshold, and as they drew closer to it the sapphires increased their constant rumble of satisfaction and anticipation. By the strain written across Ruby's face Vidarian knew the red gems treated her similarly. When they gently lowered the *Destiny* to the ground, Ariadel's eyes fluttered open, focusing clearly for the first time in days. Vidarian's fledgling fire sense felt hers questing outward, awakened by the sudden flash and rumble of the rubies and sapphires. He knelt at her side immediately, taking one of her hands in both of his. From behind them, he heard Thalnarra's hiss of indrawn breath.

When Ariadel's own fire sense touched his, she flared up in his awareness, for a split second bright and strong as she had been the day they first met. But it was a flash, momentary only, collapsing even as it reached the edges of her faltering attention. "Where are we?" With their senses entwined, he could feel the plague raging within her, the elements that made her at war with each other. He knew how much each word cost her.

"We're at the gate," he said softly, and felt the jump in her awareness as she comprehended his words. She tried to lift her head, but only for a moment—as her strength fled, so too did her sense, and she dropped away from his mind. He recklessly threw himself after her, nearly reaching out with the water magic that longed to break free inside him. With a grasp of will that darkened his vision for a split second, he held it back, to the fury of the still growling sapphires. He closed his eyes, mastering them, snarling inside his mind, then brushed his thumbs across her fingers and said, "I'm going to open it."

With a force that would have thrown her to her feet had she the strength, Ariadel writhed in the flight craft, every fiber of her being shouting resistance. When her energy fled again, she collapsed back, again winking out of his awareness—then slowly flickering, fighting back up again. "The gate . . ." she trembled as she fought to get the words out, ". . . must . . . not . . . be opened!" Her body had nothing left, had burned through its reserves in their passage to the gate, yet in the depths of her soul's urgency was the strength to fight.

Vidarian was quiet for a long moment, consumed by the sound of her breathing—knowing as he had never known any other truth that he was not capable of hearing it cease. "Ariadel," he said finally, "you'll die."

"If I die, I die in a world I understand, by the teachings that have shaped my entire life. You don't know what you're asking me for," she said. Even as the strength had welled up within her, now it fled, leaving her a swiftly collapsing shell.

"I'm asking you to live," he said.

"Not at this price," she whispered. "No one life is worth this price."

"You don't . . . !" He stopped himself and breathed, swallowing the flash of sudden anger, warned by the renewed pulsation of the storm sapphires. "You don't know the price," he said. "We only know what we've been told. I know that this is right."

Her eyes were fading, exhaustion settling across her features. She shook her head as her eyes drooped. "I can't be this," she said, her eyes pleading for understanding he couldn't find in himself. "You have to let me go." And then her eyes shut, her consciousness pouring through his Sense's grasp, flowing down into darkness.

"How can you ask me to let you die?" he whispered. And a whisper in his mind answered—

What are gods for, Vidarian, if not for cruel choices?

Her spitefulness bounced harmlessly off of the wall of his grief. "It wasn't the *Quest*," he choked, seizing Ariadel's hands in his, "it was you." He looked up and into Ruby's ashen face. "I'm losing her!" He lifted her in his arms and stood, turning toward the gate.

// *I can't let you do that, Vidarian.* // Thalnarra's voice was quiet smoke in his mind.

He turned back.

// *We came to support you,* // the gryphoness said, indicating the gryphons behind her. // *But not in making catastrophic decisions. I did not aid you so that you could do this!* //

"But you aided me," Vidarian said. "And for that I thank you." As gently as he had ever moved in his life, he laid Ariadel in the blankets again. Her pulse fluttered under his hand, time escaping. He stood, swift, and drew his sword.

The gryphons behind Thalnarra hissed in promised menace, but she flicked her beak, warning them back. // *Do you know what you're doing?* // she asked.

Her simple question, untouched by emotion, nearly undid his resolve. As Ariadel had writhed under the weight of her priesthood, so too did he falter under the specters of his father, his mother, his legacy. Regardless of its outcome, he knew his family's dynasty to have ended here, the thought of which threatened to still his hand. "What I have to," he said only.

// *If you think that I'll hold back out of pity, you're wrong,* // she warned.

"I'd be insulted if you did."

She leapt at him, claws outstretched, lashing out with a whip of searing fire energy. Vidarian fell to one side, half canniness and half clumsiness, stunned by the sudden leap. He spun away from her claws, but yelled as the flames washed over him, searing his face. Had he been in the center of the fire lash, he'd no longer be standing.

He pivoted hard on his right knee, darting in just behind the flames with a fast overhead slice of the sword, pairing it with a surge of water energy that leapt ahead of the blade and reached for the heart of her fire. But as his water sense extended away from him, the sapphires surged up, dizzying him, knocking him back. He aborted his attack and spun again, regrouping, while wrapping his mind around the sapphires.

Thalnarra gave him no time. In she lunged again, black talons as thick as his wrist flashing out for his intestines. This time the pulse of her energy was round, a cylinder of force large enough to swallow him entirely. But preceding the deadly heat itself was an aura of electricity, a warning, defining its periphery. Vidarian dove away and felt the edge of the attack just clip him, hot enough to curl the ends of his hair and fill his nose with the smoke of its burning. He had dodged her twice, but knew he couldn't be so lucky again.

Vidarian seized the sapphires with his mind and shook them, jolting them into furious action—and released their energy directly into Thalnarra's face. She roared in astonishment and fury, recoiling her own fire energy in a barrier against the stones' onslaught.

"I never asked for this," he said. "Your people had to throw prophesy into it."

// Humans, // Thalnarra said, and the thought was rimed with insult beyond his comprehension. // Shut up and fight. // She leapt at him again, the powerful spring of her hind legs bringing her to him instantly, a thousand pounds of deadly creature with equally deadly mind oriented on his defeat. His heart and animal mind cried out in terror and urged escape, but he held them back, raising his sword before him like a talisman, a wreath of water energy wrapping the blade. The wave of elemental attack she directed at him this time was a sphere of fire energy that exploded into lethal spines as it neared him— in desperation he threw up the strongest wall of water energy he could summon, recklessly spending the fury of the sapphires into it as well.

Their energies met, resisted each other—and Thalnarra fell back, her wings flaring.

There in the moment, his mind and body tuned for survival, his spirit screaming out with the need for victory, he caught Thalnarra's gaze, and was stricken with the sensation of staring deep into her very being. Where he was attuned for the precision of his purpose, his every thought directed toward opening the gate to save the life of the woman he loved, Thalnarra was divided; distracted. She questioned. In that instant he knew the purpose of the gryphon battle ritual; it was much more than a barbaric grasp for dominance.

Truth bloomed, and the world dropped away while he seized it like an iron brand.

Something within him snapped, and both the storm's mad energy—a roar of water—and the fire's spiraling heat poured out of him, melting together, becoming one, becoming nothing. Before him, coiling around his blade, that nothingness opened up, a gulf that tore at reality. Here the Starhunter seized, boiling up from the opening. Thalnarra stared, transfixed as the Vkortha had been, and the goddess of chaos reached for her existence.

With a growl, Vidarian held her back, threading the energies apart again with his mind, but he seized on Thalnarra's distraction. When his sword arm came up, one of the gryphons screamed, an eagle's defiance, nearly startling him into dropping his wrist the full length. Instead, he stopped the arc of the blade with the strength of his arm and the reach of his water energy, seizing it in place. The edge hovered less than half a handspan from Thalnarra's exposed throat. He looked up at the remaining gryphons.

"Will you all stand against me?"

"Would it stop you?" Ruby asked, and her smile, full of sharpness and grief, filled his eyes with sudden water. She walked to him, the confident sway of a ship captain in her step, and placed the rubies in his hand.

"No," he said, "it wouldn't." And he willed the gate open.

The gate was a gaping maw, a depthless ocean, an unmaking. Here at the threshold between worlds the gemstones in Vidarian's hands warred against each other, arcs of electricity crackling between them and the gate as their energies flared and flickered.

Set me free, she whispered, and the sound vibrated from the gate, prickling every inch of his skin. *Set us free, Vidarian.* Her presence loomed just beyond the gate, her energies pressing it outward in an urgent bubble of near emergence.

It was a mouth between worlds, a maw in the face of the universe, and before it all thoughts threatened to slip away from Vidarian. As he stared into the opening it was as if he looked into the night sky, doubled and tripled and quadrupled and onward into infinity, endless universes of which theirs was the tiniest speck.

You see, the Starhunter said. *There are plenty of stars to eat. I really don't understand the problem with taking a few. If I wasn't supposed to eat them, they wouldn't be so delicious.* And there before him one of the stars very deliberately winked out.

It was his own mortal terror that drew him back into the moment and gave him the consciousness to release what the gate had held, back into the world.

A concussive force knocked him back, and he curled his body just enough to shield Ariadel with his chest and arms. The ground impacting his head sent a new kind of stars blasting across his vision, and all was black. By her yell of warning and the thud beside them, he knew Ruby had fallen near as well. Above them, the thundering of wings—thousands upon thousands of wings flooding outward from the gate, the wind of their passage rushing outward and pinning him to the ground.

Storms opened up around them, tearing after individual pairs of wings and the creatures that bore them. The sky broke with lightning centered in halos around individual flying figures, while others were wreathed in circles of fire. Most destructive of all, but thankfully rarest, some of them tore at the earth with powerful magic that effortlessly ripped trenches into the ground deep enough to swallow them all alive.

Then, just before the gate, the ground rose up, and Vidarian wrapped his arms around Ariadel, gathering himself to leap. He looked at Ruby, who knelt beside him, ready to take cover as well. But the clay and rock, still topped with the grass that had been below them a moment ago, swung up in a protective curve, sheltering them from the destruction.

A creature that was almost human but significantly not so ducked under the arc of the protective mantle with them. She—somehow he knew it was a she—was covered with brown and black speckled feathers, a pair of massive wings folded at her back like a great cloak. As she crouched, he saw that her feet terminated in birdlike claws, and her hands also bore more delicate ones. Large golden eyes, twice again too round to be human, looked out at the chaos atop a compact black-tipped beak. Her clothing was an ancient style he'd never seen before, a kind of wrap that accommodated her wings, and a gold pendant hung suspended in the middle of her forehead.

When she was satisfied that the wall of earth would protect them, she turned to him. "*Isri*," she said, and he wondered how they would understand the creatures' language, but she said, "My name is Isri," in clear, unaccented trade-tongue. "I am elder mindspeaker for the Treune seridi. You are gate-opener. We've been expecting you for some time!"

"Pleased to meet you," he shouted, and at the sound of his voice Ariadel stirred in his arms.

Her eyes slowly opened, unfocused at first, then fixing on him. His heart leapt and his eyes stung. Then her soft expression of love as she saw him, so welcome and familiar, transformed with the arrival of conscious thought to horror, and betrayal. Her hand came up, shaking, to touch his face. "Vidarian," she whispered, her voice rasping, "what have you done?"

A gurgling cough behind them turned both their heads. When Vidarian looked up from Ariadel and saw Ruby's ashen face, and how she fought to remain standing, his heart shouted astonished denial.

All things, the Starhunter whispered, returning to his mind with ease and solidity, *and their antithesis*.

The wound at her side was darkening with blood, suddenly overcome as if it had been ripped open anew. Out of some instinctive reach for power,

Ruby extended her elemental sense—a massive arm of it that lit her face with shock. Vidarian automatically raised his own in a shield—and was crushed to the ground under the weight of the energy that poured out of him. He stemmed it back, and even in restraint it was as if the sea energy poured from him in a torrent, wild and near uncontrollable.

"It's . . ." Ruby gasped. "The healing magic . . . it's all wrong. . . ." And at once Vidarian realized that the infused poultice would now have its energies thrown out of balance by the same shift that had many-times multiplied their own elemental energy. And it was killing her.

Ariadel, by contrast, was rising under her own strength, leaning toward Ruby, her eyes streaked with tears. Vidarian turned to Ruby, and the breath stopped in his throat.

"No sentiment, please," Ruby said, her neck straining. "But I did tell you . . . I wanted to die on my ship," she said, and fell to the ground. Vidarian dove after her, his head swimming, looping his arm under her neck. Her muscles were slack, her eyes shut, her head lolling. And there, as Vidarian clasped her nerveless fingers, the Queen of the West Sea departed the world, the rush of her powerful elemental presence winking out before him.

"She's gone," he said.

CHAPTER THIRTY
SKYSHIP

They returned to the clearing and the gryphon camp. Ariadel had lapsed into a silence from which she could not be moved. The gryphons—including Thalnarra, to Vidarian's surprise—had quietly rallied around him. // *Your truth was stronger than mine,* // Thalnarra had said only, and would speak no more of their duel. They'd bound Ruby's body in bandages. Her last words weren't precisely a request to be returned to her crew, but Vidarian knew it was what she would have wanted.

The camp's activity had now doubled with the arrival of the seridi, and only the fast organization of their leaders kept it from tripling or more. Like the gryphons, the seridi seemed to be organized by element and led by elders; these, wearing pendants like Isri's, clustered around the gryphons from Thalnarra's pride, conferring. Catching up, Vidarian thought, on two thousand years of gossip. Meanwhile, thousands more of the creatures were spreading out in all directions, hurrying to create or find shelter and sustenance for over a million refugees. Small mixed teams of gryphons and seridi were dispatched to the gryphon prides and the priestesshoods.

Except for Isri, the seridi uniformly deferred to him to the point of stopping whatever they were doing, and so Vidarian eventually distanced himself from the camp. His pursuit of solitude eventually returned him to the gate and the little flight craft that still sat beside it, nearly forgotten. By some silent agreement the gryphons had sent Altair and Isri to follow him, and he couldn't bring himself to stop them.

Vidarian went to the craft and rested his hands on the bow. Just below its curved surface, encircling the entire craft, was a row of stones he'd never noticed before; he'd assumed they were large nails. But now each of them glowed softly with an internal energy, a pale blue light. As he knelt to examine them more closely, Isri joined him at the craft's side.

// *It was a skyship, long ago,* // Altair said.

"That's right," Isri replied, her hands passing gently over the ship's hull as if swallowed by a memory. She seemed to delight in every physical sensation—the wind, the warmth of the late afternoon sun, the scent of the trees. Now she hopped adroitly into the craft and knelt, inspecting wooden cases set into the shallow deck. Vidarian had thought that they contained ballast or some kind of stabilizer. But when Isri flipped a series of catches and opened them, she reached in and pulled up a slender mainmast made of a light, flexible metal Vidarian had never seen. Still rigged to it was a sail made of light translucent silk, and when she straightened the mast, it snapped loudly—and firmly—into place. Intrigued, Vidarian climbed into the ship after her to get a closer look.

As if this weren't enough, while he inspected the main, Isri proceeded to open two more cases hidden in front of the benches to the fore of the craft, unpacking two more sails and even slimmer masts. These folded out over the sides, unmistakably mimicking birds' wings.

The little skiff was hardly the *Quest*, but suddenly it was a piece of something like home.

"May I?" Vidarian managed.

In answer, Altair raised a foreclaw, and the blue cabochons set into the hull pulsed into life one by one as his magic touched them. With a soft groan, the craft lifted just off the ground beneath Vidarian's feet, and he scrambled to take hold. There was no wheel, but a slim capstan just before the galley had yet another clever catch system that, when opened, revealed a control mechanism shaped to fit a human hand.

The ship was rising, and he only had a few seconds to decipher the controls. One was clearly a barometer, and another delicate device set beside it he suspected was an altimeter, this one built into the ship. Now the ship was higher off the ground, its bow even with Altair's head. Vidarian touched a cylindrical switch at the bottom of the panel and heard a clunk below and aft. A long rudder—more a fourth sail, composed of a springy metal spar and another sail—had unfurled below them, steadying the ship. Vidarian thought about the Sky Knights and how they had dominated the air, giving the Alorean Empire unprecedented advantage over the surrounding territories. "This changes everything," he breathed.

// *You changed everything,* // Altair said, then dipped his beak in a small salute. // *Good flying, brother.* // The title lifted Vidarian with a surprising flush of pride and affection.

When they reached the tops of the trees, Isri shocked him by leaping over the starboard rail. He kept his hand on the rudder control to steady the craft, then ran to the side while it floated. Below, the seridi had snapped open her barred wings and was soaring gently over the forest canopy. While he watched, she gave a few powerful flaps of her wings and glided ahead, then up, riding the wind.

They were still rising, and Vidarian returned to the controls, finding one that seemed to increase the power of the air-stones, propelling them forward, and another that lessened it. There were none at the capstan for turning the craft or changing its altitude, and it took him a few moments to realize these were controlled by the three sails and traditional shiplike rigging. Managing the ropes and sail, drawing them back and checking knots, the scents of rope and wood and wind, dropped him in gentle, old memories.

Long ago, his family had owned a skiff not unlike this one, a small training vessel on which his father had taught Vidarian and his brothers how to sail. If he looked out over the bow, out instead of down, he could imagine he was on the sea, not in the sky.

Shortly he had the craft leveled out and floating. The side-sails were new to him, but after a few alterations in the rigging he found that a slight backward curve and a low propulsion setting allowed the ship to float gently where it was, teased by the breeze but not moved. Below, the world unfolded; forest melted into grassland, grassland rose into hill, hill spread into jagged coastline. And the sea—which had so shaped his existence, he'd thought—crashed there, distant and strange.

A pulse of wings on air drew his attention back to the here and now. Beside him, out in the air, Isri hovered. Her feathers were lifted in what he'd learned meant excitement in a gryphon, and her breathing was fast but steady. Watching the glisten in her eyes, Vidarian found a sudden jealousy for her and the gryphons' direct experience of the exhilaration of flight.

"May I?" she called, her wings beating twice every few seconds to hold her in the hover.

"Please," Vidarian answered, doing his best to hold the craft steady in the high wind.

He thought the mechanics of landing on a ship that floated in the air would be complex, but she must have done this before, and he stopped himself from the dizzying contemplation of when that might have been. With an ease she hadn't shown on takeoff, she dove and then looped in a quick arc, bringing herself directly on top of the *Destiny*. Then she folded her wings and dropped, one foot outstretched and the other ready to brace for impact, into a neat landing on the bench beside Vidarian. She gave one quick flap to steady herself, mantling like a hawk, and then her wings flipped back and closed with a whisper of soft, sleek feathers. With a lightness that spoke of birdlike bones, she hopped into the bench seat next to Vidarian. Her feathers smelled of sun-warmth and spice.

Vidarian was looking at the sun, staring into the sun where it now sunk into the sea in a pool of searing, liquid light, and for a long time Isri followed his gaze silently. But as the spots it burned into his eyes turned deeper and darker, he realized he was trying rather pathetically to punish himself and looked away, tracing his returning vision up the coast.

In the distance, a flash of unnatural lightning that came from near the ground revealed the location of one of the seridi that had flooded out of the gate, wreaking havoc wherever they passed.

"Why are they doing this?" Vidarian asked, his throat dry from the altitude.

"They're mad," Isri replied. "For every year that my people remained trapped with the Starhunter, it seemed one of us lost the battle to retain our sanity. Her massive and chaotic mind eroded our own."

"Why would you give yourselves to such a thing?"

"We didn't know we would survive the passage into the gate," she said. "When we lured her through, we thought it was to certain death. None had ever survived passing into the gate when a destination had not been opened on the other side. The Starhunter kept us alive—we were her bargaining chip if she were to ever be released again."

"And I fell into her hands," he said, remembering Ariadel's silence like a knife between his ribs. "The gryphons and magic-users here insisted that the gate should be sealed, not opened."

She turned to him, her pupils pinning like a gryphon's with shock. "And leave us trapped there for eternity, all condemned to the slow descent into madness?" When he didn't answer, she said, "You have set us free. Whatever paths lay ahead of you, you must know that you have the gratitude of an entire race, trapped for untold time between worlds."

For the first time since the awakening of his magic—and it now felt to be wholly *his* magic, as it never had—the weight of the Starhunter was lifted from his mind. A hollowness he felt in the world itself said that she was there—her ambiguity, her truth—but she was no longer his alone to bear. And he wondered if it was this relief he had sought all along. Had he really opened the gate for Ariadel? Had the Starhunter herself contaminated his thoughts?

In the quiet that had settled on his mind, he knew the singularity of purpose that had filled his being for that one moment. It was Ariadel's life that had compelled him, for good and for ill. And he knew that if it were left to him again, he would again release chaos into the world if it meant correcting an imbalance that he'd known in his heart threaded reality itself without her.

"It's beautiful," Isri said, looking out at the sunset spilling light and brilliance across the distant ocean far below and to the west. She closed her eyes, and the gentle wind lifted the feathers around her face.

The future was nebulous—two thousand powerful magic-wielders released into the world, the disruption of healing magic, ships that could fly—but suspended as he was among the clouds, the deep blue sky filled with fire and light, the richness of a new land spread beneath them . . . in that moment, at least, Vidarian agreed.

AUTHOR'S NOTE

Have you ever thought about doing something for most of your life, then actually sat down to do it and found yourself overwhelmed with the moment? That's me right now. How do you live up to that kind of self-induced hype? How does one write an author's note? Gryphon physics, no problem, but here I am talking to you, by default the awesomest and most important person, the Dear Reader, and I am verklempt. I can say: I hope you enjoyed the ride.

Every book has two stories: the one you see, between the pages, and the story that led to the book's creation, its long journey to reach you on your couch or in the bookstore. This second story is invariably large in cast. I owe a great deal to my parents (Verl, Patricia, and Diane), who, however disturbed by my young fixation with medieval paraphernalia and lack of fashion sense, withheld their comments long enough for Fantasy (and its sister Technology) to deeply take root. My husband, Jay, relentless cheerleader, finest imaginable partner, formidable talent in his own right. Scott Andrews, publisher of *Beneath Ceaseless Skies*, which printed "Stormchaser, Stormshaper," the short story that led to Andovar's "discovery." Michael DeLuca and Justin Howe, comrades-in-arms with Jay, Scott, and myself in the Homeless Moon. Jeanne Cavelos, Susan Sielinski, and the passionate if decidedly odd crew of the Odyssey Fantasy Writers Workshop, especially the class of 2005, who read parts of this manuscript. My sister Kim, amazing font of love and wisdom, who persisted in hunting down my work. Lou Anders, whose praises are sung by many, yet still fall short of a multifariously talented reality. Dehong He, whose cover art brings this world alive beyond my wildest imagining. The most excellent production folk at Pyr: Jill Maxick in marketing, Catherine Roberts-Abel in production, Bruce Carle in layout (whom you can thank for the beautiful fonts). Gabrielle Harbowy, copyeditor extraordinaire.

Beyond Brenda Cobbs and Kristin Jett, to whom the book is dedicated, this world that I now call Andovar has a peculiar history. It was 1995, I had just started high school, and had also discovered how to cycle America OnLine trial discs for handfuls of Internet hours (sorry AOL). On the fantasy and science fiction message boards I met Kristin—whose parents, ten years later, would be persuaded I was not an axe murderer—and Brenn. Together we roguishly decided that the available fantasy roleplaying groups were not for us, and so I started chiseling out a world map, various fantasy species (the main characters were all gryphons), and mythical histories. Brenn provided the Cherokee word for "home"—*qinasev*—and "Di'Quinasev," our "second home," was born. Our motley crew of e-mail storytellers grew at one point to forty crazy people spread all over the world, telling stories about folk and creatures that don't exist. Some friends by now have reconnected or never lost touch (Melissa, Zack, Cody, Annalise, Nicole), others still wander (Buffy "Skylance," we miss you)—but without them this world would never have caught fire.

The Internet has already given its share of interesting stories for book publishing, but for me its core message is that all art is interactive. I now create fantasy worlds for gamers who connect with each other through symbolic realities across vast geographic distances, but the fact is that, technology aside, fiction has always done this. In fantasy we find our humanity, and reach out to each other with a personal electricity that will light up the world, if we let it. Thank you for joining the quest.

ABOUT THE AUTHOR

ERIN HOFFMAN is a videogame designer, author, and essayist on player rights and modern media ethics. She lives in northern California with her husband, two parrots, and an entirely too-clever miniature dachshund. For more about her work, and the world of Andovar, visit www.erinhoffman.com.

_{}~~~